ZOO TIME

Fiction

Coming From Behind
Peeping Tom
Redback
The Very Model of a Man
No More Mister Nice Guy
The Mighty Walzer
Who's Sorry Now?
The Making of Henry
Kalooki Nights
The Act of Love
The Finkler Question

Non-fiction

Shakespeare's Magnanimity (with Wilbur Sanders)
In the Land of Oz
Roots Schmoots: Journeys Among Jews
Seriously Funny: From the Ridiculous to the Sublime
Whatever It Is, I Don't Like It

ZOO TIME

Howard Jacobson

B L O O M S B U R Y
LONDON · NEW DELHI · NEW YORK · SYDNEY

First published in Great Britain 2012

Copyright © 2012 by Howard Jacobson

The moral right of the author has been asserted

Extract from *Women* by Charles Bukowski reproduced by kind
permission of David Grossman Literary Agency

Bloomsbury Publishing Plc
50 Bedford Square
London
WC1B 3DP

www.bloomsbury.com

Bloomsbury Publishing, London, New Delhi, New York and Sydney

A CIP catalogue record for this book is available from the British Library

ISBN 978 1 4088 2868 7 (hardback edition)
ISBN 978 1 4088 3182 3 (trade paperback edition)

10 9 8 7 6 5 4 3 2 1

Typeset by Hewer Text UK Ltd, Edinburgh
Printed in Great Britain by Clays Ltd, St Ives plc

To

Jenny and Dena

and

Marly and Nita

'Will any man love the daughter if he has not loved the mother?'

James Joyce, *Ulysses*

ONE

Monkey

He Stroke She

When the police apprehended me I was still carrying the book I'd stolen from the Oxfam bookshop in Chipping Norton, a pretty Cotswold town where I'd been addressing a reading group. I'd received a hostile reception from the dozen or so of the members who, I realised too late, had invited me only in order to be insulting.

'Why do you hate women so much?' one of them had wanted to know.

'Could you give me an example of my hatred of women?' I enquired politely.

She certainly could. She had hundreds of passages marked with small, sticky, phosphorescent arrows, all pointing accusingly at the pronoun 'he'.

'What's wrong with "he stroke she"?' she challenged me, making the sign of the oblique with her finger only inches from my face, wounding me with punctuation.

'"He" is neuter,' I told her, stepping back. 'It signifies no prefer-ence for either gender.'

'Neither does "they".'

'No, but "they" is plural.'

'So why are you against plurality?'

'And children,' another had wanted to know, 'why do you detest children?'

I explained that I didn't write about children.

'Precisely!' was her jubilant reply.

'The only character I identified with in your book,' a third reader told me, 'was the one who died.'

Only she didn't say 'book'. Almost no one any longer said 'book', to rhyme with took or look, or even fook, as in 'Fook yoo, yoo bastad', which was the way it was pronounced in flat-vowelled lawless Lancashire just a few miles to the north of the sedate, sleepy peat bogs of Cheshire where I grew up. Berk, was how she said it. 'The only character I identified with in your *berk* . . .' As though a double 'o' was a hyperbole too far for her.

'I'm gratified you found her death moving,' I said.

She was quivering with that rage you encounter only among readers. Was it because reading as a civilised activity was over that the last people doing it were reduced to such fury with every page they turned? Was this the final paroxysm before expiry?

'Moved?' I feared she might strike me with my berk. 'Who said I was moved? I was envious. I identified with her because I'd been wishing I was dead from the first word.'

'*Were* dead,' I said, putting on my jacket. 'I'd been wishing I *were* dead.'

I thanked them for having me, went back to my hotel, polished off a couple of bottles of wine I'd had the foresight to buy earlier, and fell asleep in my clothes. I'd agreed to go to Chipping Norton for the opportunity it afforded me to visit my mother-in-law with whom I had for a long time been thinking of having an affair, but the stratagem had been foiled by my wife uncannily choosing that very time to have her mother visit us in London. I could have caught the train back and joined them for dinner, but decided to

4

have a day to myself in the country. It wasn't only the women at the reading group who wished they was dead.

Getting up too late for breakfast, I took a stroll through the town. Nice. Cotswold stone, smell of cows. ('Why are there no natural descriptions in your novels?' I'd been unfairly interrogated the day before.) Needing sustenance, I bought a herby sausage roll from an organic bakery and wandered into the Oxfam bookshop eating it. A chalk-white assistant with discs in his earlobes, like a Zambezi bushman, pointed to a sign saying 'No food allowed on the premises'. A tact thing, presumably: you don't fill your face when the rest of the world is starving. From his demeanour I assumed he knew I was a hater of Zambezi bushmen as well as women and children. I put what was left of the sausage roll in my pocket. He was not satisfied with that. A sausage roll in my pocket was still, strictly speaking, food on the premises. I stuffed it slowly into my mouth. We stood, eyeing each other up – white Zambezi bushman and Cheshire-born, London-based misogynistic, paedo-phobic writer of berks, buhks, boks, anything but books – waiting for the sausage roll to go down. Anyone watching would have taken the scene to be charged with post-colonial implications. After one last swallow, I asked if it was all right now for me to check out the literary-fiction section. *Literary*. I burdened the word with heavy irony. He turned his back on me and walked to the other end of the shop.

What I did then, as I explained to the constables who collared me on New Street, just a stone's throw from the Oxfam bookshop, I had to do. As for calling it stealing, I didn't think the word was accurate given that I was the author of the book I was supposed to have stolen.

'What word would you use, sir?' the younger of the two police-men asked me.

5

I wanted to say that this more closely approximated to a critical discussion than anything that had taken place in the reading group, but settled for answering his question directly. I had enough enemies in Chipping Norton.

'Release,' I said. 'I would say that I have *released* my book.'

'Released it from what exactly, sir?' This time it was the older of the two policemen who addressed me. He had one of those granite bellies you see on riot police or Louisiana sheriffs. I wondered why they needed riot police or a Louisiana sheriff in Chipping Norton.

Roughly, what I said to him was this:

Look: I bear Oxfam no grudge. I would have done the same in the highly unlikely event of my finding a book of mine for sale second-hand in Morrisons. It's a principle thing. It makes no appreciable difference to my income where I turn up torn and dog-eared. But there has to be a solidarity of the fallen. The book as prestigious object and source of wisdom – 'Everyman, I will go with thee and be thy guide' and all that – is dying. Resuscitation is probably futile, but the last rites can at least be given with dignity. It matters where and with whom we end our days. Officer.

Before they decided it was safe, or at least less tedious, to return me to society, they flicked – I thought sardonically, but beggars can't be choosers – through the pages of my book. It's a strange experience having your work speed-read by the police in the middle of a bustling Cotswold town, shoppers and ice-cream-licking tourists stopping to see what crime has been committed. I hoped that something would catch one of the cops' eye and make him laugh or, better still, cry. But it was the title that interested them most. *Who Gives a Monkey's?*

The younger officer had never heard the expression before. 'It's short for who gives a monkey's fook,' I told him. I had lost much and was losing more with every hour but at least I hadn't lost the northerner's full-blooded pronunciation of the ruderies, even if Cheshire wasn't quite Lancashire.

'Now then,' he said.

But he had a question for me since I said I was a writer – *since I said I was a writer*: he made it sound like a claim he would look into when he got back to the station – and as I obviously knew something about monkeys. How likely did I think it was that a monkey with enough time and a good computer could eventually write *Hamlet*?

'I think you can't make a work of art without the intentionality to do so,' I told him. 'No matter how much time you've got.'

He scratched his face. 'Is that a yes or a no?'

'Well, in the end,' I said, 'I guess it depends on the monkey. Find one with the moral courage, intelligence, imagination and ear of Shakespeare, and who knows. But then if there were such a monkey why would he want to write something that's already been written?'

I didn't add that for me the more interesting question was whether enough monkeys with enough time could eventually 'read' *Hamlet*. But then I was an embittered writer who had just taken a battering.

The Louisiana sheriff, meanwhile, was turning the evidence over in his hands as though he were a rare-book dealer considering an offer. He opened *Who Gives a Monkey's?* at the dedication page.

To the fairest of the fair:
my beloved wife and mother-in-law

'That's coming it a bit rich, isn't it?' he said.

'What is?'

'Saying that you love your mother-in-law.'

I peered over his shoulder at my dedication. It was a few years since I'd come up with it. You forget your dedications. Given enough time you even forget your dedicatees. 'No,' I said, 'it's my wife who's the beloved. To my beloved wife, *and* to her mother-in-law. The adjective applies only to the first of them.'

'Shouldn't you have put a comma before the *and*, in that case?'

He jabbed the page with his finger, showing me where he thought the comma ought to have gone.

Oxford, I remembered, had its own rules for where commas go. 'The Oxford comma' had long been a matter of fractious controversy inside the university, but I hadn't thought the constabulary was hot on the subject as well. No doubt Oxford also had its own rules regarding the doubling of epithets. Wasn't there a word for the rhetorical device I'd inadvertently – assuming it had been inadvertence – deployed? Something like zeugma, only not zeugma. Maybe the policeman knew.

'Listen,' I said, 'as you appear to be an unusually discerning reader, can I make a present to you of my book?'

'You certainly cannot,' he told me. 'Not only would I be guilty of taking a bribe if I accepted it, I would also be guilty of receiving stolen property.'

In the circumstances I considered myself lucky to have got off with a caution. Those were no small transgressions: stealing a book, leaving out a comma, and scheming to misappropriate my wife's mother.

2

V&P

They hadn't come with a comma between them, that had been the problem from the start.

Vanessa strode into the shop I was managing one lightless Tuesday afternoon in February when my assistants had gone home – clip-clop up the cold stone steps of the converted Georgian town house that was Wilhelmina's – and wondered if I had seen her mother. I asked her to describe her mother. 'Tall' – she made a sort of pergola of her arms. 'Slender' – she described what looked like two downpipes on a building – 'yet high-breasted' – she looked down at her own chest, as though surprised by what she saw. 'Vivacious' – she shook an imaginary orchard. 'Red hair, like mine.'

I scratched my head. 'I don't think so,' I said. 'Could you be more specific about her appearance?'

Whereupon, talk of the devil, she arrived, clip-clop up the stone steps, as tall as a pergola, as slender as a downpipe, yet high-breasted, as vivacious as an apple orchard in a tornado.

And red hair, which just happened to be my weakness. Red hair styled in a near psychedelic frizz, almost comically, as though she knew – as though they both knew – that with beauty like this you could take all the liberties with your appearance you liked.

Two burning bushes, two queens of the music hall, red-lipped to match their hair.

A word about the shop I was managing. Wilhelmina's was the most sophisticated women's boutique in Wilmslow, a whisperingly affluent town mingling comatose blue-bloods and the newly and tastelessly wealthy, just a few miles to the east of Chester. Not only was it the most sophisticated, most stylish and most expensive boutique in Wilmslow, it was the most sophisticated, most stylish and most expensive boutique in the whole of Cheshire. Beautiful women from all over the north of England, unable to find anything that did justice to them in Manchester or Leeds, never mind Chester, dressed themselves from head to toe with a wink and a nod from us. I say 'us' because Wilhelmina's was a family concern. My mother had started it and had entrusted it to me, in what she grandly called her retirement, while my younger and more suitable brother was being trained at a local business college with a view to his taking it over permanently. I was the dreamer of the family. I did words. I read books. Which meant I couldn't be trusted. Books distracted me, they were an illness, an impediment to a healthy life. I could have applied for a disability badge for my car, permission to park anywhere in Cheshire, so incapacitated by books and words was I. Indeed, I was doing words, ignoring customers and reading Henry Miller who at the time was my favourite writer, when Vanessa, followed by her mother, no comma, clopped up my stairs. It was as though characters from *Sexus* and *Nexus* had suddenly come alive, like the toys in the *Nutcracker Suite*, on the shop floor of Wilhelmina's.

You could say I saw more of the mother, first off, than I saw of the daughter, given that she appeared twice, first in words, then in person. And words affect me more than persons do. But Vanessa had made her own impression. Tall, slender, vivacious, yes,

10

flamboyant even, but angry about something too – not improbably about having such an attractive mother – and not just incidentally angry, more as though her frame had been overstrung, taut, vibrating, in a way that reminded me of a description of a schooner's rigging I had read by Joseph Conrad, the schooner being his first command. One of those descriptions that make you want to be a writer (though don't explain why you might want to be a writer like Henry Miller). The ship's quivering, I took it, was in reality the young commander's own. So maybe that was true of Vanessa and me too. The sight of her set me trembling. My first command. Correction: *her* first command. But I haven't imposed any anger of my own on her. It was all hers, the condition of her nature, as though she had to rage the way a sunflower had to turn its head. Besides, I had nothing, at that particular moment, to be angry about. I was in sole possession of a shop illuminated – someone might as well have lit flares – by the blazing red presence of Vanessa and her mother.

To this day I can remember everything Vanessa was wearing – the high black patent shoes, minimal so that you got to see her arches and her instep; the paper-fine leather coat belted so tight that it did what I thought only a pencil skirt could do, which was to make a still point of tension of her behind, a tremulousness, as though some law of gravity or protuberance were being defied; the V of its fur collar, like the vagina of a giantess; and pushed back a little from her red hair a Zhivago hat – Anna Karenina was who I saw (who else?) – the air from our fan heater winnowing its fine hairs, as though a Russian bear had stepped in out of the wind.

She wasn't expensively dressed, at least by Wilhelmina's standards. These were all top-of-the-range high-street garments, but the high street is only ever the high street. So I must be forgiven for imagining what she would have looked like had *we* dressed her.

Zandra Rhodes, I'd have put her in. She had the stature and the jawline. And could carry the brightest colours. And the boldest jest. But she wouldn't consider it, even when she became my wife and could have the benefit of my fashionable expertise gratis, as she wouldn't consider any of my suggestions.

As for Poppy, her mother, well, she was attired identically. They presented themselves to the world as sisters. Except that where the hem of Vanessa's coat was if anything a fraction too long, Poppy's was decidedly *more* than a fraction too short. But then she had lived for a while in America and American women were then, as they are now, beyond help when it comes to hemlines. How old would she have been when she first walked into Wilhelmina's? Forty-five or –six. Making her, when the police apprehended me in Chipping Norton, knowing in their bones that I was on a pervert's errand no less than on a thief's, in her middle sixties. A wonderful age for a woman who has kept an eye on herself.

Back in Wilmslow, she closed the shop door behind her, looking around.

'Ah, here she is, *ma mère*,' Vanessa exclaimed, as though after her description I needed telling who she was.

They kissed. Like herons in a park. One of them gave a little laugh. I couldn't have said which. Perhaps they shared one laugh between them. And here's the thing to consider when weighing up the rights and wrongs of my behaviour: how could I not fall in love with the daughter and the mother when they came to me so indissolubly bound?

'Well, there's certainly no mistaking who you are,' Poppy said to me once she was able to distinguish herself from her daughter.

I raised an eyebrow. 'Should there be?'

'You even raise your eyebrows like her.'

'Like whom?'

Vanessa blew out her cheeks with impatience. This was evidently as long as she could bear a confused conversation to continue. 'My mother knows your mother,' she said. Meaning, now can we get on with the rest of our lives?

'Ah,' I said. 'Well?'

'Well what?' Don't ask me which of them asked that.

'No, I meant does your mother – forgive me –' turning from the daughter – 'do *you* know her well?'

At that moment a customer emerged from the dressing room wanting to be pinned up. How long had she been in there? All day? All week? This was too much for Vanessa who, having been in the shop all of three minutes herself, felt she had been there the whole of her life. 'If we go and have tea might your mother be here when we return?' she demanded to know.

'No. My mother is on holiday.' I looked at my watch. 'Probably on the Nile right now.'

Poppy looked disappointed. 'I told you,' she said to her daughter, 'that we should have rung first.'

'No, I told you.'

'No, darling, *I* told *you*.'

Vanessa shrugged. Mothers!

'I'm sorry,' I said, looking from one to the other. 'Have you come far to see her?'

'Knutsford.'

I expressed surprise. Knutsford was only a short drive away. Given their agitation, I expected them to say Delhi. Vanessa read my surprise as anger. Angry women do that. They think everyone is at the same temperature they are. 'We are new to the area,' she said. 'We are not yet used to the distances.'

Knutsford is of course the town on which Mrs Gaskell, a one-time resident of the area, based her novel *Cranford*. And this sounded like a scene from *Cranford*. 'We are new to the area.' *Imagine, reader, the perturbation in every heart when the new residents were introduced on the first Sunday after Easter to the parishioners . . .*

Which was nothing compared to the perturbation in mine. New to the area, were they? Well, in that case they would need someone who was old to the area to put them at their ease.

How it was that Poppy knew my mother, who was considerably older than her, I discovered later. Not that I was curious. Mere plot, how people come to know one another, on a par with why the butler did it. Something to do with an older sister (Poppy's) who'd died in tragic circumstances – car crash, cancer, cranial palsy – one of those. Something about my mother having gone to school with her, the older sister. Who cared? Poppy, returned to Cheshire, wanted to pick up the connection again for her sister's sake, that was all.

Mills & Boon.

'Tasty shop,' she said, looking about her for the first time. 'A girl could get into trouble in a place like this.'

Girl?

HarperCollins.

'Thank you,' I said. 'My mother's taste. She's rarely here now. I keep an eye on the place for her.'

I was trying for insouciance. People who think of themselves as writers cannot believe that any other calling can be of interest. Only once they'd been apprised of the fact that I went home at night and wrote sentences in a lined notepad would Vanessa and Poppy want to know me better. As for shopkeeping – oh my Lord, I did that from a distance, through the back of my neck, while I wasn't looking. But I couldn't come straight out with it and say I was a novelist because then one or other of them, or most likely both of them together, would say 'Should we know anything you've written?' and I didn't want to hear myself reply that I wasn't a novelist in the crude sense of having actually produced a novel.

Even allowing for my naivety, that's a measure of how things have changed in twenty years. Then, no matter with what foundation in truth, it was possible to believe that being a writer was a glamorous occupation, that two beautiful women might travel up again from Knutsford sometime soon to renew their acquaintance with a man in whose head words cavorted like the Ballets Russes. Now, one has to apologise for having read a book, let alone for having written one. Food and fashion have left fiction far behind. 'I sell suits by Marc Jacobs in Wilmslow,' I'd say today if I wanted to impress a woman, 'and when I'm not doing that I'm practising to be a short-order chef at Baslow Hall. This fiction shit is just a way of killing time.'

Had I known then what I know now I would have burnt my books, boned up on Balenciaga, and held on to the shop for dear life, instead of letting it pass to my younger brother who lived the life of Casanova from the day he got it.

3

Me Beagle

To Vanessa and to Poppy, anyway, my first novel was dedicated. It was theirs. My beloved Vanessa's comma, and Poppy's.

Or forget the comma.

An elegantly profane novel, told from the point of view of a young and idealistic woman zookeeper – hence its lingering interest to women's reading groups, who found less not to identify with in it than in my later work – *Who Gives a Monkey's?* made a bit of a splash when it was first published thirteen years before it found its way on to the shelves of Oxfam. The title, as I should have realised, and as my publisher should have warned me – but he might already have been contemplating a suicide of his own – was nothing if not a hostage to fortune. Who gives a monkey's fuck? – 'Not me!' some tart reviewer was bound to say. And one did. Eugene Bawstone, the literary editor of one of those giveaway London newspapers no one wanted to be given. But as he had cracked the same mirthless joke in a review of a revival of Albee's *Who's Afraid of Virginia Woolf?* and no doubt said the same to King Lear when he asked 'Who is it that can tell me who I am?' and, more to the point, as no one read him anyway, his *jeu d'ennui* did not succeed in halting the novel's gentle progress.

I had some insider knowledge of zookeeping on account of my having gone out for a while – before V&P (I should date everything

16

from their arrival: BVPE meaning Before the Vanessa and Poppy Era) – with a woman who worked in the chimpanzee breeding centre at Chester Zoo, home to the largest colony of chimps in Europe. As a child of Wilmslow and Wilhelmina's, brought up to think of women as exemplifying civilisation at its most delicate and refined, I was stirred to madness by the thought of the untamed jungle on our very doorstep. There I was, tying pretty bows around boxes of the laciest, most feather-light creations, yet just down the road apes and monkeys were riding one another with an abandon that made a mockery of the very idea of clothes at all, let alone haute couture. Push-up ruffle bra-dresses by Prada! Versace metallic skirts in chartreuse green, slit to the waist! Garter belts by La Perla! Who were we kidding?

Mishnah Grunewald was the daughter of an Orthodox rabbi, much given to weeping and mysticism, whose family had got out of Poland just in time. She had turned to chimpanzees in rebellion against the stories of persecution with which her relations had persecuted her. 'I haven't left the fold, I just want the space to question,' she told me. 'And nothing calls Judaism into question quite like monkeys.'

'Not even pigs?'

She threw me a cross look. 'Pigs, pigs, pigs! The one thing everybody thinks they know about Jews – their aversion to pigs. You, however, Guy *Ableman*, should know better.'

'Me?'

I was no more in denial about being Jewish than she was. It simply never entered into the scheme of things for me. As it never had for my parents. Jews? Were we Jews? Fine, but just remind us what Jews were when they were at home?

Here's the proof I wasn't the genuine article. A genuine fired-up apocalyptic Jew, who thought about being Jewish every hour he was awake and most of the hours he wasn't, could never have resisted concluding that sentence with a bitter, deracinated joke.

'So what were Jews when they were at home – *wherever home was?*' But I knew where home was. Home was Wilmslow. We'd been there for centuries. Look up the Wilmslow Ablemans in the Domesday Book if you doubt my word. There you'll find them – my great-great-great-great-great-great-grandparents: Leofrick and Cristiana Ableman. Yeomen retailers.

Mishnah threw me a 'whatever' smile, though 'whatever' was not yet in common usage. I'd been smiled at like that before – by the Felsenstein twins and Michael Ezra, boys I'd flunked football and metalwork with at school. The bonding, *we're all in this ancient shit together* smile, whatever my denials. They had even called me boychick which, as a boy lacking affection – only words loved me – I hadn't minded. Michael Ezra, I minded, but that was later, and for other reasons.

Mishnah Grunewald, with purple eyes and hair as is a flock of goats – straight out of the Holy Land she seemed to come, without a trace of her family's long sojourn in Eastern Europe on her, whereas I was as colourless as pewter, of the same washed-out hue as the Polacks who'd tormented her family for centuries, which is not to imply, for Christ's sake, that I was a bit of a Jew-baiting Polack myself – Mishnah Grunewald smelt of the animals whose confidante she had become, an odour of unremitting rutting that turned me into a wild beast whenever I got to within sniffing distance of her presence. 'You're worse than Beagle,' she used to tell me, Beagle being the dominant male at the breeding centre. I pictured him with a blazing red penis that he was forever working at, much like myself. Though she was matter-of-fact about her work, Mishnah had only to let drop some circumstantial detail of her life in the zoo, such as that she'd once had to lend a hand in the tiger cage, masturbating the wild cats, for all reason to desert me. What was she doing masturbating wild cats? That was just something they did, to keep the zoo quiet.

Honestly? Honestly. Tigers? Yes, tigers. How did that make her feel? Useful. How did it make the tigers feel? You'll have to ask them. And Beagle – did she ever masturbate Beagle? This I demanded to know as I clawed at her clothes. I imagined him looking into her Song of Solomon eyes, his jaw hanging, a chimp besotted with one of the daughters of Canaan, as I was. The answer was no. You didn't do that to monkeys. They were too dangerous. Whereas tigers would go all dopey. 'So which am I,' I asked her, 'an ape or a tiger?' In the end I insisted that she call me Beagle during lovemaking, so there would be no mistake.

Who Gives a Monkey's? was only ostensibly Mishnah's story. Its real subject was – no, not the fine line that divided animals and humans, nothing so trite – but the greater inhumanity and self-disloyalty of humans. Apes knew rage and spite and boredom right enough, but they were not cynical as mankind was. Crazed with undifferentiated lust they might have been, but they were serious in their monkeydom, understood what being of their species entailed, weren't forever jumping ship and crossing over the way humans did, and cared for one another. They even showed a protective love to Mishnah which she assured me she had never met the equal of in her own species. 'What about me?' I'd asked. She laughed. 'You're more feral than any animal in Chester Zoo,' she said. It was the nicest word any woman had ever used of me. Not zoo, though I loved the extra vowel she gave it – zooo, not zo or zuh – but feral. Feral! From the Latin for an unruly beast. Guy Feral. Feral Guy. But I turned it against myself for the sake of art. *Who Gives a Monkey's?* told of unbridled selfishness and moral slippage in the world of men. If Mishnah was the heroine, I was the villain – a man ruled by pointless ambition and a blazing red penis, at whose behest he stumbled blindly into the zoo theologians call hell.

Or was that unfair to zoos? Didn't the undifferentiated lust of their inmates make zoos a paradise? Here was my point: the chimps weren't kinder to one another *in despite* of their libidinousness, but *because* of it.

I wasn't some prophet of unbridled sex. I joined words, not bodies. But I remembered what the novel owed to sex, that sex was integral to it, that prose trumped verse because it celebrated our lower instincts not our higher, except that my point was that our lower instincts *were* our higher instincts.

'Gerald Durrell meets Lawrence Durrell,' the *Manchester Evening Chronicle* quietly enthused. *Cheshire Life* was more uninhibited in its praise – 'At last Wilmslow has its own Marquis de Sade.' You can't buy notices like that. I was even invited to give the annual lecture at Chester Zoo until the head keeper read the book and discovered it ended in a scene of man-on-monkey mayhem in the chimp enclosure.

Mishnah Grunewald, whom I'd stopped seeing years before, and could barely remember, to be honest, now I had Vanessa and Poppy constantly before my eyes, wrote to say she felt she'd been betrayed. Had she known I was planning to make a tasteless priapic comedy out of her profession she would not have taken me into her confidence, let her alone her bed.

What had particularly annoyed her was the epigraph I had cobbled together from some throwaway sentences by Charles Bukowski – 'I ate meat. I had no god. I liked to fuck. Nature didn't interest me. I never voted. I liked wars. History bored me. Zoos bored me.'

'How could you write those things about me?' she wanted to know.

I wrote back to explain they had nothing to do with her. The remarks were not attributable to any living person. In so far as they were the views of anybody, they were the views of the chimp,

Beagle. And if *he* couldn't say zoos bored him, who could?

But she had no feeling for fiction. Who does any more? She took the 'I' in the novel for her and therefore supposed that every thought expressed was intended to be hers. 'You of all people know that zoos don't bore me,' she wrote. 'That's the part that hurts.'

I buried my face in her writing paper. The ape-enclosure smell of it drove me half mad with desire, though I was married to Vanessa by this time. Vanessa, too, though she'd never been near a zoo, drove me half mad with desire. On her I smelt her mother.

Who Gives a Monkey's? was shortlisted for a small prize administered by the estate of a Lancashire mill owner with a taste for local literature and discreet pornography, and was chosen by the arts editor of the northern edition of the *Big Issue* as his Book of the Year. Even the homeless, it appeared, recognised something of their essential nature in my novel. Then it fell into the literary equivalent of those same piss-soaked doorways in which the homeless laid out their cardboard beds – the black hole known as back list.

While I could chalk Chipping Norton down to spur-of-the-moment kleptomania brought on by professional stress – my own fault for succumbing to the hubris of supposing I could charm a book group, but stress is stress whoever is to blame for it – I couldn't pretend I wasn't in other ways behaving strangely. I was tearing off my fingernails, I was pulling hairs out of my moustache, I was peeling the skin from my fingers. When a caged parrot does the psittacine equivalent of one or all of these things, Mishnah had told me, he is diagnosed with depression or dementia. You open the cage and let him fly away; though by that time he has probably forgotten what it was about his freedom he has missed.

I the same. Had anyone opened my cage I wouldn't have known where to fly. Well, I would: I would have flown to my wife's mother's place. But then she wasn't my purpose, she was my consolation for having lost my purpose.

By purpose, understand readers.

I wasn't the only one. No one had readers. But every writer takes the loss of readers personally. Those are *your* readers who have gone missing.

When you have no one to address you address yourself. This was another way in which I was behaving strangely: I was self-communicating, speaking words to no one in particular and not always realising I was doing it. Moving my lips to no effect, and certainly not in the hope of initiating a conversation, usually on long directionless walks through Notting Hill and Hyde Park – for I had moved south on the strength of my early, illusory success – unconscious of the world unless I happened to find myself outside a bookshop in the window of which not one of my books was to be seen. A writer found moving his lips outside a bookshop that doesn't stock his titles is automatically assumed to be uttering menaces and maledictions, or even plotting arson, and I didn't want people to think things had got as bad for me as that.

Whatever it looked like, I wasn't talking, I was writing. Mouthwriting, I suppose you'd have to call it – practising the sound of sentences when I wasn't anywhere I could write them down. This is called having a book on the go but the worrying part was that the book I had on the go was about a book I had on the go about a writer mouth-writing about worrying about mouth-writing. And this is when you know you're in deep shit as a writer – when the heroes of your novels are novelists worrying that the heroes of their novels are novelists who know they're in deep shit.

You don't have to be a psychiatrist to see that stealing your own books symbolises sleeping with your mother-in-law.

Help me, someone, I was saying.

4

Death of a Publisher

Things had not been going well in my neck of the woods: not for me, on account of being a writer whose characters readers didn't identify with, not for my wife who didn't identify with my characters or with me, not for Poppy Eisenhower, my wife's mother, where the problem, to be candid, was that we'd been identifying with each other altogether *too* well, not for my local library which closed only a week after I'd published a florid article in the *London Evening Standard* praising its principled refusal to offer Internet access, and not for my publisher Merton Flak who, following a drunken lunch in my company – I had been the one doing the drinking – went back to his office and shot himself in the mouth.

'I suppose you think all this has got something to do with you,' Vanessa, mysterious and beautiful in black lace, whispered at the funeral.

I shrugged through my tears. Of course I thought it had something to do with me. I thought everything had something to do with me. I was a first-person person by profession. 'I' was the first word of *Who Gives a Monkey's?*. It was also the last. 'And yes I said yes I will I' – no matter that it was a monkey, or might have been a monkey, who was saying it. And the truth is, you can't imagine yourself into the 'I' of another person, or indeed another creature, without imagining yourself.

But even though I was the last author to talk to Merton Flak alive, the fact that he had a gun in his filing cabinet at least proved he must already have been thinking about doing away with himself. Nor did I think I was wholly to blame for the crisis in publishing, the devaluation of the book as object, the disappearance of the word as the book's medium, library closures, Oxfam, Amazon, eBooks, iPads, Oprah, apps, Richard and Judy, Facebook, Formspring, Yelp, three-for-two, the graphic novel, Kindle, vampirism – all of which the head of marketing at Scylla and Charybdis Press mentioned in her eulogy (with some embarrassment, I thought, since she was an inveterate Yelper herself and blogged regularly on weRead) as contributory to poor Merton's taking the drastic step he had. Of these, I was as much a victim as anybody else.

Metaphorically speaking, at least, we all had pistols in our filing cabinets. Even those publishers who still had writers, even those writers who still had readers, knew the game was up. We laughed at what wasn't funny – dry, cancerous explosions, like the guffaws of crows – and fell into moody silences, as though anticipating the death of someone we loved, in the middle of what in better times would have been animated not to say scurrilous conversation. We had stones in our gall bladders, our spleens were engorged, our arteries were clogged. At one time, war or plague would have thinned our population out. Now, unread, we were dying of word-gangrene. Our own unencountered words were killing us.

But there was no solidarity in disaster. We dreaded gatherings and parties in one another's company for fear of encountering someone exempted from the common fate, someone who had broken rank, had received a sliver of good news, a whisper of interest from the gods of television or film, an endorsement from E. E. Freville, otherwise known as Eric the Endorser, a man who at one time would have given anybody a puff for a glass of cheap white wine but after hitting the endorsement jackpot with a succession of Nobel Prize-winners ('Unputdownable'; 'I laughed till I cried, then I cried till I laughed'; 'A page-turner of page-turningly epic proportions') had become a literary personality in his own right and was now said to be reading books before endorsing them. I myself, on account of a number of extraordinarily favourable not to say bizarre reviews I had suddenly started to get on Amazon – 'Cross Mrs Gaskell with Apuleius and you come up with Guy Ableman,' was one of the more recent – had become an object of mistrust to other writers. What was I doing different? Why did I have readers? I didn't, as it happened, I just had stars on Amazon. To tell the truth, though no one believed it, every time a new and more extravagant review appeared – 'A verbal *spermfest*! With his latest novel Guy Ableman surpasses anyone who has ever dipped a pen in the incendiary ink of erotic candour' – my publishers reported a drop in sales.

'Strange,' Merton had admitted, 'but it would seem that people don't want to be told what to like.'

'You mean in the way of erotic candour?'

He swatted the phrase away. 'I mean in the way of anything.'

I had a suggestion. 'In that case, why don't we submit our own reviews to Amazon saying that my books are ratshit?'

He wouldn't hear of it. People didn't want to be told what *not* to like, either. And besides, slagging himself off on Amazon in the hope of increasing sales was an impropriety no serious writer would ever live down. 'It could even be illegal,' Merton reckoned, looking around to be sure no one was listening.

That last lunch I had with him, in a restaurant the size of a matchbox, was our first for more than two years. But for his rubbish wardrobe – British Home Stores chinos of the sort wives buy for husbands and on which he'd wiped his hands of hope a thousand times too often, and some sort of trekking jacket found in one of those safari shops at the Eros end of Piccadilly – I wouldn't have recognised him. He had lost half his teeth and all his hair. Never a talkative man even when times were good and the Pauillac flowed, he sat slumped over his food, a barely touched glass of house wine in front of him, not eating his beetroot salad, his elbows digging into the diners on either side of him, revolving his head violently as though wanting to shake out more teeth. 'Mmm,' he said, whenever our eyes or knees met. Not knowing what else to do, I began ripping at my fingernails under the table.

There are 'mmms' which denote quiet acceptance of the state of things, the slow workings of reflection, or simply embarrassment. Merton's 'mmms' were none of these. Merton's 'mmms' indicated the futility of speech.

For which reason they were infectious. 'Mmm,' I said in return.

In the old days when a publisher took one of his writers out to lunch he'd ask how the work was going. But now, like all publishers, Merton dreaded hearing. What if the work was going well? What if I had a book to show him? What if I was expecting an advance?

Eventually – as much to bring the afternoon to an end as to start a conversation, because the way things were going I would soon have no fingernails left, and because I cared for Merton and couldn't bear what he was going through – I said something. Not, *Christ, these chairs are uncomfortable, Merton,* not *Do you remember when you used to take me to L'Etoile and we ate cervelle de veau, not spotted dick?* but something more sympathetic to his state of mind. A couple of senior publishers – immediately castigated as dead white males – had gone public that weekend about the decline in the literacy of new writing: manuscripts turning up misspelt, ill-punctuated and ungrammatical, an uneducated jumble of mixed metaphors, dangling participles and misattributed apostrophes, less where there should have been fewer, mays where there should have been mights, mights where there should have been mays, theres for theirs and theirs for theres. We hadn't only forgotten how to sell books; we had forgotten how to write them. I didn't doubt that whatever else was at the root of Merton's depression, misattributed apostrophes weren't helping. 'You look,' I said, putting my paper napkin to my mouth, as though I too was in danger of losing teeth, 'like a man who hasn't read anything halfway decent for a long long time.'

I wanted him to see I understood it was hell for all of us.

'No, the opposite,' he said, probing the corners of his eyes with the tips of his fingers. He might have been trying to prise oysters out of their shells, except that he couldn't any longer afford oysters. 'The very opposite. The tragedy of it is, I've had at least twenty works of enduring genius land on my desk this month alone.'

Merton was famous for thinking that every novel submitted to him was a work of enduring genius. He was what was called a publisher of the old school. Finding works of enduring genius was why he'd entered publishing in the first place.

'Mmm,' I said.

Talking works of enduring genius made Merton almost garrulous. 'It would be no exaggeration,' he exaggerated, 'to say that eight or ten of them are masterpieces.'

I pulled a couple of hairs out of my moustache. '*That* good?'

'Breathtakingly good.'

Since none of these was mine, no matter what they said on Amazon, I had to labour to be excited for him. 'So where's the tragedy?' I asked, half hoping he'd tell me that the authors of at least four or five of them were dead.

But I knew the answer. None was suitable for three-for-two. None featured a vampire. None was about the Tudors. None could be marketed as a follow-up to *The Girl Who Ate Her Own Placenta*.

It was even possible that none was free of the charge of dangling a participle. Though Merton was a publisher of the old school, the new school – which held that a novel didn't have to be well written to be a masterpiece, indeed was more likely to be a masterpiece for being ill-written – had begun to wear away his confidence. He didn't know what was what any more. And whatever was what was not being submitted to him.

'Do you know what I am expected to require of you?' he suddenly looked me in the eyes and said. 'That you twit.'

'Twit?'

'Twit, tweet, I don't know.'

'And why are you expected to require it of me?'

'So that you can do our business for us. So that you can connect to your readers, tell them what you're writing, tell them where you're going to be speaking, tell them what you're reading, tell them what you're fucking eating.'

'Spotted dick.'

He didn't find that funny. 'So why particularly me?' I asked.

'Not just you. Everybody. Can you imagine asking Salinger to twit?'

'Salinger's dead.'

'No bloody wonder.'

He fell silent again, and then asked me if I used the Internet. *Used the Internet* – you had to love Merton, he was so out of touch.

'A bit.'

'Do you blag?'

'Blog? No.'

'Do you read other people's blags?'

'Blogs. Sometimes.'

'The blog's the end of everything,' he said.

The word sounded uncouth on his lips. It was like hearing the Archbishop of Canterbury talking about taking a Zumba class. The blog belongs to yesterday, I wanted to tell him. If you're going to blame anything you should be blaming myBlank and shitFace and whatever else was persuading the unRead to believe everybody had a right to an opinion. But it was rare to hear Merton open up and I didn't want to silence him almost before he'd begun. 'Tell me more,' I said.

He looked around the room as though he'd never seen it before. 'What's there to tell? Novels are history, not because no one can write them but because no one can read them. It's a different idea of language. Go on the Internet and all you'll find is —' He searched for a word.

I offered him expostulation. A favourite word of mine. It evoked the harrumphings of bigoted old men. Only now it was the bigoted young who were harrumphing.

Merton seemed happy with it, in so far as he could be said to seem happy with anything. 'Novelists find their way to meaning,' he said. I nodded furiously. Wasn't I still finding my way to mine? But he was speaking to the unseen forces, not to me. 'The blog generation knows what it wants to say before it says it,' he continued. 'They think writing is opinionated statement. In the end that is all they will come to expect from words. My own children ask me what I mean all the time. They want to know what I'm getting at. They ask the point of the books I publish. What are they on about, Dad? Tell us so we don't have to read them. I can't come up with an answer. What's *Crime and Punishment* on about?'

'Crime and punishment.'

He didn't appreciate my facetiousness. 'So you think their question is fair? You think a novel is no more than its synopsis?'

'You know I don't.'

'Do you have children? I can't remember.'

'No.'

'You're lucky in that case. You don't have to see how badly

educated they are. You don't have to see them come home from school having read a scene from *King Lear* – the one in the rain, it's not considered necessary to read about him when he's dry – and thinking they know the play. It's about this old fart, Dad.'

'So what do you say to them?'

'I say literature is not *about* things.'

'And what do they say?'

'That I'm an old fart.'

These were more words than I'd heard Merton utter in a decade. But they were to be his last. 'Mmm,' he said when he saw the bill.

Later that afternoon, without twitting about it to anyone, he did what he had to do.

If you discounted the book-stealing, the mouth-writing and the hair-pulling, I was in better shape than many. I was certainly in better shape than poor Merton. I still dressed well, couture being in my veins, bought expensive shoes and belts, and tucked my shirt into my trousers. (Slovenly dresser, slovenly writer.) But by no stretch of the imagination could I have been said to look like someone who was thriving. I was in my forty-third year – ancient for a twenty-first-century novelist, and certainly too ancient to go on appearing on any of those lists of writers under whatever that I had once graced – but I could have passed for someone ten or twelve years older. I'd let my gym membership lapse, upped my wine consumption to more than two bottles a night, and stopped trimming my eyebrows or having my hair cut.

Anyone would have thought I didn't want to see out. (Which in point of fact I didn't.)

But more worrying was that no one wanted to see in. I was like a garden no one gave a monkey's fuck about.

5

Me, Me, Me

Make allowance for the self-pity intrinsic to a dying profession. In truth, Vanessa gave sufficiently a monkey's fuck as to say she thought I needed a holiday. And never mind that she'd been saying I needed a holiday, needed to be off, needed to be somewhere else, needed to be somewhere she wasn't, for the nearly twenty years we'd been together.

'A holiday from you?'

'From your work. From yourself. Be somebody other for a while.'

'I'm always somebody other. Being somebody other *is* my work.'

'No it isn't. You're always you. You just give yourself different names.'

I sighed the marital sigh.

'Don't make that noise,' she said.

I shrugged the marital shrug.

But she was flowing. It was exhilarating, like being swept away in a warm river. 'Get away from yourself. And if you think you need a holiday from me as well, then take one. I won't stand in your way. Have I ever? Look at me. Be honest with me.' She slipped her hand between my thighs. 'Be honest with yourself. Have I ever?'

In the excitement I forgot the question. 'Have you ever what?'

She withdrew her hand. 'Stood in your way.'

'No,' I said.

'Thank you for being honest.'

I waited for her to slide her hand back. Wasn't that how a wife was meant to reward a husband for his honesty?

'But this isn't a green light for one of your literary flings,' she went on. 'I'll know. I always know. You know I'll always know. You get soppy with me on the phone and shitty garage flowers start arriving twice a day. In which case enjoy yourself, just don't expect me to be here when you get back.'

'*If* I get back . . .'

That might sound like a man looking for a way out. But I wasn't. I loved Vanessa. She was the second most important woman in my life. What I was looking for was something to write about that somebody not me wanted to read about. If she left me I'd have been heartbroken, but at least heartbreak is a subject. It's not abuse but it's still a subject.

'Don't threaten me with empty threats,' she said. If I was running low on ideas she was running low on humour. Not that jokes had ever been her strong suit. She was too good-looking to be a joker. At forty-one she could still walk on seven-inch heels with blood-red soles without her knees buckling. And you need serious concentration for that.

'Come with me,' I said, picturing us strolling arm in arm down some Continental promenade together, she towering over me in her sado-spikes, men envying me her legs. Our stopping every now and then for her to stoop and slide her hand between my thighs. Men envying me that.

'I can do fine on my own,' she reminded me.

'I know you can do fine on your own. But life isn't all about you. *I* don't do fine unless you're with me.'

'You, you, you.'

'Me, me, me.'

'And where would we go?'

'You choose. Australia?'

Now that *was* picking a fight. We'd been to Australia the year before, to the Adelaide Festival – where else? – in the hope I might get a book about a writer going to the Adelaide Festival – where else? – and had very nearly come unstuck. The usual. Fan of writer in need of a fillip (fan is even called Philippa: get that) tells how she's trembled over every word writer writes whereupon writer checks the coast is clear, takes fan outside and trembles over every button on her dress.

Did Vanessa know? Vanessa knew everything.

'Vanish again,' she warned me, during a getting-to-know-everybody breakfast in the Barossa – Philippa, whom I knew well enough by this time, sitting opposite in all her prim lasciviousness: such dirty girls, these word tremblers – 'and you'll be going back to London on your own.'

'What are you proposing – that you stay here? You'd go mad here.'

'No, that's you. *You'd* go mad here. You already are mad here.'

'And you're telling me you'd keep chickens and grow wine?'

'I'd get some peace.'

Ah, peace! The one person you don't get married to, if it's peace you want, is a writer. You'd have more chance with a bomb-disposal expert.

So my suggestion, when we were back home, of an Australian holiday, was purposely provocative. Novelist provokes wife – there was surely a novel in that.

In the event we stayed in London and talked about a divorce.

'Don't threaten what you can't deliver,' she said.

Actually, the idea was hers. I reminded her of that. Divorce was the last thing I wanted. I still enjoyed her bruising company, still got a kick out of looking at her. Her face was like a small hall of mirrors, all sharp edges and bloody reflections. When I looked at my face in hers I saw myself cut to ribbons.

The halo of red hair around her head – the blood fountaining from mine.

The slightly snaggled front tooth, which looked loose but wasn't – the state of my brain.

So why had I vanished into the South Australian night with Philippa whom I did not get a kick out of looking at? Because she was there. And because I had a reputation for wildness to keep up. Don't ask with whom. With myself.

And because Vanessa threatening to divorce me was exciting.

'You don't have to tell me it's my idea,' she said. 'All your ideas are my ideas.'

'I grant you that. I don't have any ideas. I'm not a philosopher. I'm an anti-philosopher. I tell tales.'

'Tales! When did you ever tell a tale unless I gave it to you.'

'Name a tale you gave me, Vee.'

'One!'

'Yes, one.'

'Do you know what,' she said suddenly, turning her face from me as though any sight had to be better, 'I hate your mind.'

'My *mind*?'

'What's left of it.'

'Is this all because I've started a new book?'

Vanessa hated it when I started a new book. She saw it as me getting one over her who hadn't started a new book because she hadn't finished, or indeed started, the old one. But she also hated it when I hadn't started a new book, because not starting a new book

34

made me querulous and sexually unreliable. At least when I was writing a new book she knew where I was. The downside of that being that as soon as she knew where I was she wished I were somewhere else.

In fact, my question hid a lie; I hadn't started a new book, not in the sense of starting *writing* a new book. I had mouth-written a hundred new books, I just didn't believe in any of them. It wasn't personal, it wasn't only *my* books I didn't believe in, it was books full stop. If *I* was over, it was because the book was over. But Vanessa wasn't aware of the full extent of the crisis. She saw me trudge off to my study, heard the keys of my computer making their dead click and assumed I was still pouring forth my soul abroad like Keats's logorrhoeic nightingale.

I even affected high spirits. 'I'm sitting on top of the world,' I sang, breaking for tea.

'No you're not,' she shouted from her room.

She was contradictory to her soul. 'I did it my way,' I sang the morning after our wedding. 'No you didn't,' she said, not even looking up from her newspaper.

If my singing irritated her, the sound of my writing drove her to the edge of madness. But so did the sound of my not writing. This was part of the problem of our marriage. The other part was me. Not what I did, what I was. The fact of me. The manness of me.

'You, you, you,' she said for the umpteenth time that night. It was like a spell; if she said the word often enough maybe I, I, I would vanish in a vapour of red wine.

We were out to dinner. We were always out to dinner. Along with everybody else. Dinner was all there was left to do.

It was one of those restaurants where the doorman comes round to greet the diners he knows. Be ignored by the doorman and it's plain you're no one. He doffed his top hat to me. We shook hands.

I held his long enough for everybody to see just how well we were acquainted. It even occurred to me to call him 'Sir' and hold my hand out for a tip.

After he'd passed on we resumed where we'd left off. 'You were saying,' I said. 'Me, me, me . . .'

'You think you're the only person out there not getting what you deserve. Do you think *I* get what *I* deserve? The spectacle of you wittering on about the extinction of the art of reading makes me sick. What about the extinction of the art of writing? Dirty-minded shopkeeper looking for sex in Wilmslow writes about dirty-minded shopkeeper looking for sex in Wilmslow. Christ, with a subject like that, you're lucky you've *got* a reader!'

'I wasn't a shopkeeper, Vee, I was a fashion consultant.'

'Fashion consultant, you! Whoever consulted you on fashion?'

I wanted to say 'The women of Wilmslow', which would have been the truth, but in the context of this argument lacked gravitas. 'My advice was frequently heeded,' I said instead. 'Though not, I accept, by you.'

'You looked after your crazy mother's shop and drooled over her customers. I saw you, remember. I was one of the customers. And as for heeding your advice – why would I want to look like a Cheshire trollop?'

She had a point.

She never didn't have a point. It was why I respected her. I'd say it was why I loved her but it felt as though I loved her in spite of her always having a point.

I scanned the restaurant. A psychologist might have supposed I was unconsciously searching for the Cheshire trollop Vanessa had refused to be, but in fact I was wondering if there was anyone here I recognised. It calmed me to think that rich and famous people had nothing better to do with their evening than I had. Ditto less rich and famous people who would be finding it calming to see me there. It's possible I was looking for them too.

Vanessa was still ranting about readers and how I should count myself lucky that I had any at all. 'If you had only one that would still be one more than you deserve and certainly one more than I've got.'

I didn't point out that the reason she didn't have a reader was that she hadn't written anything for anyone to read. And I *hadn't* been saying I was the only person out there not getting what I deserved. I'd been saying – well, what had I been saying? No more than that the roof was falling in on all of us. *No one* was getting what he (sorry: 'he/she') deserved, unless he ('he/she') was getting more than he ('they') deserved. There was, in the new scheme of things, no proportionality of reward. Either you got too much or you got too little. Which was a universal, not a particular complaint. But Vanessa didn't believe I had a right to voice a complaint of any sort. I was one of the lucky ones. I was published . . .

And there you have it. Like the rest of the world, Vanessa wanted to be a published writer. She was the promise of the future: no readers, all writers. She'd seen me become a writer, watched the empty pages fill, been present during the initial excitement of publication, and if I could become a published writer, a man shorter than her even when she wasn't wearing seven-inch heels, a man who said foolish things, fucked foolish girls, stole his own books from Oxfam and all his best ideas from her, why couldn't she? Hadn't she written a sample chapter? Hadn't an important agent said she had what it took?

'That was ten years ago,' I reminded her.

I didn't mention that the agent had his arm up her skirt while he was telling her she had what it took, or that he had since slashed his wrists – though there was no provable connection between those two events. It wasn't tact that stopped me; Larry's suicide was simply not worth mentioning. You could count on the fingers of one hand the number of people in publishing still breathing.

'Well, what time do I have to finish a novel? I'm always having to listen to the racket of you belting out yours.'

When I wasn't defending my right to make a racket, I was sorry for her. I could see she was at her wits' end, that non-production was making her ill. It was as though, without a novel on the go, her life had no meaning. Sometimes she would put her fists between her breasts, like a mother ripped from her babies, or a Medea who had killed her babies, and beg me to be quiet so she could think. I was killing her, she told me. And I believed it. I was killing her.

She kept asking me to leave the house to write, to build a shed at the bottom of the garden, to rent an office, to go away for a year. It was the noise my writing made, the computer waking – 'Boing!' – to my presence every morning, the hammering at the dead keys. She was more jealous of my computer than she'd been of Philippa. Sometimes I thought I heard her crouching outside my door, to punish herself with the noise of the detested keyboard. On those occasions I typed gobbledegook at speed to goad her still more. It wasn't my intention to torment her into greater extremes of jealousy, it was my intention to torment her into getting back to her book. In this I was as crazed as everybody else. Books were over but writing them was the only thing I valued. So long as she didn't have a novel to her name, yes, Vanessa was a dead woman.

Everyone was. You wrote or you were nothing.

'Just fucking finish it, Vee.'

'Just fucking finish it! *Just fucking finish it!* What the fuck do you think I'm doing? Get out of my life and I'll fucking finish it.'

I was lucky I wasn't a dead man myself.

You know you're in deep shit as a novelist when it's not only your heroes who are novelists having troubling finishing their novels but your wife is a novelist having trouble finishing hers.

But since the novel as a living form had had it, why did it matter what either of us was doing?

A fair but stupid question, such as someone visiting from another planet might ask. Life as a living form had had it – life with purpose, life driven by idealism or belief, life that was more than shoving down expensive grub in restaurants that were booked up two years in advance unless you knew the right people, as I did – but we still lived, still made our reservations, still sat at our favourite tables eating food we could no longer taste and could barely afford. Don't look for logic. The worse things get, the more attached to them we become.

I called the waiter over. 'André, another bottle of Saint-Estèphe.'

He returned with the wine list. He was sorry, no more Saint-Estèphe.

No more. It was the catchword of the times. Everything was running out. No more of anything. I thought of Poe's great poem of ecstatic madness – Quoth the Raven, 'Nevermore.'

'What did you say?' Vanessa asked.

I was starting to talk to myself. 'Nevermore,' I said.

She thought I was describing our marriage. 'Bring it on,' she dared me.

On the way out of the restaurant I noticed an unfinished bottle of Saint-Estèphe on a vacated table. I looked around to see if anyone was watching. Everyone was watching, there was nothing else to do *but* watch – but what the hell! I grabbed the bottle by its neck and knocked back the dregs.

The novelist as drunk. I hoped readers of mine had seen what I'd done. Then I remembered I had no readers.

'They call me mellow yellow,' I sang.

'No, they don't,' Vanessa said.

*   *   *

On the emptied street, Vanessa paused to give a pound coin to a tramp. Not any old beggar or derelict, not a drugged-up Soho layabout or a *Big Issue* seller, but a tramp of the old school, wind-burnt face, long white beard, trousers ripped all the way to his groin (so better dressed than most of my profession), a who-gives-a-monkey's indifference to whether anyone noticed him or not. He was sitting on a wooden bench outside a pub, writing in a reporter's notebook.

'He looks just like Ernest Hemingway,' Vanessa whispered admiringly, reaching into her bag.

'He seems to be writing longer sentences than Ernest Hemingway's,' I whispered back.

I wanted to see what he was writing but couldn't, with decency, get close enough. I felt slightly shamed by him, such profound concentration, such fluency of the hand, no need of a computer. Was he the last of the pen-holding, *plein-air* novelists?

In so far as she was capable of doing anything discreetly, Vanessa discreetly plonked her coin in front of him. He didn't look up or otherwise acknowledge her. I knew how he felt. There was a sentence he had to get right, and nothing else existed.

Vanessa took my arm. She was trembling. All acts of generosity on her own part moved her deeply. I even wondered if she was going to shed a tear. (*Were* going to shed a tear? *Was* going to shed a tear.)

As we walked on, the sound of a coin hitting the pavement and then rolling into the road followed us.

Vanessa jumped. Anyone would have thought she'd heard a gun go off. I jumped with her. We were all keyed up. A car's exhaust backfired and we feared another publisher had taken his life.

'If you're thinking of going back and picking it up for him, I wouldn't,' I said. 'That didn't sound like a fall to me. It was too violent. I'd say he threw it.'

'At me?'

I shrugged. 'You. Us. Humanity.'

I was secretly impressed. Not just the last of the *plein-air* novelists, but the last of the idealists for whom only art mattered.

A question that was sometimes asked: What had a woman as beautiful and confident as Vanessa, who could have married a rock star or a banker or a presenter on breakfast television – who could, for God's sake, have *been* a presenter on breakfast television – seen in me?

The answer I invariably gave: 'Words.'

In the century of the dying of the word there were still women who lusted after men to whom words came easily. And vice versa, of course, though the men who didn't have words themselves were less likely to value them, and were certainly far more frightened of them, than the women. Give a man a word or two more than the common and he'll always find a woman to revere him. Fill a woman's mouth with words and she'll scare the living daylights out of the other sex. Nothing but bags of nerves, the other sex. Every man I knew, a quivering wreck the moment a woman spoke.

Something else that was dying – men.

As both a reverer of words in men and a woman whose own words put men off – I'm talking about the words that flowed from her, not the novels she was never going to assemble from them – Vanessa considered herself lucky to have found me. She never said as much to my face, but I understood that to be the reason she had married me in the first place, the reason she had stayed with me and the reason she once flattened a young reviewer whose name was all initials and who had spoken ill of my prose style.

41

There's loyalty for you. But when I thanked her for it afterwards she denied it had anything to do with me. 'You qua you deserve all you get,' she said. 'It was your gift I was defending.'

'I am my gift,' I told her.

She coughed and quoted Frieda Lawrence at me. 'Never trust the teller,' she said, 'trust the tale.'

'That's D. H. Lawrence,' I corrected her.

'Oh yeah!' She laughed wildly.

But her point remained the same, whichever Lawrence she was quoting. The initialled reviewer had traduced the tale, the fragile thing of words spun only incidentally by me, as the farmer only incidentally grows the wheat. (And stolen from Vanessa, anyway.) That was why she trod on his spectacles: so that he would know how it felt to be the word, the wounded logos, kicked when it was down.

Things dying can have a voluptuous beauty. Only think of the dying of the day or the dying of the summer. So it was with the word. The sicker it grew, the more livid it turned, the more people of an over-refined and morbid disposition fell in love with its putrefaction.

Would I be around to see it finally pass away? I wasn't sure, but I could imagine the scene, like the burning of a Viking hero at sea — the sky, as bloody as a reviewer's nose, painted by J. M. W. Turner; the last of the verbalising men looking into the self-combusting sun, hoarsely mouthing their goodbyes; the women tearing their hair and wailing. Foremost among them, atremble in lacy weeds such as those she'd worn to see off poor Merton, my Vanessa.

Magnificent in mourning.

6

Party's Over

Mourning. We were all doing it. The trick was not to let it get you down.

After Merton died I thought it would be a good idea to see my agent to talk about what next. A living writer needs a living publisher.

Over the phone, Francis wondered what the hurry was. I could hear the alarm in his voice.

Like Merton, he dreaded the prospect of a new book. Knowing writers were coming to see them, some agents had taken to locking themselves in lavatories rather than have a manuscript handed to them personally like a subpoena. That was how far the situation had deteriorated. A good day now was one in which no one gave them anything they had to find a publisher to sell to.

But at least I *had* an agent. 'So who's representing you now?' other writers would ask me when we met at literary parties. We called them parties but they were more like wakes. Except that at a wake there'd have been more to drink, and fuller sandwiches. Maybe even sausage rolls. I evaded the question. Give another writer the name of your agent and he stroke she would try to steal him stroke her off you.

Sometimes I'd lie. 'I'm going it alone now,' I'd say.

'Can that work?' Damien Clery wanted to know.

He was the author of slightly camp, light-hearted social come-
dies set in cathedral towns – Trollope in a tutu, one reviewer had
called him – but was better known for having jumped his agent
from the other side of the desk and broken his nose. Since then,
no agency would touch him. No publisher either. For the last
four years he had been living off a charity administered by the
Scrivener. I found him frightening, not by virtue of his violence of
temper but the very opposite. He was the sweetest, mildest-
mannered novelist in London. He had golden curls, lovely
lilac-coloured eyes, and spoke melodiously. But you never knew
when he would turn feral – a word I begrudged him because
Mishnah Grunewald had used it of me, though I had never
touched an agent's nose.

'It works fine, Damien,' I confided, 'but it means you have to do
a lot of legwork. You have to deposit the manuscript on a publisher's desk by hand. No point posting it. They won't read it. You need
to make personal contact.'

'They won't let me near. There are photographs of me in the
reception area of every publishing house in the country. Security
has me out before I can even ring the bell.'

'Ah,' I said, backing away.

'I suppose I could get somebody else to deliver for me.'

'That might work,' I said. 'Though they'd still know it was you
from the name on the typescript.'

'Not if I changed it.' He gulped down a full glass of wine at
terrifying speed and then had another idea. 'Hey,' he said, 'you
wouldn't be prepared to drop off some manuscripts for me?'

I backed away further. 'Would have done so gladly,' I lied, 'but
they know me too, remember.'

'Yes, but you could say you were delivering for a friend.'

'I could. But I wouldn't be comfortable doing that if you

changed your name. Once it came out that you weren't who you said you were, we'd both be blackballed.'

'I am *already* blackballed,' he said, as though that were my fault. He looked me up and down with his lovely lilac eyes and shook his golden curls. He'd remember me, I was to understand.

Manuscrip*t*s, he'd said. That was the alarming part. *Some* manuscripts. So how many of them were there? A rejection of a single manuscript can turn the gentlest of us angry. The idea of Damien Clery carting around a whole barrowload of unpublished comic novels from publisher to publisher and being ejected before he made it past reception was even more frightening than the speed with which he was dispatching wine. When he blew his top next there was no knowing the damage he would do.

I was pleased with myself, at least, for not giving him Francis's name. If anyone was going to punch my agent on the nose, I wanted it to be me.

Convince me, Francis's expression always said these days. Give me a good reason for attending to your proposal.

I'd been toying for some years with the idea of writing a revivifying sequel to *Who Gives a Monkey's?*. *Who Gives a Monkey's About Who Gives a Monkey's?* was one idea, or maybe just *Monkey's Revisited*.

Francis breathed hard whenever I suggested this, as though it was a conversation he wasn't sure his heart would allow him to survive. 'Move on,' he always said, pouring himself water from a cooler.

He no longer poured me a glass.

I often wondered whether Francis's lack of enthusiasm for a sequel could be attributed to his not having been my agent for the original. My first agent – Quinton O'Malley – went missing on the Hindu Kush with the manuscript of my second novel in his backpack. His body was never recovered, though pages of my manuscript continued to be found scattered over a wide area for years after. Had

Quinton lost his bearings and gone stumbling through the ice with my manuscript wrapped around him for insulation, or had the novel itself sent him mad? The question, to tell the truth, wasn't much discussed. A literary agent going missing was too common an occurrence to attract speculation. And neither the Afghani nor the Pakistani police was much bothered to investigate.

Whatever his motives, I didn't doubt the soundness of Francis's advice. Most agents were telling their clients the same thing. Move on. Meaning move on from doing what you used to do, from hoping what you used to hope, or from hoping anything; move on from the fantasy that words could make a difference, could make a better world, or could make you a decent living. In some cases it simply meant move on from the idea of being represented by your agent. It wasn't just Damien Clery who was in trouble. Half the fiction writers in the country had been shown the door by their publishers; the other half made phone calls to their agents that were not returned. Writers needed silence but not a silence as profound as this.

It wasn't just back list that was a black hole. Front list was no better.

I have said: I was one of the lucky ones. Francis Fowles believed in me, for no better reason, I sometimes thought, than that we were both short. In my experience literature is a tall man's business – not fiction, maybe, but every other branch of the profession – so there was an automatic, unspoken confederacy of the short between us. Francis's enemies – publishers he had once persuaded to pay too much, writers he refused to take on, other agents whose writers he stole, literary editors who hated him because they hated everybody – called him 'the Dwarf', but he was by no stretch of the imagination dwarfish, his roundness simply made him appear smaller than he was, as my gauntness made me look bigger, but side by side we were the same size. The other thing we'd shared was constipation, each of us going so far as to recommend the other remedies, though

since the Great Decline everyone involved with books was constipated. (Literary editors the worst, but then literary editors were in
the worst position: sedentary to no creative end, jealous of every
book that landed on their table, each a further nail in the coffin of
their own unfulfilled creativity.)

Notwithstanding Francis's faith in me, I noticed that no title of
mine was visible on his shelves. In the past when I'd called on him
I'd be kept waiting in reception while he or one of his assistants
rearranged the books so that my latest could be retrieved from the
pile, dusted and displayed face out. 'Just been rereading my favourite bits,' he would say, when I entered his office. But in line with
more recent agency practice he had abandoned this subterfuge.
The party's over, he wanted me to know now. The age of sparing
a writer's feelings was past. Displayed face out on his shelves was a
new TV tie-in cookery book by Dahlia Blade, a bulimic Kabbalist
from an all-vegan girl band, and *Blinder*, the memoirs of Billy
Funhouser, a teenager from Atlanta who'd lost his sight when his
adoptive mother's breasts exploded in his face.

Francis greeted me with a sad smile in which I was to see the
ghost of better times. It was no fun for him, any of this. He'd worn
bow ties when I first met him. But bow ties no longer went with
the territory. Now, to suggest a casualness inimical to his nature and
his bulk, he wore a striped slim-fit work-shirt outside jeans. You
could tell he had no wife. No wife would have let her husband go
out in a shirt like that.

He sat down with difficulty. 'So?'

'I need a publisher.'

'For what?'

'To publish me.'

'You've got a publisher.'

'He's dead, Francis.'

He pulled a face. Dead! Who wasn't? But he did say, 'Terrible business,' and then ask, 'To publish anything in particular?'

I had another crack at *Monkey's*. Half sequel, I said, half essay, half lament.

He held his heart. 'You can't have three halves.'

'Why not? *The Monkey on My Back* – a discursive novel in three parts.'

'What would you be half sequelling, half lamenting and half discoursing about?'

I opened my arms as though to introduce him to his own room.

'My furniture?'

I laughed. 'What we've descended to. The state of the art. The mess we're in.'

He pretended not to know what I was referring to.

Denial. Who could blame him? It was deny or die.

'So how many weeks has *Blinder* been number one?' I asked, by way of making my distemper more specific.

'Don't knock it,' he said. 'Ten per cent of Billy Funhouser's royalties are going to fund a class action.'

'Against whom?'

'Against the silicone company, who do you think?'

'Class action! Are you telling me that exploding implants are blinding children all over America?'

'You'd better believe it.'

I shook my head.

But Francis always knew when he had me. 'Books are still capable of being a force for good,' he said. 'It doesn't all have to be navel-gazing.'

'Who's navel-gazing?'

'Monkeys, monkeys . . . Do you want me to tell you how one always knows a writer's in trouble as a writer?'

I didn't want him to lose faith in me as a writer. 'No, Francis,' I said. 'I know when a writer's in trouble. When he resorts to writing about writing. And do you want me to tell you how a man knows he's in trouble as a man?' (I didn't want him to lose faith in me as a man either.) 'When he starts feeling up his mother-in-law. In my case the two are not unrelated.'

In better times, when authors and their agents were expected to hit the town together, Francis had got us both drunk at the Garrick where he confided to me, among other indiscretions, his ongoing affair with a writer of historical romances with a strong factual slant. Their liaison, he'd told me, was conducted in costume. I'd fallen silent when I learned this, imagining him in petticoat breeches and a peruke. He mistook my silence for erotic envy. 'Yes, I'm having quite a time of it,' he'd admitted, looking around the room and blushing. Since then, although the carousing had gone the way of long lunches and launch parties, we'd kept up this tradition of exchanging inappropriate personal confidences – much of them coming from me, and most of them fallacious, in the cause of keeping him as my agent.

'You're feeling up your mother-in-law?'

'In a manner of speaking.'

'Does that mean you are or you aren't?'

'I am and I am not, yes.'

'Have I met your mother-in-law?'

'You wouldn't ask me if you had. She's a woman you don't forget.' I rolled my eyes, as though up and around her thighs.

He waited, chewing his thumb, for me to roll my eyes up and around some other part of her.

'What's her name?'

'What's her name got to do with anything?'

'I want to know who this person is that I wouldn't have forgotten had I met her.'

'Poppy.'

'Poppy!' He sucked in air through his teeth, as though already, on the strength of her name alone, he was as infatuated with her as I was. 'Poppy who?'

'Poppy Eisenhower.'

If it was infatuation before, it was love now. '*The* Eisenhower?'

'Could be distantly related. Her second husband was American. I don't think she was with him long enough to find out who his family was. He kicked her out after she'd posed with her cello for a poster advertising a Boccherini concert.'

'Sounds a bit unreasonable.'

I didn't tell him what Poppy had shockingly early in our acquaintance told me – that she'd posed for the poster nude. I didn't think he could take it.

But he was capable of making her nude without my help. Poppy, pose, cello, Boccherini – let's be fair: the words themselves undressed her.

He shaped one of his eyebrows into a question mark. I shaped one of mine into the answer he desired.

'So, she married again?' he pursued after a moment's lewd, musical reflection.

I shook my head.

'Then why haven't you introduced her to me? I know your wife, why shouldn't I know her mother?'

'Ah, Francis!' I said, implying I didn't dare trust her in his company, the devilish dwarf he was.

To such despicable acts of servility were writers now reduced.

He sat forward in his chair, with even more difficulty than when he'd sat back. 'Poppy Eisenhower,' he repeated. He seemed to be searching for an idea that was worrying him. 'You aren't thinking of writing about it, I hope? I know you.'

'It?'

'Her. Poppy Eisenhower, and you. The situation.'

'*The Monkey and the Mother-in-Law*?'

He put his hands together like a supplicant running out of patience. 'Guy, unless you actually want to go and live with monkeys like Jane Goodall,' he said, 'which I would not necessarily dissuade you from doing, but *unless* you're going to do that, my final word to you on the subject is forget them.'

'Monkeys with me are metaphorical,' I told him.

'That's why no one gives one.'

'All right, no more monkeys. But I like suddenly the idea of writing about my mother-in-law. Why couldn't I have come up with that? A paean to the older woman.'

'Don't. I beg you, don't.'

'Are you thinking about Vanessa?'

'I'm thinking about you. It'd be professional suicide.'

'Why? I thought older women were all the rage. MILFs, Cougars, now the MILAW. It's a winner, Francis.'

'Not the way you'd do it.'

'How would I do it?'

'Masculinistically.'

'What does that mean?'

'It means that women wouldn't like it.'

'Why wouldn't women like it?'

'Why don't women like anything you do? Because you don't meet them halfway . . . because you won't let them in . . . because you write about chimps with flaming red penises? How do I know? Stay away – that's all I'm saying. Feel her up in real life, if you must. Not on the page.'

'So no monkeys, no mothers-in-law, no masculinism . . . what does that leave?'

He had an answer ready. 'A Swedish detective.'

'I don't know anything about Swedish detectives. I've never been to Sweden.'

'A boy detective, then. You've been a boy, haven't you? Tell me you've been a boy.'

'I'm not interested in detectives, Francis.'

'What about a Wilmslow detective? There hasn't been one of those that I know of.'

'That's because there are no crimes to detect in Wilmslow. Except for parking offences and rates evasion. Or being a footballer. I suppose I could at a pinch make him a parking warden, or a rates evasion officer who has his eye on every property owned by the board of Manchester United in order to pay them back for refusing him a trial . . .'

'Sounds good . . .'

'. . . and who just happens to be fucking his mother-in-law.'

'Who just happens to look like a monkey . . . Tell me about it.'

'Poppy doesn't look like a monkey,' I said.

'I'm sure she doesn't.' He sounded very tired. He began rubbing his hand over his face. I half expected his features to be gone when he took his hand away.

'So where exactly does this leave us, Francis?' I asked, after a decent interval.

'Fucked,' he said with a laugh.

'Are you describing the industry, my future prospects, our relations, or fiction in general?'

'All of them.'

'And a new publisher?'

'You write the book, I'll find the publisher. In the meantime I'd stay where you are. But when you do give me a story, make it one I can persuade a publisher he can publish.'

'I don't like the way you say "story". You know I don't write "stories" in that sense.'

'You mean in the sense of something happening?'

'I mean in the sense of plot. People confuse plot and story. They think there's no story if there's no machination. Fucking code-breaking, for Christ's sake. Plenty of things happen in my books, Francis. Even leaving aside the wars my words wage, plenty happens. People look at one another, talk to one another, fall in and out of love. They are driven on by their psychologies and if psychology isn't story I don't know what it is. You know what Henry James said about a psychological reason being story enough for him . . .'

'And you know what H. G. Wells said about there being nothing on the altar of James's prose but a dead kitten, an eggshell and . . . something else.'

'*A bit of string*. So what's your point? That I should be more like H. G. Wells? Are you recommending I write science fiction now?'

Francis fell silent. He looked, suddenly, about a hundred.

'Write whatever you fancy. I'll do what I can,' he said.

I felt about a hundred myself.

You have occasionally to see your agent, as you have occasionally to see your publisher, but unless you are a writer of what the malignantly illiterate call 'stories' you always wish you hadn't. Frankly, a visit to your embalmer would be more fun. And would certainly hold out a greater promise of *something* after death.

I wanted to ask him if he really thought we were fucked, or if he was just playing with me. But walking past the books on his desk, the memoirs of Billy Funhouser, martyr to his mother's plastic surgery, and Dahlia Blade's cookbook for bulimics, I knew the answer to the question.

Whatever else, fiction was fucked.

7

Room at the Bottom

Talking about answers – there's an easy answer to the question when did it all start to go wrong for me. From the moment it all started to go right.

You write your first novel and you've pretty well said what you have to say. I was twenty-four when I wrote mine, twenty-seven when it was finally published – so I just made it onto the list of the hundred best male writers in Britain and the Commonwealth under twenty-eight – and I might as well have taken the Merton route there and then. Not a reflection on my work. Nothing to do with me qua me, to borrow a favourite locution of Vanessa's. It's the rule of nature.

After a prolonged courtship – something else I learnt from Mishnah Grunewald – the male black widow spider of North America mates once and then dies. Even if the female doesn't eat him he has nothing left to offer. Such things are common among males. You get one go, you give your all, and then it's curtains. The male novelist the same. You spruce yourself up, you date, you deliver yourself of all your best lines, you impregnate, and you're spent. Goodnight, sweet prince.

But where the spider offers himself to be eaten, or crawls into a corner to die, the male novelist goes on beating his meat to no effect, looking to repeat the performance that so pleased the female of the species the first time round, but without the conviction, the passion or, to be frank, the spider sperm, all the while suffering the excruciations of the slowest extinction of them all – death by creeping invisibility: a day at a time, a book at a time, the novelist vanishing from the shelves of public libraries, from the windows of bookshops, from the recollections of once loyal readers.

Funny, but the minute I think about spiders I see my old primary school English teacher, a man who didn't suffer my exhaustion of purpose but, on the contrary, at more than twice my age was still enjoying an inexhaustible book-centred curiosity. A different sort of spider, maybe, more of a dung beetle if you consider how he spent his time, but a spider was what he reminded me of whenever, on the way to visiting my demented parents, I called on him in his Cheshire cottage – a spider sitting at the centre of a vast silky web of words, devouring at his leisure.

'So what are you reading?' he would ask, squinting at me, the moment we shook hands. It was the same question he'd put to me every day at school, as though whatever I'd been reading yesterday I must by now have finished.

'Me? I'm a writer now,' I reminded him. 'I'm at the other end of the production line.'

It was a lovely Cheshire day, the light creamy, the cows in a nearby field sitting under a tree, the air quiet. It's a county you forget about, Cheshire, because nothing remarkable ever seems to happen there. Emlyn's cottage, just half a mile from the house where I was born, had holes in the roof and a garden with a lily pond in it. I don't know who cleaned it because Emlyn never stirred from the dark of his library. His wife had died. His children had moved away. It seemed an act of tact on all their parts, leaving Emlyn to his books.

He didn't respond when I reminded him I was a writer. He seemed not to want to know that. He attached no value to writing, only to reading. How that can make any sense I am unable to explain. I tackled him on it once. 'How can you love the literature and not the making of it?'

He knitted his brows. With Emlyn that phrase meant what it says. He truly did stitch his eyes and brows together, as though to concentrate what was left of his face into the part of it he read with. 'Who says I *love the literature*?' he asked angrily. 'There are books I enjoy reading. There are books I don't. What do I want with tittle-tattle about the people who write them?'

'Nothing. But I'm not talking about tittle-tattle.'

'What then?'

Good question. I paddled the musty air of his library with my fingers. 'The process . . . the doing . . . the state of writing . . .'

'I repeat what I have just said to you. What business of mine is any of it? By the time I read the book the doing is long done. The book belongs to me now.'

I understood that. As a writer I even craved it. Never mind me, attend to the words which supersede me. But I had been Emlyn's star pupil. He had hauled me up, aged ten, onto the platform during school assembly. 'This boy will go far in literature,' he said. 'Remember his name – Guy Ableman.' He even wrote to my parents to tell them to nurture my 'rare and precious gift' – a vote of confidence that was lost on them but meant a lot to me, hence my staying in touch with him over the years, so that he could observe his prophecy come to rare and precious fruition. But since it had, since books were all he cared for and now here was I writing them, couldn't he have shown me he was proud? Couldn't he have said 'Well done!' to both of us? Wasn't he even the slightest bit impressed with me for having pulled it off?

Couldn't he have given some evidence that he at least remembered me?

Apparently not. Whatever he had meant by my going far in literature, he hadn't meant or hoped that I would write it. A life devoted to literature, for him, was a life devoted to consuming it. For the act of writing itself he didn't give a monkey's. I even felt he thought — in so far as he thought about me at all — that I'd let him down rather. Crossed over from the realm of pure ideation into gross manufacture. Become a mechanic. For himself, he found sufficient satisfaction to fill and justify a life simply in reading. Homer, Tacitus, Augustine, Bede, Montaigne, Addison, Thackeray, Herbert Spencer, Spengler, Chaquita Chicklit — everyone.

That he didn't feel it demeaned him to be reading ephemeral dross, that he could with interest open *Twilight*, *New Moon*, *Eclipse* and *Breaking Wind* the minute he had closed Herodotus, astonished me.

'How do you do it?' I asked him.

'I have the time.'

'No, I mean how can you *bear* to do it?'

'You have to read a book to discover you wish you hadn't, and by that time it's too late. But do you know? — I almost never wish I hadn't.'

'So there's nothing amiss with civilisation from where you're sitting, Emlyn?'

He smiled, pulling his blanket around him. It was the smile of a man who'd seen God on his shelves. With outstretched arms he made as though to embrace his walls of books, like a Lotus-Eater pointing to the drowsy long-leaved flowers among which he slept.

That kind of spider.

The *Arachnidous bibliomani*.

*   *   *

Before he perished in the snows of the Hindu Kush with only my manuscript to keep him warm, Quinton O'Malley had warned me not to let the success of my first novel go to my head. 'Stay up there,' was his advice. 'Don't sever the roots that have nourished you. Keep working at the zoo.'

'I don't work at a zoo,' I told him.

'Then keep talking to people who do. If you come to London for a literary life you won't have anything to write about. I've seen it happen a thousand times. Stay with what you know, stay where your inspiration is. There's nothing doing here. And between ourselves there's no one worth knowing.'

He sniffed. Not complacency; blocked sinuses. Quinton O'Malley, long-faced, with the bulk of a bear, suffered the cold as no other man has ever suffered it. He froze in temperatures of seventy-five degrees Fahrenheit. Though it was a warm July afternoon when I first met him he was wearing canary-yellow corduroys tucked into grey-flecked merino socks, mountain boots, and was wound around in the wool of a small hillside of sheep. Why such a man should have ventured into the Hindu Kush there is no explaining. But this was the beginning of the Great Decline when everyone at the publishing end of literature, like everyone at the writing end of literature, was acting strangely. It would have been no more or less surprising had he walked off Brighton Pier. Though to do that he would have had to take his turn in the queue behind two novelists, a poet, and the deputy manager of Foyles.

I had sent my manuscript to him after reading that he was the best-connected agent in London, and had a particular interest in the *outré*. The godchild of T. E. Lawrence, the intimate of Thesiger and Norman Lewis, a homosexual who did nothing about it, an agent who numbered three wife-murderers (one convicted) among his clients, he had, in his younger days, hit the bottle with Dylan

Thomas, taken opium with William S. Burroughs, shared a depression with Jean Genet, and still, at seventy-whatever-he-was, gave the most louche literary parties in London. He was a member of every club including some reputed to be proscribed. He chaired every committee. If any writer was going to be honoured – whether that meant an OBE, an invitation to tea at Buckingham Palace, or freedom of the city of West Belfast – it would have to be at Quinton's say-so. Know Quinton and you knew everybody.

'There's you,' I said.

It was all I could do not to stroke him, insalubrious as he was, a man who had gone out on the tiles to get depressed with Genet!

'Oh, don't believe what you read about me. I'm an empty shell. You've read T. S. Eliot's "Hollow Men"?' He banged his chest. 'He was thinking of me.'

He saw me mentally doing the arithmetic. 'I was a baby. He heard me cough in the pram and started writing. Wind in dry grass. Rats' feet over broken glass. You're better off in Nantwich.'

'Wilmslow.'

'Wilmslow.'

I wanted to tell him – with respect, and though I wanted to stroke him for having inspired Eliot to his greatest depths of desolation, if only from the pram – that I thought he patronised me. I was his hetero-provincial writer. No doubt he laughed about me to the metropolitan wife-murdering sodomitic junkies with whom he didn't share his bed. When he first lit upon *Who Gives a Monkey's?* in a reject pile – it was a custom of his to flick through one rejected manuscript a day, just to be on the safe side – he thought the narrator was the author: a one-time Orthodox Jewish woman who gave sexual relief to tigers and bred chimpanzees for whom no sexual relief was possible, writing under the pseudonym of Guy Ableman in order to conceal her sex and the fact that her novel was in fact a true story. It was on that assumption that he took the book on. He wanted to show her off and introduce her around. The Chimp Woman. 'Think twice before shaking her hand,' I can imagine him telling his dissipated friends. I must have been a great disappointment to him when he met me. A Wilmslow boy in a suit and tie. He wound one of his many scarves around his face and wiped his nose on it. 'Well, you're a surprise, I must say,' he said.

We were in a French restaurant in Kensington. He ate with his coat on and spent the two and a half hours we were together describing the transparent Nordic loveliness of Bruce Chatwin's eyes.

I bridled at Nordic. Not sure why.

'You have the opportunity,' he told me over strong coffee, 'to lead a new generation of decadents. But stay in Northwich.'

'Wilmslow.'

'Wilmslow.'

'I have to get out,' I said. 'Bruce Chatwin didn't stay in Sheffield.'

'Probably his biggest mistake. He told me that once.'

'That he wished he'd stayed in Sheffield?'

'Not in so many words.'

'Well, not me. I have nothing to write about up there. I have exhausted the place.'

'Come, come,' he said, coughing – rats' feet over broken glass – and ordered us both a brandy. 'Provincial life didn't fail George Eliot.'

'But it did nothing for Henry Miller,' I said.

'And who would you rather be?'

I lacked the courage to say Henry Miller, in case George Eliot, too, had been a drinking friend of his.

'Tell me what else goes on in your neck of the woods,' he

persisted. I had the feeling he wanted to hear about incest and bestiality.

'Nothing of the sort you would find interesting.'

'You'd be surprised what I find interesting. Think. What great events are there? What magnificent institutions? You've opened our eyes to Chester Zoo. What next?'

I happened to know there was an annual transport festival in the east Cheshire town of Sandbach, held in commemoration of Sandbach's long history as a manufacturer of commercial vehicles. We'd once dressed the Transport Queen in the family boutique, free of charge, to show her unbounded gratitude for which she'd let me undress her again at the back of the Foden trucks showroom when the carnival was over. I was fifteen at the time. She was nineteen. I disgraced myself. But now that I had become a successful writer she was writing to me, inviting me to try again.

Fame!

'Well, there's a start,' Quinton said when I mentioned this to him. 'Love among the autoparts.'

'Don't you think it's a bit small time?'

'I most certainly do. And hurrah for that. You've put the monkeys of Wilmslow on the map —'

'Chester.'

'Chester. Now do the same with the beauty queens of Middlewich.'

'Sandbach.'

'Wherever.'

'I'm not sure I can write another novel from the woman's point of view,' I said.

'Then tell it from the man's.' He roared with rattling laughter. At the idea of a man having a point of view? Or at the idea of my being one?

But his was a persuasive personality. So I did as he suggested, delved into my own erotic history, researched the Foden steam lorry, and told the tale from the point of view of a man with a blazing red provincial penis – Sandbach man, as libidinous as a cage of unmasturbated chimpanzees, breathing in the fumes of the trucks for which the town was famous.

I never found out what Quinton thought of it. Had it killed him? Had the sheer unforgiving, unremitting *straightness* of it finished him off in the cold? True, he wasn't morally particular about those he represented. Three wife-murderers, don't forget. But Sandbach man could have been a step in the direction of unre-constructed, non-Nordic hetero-proletarianism too far.

Who knew what Quinton thought, or even if he thought anything? Maybe he'd only ever taken the manuscript away to line his boots.

I went ahead with its publication agentless anyway, suggesting to Merton, who had published my monkey novel, that as no one could now prove otherwise, we take the killer route on the jacket. *This book is dangerous. Think twice before you read it – especially at altitude.*

But Merton no more liked putting the word 'dangerous' on the jacket of a book than he liked putting the word 'hilarious'. 'Another life-changing masterpiece from the prize-winning author of *Who Gives a Monkey's?*' was what he plumped for instead.

People compared me to John Braine and Alan Sillitoe. *Tuesday Night and Wednesday Morning* meets *Room at the Bottom*. Which was a comedown, I thought, from Apuleius and the Marquis de Sade. Though one reviewer did say that he thought the screams of chimps on heat were following me around the north-west of England, while a second (who turned out to be the same person, reviewing me under another name) wished I'd stuck with the territory I knew best – the monkey house. In a third review, for the *London Magazine*, again under another name, Lonnie Dobson, aka Donny Robson, aka Ronnie Hobson, delivered his most deadly verdict. 'In his debut novel Guy Ableman made an entirely unsuccessful job of imitating a woman; in this his second, and we can only hope his final novel, he has made an entirely unsuccessful job of imitating a man.'

Shortly after publication I ignored poor frozen Quinton's advice and moved to London. At first, this pleased Vanessa and her mother who were city girls at heart. But gradually they began to wonder if they'd done the right thing. In Cheshire they had the air of louche women who'd been expelled from somewhere else and were only waiting for their reputations to catch up with them and they'd be off. In the city, everyone looked like that. They were still a sensational pair, but they didn't bring the traffic to a halt.

Me neither.

There is a school of thought that has it that London was the end of me. But there is also a school of thought that says I never began. My work changed, that much we can agree about. It lost some of its raw verve. It became more orderly in its disorderliness. Wandering about the streets of Wilmslow with a cigarette dangling from my bottom lip I'd been able to believe I was anathema to respectable society and wrote accordingly. The minute I settled down to write in London I felt respectability settle on my shoulder. 'For a man of the big cities,' Henry Miller once wrote, 'I think my exploits are modest and altogether normal.' That's what big cities do: they normalise what elsewhere would be thought outlandish. The monkeyman who had become my trademark hero cut a poor dash in west London. Wilmslow and Sandbach, if they didn't quite excuse, at least explained him to a degree. He was like the beast of Bodmin Moor, a creature made fascinating by his out-of-placeness.

But once transport him to the pubs and clubs and lonely-wife bars of the capital and the fascination ebbed away. What made a man a rough diamond in the north, made him just one more loutish boor in Westbourne Grove. He was like too many men trying to go to seed in the big city.

But it would have made no difference had my third and fourth novels been works of genius – *Middlemarch*, *Cranford* and *Sexus*, *Plexus* and *Nexus* rolled into one. They would still have vanished within weeks of being published, and would barely have lasted longer when – and not so much when as if – they got their second wind as paperbacks. Readers had changed. Expectations of the book had changed. In a word, there were none.

When did my books stop appearing in the bookshops? Where did my oeuvre go? My question was a general one: every novelist in the country capable of writing sentences with conditional clauses in them was asking it. We were all being written out of history. Was three-for-two to blame? Was it the celebrity memoir? It had all happened so quickly. Your work was on display in alphabetical order of title, spines showing, as though for all eternity, then it wasn't. It coincided with bookshop staff not knowing who you were. One day their eyes fell out of their heads with the excitement of seeing you. The next they didn't know you from a mere member of the non-book-buying public. 'Name,' they'd say when you turned up to sign books. 'How do you spell that?'

Was it happening to Kundera? Was it happening to Gore Vidal? 'That's V, i, d, a, l.'

Mailer was dead, Bellow was dead, Updike was dead. Was it having to spell their names in Borders that had killed them?

And now Borders itself was barely breathing.

There were no doubt a thousand explanations for this, but paramount among them was Flora.

8

So What Are We Going To Do With You?

Had I needed to plead mitigating circumstances for shoplifting one of my own titles, I'd have added Flora to the extensive list. Not Flora the margarine, but Flora the legendary paperback publisher in whom the art of unpromoting any male novelist who wrote in the first person, made light of life or described intercourse with a woman from the man's point of view, was honed to the highest level of sophistication. In her younger days, Flo McBeth had put together her own imprint of nineteenth- and early-twentieth-century women writers whose husbands, brothers or fathers had refused to allow their manuscripts to leave the house. What was remarkable was not only the quality of the work Flo and her staff rescued from obscurity, but the apparent frequency, even as recently as 1940, with which men of all classes of society – afraid for one reason or another of their womenfolk's creative spark – had repressed it. Flo's enemies wondered aloud if some of these recovered works were frauds, but if they were then who had written them? Flora herself? In which case her skills as a pasticheur were no less prodigious than her skills as a publisher. Either way, she was able to quit the world of books as a young woman, wealthy, with an unequalled reputation and a CBE. Then, after a retirement which she was said to have found irksome – she'd made the book person's mistake of going to live in the country (rolling fields, smell of hay, silly sheep, baa baa, and time to read all one *wanted* to read) – she was back in the role of publisher of a paperback list that had always been boldly masculinist in spirit, that's to say comprised books she *didn't* want to read.

It was a strange appointment all round. Was the Swedish group who had bought Scylla and Charybdis Press looking to have it quickly wound up? And what was Flora herself up to? Was she avenging those generations of silenced women by extinguishing in men the same spark that men had attempted to extinguish in them? No one knew her motives, and certainly none of the writers she'd taken over was prepared to speculate for fear she would unpromote them even more than she already had. Flora it was, anyway, who at the age of sixty had made a notable return to the profession just in time for the paperback edition of my third novel.

In fact, for all that it had been a mistake to set it in Westbourne Grove, *The Silent Shriek* hadn't gone down too badly in hard covers. 'A novel that subtly enacts its own futility' was the worst Jonny Jobson had found to say about it in the *Yorkshire Post*. Not exactly complimentary, but after what he'd written about *The Lawless* (my novel set in Sandbach) I felt I was on my way back up again. It didn't sell more than a couple of thousand copies, but then no one expected hard covers to sell more than a couple of thousand copies. Paper covers hardly much better, come to that. Paper was simply a second bite at an apple that had gone rotten. Only with Flora there wasn't even an apple.

'So what are we going to do with *you*?' she called me into her office to ask.

The emphasis carried the distinct implication that she'd known exactly what to do with everybody else.

'Market the balls off me,' I suggested.

Risky, that. But I'd been determined not to go down in Flo's presence without laying my virility on the table.

'Believe me, Guy . . .' she said, laughing and letting her office chair take her a long way back, as though she didn't mind my seeing what a strong jawline she still had for a woman her age.

She was a walker and a mountaineer, small and wiry with good calf muscles which she showed off by wearing hiking shorts to work in all weathers. Hiking boots, too, with which she was rumoured to have kicked a number of her male authors who'd expressed dissatisfaction with the manner in which she hadn't marketed them.

Me, she didn't kick. Unless you call it kicking to suggest I find at least three young women writers to endorse the novel it was her bad luck to have to find a way of bringing to the attention of a book-bored public in paperback.

I suggested E. E. Freville. Eric the Endorser. He used to be a fan of mine, I told her.

'Darling, he used to be a fan of everybody's. But he's not a woman and he's not young, and anyway he's A-list now and will only endorse a book if we can guarantee him a print of fifty thousand and a window in Smith's.'

'So guarantee it.'

She made a fist around a paperweight and snorted. 'Let's get back to these girls,' she said. 'Ideally under twenty.'

'Flo, I don't know any girls under twenty. I don't know *anybody* under twenty.'

'I wouldn't boast about that.'

'Besides,' I said, 'a writer under twenty would barely have been walking when my first novel came out.'

'That sounds a positive recommendation to me,' she said, raising herself on the arms of the chair, once, twice, three times, and taking deep breaths as she did so.

There's a pinnacle of naked insult which is so breathtaking that you must admire the view, no matter that it's you who's being thrown from it. I wondered if I ought to applaud her. 'Bravo, Flo!' Instead I asked if she could recommend any young women of the age she suggested.

She pretended to think about it, using a couple of paperweights to exercise her biceps. 'Well, here's the whole problem,' she said after she had pumped herself up sufficiently, blue veins starting out of her forearms, 'would any of them like you?'

'Do they have to like me?'

'Your work, darling. Would any of them *get* it?'

'Identify with it, you mean?'

I wondered if 'identify' was an exclusively female concept, like hormonal or moody, so angry did my use of it make her.

'Try "empathise", darling,' she said.

You always knew when an interview with Flora McBeth was finished. She would make small rapping movements on her chest with her fist, and her voice – though always becomingly hoarse, like syrup passing through muslin – would start to sound as though sand had somehow got into a hairdryer.

Two weeks later she rang to say she'd found a bright young thing called Heidi Corrigan who was prepared to say I was one of her favourite farceurs over forty.

I skipped the 'prepared to'. 'I'm not a farceur, Flo,' I said.

'Doesn't matter in the least. No one knows what the word means anyway.'

'There's another problem with Heidi Corrigan,' I said. 'Her mother was the publicity director here when S&C published my first novel. She sometimes brought Heidi into the office. Pretty little girl. I sat her on my knee while I discussed strategy with her mother.'

'Which shows no affection is ever wasted in this business, darling. But don't worry – I won't tell.'

'I'm not worrying. I just want to know how it helps to have a quote from Heidi Corrigan?'

'Helps the Pound Shop.'

I don't recall exactly, but this could have been the conversation that caused me to begin pulling the skin away from my cuticles. 'The Pound Shop!'

'Well, I'm not making any promises. They might not go for it.'

'But a quote from an adolescent on the back of a book jacket could persuade them – is that what you're telling me?'

'Who said anything about the back? We're talking front. Wider, younger audience, darling.'

'She's only published two short stories.'

'*C'est la vie literaire.*'

'Flora, I'd rather drown myself.'

Whereupon, like everything else, the line went dead.

But she responded to my wishes. The book went out without a word from Heidi Corrigan on the front or back, but where it went out *to* was anybody's guess. Certainly not the Pound Shop.

That's not quite the end of the story. I did find out where one copy landed. It landed on the desk of Bruce Elseley, a novelist some twenty years my senior – and therefore even deader meat than me – who on two previous occasions had written to my publishers accusing me of plagiarism. Nothing had come of these accusations, perhaps because he'd asked my publishers for action to be taken against at least a dozen more of their writers, each of whom he accused of stealing from him. That he'd have had more chance of receiving satisfaction had he chosen only one novelist per publishing house to accuse, I could have advised him were I in the business of advising him anything other than to keep up the erotic self-asphyxiation – an exquisite but dangerous form of auto-pleasuring which I mention only because Elseley was widely known to be a solo fetishist who'd already had to be cut down from a hook on the inside of a hotel door in Wales where he'd been attending a literary festival.

This event, to digress, had serious repercussions not just for this literary festival but for literary festivals in general. Most of them relied on local goodwill and sponsorship to survive. At the level of the rotary club and mayoral committees there had always been a mistrust of a festival devoted to books – it felt a contradiction in terms to them: how could one be festive about a book? – so when one of the invited writers was found half choked to death in his hotel bedroom, wearing ladies' fishnet stockings and with an orange from the Co-op in his mouth, their deepest suspicions were confirmed. The question had now to be asked whether the community wanted to go on being associated with literature.

'One more trial year,' was the concession the festival organisers were able to wring from the town, which meant that no further chances could be taken with the likes of Bruce Elseley.

This also led to hooks being screwed off the doors of every hotel and bed and breakfast in Cheltenham and Hay-on-Wye whenever writers were known to be in town.

Whether Elseley's belief that he was being stolen from intensified as a consequence of this exclusion from the festival circuit I cannot say, but it doesn't take much imagination to suppose it must have. It wasn't long afterwards, anyway, that he managed to get hold of my address and began writing to me directly. *The Silent Shriek*, he claimed, was a direct steal from his novel *Darkness Visible*, whose title he had himself stolen from William Styron who had taken the phrase from Milton. Unlike Styron's *Darkness Visible* which was an elegantly written memoir of madness, Elseley's was a slapdash chronicle, written in present-tense diary form, of the three-year period in the sixth century when an erupting volcano blackened the entire face of the earth, destroying crops and domestic animals, poisoning water, causing women to miscarry and men to lose their wits and hang themselves. Since my novel was a satire set in Shepherd's Bush about a failed feral writer working in a pet shop that was staving off bankruptcy by selling lemurs smuggled in from Madagascar, I didn't see he had a case. But once every six or seven months another letter arrived, each more rancorous and menacing than the last. And then, shortly after Merton died, I received a postcard of a Goya beheading, on the back of which was painted, in what looked like a mix of green ink, sperm and faeces, the words

HA! THIS IS WHAT HAPPENS TO THOSE WHO SHELTER THIEVES.

I showed it to Vanessa.
'I know how he feels,' she said.

9

Same Old Same Old

Had it not been stolen twice already, the one thing I would have nicked from Elseley was his title.

Milton was describing Hell when he coined the phrase 'darkness visible'. 'Region of sorrow', 'torture without end'. I knew the very place he had in mind – Chipping Norton.

But every writer had his own Chipping Norton to endure. Day by day the darkness thickened around us.

So was my mother-in-law a symptom or a solace?

Was she the proof that without the ballast of an honourable profession to steady me, I was sinking morally? Or was she just there to make it all feel better until the darkness finally descended?

Maybe I didn't have to decide. Francis's bold warning – 'Don't do it, Guy' – turned her at once into a solution. Fiction was fucked but that didn't mean there was no more fun to be had making it. Stay away, Francis had counselled me. If not in life, then at least in art. They would hate me for it. Why? Search me. Masculinism, Francis said. By which I took him to mean braggadocio. No one wanted to read about a man filling his boots any more. Once upon a time it had been all the rage – Henry Miller, Frank Harris, J. P. Donleavy – men having it away in sentences as ponderous as they were priapic. Finished, Francis had pronounced. The swordsman hero flashing his prose around, writing with a pen dipped in hot semen, was dead in the water.

Well, we'd see about that.

Art is renunciation, someone once said. Here was another view. Art is indulgence. I wasn't the first to think that. Decadence went back a long way. But these weren't decadent times. Defeat is not decadence; death is not decadence; even Richard and Judy were not decadence. We were too inert to be decadent. Fiction had been fucked by too little, not too much; by caution, not wickedness. Could I put a bit of evil back? Did I have what it took to unbuckle against the forces of the great god Nice and let it all hang out?

As for the ethical question of whether it was right for a man to feel up his wife's mother, that was dissolved in the prospect of there being a book in it. The calculation wasn't cynical. I wasn't after Poppy to write a book. I had *always* been after Poppy. But if I could have Poppy *and* write a book −!

The odd part was that there was any desire left in me to write a sentence, never mind a book. Yet there was. An intense desire − akin to lust or hunger − which all the militant women's book groups in Chipping Norton couldn't expunge. Explain that! I couldn't. But I wasn't alone. The more a book of one sort or another was identified as surplus to cultural requirement, the more of them were written. Books that no one wanted to read were running at plague proportions. If there was a book to be made you made it − and wondered who the hell would read it later.

It was like lighting a candle in the dark. You knew it was no match for Hell's own 'ever-burning sulphur', you knew the darkness would snuff your little light of hope out in the end, but at least for the hour it burned, *you* didn't.

I even had a title. It's a big moment when you hit on a title and know it's the one. I can still remember when I first thought of *Who*

Gives a Monkey's? and announced it to Vanessa. She was in the bath, with her feet in the air, sanding her heels with Sicilian pumice. 'That's one shit title,' she said, though when the book did well she claimed she'd thought of it. She could even tell me where she was when it came to her – in the bath with her feet in the air, rubbing Sicilian pumice into her heels.

Like a monkey. Hence . . .

This time, for an assortment of reasons, I didn't convey my excitement to her. Instead, I rang Merton with the news and got his secretary. 'Merton's gone,' she reminded me.

'Gone?'

'Passed away.'

'Oh God, Margaret,' I said, 'I'm so sorry. I'm so used to his being there I forget he no longer is.' We'd actually talked at the funeral. She'd cried on my shoulder. We'd hugged each other. I even remembered the belted raincoat she'd worn. She'd creaked in my arms. I'd sniffled in hers. In a strange way – *Lust und Tod*, I suppose – it had been arousing. She was a good-looking woman with a narrow waist, reliable but with a suggestion of being willing to go out on a limb for you, like a secretary in a fifties Hollywood movie. We looked deep into each other's affliction. There'd never be another Merton, we agreed. It was a miracle we hadn't kissed. Unless we had and were both in denial about it.

I could hear her tears welling again down the phone line. I hoped it wasn't guilt.

'Are you all right, Margaret?' I asked.

'Yes, yes, fine. Are you?'

'Yes, I am. But I'm shocked to have forgotten that Merton has gone.'

'It's understandable,' she said, 'you're not alone. It's nice that people can't think of him as dead. I can't.'

Unless they couldn't think of him as dead because it was so long since they'd thought of him as alive.

Until a replacement could be found, Margaret explained, Flora McBeth was looking after his authors. Did I want to speak to Flora? She laughed a wild laugh, as though she knew the effect Flora's name would have on me. It was an exciting laugh. Full of irresponsibility, which is an enticing promise in a normally responsible woman. It was as if – though customarily covered up – she were showing me her legs. I was sorry we hadn't kissed. If indeed we hadn't.

A few moments must have passed in ruminative silence.

'Well?'

'Well what, Margaret?'

'Do you want me to put you through to Flora?'

I did not.

There was a rumour that high among the explanations of why Merton had taken his life was Flora.

Because he was fucking her?

Because he was afraid of her?

Because he was fucking her and afraid of her?

No one knew. And if anyone did, he stroke she was afraid to say.

Something made me think about Margaret.

I emailed the title to Francis. *The Mother-in-Law Joke.*

'The joke being,' I wrote, 'that it isn't.'

'Isn't what?' he emailed back.

'A joke!'

'I never thought it was,' came his reply.

'My aim,' I emailed in return, 'is to write a transgressive novel that explores the limits of the morally permissible in our times. Who are the great blasphemers of our age? Not poets and writers any more. Stand-up comedians. My hero is a stand-up comedian. First line of novel, he walks on to the stage, says *Take my mother-in-law – I just have*. Audience gets up and leaves in disgust. What do you think?'

I received no answer, not even an out-of-office reply. A day, two days went by. I was bound to be concerned. The way things were, if you didn't hear from anybody for a couple of days you assumed they were lying face down on their office floors with their brains dotted around them.

On the third day Francis got back to me. It seemed he'd been chewing the idea over.

'I beg you!' he wrote. 'And anyway . . .'

'And anyway what?' I wrote back.

'And anyway you're culturally up the shoot,' he replied. 'You're behind the times. The audience wouldn't leave in disgust. Might not laugh, but wouldn't walk out. Material not offensive enough.'

'Not offensive enough! What does he have to do – take his dick out?'

Good job I didn't try that line on Vanessa; she'd have said I'd been taking my dick out in public for years.

And no, that wasn't funny either.

Francis was cooler. 'Taking dick out just same old same old. You're barking up wrong tree. No reason you should listen to me, you're the writer. But if you have to go in this direction – and don't expect me to find you a publisher if you do – but if you must, if you really *must*, then here's how I see it. First of all drop "explore". Exploration fine when you're exploring Antarctica, otherwise suicide. Cut to chase. Make hero climate scientist, not comedian – funny not selling. As for the sex – wish you wouldn't, but anal is still big. Non-procreative. There's a school of thought that sees anal, so long as it's consensual, as non-sexual. Can you have anal sex

76

and still be called a virgin, etc? Have it happen on global warming trip to Afghanistan. Wife suspects, employs depressed detective, ex-SAS, depressed detective confirms and tries to fuck her, she goes berserk, has history of going berserk, knifes him.'

'The detective?'

'The husband.'

'What about knifing the mother?'

Our emails were running hot now.

'Like it, like it. Mother had abused her. Knifes both. Knifes all three if you like. But you'll need redemption. Afterlife big. Limbo and purgatory all rage. Explore that if you must explore something. You'll enjoy this if you let yourself. Always thought there was an other-dimensional thriller writer in you, trying to break out. Have fun with your researches, lucky bastard. Poppy Eisenhower – phwah! Still say you shouldn't, but my best if you must. f.'

'Hear you, but where did you get idea I ever wanted to write thrillers of any dimension? I abhor that crap. You know I abhor that crap.'

The next I heard was by text via his BlackBerry. 'Methinks the novelist doth protest too much.'

'A middle-aged tart said that,' I texted back.

His reply was instant. 'Thought middle-aged tarts your forte. Just don't forget Afghanistan and Afterlife. 19th-century Afghanistan be best. Can't go wrong with history. But written in present tense. f.'

I skipped the 19th-century suggestion and had a better idea than anal. I'd do love. I didn't care what Francis thought. Loving your mother-in-law was as disruptive of society as an anal fuck any time. Everyone was anal fucking. I'd had them anal fucking in the zoo, and anal fucking again in Sandbach. Anal was the new vaginal. But how many people were head over heels in love with their wives' mothers?

Not offensive enough? Me!

Same old same old? Wait until I bought Poppy roses, told her I couldn't get her out of my mind, swore to her that I'd adored her from the moment I first saw her.

Wait until I slid her dress off – unless, unless that was to drop back into the conventional. Yes. Wait until I slid her dress off then slid it back on again telling her I respected her too much.

She was sixty-six and out of bounds. I'd show them fucking transgression!

And I had a better idea than Afghanistan as backdrop, or the Afterlife as postscript. Australia. Where things had happened that shouldn't. Tell it the way it was, Guy. Telling it the way it was was dirty.

Are There Monkeys in Monkey Mia?

It had been in Australia that I'd first tried it on with Poppy. The same Adelaide Writers Festival trip on which I'd unbuttoned Philippa in a vineyard. Did I mention that Philippa was a New Zealander? A lecturer – hence her interest in me as a living practitioner – in Unglish Luht. It had taken me a while to know what she was talking about. Even when she told me she wanted to suck my pruck I wasn't entirely sure. It was Philippa, anyway, who'd heated me up for Poppy. That's often the way of it with sex, if you're a man: it's like dominoes – with the first act of venery every objection to the others collapses. Once you've been bad with A there's nothing to stop you being bad all the way down to Z. And a wife's mother is Z plus plus.

Poppy had accepted Vanessa's invitation to spend time with us in Australia. She hadn't fancied Adelaide. She couldn't picture it. It sounded flat, she said. She liked the sound of Western Australia better and wanted us to join her there. So we flew to Perth and spent a week together in a hotel overlooking the Swan River while Poppy recovered from her jet lag. The heat suited them. In their sun hats and striped blazers, they looked like sisters, a pair of bold English adventuresses who'd somehow wandered off from Henley, but who, now they were here, wherever here was, feared nothing but any man dividing them. They linked arms, showed their faces to the sun in an identical manner – the same squint, the same submission to sensation – shopped for similar garments and gasped for tea simultaneously, at precisely 4.13 p.m., as though joined by a single throat. There is still something colonial about Perth; following behind them, carrying their parcels and enjoying the synchronised sway of their hips, I felt like their 'boy'.

I loved watching them from this respectful distance. I felt affectionately towards them as a pair. Mothers and daughters appeal to men of my sentimentalising erotic bent. Once, observing them staring across the Swan River to South Perth, I recalled Norman Mailer – another of the great sperm-chuckers of yesteryear – likening his wife and Jackie Kennedy talking at Hyannis Port, the site of the summer White House, to 'Two attractive witches by the water's edge'.

'Witches' caught my two. Or at least it caught me, a man ensorcelled.

Then, suddenly, Vanessa announced that we were hiring a camper van and driving to Broome. Poppy's wish, and Poppy's wishes were to be indulged.

She'd read about Broome – about the pearl fishing, the great swathe of iron-flat beach on which you could ride a camel, the mangrove swamps with osprey flying over, the giant goannas lolloping down the main street with their tongues flicking, the unrelenting heat. We could have flown straight to Broome and been on that camel the same afternoon, but Vanessa too had wishes which, post-Philippa, I was in no position to challenge. Vanessa wanted to see the outback. There'd been rain and the desert was alive with wild flowers. When Vanessa said 'wild flower', Poppy's face became one; just as, when Poppy said 'wildlife', Vanessa's nostrils dilated. They fired what was feral in each other, without due regard to the effect it had on me.

I had no desire to do this journey. I had come to Australia to wave my literary distinction around, to be seen, to be applauded, to be appreciated, fulsomely and unambiguously, by the likes of readers such as Philippa; I hadn't come to vanish into the obscurity of the bush, no matter how alive with wild flowers. The driving worried me too. I had never thrown a car around the lanes of Cheshire the way my brother Jeffrey did. I drove in a stately, some-what elderly manner, always afraid that the girth of my car exceeded the width of the road. How I'd handle a camper van big enough to afford privacy to three people, I wasn't at all sure, but Vanessa, always more the man of the family than I was, said she'd look after the getting us there. All I had to do was sit quietly, not write or talk about writing – not so much as take a note: work was verboten now I'd had my festival – and navigate. The navigation would be easy: facing the Indian Ocean you threw a right out of Perth and after three days you reached Broome.

Poppy sat in the back seat, reading. A miracle to me that anyone could read in a moving vehicle without going down with a migraine – Vanessa had to stop the van every time I needed to turn a page of the map – but even more of a miracle was the fact that Poppy was reading at all. She had always pretended that she didn't read, especially fiction, but suddenly she was eating the stuff. And what she ate – let alone the speed at which she ate it – struck me as in reverse ratio to the needs and interests of a woman her age.

'Aren't you a bit old for books with lipstick-pink covers?' I asked her, while Vanessa was filling up with diesel.

'Old!'

It was good I had annoyed her. In love – in unnatural love, anyway – annoyance is the prelude to indiscretion.

'Old as in mature. Old compared to the characters in the books you're reading.'

'How do you know the ages of the characters in the books I'm reading?'

'I can tell by the jackets.'

'Never judge a book by its cover, you should know that.'

'But that's exactly how *you* judge. I've watched the way you choose them.' (Good to tell her I'd been watching her.) 'You only choose the ones with lipstick-pink covers.'

She rapped me across the knuckles with her reading matter, as though it were a fan. 'Not everyone is an Einstein,' she said.

I looked her boldly in the eye. 'And not everyone is an Eisenhower,' I said.

The strange thing was that Vanessa was able to talk to her mother knowledgeably about these books though I knew to a certainty that Vanessa hadn't read them. So where did her information come from? Was it in the ether? Did that explain why some books – almost all of them for women – suddenly swept the world? A thousand miles from the nearest bookshop, without radio or news-papers, out of contact with gossip or opinion, Vanessa and Poppy were able to discuss the latest blockbuster. No wonder telepathic heroines were popular. Between women a telepathy of crass fictional taste existed. I saw it with my own eyes.

I didn't raise the subject with them. Whenever Vanessa was at the wheel of the camper I did as she had told me and clammed up. The quiet was welcome to me, too. I was able to sit and think about the writers I'd met in Adelaide, literary heavyweights some of them, in the taciturn vein of international novelists, not wanting to waste their words on mere conversation. The biggest hitter of them all, a huge Dutchman who wrote elegantly slender novellas for which he'd won a Nobel Prize and was said to be put out that he hadn't won a second, had been flown to the festival first class and housed at great expense only to announce, an hour before his gig, that he didn't talk in public. So he sat on the stage of Adelaide Town Hall with his belly hanging between his knees, and his audience sat in their seats with their hands clasped on their laps, and so the hour would have passed, with each staring at the other in silence, had someone not thought of showing slides of the bridges of Amsterdam. When it was over they gave him a standing ovation.

Rumour had it that no visiting writer to Adelaide had ever sold more books. The less a novelist said about his work, apparently, the more the public wanted to read him.

'A lesson it would do you no harm to learn,' Vanessa said at the time.

About halfway to Broome, Poppy saw a sign to Monkey Mia and wanted to make the detour. 'It's a bit more than a detour,' I warned her. 'If I'm reading the map right it's over four hundred kilometres once we leave the highway.'

'You *won't* be reading the map right,' Vanessa said. 'Turn it the other way round. Four hundred kilometres off the highway is Indonesia.'

'Trust me,' I said.

Poppy recalled reading that they had dolphins at Monkey Mia. You could swim with them and stroke their bellies. She thought that some of them stroked yours.

'What with – their flippers?' I wondered.

Vanessa thought I was being sarcastic to her mother. She couldn't have been more wrong. I was off on some anthropomorphic fantasy. *I am a dolphin.*

'Then we're going,' she said.

'It'll take all day to get there,' I pointed out.

'Ah,' Poppy said. 'Then let's not.'

'No, let's,' Vanessa insisted. 'It's your holiday.'

So she swung left off the highway and drove and drove.

'Beautiful country, don't you think?' I remarked after a couple of hours of silence. 'Pristine. You'd think you were the first people ever to come here if it wasn't for the road. Even the dirt looks clean and virginal. I feel like Adam.'

'Adam didn't have a camper van,' Vanessa said. 'And you agreed you wouldn't do any writing on this trip. Especially not natural description, which I thought we'd agreed you should leave to others.'

Poppy was sympathetic to me. Perhaps to show there were no hard feelings after our falling-out over book covers. 'I think that's cruel of you, Vanessa,' she said. 'I know what Guy means. The dirt does look virginal.'

Something about the way she pronounced me. Something about her breath on the back of my neck, warm with the letters of my name. Something about *virginal*. Did she feel like Eve?

'Do you think there are monkeys at Monkey Mia?' she asked about an hour after that.

'Doubt it,' I said. 'Just dolphins.'

'Don't say monkey to him,' Vanessa said. 'Don't start him off.'

'Why, is he an expert on monkeys?'

'He's an expert on how his career went wrong.'

'I didn't think your career had gone wrong,' Poppy said to me.

'Precisely,' Vanessa said.

An hour after that, Poppy unscrewed the cap of her brandy flask. It was six o'clock and wherever she was in the world at six o'clock she had to have a drink. Wilmslow, Chipping Norton, Primrose Hill, Monkey Mia – six o'clock was drinkies time.

'Anyone?'

'No thank you, Mother,' Vanessa said, 'I'm driving, in case you didn't notice.' Her mother's drinking infuriated her. Six o'clock the first drink. Six thirty drunk. It was the only weakness which

84

the one had that the other didn't. The six o'clock tipple followed by the six thirty falling over.

My own mother was the same. Though Poppy was considerably younger, our mothers inhabited the same social sphere and got drunk at exactly the same hour and speed. Allowing for the international time difference, she too would have been falling about pickled in Wilmslow right now. As my father would have been finding ways of keeping her upright. I had never liked my father much, but his attentiveness to my mother had always impressed me. On one occasion, in my presence, he actually tied her with his belt to a lamp post in the middle of Chester while he went to get the car.

I couldn't have been more than seven or eight years old at the time. 'Come kiss your mother,' my mother said, and when I went to kiss her she hissed furiously in my ear, 'Now free me!'

Did such memories contribute to the passion I had formed for Poppy?

Who can say? But I did accept a brandy, which she handed me with not altogether steady, painted fingers in the same silver cup – it was the cap of the flask – from which she'd been drinking. Thus, in a manner of speaking, did our lips touch.

'Are there monkeys at Monkey Mia?' she asked. And went on asking it, with increasing frequency, the more brandy she drank, until she fell asleep within sight of our destination.

It was the first thing she said when she opened her eyes and found herself in the campsite. 'Is this Monkey Mia? Are there monkeys here?'

Comedian

Was he subtly joking, the giant Dutchman who refused to address his enraptured audience of readers in Adelaide Town Hall? Was his hour of silence in fact an act of the most vertiginous volubility, a Dadaist gesture calculated to put to shame the legions of more obviously garrulous authors like me who trooped their wares – running a gag here, throwing in a comic anecdote there – from one festival to another?

I thought about him a great deal on the road to Broome, as a way, partly, of taking my mind off Poppy whose presence in the hot intimacy of a camper van, in which the three of us curled up to sleep at night separated only by a flimsy curtain, was a severe trial to me. But he troubled me on his own account, in the time I had to think about him, while Poppy and Vanessa crooned in unison over every flower the newly watered desert threw up, because he called into question the whole enterprise of the travelling showman novelist. No, he'd said – except that he hadn't said anything – no, he would not play the comedian.

Dadaist gesture or not, his silence changed the game. He was a writer. He wrote. And if those who queued to look at him called themselves readers, then let them read. The rest was nothing.

Whereas our message – those who talked as though a

prohibition against speaking had just been lifted – what was that? Behold, beyond the page, what entertainers we were.

But there was no beyond the page. Beyond the page was no business of our readers. And if we *made* beyond the page our business, no wonder that the page was no longer being turned.

A plain logic demanded that we ask ourselves this question: if we wanted to play the comedian why didn't we just call ourselves comedians and dispense with the vestigial bookishness? We were finished, anyway. Comedians had taken over. The best of the stand-ups worked from scripts that might as well have been short satiric novels; they saw as novelists saw, they enjoyed the rhythm of the language, they deployed exaggeration and bathos as we did, they excoriated, they surprised, they caught laughter on the wing, in the moment it threatened to tumble into terror. They were predictable and complacent and self-righteous, too, but then who wasn't? What is more, they had a slavish following. Where had all the readers gone? Wasn't it obvious? They were watching stand-up comedy.

Had Vanessa not warned me against discussing my career while she was driving I'd have told her I was getting out. No, not out of the van, Vee, out of literature. And where would I go? The stage, the stage . . .

Take my mother-in-law . . .

In the event, I just sat and navigated. The miles went by; every now and then Vanessa stopped the van so that the two women could get out and pluck a desert pea, or fix their binoculars on a wedge-tailed eagle who felt about the prospect of sinking his teeth into their browning flesh pretty much as I felt, and once we had to pause to catch our breath after nearly running into a troop of tarty emus with hair cropped like Vanessa and Poppy. They teetered across the road and looked back at us with contemptuous

87

expressions, not in anger that we'd almost killed them but as though they were out on a hen night and we, the stags, had just thrown them a pathetic chat-up line. Fuck you, they said in Emu. And faced with such natural wonders I never did figure out a way to change my career.

Now, a year or so later, with my name mud in Chipping Norton, with fellow writers and publishers dropping like flies, with bookshops closing up and down the country, and agents hiding from their clients, here I was tearing at the skin behind my ears and still wondering. In that time, stand-up had bloomed like wild flowers in the Great Sandy Desert. Who were the unacknowledged legislators of the world? Not poets or novelists. Comedians. Who took tea at 10 Downing Street? Not poets or novelists. Comedians. Their jeering was the jeering of the age. They *were* the age. Well, it was too late now for me to make a change. I no longer had the cojones. Maybe I'd never had the cojones. All very well to talk about it as an option, but what if one became a writer out of timidity, as a way of being a performer without having to perform? Were comedians just novelists with balls? Granted a bolder personality, would D. H. Lawrence have been W. C. Fields?

Funny might be ruling the world but, as far as the novel went, it was a dead letter. You can't have funny where you have sacred, and someone somewhere had left the windows of the novel open for sacred to spirit itself in on broken wings. And what was the sacred, anyway, but the cloak the funereal threw over their turgidity? Eugene Bawstone – the literary editor and sacristan who had greeted my first novel (*Who Gives a?*) with a two-word review: 'Not me!' – a man whose shy, depressed demeanour and Bambieyed good looks had earned him the nickname 'the Princess Di of English Letters' (though I can avouch that there was nothing promiscuous about his reading), was rumoured to have written to each of his reviewers by hand, telling them they were no longer to use the words funny, riotous or Rabelaisian when writing for him. The quality he looked for in literature being 'weightlessness', he had never found a novel funny, riotous or Rabelaisian in his life (and that included anything by Rabelais) and assumed his reviewers were either lying or showing off when they claimed they had.

'Have you ever wondered,' I once asked him at a party, 'whether the fault doesn't lie in you?'

I now realise, though I didn't know it at the time, that I must have been drunk. Drunk and riotous.

He raised his sad eyes prettily to me. Was he going to confide the details of his personal unhappiness, I wondered. Or was he going to slip his hands down the front of my trousers?

'What fault are you referring to?'

'The inability to feel pleasure. Psychologists call it anhedonia.'

'Psychologists! Are you saying I should be sectioned for not finding what you write diverting?'

I thought about it. A strange negative energy came off him, as though he possessed the gift of sucking vitality from the room. I felt the breath of life leaving my body. It was either him or me. 'Well, I hadn't quite put it to myself like that,' I said with brutal unsubtlety – what could I do? he brought out the brute in me, just as Diana must have brought out the brute in her men – 'but now you mention it, yes, I think the madhouse might be the only place for you.'

'In a straitjacket?'

His voice possessed that very quality of weightlessness he admired so much in literature.

'You are,' I said, 'already in a straitjacket.'

A week later he was found dead, slumped at the wheel of his car, in an underpass in Paris. He wasn't, of course, but a man can dream.

Wrong to blame it all on Bawstone. No publisher with a business brain allowed the word 'funny' to appear on a book jacket. Merton had banned it from his list years before. He tore his hair when anything made him laugh. 'What am I going to do with this?' he'd ask. It was even possible that something had made him laugh just before he took his life. Maybe I had. Maybe I'd asked him what chance he thought I had of winning the Nobel Prize for Literature.

All this apart, the comedy phenomenon needed explaining: if no one wanted funny, why the triumphant march of the comedians? Something didn't make sense.

Take my mother-in-law . . .

What if Francis was wrong? What if a comedian who fucked his mother-in-law was the hero of sexual transgression everyone was waiting for?

It's hard to embark on a story uncertain whether your hero is a comedian or a climate scientist. There comes a moment, and it comes early, when you must make the leap and see the story through with him.

What did I know about climate science? If it was hot in my study, I put on the air conditioning. If it was cold I imagined lying in the arms of my wife's mother. Climate science.

Anything further would entail research and I didn't do research. In this I was out of step with my neutered associates. Research was what desperation had driven them to. Especially research into the latest developments in epigenetics, particle physics or quantum mechanics. There'd been a time when novelists were proudly indifferent to all of this. The boffins did matter, we did the human heart. But we'd lost faith in the human heart, which meant we'd lost faith in ourselves. We weren't important, they were. If we could hitch a ride on their wagon, maybe we'd get to where they were going. And where was that? Search me. Relevance? Contemporaneity? An audience?

Whatever we were hoping, we no longer stood up for ourselves. It wasn't even a two-way street – we'll bone up on you if you bone up on us. The scientific community's response was that we weren't worth boning up on. You aren't where it's at, sunshine. So any twopenny-halfpenny proponent of string theory believed he could do his job and not acquaint himself with the uses of metaphor or the seven types of ambiguity; any climatologist could draw his graphs in serene and unchallenged ignorance of *Henderson the Rain King*.

Well, if they weren't reading us, I at least was not reading them. Whatever else he was or wasn't going to be, my hero wasn't going to be a climate scientist.

Take my mother-in-law – I just have.

It was that word 'just' I found hard to resist. The idea of a comedian coming out to entertain his audience with the smell of his mother-in-law still on him. It was a disgusting concept which confirmed Vanessa's view that I was a disgusting person.

'Person or author?' I'd always asked, to be on the safe side.

She never missed her cue. 'Both.'

And that was leaving my disgusting thoughts about her mother out of it.

If my tentative hero had the taste of his mother-in-law on his fingers, I had the taste of his fear on me. The scene described itself. A comedy club in Chester, housed in the back of a riverside pub. Monday. First-timers' night. Thirty people in a grimy room, simultaneously desperate to laugh and not expecting to be amused, their feet in puddles of warm beer. Not being a beer drinker myself, I associate its smell with human hopelessness. Warm beer, rats' piss, failure. My hero would be smelling of all three. I saw him gnawing his fingernails behind the torn black sheet which served as a curtain. Then out into the limelight, tapping the microphone because that was what he'd seen real comedians do.

Take my mother-in-law – I just have.

Not a laugh to be heard. Too subtle for a Chester audience? Too gross? Francis said not. Francis said not gross enough. But Francis wasn't Chester. *Get off the stage*, I heard them shouting, anyway. *Don't give up your day job.*

In which event I could have it both ways. My first-person narrator would be a comedian *and* a comedian manqué, a comic who never was. He would try out his riff and keep his day job, and his day job would be mine, he would do what I had done before the rabbit hole of publication had opened for me to fall through like that pervert Lewis Carroll's Alice – he would be in the ladies' fashion business, tending his parents' shop. A fashion consultant.

This had been my world. I knew it inside out. Certainly I understood it better than I understood Chester Zoo, the wild smell of Mishnah Grunewald on my skin notwithstanding. I even began to wonder whether that was when it all went wrong: the day Mishnah called me 'feral' and I went in search of the monkey in myself. As a novelist, never mind as a man, wouldn't I have done better had I stuck with retail? Quinton's words: don't sever your roots, stick with what you know.

Without question, Vanessa would be scathing. The moment I put my hero in charge of a lacy little boutique in Wilmslow she'd accuse me of shedding the last pretence that I was interested in somebody not myself. 'Solipsistic shit!' she'd called me when I'd written as Mishnah Grunewald – a Jewish woman zookeeper. 'Solipsistic shit!' she'd called me when I'd written as an unprincipled van salesman on the loose in Sandbach. She was hardly going to think any better of me when I wrote as a comedic Wilmslow fashionista with artistic pretensions and parents identical to my own.

But then Vanessa was not going to see this novel until it was too late for her opinion to count. Normally I presented her with a typescript hot from my computer. But how do you give your wife a novel about a man – a comedian or a fashion consultant – who's in love with his wife's mother? I'd deny the similarity of course. *This is a work of fiction, Vee, for Christ's sake. Any resemblance between the characters and persons living or dead* . . . But she'd never swallow that. In her soul Vanessa didn't believe in fiction. Her own work-in-progress, now in its second decade of non-completion, didn't even bother to change names. The heroine was Vanessa, the bad guy was Guy. Once you changed anything, Vanessa maintained, you lost the ring of truth. So I had no hope of persuading her that I had entirely made up the story of a Cheshire-born shop assistant who'd formed an unnatural attachment to the mother of his wife, a woman in all particulars identical – because I too loved the ring of truth – to Vanessa.

Which left me with only two courses of action: either I'd risk ending the marriage, or I'd not write the book.

A no-brainer – as people with no feeling for language, readers who didn't read me, readers who didn't read anyone, the wordless walking brain-dead – chose to put it. A no-brainer.

12

Little Gidding

In my head I called him Gid, my comedian who wasn't. Gid, short for Gideon, not to be confused with Guy, short – in mock-heroic Vanessa-speak – for Guido.

Guido was what she called me the first time we slept together. *Geeeedo!* Like Sophia Loren wheedling her way into the forgiveness of Marcello Mastroianni. She climbed on top of me and blew the name into my eyes. *Guido, Guido* . . . At a stroke, Wilmslow became Naples. I could smell the pungent lava of Vesuvius floating on the lavender-blue waters of the Mediterranean. See Wilmslow and die. With Vanessa astride me, death would not have been so terrible. Life with Vanessa astride me was better even than death though, and life crooked its libidinous finger at me. *Guido, Guido* . . .

I believed it. I *was* Guido. I even began to dress differently. More Italianately. More Armani than Boss. Soft black crêpe. The jacket like a second skin. *Guido, Guido* . . . And I was fool enough to think Vanessa believed it also. Maybe she had, at first. But eventually the name snagged on the ridiculousness of things and became ridiculous itself. 'Use your nose on me, Guido,' I recall her saying. I bridled at that, I'm not sure why. Was it the idea of being sexually adroit only by virtue of my nose? I acceded, nevertheless, and even enjoyed it, but I was never entirely free of the sensation that she

94

was making light of me, even denying me, phallically. Henry Miller wouldn't have minded, but D. H. Lawrence would. Eventually, when Vanessa called me Guido I did not see the Bay of Naples, I saw Mount Derision, and below it the Slough of Despond.

I say 'eventually' as though it just happened over time, but in fact Vanessa hit upon a very particular usage of Guido that took the gloss off it. We were a few years into our marriage. I'd published a brace of novels, the first of them still generating sufficient interest for me to be invited to the sort of festival that would put up a poetry tent in a field, next to the hamburger and noodle stalls, as a diversion, mainly for the older visitors, from the main business which was music. I didn't enjoy these gigs. Not my sort of readers, that's if they were readers at all. They sat on cushions on the grass expecting someone to recite something with easily graspable rhymes and hypnotic rhythms, in the spirit of the music from which they were taking a short break. The writer on before me did lineless free association on the spot, as the spirit moved him. 'Heroes, zeros, losers, users, holding hands, folding wands, kissing, missing, missing what? missing nought, in love no ought, whatever teachers taught, bodies warming, love-ties forming . . .'

Amazed that anyone could detect in language the consonance of terminal sounds, the woodland folk banged their little hands together.

'Shouldn't be here,' I whispered to Vanessa as we stood at the back of the tent drinking beer from biodegradable plastic cups. 'This is no place for prose.'

'Whooh!' she shouted, punching the air with her free hand. Not in response to my words but the performance poet's. As someone who sweated hard over every line and had nothing to show after four hours at the computer but a few random swear words addressed to the readers she didn't have, she was bowled over by the impromptu.

'Don't do that whooing shit,' I told her.

'Why not? Because it's not you I'm whooing?'

'Because it's not seemly, for one. And two, because he's crap.'

'Whooh!' she shouted. 'Yeah!'

The impromptu poet was so touched by her appreciation that he began to hymn her beauty. 'Lovely lady, be more bravely, come into my parlour, a little farther, still more farther, fuck your friend (unless he's your father) . . .'

I had agreed to do this gig only because Vanessa fancied the idea of a trip to the country.

'Let's camp,' she'd said.

I thought about it. 'Let's not,' I'd said.

'Go on. It would be such fun. We could build a fire. We could cook sausages. I could suck your dick under the moon.'

'You could do that in our garden.'

'You have no poetry in your soul, Guido.'

This was why she was paying me back, first by whooing at the performance poet and then by joining a small queue to buy a collection of his poems.

'How do you collect poems you make up on the spot?' I wanted to know.

'Don't be cretinous,' Vanessa said.

'How am I being cretinous?'

She didn't tell me. I was too cretinous to be told. But after I'd done my reading – ten pages of my most dense discursively lubricious prose containing references to characters the audience knew nothing of and events they couldn't possibly comprehend, which might be why there was barely any audience left by the time I'd finished – she picked up the word again. 'Cretin,' she said.

I was sitting staring into space behind my pile of books for which there was, to no one's surprise, not a single taker. I could smell burgers and pizza. I could hear jazz. Opposite me flags fluttered and the litter police made sure that people graded their crap before putting it into bins. Though there was no bin I could discern for the crap impromptu poet's crap impromptu poetry. Other than me, everyone was being lovely to everybody else, twittering like little love birds.

'It's not me that's the cretin, Vee,' I said. 'Illiterate twats.'

'What did they do wrong? They came, they sat, they listened –'

'– they left . . .'

'What did you expect, you cretin?'

'Knock off the cretin,' I said.

'I won't. Guido Cretino.' She laughed at her own music. Vee the performance poet. 'Have you met my spouse, the distinguished louse, writer of fiction with his *dick*tion, Guido Cretino?'

And the name stuck.

A rule of thumb when choosing a name is that it should look arresting on the page. I'd never been a Bill and Mary novelist. Life is banal enough, in my view, without a writer replicating it. But you can also strive too hard. Beaufield Nubeem, for example, or Tyrone Slothrop. Gideon was feasible and yet still caught the eye. Erudite reviewers would make something of the biblical Gideon being a feller of trees, God's agent in the slaying of the Midianites. Thus, a feller of the decencies. In fact, I only ever chose a name for its sound and its appearance, not its meaning. Only after the reviewers had been to work did I know why I'd called X, X. And by that time it was too late to disabuse them. Gideon worked for me aesthetically, and because I could abbreviate him to Gid, which worked for me because it looked like gad, as in the gadfly – a small sexual irritant, goading his mother-in-law into what he hoped at last would be sexual frenzy.

Goading, giddying, Gidding.

'Little Gidding', someone at the *TLS* was going to notice, the last of Eliot's *Four Quartets*. 'Is Guy Ableman telling us he has finally come to feel what Eliot called "the laceration / Of laughter at what ceases to amuse"?'

Finally?

That 'Little Gidding' was also an ironic reference to any one of a number of Henry James's flaccid heroes – those still waiting for their lives to start, for the beast in their jungle to rouse himself and leap, for the sacred terror of which they walked in fear to strike and tear their throat – I could count on the *London Review of Books* to point out.

Such dense literary affiliation, and all I was after was a gadfly name that sounded teasingly like my own.

Gid, anyway – maybe Little Gidding was better after all – Little Gidding – or why not simply Little Gid? – would manage, as at his age I managed, Wilhelmina's of Wilmslow. I'd have, eventually, to fictionalise that – the Wilhelmina's and the Wilmslow. I was only *lending* him my past. But for the time being we were in this thing together, running the shop, with the assist-ance of a couple of competent and voguish girls with no A levels, while our parents, cruising the world on its profits, wondered what to do with it – sell, come back and run again themselves, or pass down to the next in line, in my parents' case to me, an ingrate fantasising about being Henry Miller while waiting for my younger brother to finish his business education, in Little Gid's a more contented personality who did occasionally, without any reason to suppose he had the aptitude, think about being a comedian.

Whatever its congeniality to either of our personalities, Wilhelmina's was, as I like to go on remembering, for I hadn't always been down on my luck, an aromatic and exclusive boutique, stocking demonstratively upmarket clothes – the Rifat Ozbeks, Thierry Muglers, Gallianos, Jean Paul Gaultiers and of course Dolce and Gabbanas of the day – to women who would rather shop locally than have to find somewhere to park their Lamborghinis in Manchester, Liverpool or Chester, not that they'd find what Wilhelmina's sold in Liverpool or Chester. Being younger than me – a novelistic ruse devised to throw auto-biography hunters off the scent – Little Gid would number footballers' wives among his clients. And if they weren't football-ers' wives when they went in to his shop, they sure as hell would look like footballers' wives when they left. Either way, they trusted him. They put themselves in his hands. Gid Pet, they call him. Gid Darling. Gid Angel. They felt that that something that had rubbed off on him, rubbed off on them. He accompanied his parents to Paris and Milan, then later he would go on his own. Met couturiers. Met models. It was worth going into Wilhelmina's just to sniff the catwalks of Europe on him.

On me, too, for the brief time I did what he did. Guy Dear. Guy Angel. My heart wasn't in it but I was fashionably thin, liked putting my hands on women's bodies, and had pretty much the same taste as our clientele. Which did not yet include footballers' wives. They were not a discrete species in my time. The difference between Little Gid and me wasn't only a difference of chronology but of class. My Wilhelmina's was genteel. By Little Gid's time chav had happened. Jean Muir had lost her rail to Versace. But the designer labels, the trips to Paris and Milan, the couturiers, the models – these I too enjoyed in a provisional, Henry Millerish sort of way, by which I mean I wished the fashion houses had been whorehouses, actual whorehouses with real, working, thirty-pound-an-hour whores in them, for whorehouses belong to literature as couture never can. Like attracted like, anyway, so any number of well-turned-out women made the trip to Wilmslow if they didn't already live there. Half of Lancashire, half of Staffordshire, all of Cheshire. Hence Vanessa, who had idled with the idea of being a model herself, as she idled with the idea of everything, and might have made it but for those incipient literary ambitions which have done, and I don't doubt will continue to do, long after we are dead, such damage to us both. And hence her mother, Poppy, who for a short while had *been* a model, of a sort, and who was loosely connected to my mother, Wilhelmina.

As *for* Wilhelmina and my father, they had relinquished the business and they hadn't. No matter how many times they sailed away, they always sailed back again, partly to check whether I'd run it into the ground, or run off with the staff, partly because they missed the razzamatazz – the whizzing off to Paris, the London parties, the sound of champagne corks popping in Chester.

Little Gid's fictionalised folks, I fancied, would be less concerned about him. He would have more of a flair for fashion than I ever had. And he would actually *enjoy* running a shop. There are such human beings. They take pleasure in what's called 'meeting people'. They enjoy making a sale, cashing up, reordering, doing the books – commerce, accountancy, money as and for itself. My brother Jeffrey – Jeffrey Darling – was such a person. He drove a BMW sports coupé through the lanes of Cheshire, the snow-white cuffs of his shirt protruding from his Gucci jacket, humming happily to himself. He dreamed clothes. I haven't invented that. He told me once that he dreamed beautiful clothes. 'And what are your nightmares about?' I asked him. 'Hideous clothes.'

The last time we talked there was a chance he would soon have his own TV series. Or at least one half of a TV series. *The Town Mouse and the Country Mouse* — a tale of two fashion retailers, one in Manchester, one in Wilmslow, and the differing demands their customers made of them. It didn't seem to have much meat on its bones televisually to me, but what did I know about television? And if it didn't eventuate, it didn't eventuate. Jeffrey Sweetheart was cool about it.

So Little Gid, were I ever to put flesh on his bones, would have a bit of Jeffrey in him, visually and in relation to the joys of retailing, at least. His head would not be in the clouds. He would hear when people spoke to him. He would remember to reply. He would not be so transfixed by words — on labels, on a passing vehicle, in a newspaper that had been brought into the shop — that he would forget he'd left someone in the dressing room waiting to try on the same garment in another size. He would not, in short, be a writer. Which meant it was always possible I'd be able to stitch him up a happy ending here on earth, whatever Francis's advice to the contrary — that's if nothing terrible happened on account of his fucking his mother-in-law, which I couldn't at this early stage of the narrative guarantee.

13

Viscera

It's a curse, the writing impulse, if it gets you early, and if it doesn't get you early it isn't a writing impulse. Don't listen to anyone who tells you they discovered they had literary talent late on. Either they're lying about the chronology, or the talent they are talking about they don't have. The impulse to write is an impulse to alter the conditions of your childhood. Not to falsify them, but to make the world other than the hellhole it looks to you when you're young. Show me a happy child and I can imagine all manner of future occupations for him – in sport, in politics, in fashion retailing – but none of them in literature. Novels are born out of misery, which is why the best ones aren't miserable, no matter that misery is a seller. The fact that the novel has been written is evidence that the misery has been overcome.

Misery of the succumbed-to sort you can get in life.

So I began with the highest of ideals. I would make the world a better place than it was, if not to live in then to read about.

By better I didn't mean more wholesome. I meant full of the rudery we were too scared of in Wilmslow. It could be that I'm talking only about myself. Full of the rudery, in that case, that *I* was scared of. If I could master rudery, I thought, I'd master life.

And death.

I pinned photographs of writers considered beyond the pale of polite society to my bedroom wall. Jean-Paul Sartre, William S. Burroughs, Henry Miller, Leonard Cohen, Brendan Behan, Dylan Thomas, Norman Mailer. All devilish, existential blasphemers in their way, all men in pain, like me, though I was but a boy in pain.

Henry Miller topped the list. He splashed filth about like a graffiti artist in words. But he was a philosopher of sorts as well. He'd splash filth about then cogitate over what he'd done. Fourteen was young to be reading Henry Miller and I doubt I understood it all. I certainly wasn't always able to picture what he was doing with the women. But you can tell when a writer dares you to say he's gone too far — *too far? so you know what's far enough?* — and I applauded the enterprise. I'd go too far, I promised myself, when my turn came.

I'd been introduced to these writers by a temporary school-teacher, Archie Clayburgh, a sort of parody Englishman who wore a monocle to teach in and drove to school in an Austin A40, wearing goggles. He was an author in his own right, a contributor to *Playboy* and *Penthouse* and *Forum*, though to our chagrin we discovered that only after he'd left the school. Not impossibly, the headmaster discovered it before us and that was *why* Archie Clayburgh left the school. Piers Wain, the teacher Archie Clayburgh temporarily replaced, had been badly teased by us before his nervous breakdown, on account of the gentleness of his manner and the strange way he had of pronouncing the name Brontë, caused partly by his not being able to handle the letter r, and partly by his reading the diaeresis as an injunction never to allow the word to end. That his career and character were defined by this queer pronunciation only shows how often he invoked it, the novels of Charlotte, Emily and Anne Bwontaiaiai being his life's passion and more or less the only works of fiction he encouraged us to read. If we listened to Piers Wain the English novel began in 1847 with the publication of *Jane Eyre* and *Wuthering Heights*, flourished in 1848 with the publication of *The Tenant of Wildfell Hall*, and died in 1853 with the publication of *Villette*.

'Novels for girls with migraines,' was how Archie Clayburgh dismissed them when we told him what we'd read with Mr Wain.

He brought a giant hourglass into his lessons and upturned it when he began speaking. If no one laughed before the sand ran out, or if no one showed that he'd been shocked or sickened to his stomach – either by retching, fainting, or asking to be excused – he would acknowledge he had failed as a teacher and hand in his notice. His favourite word was 'visceral'. 'You don't just read with your heads, boys,' he'd tell us, 'you read viscerally, with your bowels.' And if we hadn't laughed before, we'd laugh at that.

Archie Clayburgh knew he couldn't get us to read more than selections of his favourite retch-making writers in class, but he made sure they were available in the school library, though they were locked away behind glass doors and we had to sign to take them out.

When Mr Wain returned, *Tropic of Capricorn* and *Beautiful Losers* vanished from the library and we all went back to getting headaches when we read.

But with me, at least, Archie Clayburgh succeeded in his aim. I read raucously from then on. Words no longer made me wince with their intrinsic excruciation. Words now frolicked lewdly before my eyes.

My father, a small man with feeble eyesight and no hair, not even where his eyebrows should have been, wasn't sure what he thought of my having writers on my wall. 'Who's this?' he'd ask, on one of his rare visits to my room – it always felt as though he'd got lost in his own house and only stumbled on me by chance. Invariably his squint rested on what was then a famous photograph of the novelist James Baldwin. I think my father wondered what I was doing with a portrait of a black man in my bedroom, and I think he spotted something else not quite right about Baldwin, namely that he was a homosexual, and he must have asked himself whether his being on my wall meant that I was a homosexual too.

It occurred to me that if I gave him Henry Miller or Leonard Cohen to read he wouldn't fear for me on that score, but he wasn't a reading man. He wasn't an anything man, my father. He existed to be at my mother's service, much like a dog, and that was that. She called and he went running. When I pictured them having sex, which was all the time when I had a Henry Miller on the go, I couldn't get beyond the image of his sniffing her. But they had me and Jeffrey Dearest so he must have done more than sniff her, twice at least.

As a matter of disinterested enquiry, could this picture of him sniffing have been behind the sniffing I thought of getting Gideon to do when he walked out on to the stage? Was there, after all, though I prided myself on freedom from all filial feeling whatsoever, some buried Oedipal sexual disgust in me?

I thought about it and then thought not.

My mother was as much a mystery to me, from the progenitive point of view, as my father. It was impossible to believe I had issued in any normal way from either of them. She had what the people of Wilmslow characterised as oomph. Not just get-up-and-go but an overdeveloped instinct for emphasis and play. She dominated every conversation, whether in the house, in the shop, in the street, at a restaurant or indeed at any social gathering, throwing her arms about, pulling faces, rolling her smokeless artificial cigarette between her lips – she went to sleep chewing on that cigarette

– and laughing wildly. And this before the six o'clock drink. She was, of course, immaculately turned out at all times, favouring little suits, usually Chanel, with short jackets and tiny barrel skirts, frequently worn with a matching French beret from which a small point of steel protruded like a radio mast. Was she a transmitter for some faraway planet? That would have been as good a guess as any. Certainly she wore sufficient metal, around her wrists and even stitched into her gloves like chain mail, to make magnetic contact with an alien people hundreds of thousands of light years away.

Alternatively, her drawing power existed solely to pull people into the shop, and once they were inside it was highly unlikely they would ever get out again until they'd spent a minimum of a thousand pounds on a scarf.

She was a chain-smoker before chain-smoking went out of style and dripped ash without apology onto the shoes of her customers, onto the clothes they bought, into the change she gave them. Latterly, she smoked an electronic cigarette which hung perilously from her lower lip and glowed like a second set of antennae.

Her attitude to my having writers on my wall was that I was in understandable rebellion against the boisterous materialism of which I was the beneficiary and would eventually grow out of it. That I went to the University of the Fenlands was a source of pride to her, as I was the first person in the family to go to a university anywhere, but she would have been no less pleased to see me enrolled at Wilmslow Business College, an ambition she saw realised in Jeffrey.

Such were the intimate characters of the mild-mannered novel that was my life, and I bring them forward not in any way to disparage them but in order to explain why that novel had to be rewritten viscerally by me.

* * *

But I hadn't written a word of any sort I'd have dared show a living soul before Vanessa Green and Poppy Eisenhower turned up uninvited. If Archie Clayburgh was the tinder, they were the lighted match.

They came again to the shop, their hair aflame, about a fortnight after their first visit, this time as customers. Vanessa bought Bruce Oldfield trousers, in all likelihood to annoy me. Trousers were a terrible waste, given her legs, and these were too full, giving her the look of a clown, but my mother had taught me to exploit a customer's tastes, however appalling. 'You never dislike what they like,' she told me. 'You don't set up a conflict in their minds by suggesting something you think looks better. That just allows them to shy from the choice and buy nothing. Tell them they look nice in what they think they look nice in and then get them to buy two of it.'

Poppy bought two silk shirts by Donna Karan. One was very nearly see-through and it was all I could do not to enquire about the circumstances in which she planned to wear it. Certainly none I could imagine in Knutsford or its environs.

They bought their clothes separately, Poppy Eisenhower signing a cheque, which I accepted though it exceeded the limit guaranteed by her cheque card, Vanessa paying by credit card. She had not, I noted, changed her name to Eisenhower. She remained Vanessa Green. Their having different surnames added to their intrigue, but added, I thought, to her mother's intrigue more.

They were disappointed my mother was still away, but by this time I had put them in touch with each other so that I'd be free to think about other things in her company. By 'her' company I mean Poppy's. Even at that stage I was interested in her – not I think *more* interested than I was in Vanessa, but interested to the same degree. The problem with Gideon as a character was that if he wasn't a writer – and I knew Francis was right about that at least: that I couldn't make him a writer – then I didn't see how he'd be up to the subtleties of sinfulness which I, as a writer of rudery in-waiting, a writer to my soul no matter that I'd submitted nothing for publication, brewed up whenever I looked at the two women. You had to be a writer to invite the trouble, you had to be a writer to be prepared to put your life into a sort of suspense while the story of what would happen had its way with you. As a non-writer, as someone like my brother Jeffrey, say, Little Gidding would follow his heart not his curiosity, would make a decision calculated on what promised to make him happy. Whereas I didn't give a fig for happiness. I was after bigger, dirtier fish.

I did the conventional thing at first. I asked Vanessa out. But even this needed to be a rigmarole. Not a rigmarole of mere plot, a rigmarole of dangerous duplicity. Poppy had given me their contact details to pass on to my mother, so I knew where they lived. On the pretext that I thought they'd left a pair of gloves in the shop, I drove out to Knutsford and knocked on their door. They lived, of course, in a cottage. Mossy-roofed. A bird of some description sang in a bare tree in their garden. Winter flowers of some description grew in a wooden trough. Enough with the nature writing. It must have been about seven o'clock. When I knocked on their door I heard shouting. I thought one of them was saying to the other, 'Not in your underwear you don't,' but that could have been a transference from my own demented hoping.

Eventually I heard a rapping on an upstairs window and looked up. Vanessa was twitching the curtains as though signalling to an invading force in the North Sea. I waved. She mouthed something bad-tempered at me which I couldn't understand. I held up the gloves. She looked astonished. She told me later she thought I'd driven over with the gloves to see if either of the women wanted to buy them or, if both of them did, to offer them a single glove each. Which, when you think about it, was essentially the mission I was on, whether I knew it at the time or not. Unless I saw the women as the gloves, my fingers . . . But that was going too far, too soon.

He's keen, was what Vanessa told me she thought. Meaning keen to make a sale.

She came downstairs and opened the door just wide enough to pass a pound note through. Her red hair was uncombed and she emanated cigarette. It was an emanation I liked on women. All the models at the fashion shows had more nicotine in their bodies than protein. Some were scarcely more than walking cigarettes. They'd come off the catwalk, undress and light up. It would get so smoky backstage that they had to stand by the fire exits or hang out of the windows in their tiny pants, choking. One night in Milan I took out a yet-to-be famous model, Minerva, whom I'd met at an after-collection party. That was one of the perks of Wilhelmina's. You didn't get to the best parties but you got to the second tier where you could talk to models who were second tier themselves, but beautiful enough for you if you lived in Wilmslow. Minerva ate steamed broccoli and tobacco. She moved her head like a giraffe's, as though sniffing out whatever grew on the tops of trees. Throughout the most expensive meal I'd ever bought – I remember calculating that I could have ordered dinner for eight in Wilmslow for the price of each floret of broccoli – Minerva coughed in my face. I breathed her in as though she were a rare flower. Had she had her mother with her doing likewise I might well have fallen fatally for them both.

'Yes?' Vanessa asked.

I put my face as close to her smoky mouth as I dared.

Something told me to give up the glove idea. 'Just passing,' I said. 'I wondered if you were up for a drink.'

'Here?'

I never knew what she meant. On her lips even the simplest words became an enigma. *Here?* What did *here* mean? On the doorstep? In the street? In Knutsford, in Cheshire, in England, in Europe, in the universe?

My mouth must have fallen open. 'I can't let you in,' she said.

'I don't expect you to let me in,' I said. 'I meant a drink outside.'

She was having the same trouble with me. 'Outside?' In their garden, on the street, in the gutter?

'A pub. A bar.'

'I don't go to pubs or bars.'

'I don't either,' I said. 'A meal?'

'I've eaten.'

'A burger? Fish and chips?'

'That's food. I've just said I've eaten.'

Gideon in his comedic phase might have scratched his head and said, 'How about a fuck in that case?' but I was no comedian. I was twenty-four and writing the novel of what was happening in my head.

It's true that Henry Miller might also have asked her for a fuck. In fact Henry Miller might well have asked to see her cunt, but I wasn't yet Henry Miller either, more was the pity.

In the event, what I did would probably have shocked Henry Miller, Leonard Cohen and Norman Mailer rolled together. I asked, since she didn't want to come out herself, whether perhaps her mother did.

I expected her to query 'did'. '*Did* what?'

Did want a fuck, I decided against saying.

14

OCD

It was a shame we didn't make it to Monkey Mia until dark. It meant that we missed out on being scrutinised by the pelican who guarded the beach. Before you could get to what else Monkey Mia had to offer, you had to pass the pelican. And if he didn't like you you could kiss goodbye to the dolphins, never mind the monkeys.

Although under normal circumstances she would not be parted from her mother, Vanessa couldn't face having her sleeping in the van with us that night. Drunk, Poppy snored. Not a loud snore but loud enough to spoil the outback experience for her daughter. We were in a complex of lodges and cabins, bars, cafés, restaurants; we parked the van where we could avail ourselves of the most modern conveniences known to camping – had we asked, they'd have piped red wine into us through our taps – but we were still half a thousand kilometres from the highway, on a promontory protruding like a nose from the coastline of Western Australia far into the Indian Ocean. We were a long way from anywhere. Vanessa had come here to get away. From me, from my writing, from her own writing, from the morbidities of London where, even before Merton took his life and our favourite independent bookshop closed its doors, the prognosis for civilisation had been made and was declared terminal. It would be good to hear the silence, she said. Or the sound of life that wasn't human life. I wasn't sure what she expected to hear. The waves? The pelican opening and closing his beak, click-clack? The night-time cries of dolphins? She didn't know what she wanted to hear, only what she didn't. Number one was her mother snoring. Number two was me on any subject.

So we moved her mother into a lodge. She was awake by this time and wanting dinner. 'Sleep,' Vanessa said. Her words had an uncanny effect on Poppy. If Vanessa said sleep, she slept. Ten minutes after seeing her in, ascertaining where the switches were and how the air conditioning worked, she was flat out on the bed, snoring.

'See,' Vanessa said.

On me too her words worked hypnotically. I saw.

We ate dinner at wooden tables looking out into Shark Bay. The air was warm and silky. The sea barely moved. 'It smells like baby out here,' I said.

'Like a baby?'

'No, not like *a* baby. Like baby. The essence of newborn baby that you get when you smell its head.'

'Christ, I hope you're not thinking of writing that down.'

I was, but didn't dare to now.

'I'll tell you what I can smell,' Vanessa said. 'Dolphin.'

'What does dolphin smell like?'

'Breathe in. Can you smell it now?'

'Yes,' I lied. In fact, what Vanessa could smell was the barbecued barracuda at the next couple's table. Unless it was their baby.

Every now and then Vanessa gestured to the sea and said, 'Look!'

I looked but couldn't see anything.

'There! Do you see?'

Dolphins.

For my money what she saw could as easily have been monkeys. From this distance and in this light any oil-slick grey dolphin rolling over and waiting to be tickled in Shark Bay would not have been visible. But Vanessa was in marvelling mode. She looked up at the stars. She inhaled the night. You can tell from the night when you're far from anywhere, and this was a night a million miles from everything. And then a shooting star shot by, just for us.

'Christ, Guido,' she said, taking my hand, 'isn't it something?'

'It's something all right,' I said.

We kissed. Not bad after all those years of marriage, still kissing. Kissing was a skill we'd retained. She'd long stopped smoking but whenever I kissed her I remembered the tobacco taste of our first embraces. It was possible that I continued to kiss her passionately in order to seek out that very memory. Call it a Proustian kiss, then. Amplitudinous and digressive. And of course weighed down with the melancholy of time.

Was she kissing me for the same reason? Who could say? I'd never understood why she'd kissed me in the first place. She hadn't appeared to like me. She disagreed with most of my opinions, didn't think I had it in me to be a novelist – on the grounds that I didn't understand her and was therefore unlikely to understand anyone else – refused on principle to wear the clothes I wanted her to wear, and regretted the disparity in our height. Could she have kissed me to stop me kissing her mother? Or to stop her mother kissing me? It had occurred to me over the years that she'd married me telepathically, by proxy or in answer to some sort of uncanny mother-daughter transference of affection, or simply to afford vicarious pleasure to Poppy. For that theory to have worked I'd have needed evidence that Poppy had wanted me for herself, only our age difference a barrier, but I had no evidence of the sort. If anything, she'd been as uninterested in me as her daughter – even the night she agreed to go drinking with me in Knutsford – and didn't change her attitude in any marked way, as Vanessa definitely did, when Quinton O'Malley rescued *Who Gives a Monkey's?* from the reject pile, sold it to Merton Flak who hailed it as a masterpiece and I became a shooting star myself.

It was also possible that Vanessa had loved me deeply but unconventionally, and I had not been unconventional enough to appreciate it. Except that I had stayed in love with her, no matter how great the provocation and temptation not to, and if that wasn't appreciation what was it?

Our Monkey Mia kiss, however it was to be interpreted, came to an end when a motor yacht with lights blazing and loud music blaring hove out of the night and dropped anchor right in front of us, exactly where Vanessa swore she'd seen the dolphins doing cartwheels.

'All we need!' she said, as though this was the last in a series of intolerable vexations. That was Vanessa – the smallest irritation drove out all memory that she'd ever enjoyed a moment's happiness in her life.

I suggested we move tables but there was no escaping the glare or the racket.

Vanessa's father, in the brief time she'd known him, had been a sailing man and she'd inherited from him a hatred of anything that needed an engine to propel it through the water. You had a sail, or you rowed, the rest was parvenu grossness. Just before we left London, Garth Rhodes-Rhind, a crossover fantasy writer – which meant he moved implausible characters from another world and time into an implausibly rendered present, or vice versa as the fantasy took him – had thrown a bragging party in Docklands on a motor launch. 'Launch on a Launch', the invitation read. The boat, of which he was said to have bought a major share with the sale of the world rights in a novel about a thirteenth-century alchemist with a striking profile and second sight who'd blundered into contemporary Clerkenwell where alchemy was/is all the rage, was a crude pink floating brothel of a vessel which, at least for this one night, he called *Lulu* after the publicity girl for whom he threw over his wife on the strength of royalties from the previous cross-over fantasy about a Clerkenwell banker with a striking profile and early-onset Alzheimer's who'd gone back in time to a thirteenth-century monastery on the summit of Mont Ventoux. There were security men on the boat to stop the wife gatecrashing the party. 'Don't you ever think of doing this,' Vanessa had said to me, squinting viciously through her flute of *Lulu*-tinted champagne.

'Running off with the publicity girl or preventing you from attending the bash?'

She shook her head, a gesture which comprehended everything she loathed about the venue. 'Don't be smart with me, Guido,' she said. 'You know what I'm saying.'

'Vee, what sign have I ever given you that I would like a motor-boat? I can't swim. It makes me seasick to have a bath.'

'Wait till you earn what Garth Rhodes-Rhind earns.'

I rode with the punch. 'I won't be buying a boat.'

We left it at that, though I sensed she went in fear of what I would buy should I suddenly start earning big, whether I wanted a motor launch or not. A fear that caused its own friction, not only because I resented her thinking there was a vulgar plutocrat hiding out in me, but because we both knew that Garth Rhodes-Rhind's earnings from urban fantasy were beyond a writer whose genre was the Wilmslow dissolute, no matter that there were some who viewed that as urban fantasy on my part.

Thus, either way, I felt a failure to her, and indeed to myself. Not least as I had known and helped – well, met and spoken to – Garth Rhodes-Rhind when he was penniless and had encouraged him to believe he could amount to something – though not very much – if he persisted, never for moment believing that he would.

Disheartened by the noise of the motor yacht, we went to bed in the van. In the morning we decided we'd have breakfast in the same restaurant rather than the van so that Poppy could enjoy the view she'd missed out on the night before. She was well rested and looked rather lovely in a safari dress with lots of pockets that complemented Vanessa's. A miracle they could do that without consulting each other, not just choose to wear identical dresses in different colours, but put their hair up similarly, and both wear Roman sandals.

They looked like the mistresses of big-game hunters. In the pockets of their dresses they carried their lovers' bullets.

The owner of the motorboat was out on deck, wearing a powder-blue sailor suit and giving orders. Provisions were being ferried aboard. Crates of champagne and baskets of lobsters, I assumed. In between taking receipt of these, he'd walk up and down, examining the boat, tugging at ropes, checking the paint-work and shaking his head in anger when he found a scratch. This was what you did if you owned a motor yacht – housework, only at sea.

He appeared to be a man in his forties, overcooked by the sun, so that while he cut a youthful figure you could tell, even from a distance, that close up he'd be prematurely aged. Ill-tempered, too, in the way of the idle rich. Be careful, as they say, what you wish for, and he'd wished for a boat whose appearance and well-being now took up every minute of his time.

He had a phone in each hand and another on his belt. All three were ringing.

Vanessa and Poppy drank their tea and laughed at him as he made his round of minute housewifely investigations.

'God, aren't men neurotic!' Poppy said.

'OCD if ever I saw it.'

This was designed for me to hear. I suffered from an extreme form of obsessive compulsive disorder whenever I had a book on the go. I believed I would no sooner write a sentence than I would lose it, either to the four winds if I was writing outside, or to the ill will of a computer when I was at my desk. So I made multiple backups of everything I wrote, writing on paper what I'd typed into a machine, saving on a multitude of external hard drives what I was not prepared to trust to the internal memory of my computer. In the days of carbon paper I'd hide a minimum of four copies of every page I'd typed and leave a note in a sealed envelope for Vanessa, telling her where to find them in the event of my death. Later, I did the same with flash drives of which I kept about a dozen active, depositing them in the pockets of jackets I didn't wear, Sellotaping them to the backs of paintings, concealing them in Vanessa's underwear drawer, hanging them from loops of string behind our bedhead. And the whereabouts of these were logged in a folder marked for Vanessa's attention. If I die, this is where my work is to be found.

When *Who Gives a Monkey's?* was published Vanessa presented me with a soft Italian briefcase embossed with gold lettering. Not my initials – GA – but OCD.

She thought she had married a madman, but if I was mad to suppose that writing was an open invitation to death to seize me, then every other writer was as mad as I was. You no sooner join two words together than you fear your life will soon be over, not because writing wears out the heart but because the act itself, with its wild gamble on futurity, is so presumptuous. Time does not wait for a writer to polish his periods. Even to start a sentence is to send out a challenge to the gods. 'I will live beyond my physical existence, my words will put me among the immortals.'

Comes back the booming answer, 'Oh no they won't!'

Was it because she had failed to start a book she was never going to finish that Vanessa failed to understand the necessary morbidity of writing? She hadn't, brick by brick, built her overweening Babel. She sketched an idea and went to bed. She tried a line of dialogue and tore her hair. Nothing followed. She didn't do joined-up sentences. So the gods would let her live. She didn't threaten them.

We spent the morning at Monkey Mia playing with the dolphins. On the beach at first, waiting for them to roll out of the sea and cavort with us under the eye of the pelican. Then later in a little rowing boat which they buffeted mischievously, disappearing under us as the fancy took them, cuffing our oars, sometimes making as though they wanted to come aboard, eyeing us sideways like parrots on a pirate's shoulder.

'Oh, Mother, Mother, look!' Vanessa cried.

'Aren't they darlings,' Poppy cried in return.

I couldn't have said what posed the greater risk to our stability, the frolicsomeness of the dolphins or the eurhythmic throbbings of Vanessa and her mother, through whom a single vibrating chord of sympathy with God's creatures seemed to pass.

Myself I found them scary. Vanessa and her mother *and* the dolphins. By what right had we declared dolphins magnanimous in all weathers, not the remotest danger to us, when we knew that no creature under the sun could be relied upon never to turn nasty – to one another, never mind to us? It demeaned them, in my view, attributing to them nothing but benign intention, interpreting those strange snouty grimaces as smiles of fondness for *Homo sapiens*. One of these days, I thought, as I sat rigid in the little rowing boat, one of these days the terrible truth about what dolphins really think of us will come out. I was glad when we were back on dry land. But Vanessa and Poppy wanted never to leave. Our plan to drive off that afternoon was abandoned. We would stay another night, sleeping off the excitement before meeting again, in what was now our usual place, for dinner.

Poppy was already tipsy.

'So where are the monkeys?' she asked.

'Do you think it's drink or do you think it could be early-onset dementia?' Vanessa whispered to me.

'It's excitement,' I said. 'It's been a long day, after a long drive.'

'And it's been a long life,' Vanessa said. I knew what came next. If *she* went silly she hoped someone would knock her on the head and finish her off. Was it time to be thinking of doing that to her mother? It half crossed my mind that she meant it, that she'd brought Poppy all this way in order to tip her into Shark Bay where the dolphins could eat her and return her to the diurnal round of nature. Who'd know it wasn't an accident?

But she'd had her chance to do that earlier in the day and she hadn't taken it. Anyone seeing them together in the boat could have mistaken them for lovers, Vita Sackville-West and Violet Trefusis, only more red and Rubenesque, their faces touching, their fingers on each other's shoulders, consumed together by the wonder of it all.

Poppy looked sumptuous, tipsy or not. In the heat, her dress clung to her thighs. Breast for breast there was nothing to choose between Vanessa and her mother – full and soft as a goose-down pillow, both of them (though Poppy's rose and showed a little higher), and unfair, shocking, even deranging, on women other-wise so slender – but for all the difference in their ages, Poppy won it when it came to thighs. Who can ever say what it is that makes that part of a woman suddenly more than a man can bear to look at? Underneath the dress her flesh was not the flesh of a young woman. I had seen her in a bathing costume and knew that her skin had lost its youthful spring. It was mottled now, ever so slightly stretched and pitted, a victim of over-prominent veins and cellulite. And yet the strain of her thighs against the thinness of the material that held it taut, that rounded slope that is never seen on a man's body, no matter how beautiful, the fullness of her without the fatness of her, as though a fruit could ripen for a second time, or as though one of the Monkey Mia dolphins was rolling over inside her dress – I had no defences against the beauty of it. And the tipsiness – well the tipsiness only added to her wild allure.

What I did, I did because I couldn't not do. Call it obsessive compulsive disorder. On the pretext of some natural excitement – don't ask me to name it: the appearance of a hitherto unseen planet, a sweet aroma of chilli oil and frangipani blown in on a current of warm air from an undiscovered continent, a hundred dolphins leaping balletically, as though choreographed by Neptune, from the pellucid waters of the bay – I extended my arms, clapped my hands, and under cover of the table brought one down on the living quiver of Poppy's flesh, just inches from her pelvis, but not so high up that my gesture could be interpreted as lewd. We deal in millimetres when it comes to taking liberties, and guided by the deep unconscious of filial regard, I was nanomillimetre-perfect.

15

I Am a Cello

In the beginning . . .

The night Poppy accepted my invitation to taste the delights of Knutsford with me, since her daughter wouldn't, was remarkable more for the fact of her acceptance than anything else. And that could have been attributed simply to boredom. Knutsford, for Christ's sake! Settling in Knutsford when you had hair like that.

After we'd talked about my mother I'd hoped she would quiz me about my writing practice, no matter that I hadn't written anything. Where I got my ideas from. What time I started. When I knew I'd finished. The sorts of questions they would ask me years later in Chipping Norton before telling me that no matter how *I* knew I'd finished, *they* knew when they had, which was the minute they started. But this was before the days of book groups, and Poppy would not have been a book-group woman anyway.

It's hard to credit intelligence to the non-bookish when books are the only measure of worth you have. I almost forgave my own mother the preposterousness of her personality on the grounds that she devoured airport novels when she wasn't shouting in the street, no matter that what she devoured was shopping and fucking told from the other side of the counter − *selling* and fucking. It astonished me that she was able to find so many soft-porn novels about the retail trade. Did she have them written especially for her, I wondered. She sat up in bed with a scarf tied round her head, her mouth open, her electric cigarette hanging from her lips, turning pages as though she was in a competition to be the first to finish. I don't share the general respect shown to the mechanical act of turning pages. But at least she was ingesting words, and an ingested word might stick halfway down the gullet and shock the reader into reflection. Whereas Poppy, though an intelligent and in some ways far more cultured woman than my mother, was, in this period of her life at least, book-dead. I'd dreaded, when we first began to sit down and talk in the parlour of the White Bear, that she would fail the Tolkien test in record time. I'd said what fun it was to be sitting where Signor Brunoni might have performed his magic, and when she showed she didn't know who I was talking about I told her. Travelling magician, character in *Cranford*, by Mrs Gaskell. And why might he have performed his magic here? she wondered. I stared at her. Because we were *in* Cranford, this was it, Knutsford–Cranford, surely she . . .

Surely she nothing. She shrugged the information away from her as though a fly had landed on her collar. 'Doesn't sound like my kind of magic,' she said. Whereupon I thought, here we go, Tolkien. But in fact she hadn't even made it that far up the ladder of literacy.

'What is?' I asked, with my heart in my mouth.

She thought about it. 'I've always liked Tommy Cooper,' she said.

A dozen years later her answer to the same question would have been a boy wizard.

But worse was to come. Before the evening was over she had failed the Tolstoy test.

And yet the conversation leading up to it had been propitious. She was a cellist, she told me. A serious musician whose repertoire included Bach, Boccherini, Vivaldi and Dvořák. I quivered a little. Dvořák. She asked if I played. No. I just listened. Particularly to Dvořák. She had never been a professional cellist. Not quite up to that. But she had played with an amateur orchestra in Bournemouth, and then in Washington to which her second husband, a junior diplomat named Eisenhower, had whisked her when Vanessa was still a teenager. It was in Washington that she'd done a bit of modelling, too, once famously posing nude wrapped around her cello for a poster for the Georgetown Camerata Chamber Orchestra. 'Well, not really nude,' she told me, presumably bethinking herself of our age difference, 'but it looked that way. And it brought my marriage to an end.'

'Your husband didn't like you posing nude with your cello?' I asked. Funny what husbands don't like.

'It wasn't so much that. He was jealous of the photographer who happened to be the violinist with whom I was rehearsing Brahms's Double Concerto at the time.'

'At the time he took the photograph?'

'No, at the time my husband walked in and found us.'

'Found you . . .'

'No, not that. Found us rehearsing. The sight of it maddened him so much he threw me out of the house.'

'Christ! And the violinist?'

'He threatened to kill him.'

'This is Tolstoy,' I said excitedly. 'Pure Tolstoy.'

She looked at me in bewilderment. 'Is he another of your *Cranford* crowd?'

Was it possible? Was it possible to be a good enough cellist to play Brahms's Double Concerto and not have heard of Tolstoy? Was it possible to have got beyond the age of ten, never mind the music, and not have heard of Tolstoy?

123

Unless she was teasing me. She had ironic eyes. She could have been having fun at my expense. But she didn't seem engaged enough for that. Teasing is flirting, and she wasn't flirting.

I mentioned *The Kreutzer Sonata, Anna Karenina, War and Peace. Anna Karenina* appeared to ring a bell and she must have deduced the others were books because she said she hadn't read them. 'I'm not a reader,' she said. 'Vanessa reads enough for both of us.'

I didn't say reading doesn't work like that. I didn't say you can no more read for another person than you can drink water for him stroke her.

I couldn't work her out. Didn't one artistic endeavour necessarily bleed into another? If you play Bach's Cello Suites you read Tolstoy. It was only much later that I realised you didn't have to be cultured to be a musician – or a writer, come to that. Art? Some of the most vulgar philistines I knew made art, and of those the most vulgar still wrote books. Refinement was mainly to be found among those who consumed or championed them, like poor Merton. But you don't know that when you're twenty-four and still trying to spit out your first novel.

Poppy was lying about her reading, anyway. She read avidly. Pure shit, but she read it avidly.

Ditching Tolstoy, I asked her about her life before and after the junior diplomat who dumped her in Washington. There wasn't much to tell. Her first husband had been a naval officer who'd drunk himself into an early grave. She'd loved him, on the occasions she saw him. Vanessa the same. But the two women had been alone together a great deal, so apart from missing their annual sailing holidays off the Isle of Wight they barely noticed the change when he'd gone. Vanessa hadn't liked it in Washington and was glad to fly home. She went to Manchester University for a year, read philosophy, changed to languages, changed to art history, changed back to philosophy, and then left. She hadn't liked it there either. But the absence of necessity was the real reason, Poppy explained. They'd been left money by Poppy's first husband and she'd got a good settlement from her second; they wanted for nothing; other than to dress like each other and to float about looking lovely, they were without an aim. And the cello? Yes, she still practised. Vanessa too. At home, they played Vivaldi's Double Concerto in G Minor together.

My eyes swam. 'Nude?'

Where I found the courage or the folly to ask that I will never know. I no sooner said it than I backed away in my chair, putting my hands up to my face, half as though expecting to be struck, half as though preventing the demons that lived inside me from uttering another word.

Poppy put her glass down and for the first time looked me straight in the eyes. Then she beckoned me to her with a crooked finger.

I had flushed the colour of her lipstick.

'Cheeky monkey!' she said, kissing me on the cheek.

Cellist's thighs.

I should have remembered.

Light years later, touching the living quiver of Poppy in the heat of the Monkey Mia night, that fact should have come back to me. Cellist's thighs.

I am a cello.

And my work-in-progress alter ego, Little Gid, would he be a cello too?

Some things you keep for yourself.

16

All the World Loves a Wedding

'Cheeky monkey', I am now willing to accept, was what did it. Since it was meant to be a sexual compliment of sorts – wasn't it? – I couldn't but wonder what she'd seen in me. Not what she'd *seen* in me, but what she'd seen in me that was chimp-like. From which wondering it was the smallest step to remembering Mishnah Grunewald who had called me Beagle. And there, suddenly, was the novel I knew I needed to write. Courtesy of the woman – or at least one of the two women – I needed to impress.

How strangely inspiration works! Poppy Eisenhower was – or at least she presented herself at the time as being – the least bookish person on the planet, a woman ignorant of Mrs Gaskell and Tolstoy, and yet without her I would not have found my way out of the dark of uncreativity. The Dark Lady of my Sonnets, whose idea of magic realism was Tommy Cooper saying, 'Just like that.'

It was Vanessa's belief that because I kept everything for myself I was too selfish ever to be a truly great novelist.

This was a modified version of her earlier belief that I was too selfish ever to write a novel at all.

She was amazed when I finished my first book. 'I'm walking on sunshine,' I sang.

'No, you're not,' she said.

And she was even more amazed when a publisher accepted it. But she was generous in defeat. 'I am proud of you and delighted for you,' she said. 'I see it almost as one of my own.'

'That's kind,' I said, not knowing what she was talking about. I had written it in secret, during the first two years of our marriage, either while she was sleeping or out having her nails done with her mother, or while I was standing at the till on a quiet day in Wilhelmina's.

'I mean one of my own in the sense that you could not have done it without me,' she said.

I didn't mention Poppy's all-creating touch.

And she was right about the part she'd played. For all my exalted literary ambitions, it was wanting to stick it to Vanessa, to confound her view of me as a fantasist, that turned daydreaming into actuality. Just as one should never discount, when fathoming the origins of art, the influence of an uneducated mother-in-law, one should never underestimate, when measuring ambition, the influence of a jeering wife stroke husband. For jeering, too, is conversation, and conversation, for a writer such as I am, is the midwife of creation.

There's a word for it. Maieutics. Sounds as though named after a goddess — Maieusis. I didn't mention this to Vanessa, knowing that that was how she would henceforth want to be addressed: as the goddess Maieusis.

'And also mine,' she went on, 'in the sense of its being the nearest I will get to mothering a child.'

Neither of us wanted a child. Not wanting a child was the only thing we agreed about. I sometimes thought it was the reason we got married, the wellspring of our union – not to engender life. So it seemed a contradiction, on her part, if not a betrayal, to be thinking of my book as offspring.

We fell out over what to call it. My working title, *The Zookeeper*, wasn't her idea of what you call a child.

'Nor mine,' I said. 'But it's not a child.'

'It is to me,' she said. 'Can't you give it a child's name?'

'Like what?'

'*Vanessa*.'

'You're not a child.'

'I was.'

'It's not about you.'

She laughed one of her deep, guttural, scornful laughs. 'Ah, darling,' she said, shaking her head, 'why are you in such denial? It's about me on every line, admit it.'

'Vee, you haven't read it yet.'

'Do I need to?'

'If you're going to go on thinking it's about you, yes.'

She treated me to one of her archest expressions, eyes dancing, lips pleated. The prelude in some households, I didn't doubt, to domestic violence. In our household such an expression *was* domestic violence. But you couldn't be married to a woman like Vanessa and not pay a price for it.

'So what *is* it about?' she asked.

'Animality, sensuality, cruelty, indifference.'

She laughed animalistically, sensually, cruelly, indifferently. 'My point precisely,' she said. 'I know how you see me.'

'Vee, it's set in a zoo. I don't see our life as a zoo.'

'A zoo? You've never been inside a zoo in the time I've known you. You've never taken me to a zoo. You've never so much as mentioned a zoo. You don't like animals. You won't even let us have a cat. A zoo? You?'

I hadn't told her about Mishnah Grunewald. Vanessa wasn't a wife who liked hearing about her husband's past. We were Adam and Eve. Before us, nothing.

'I have a rich imagination,' I reminded her.

'And what happens in this richly imagined zoo?'

'Zoological things.'

She paused. 'It's about your dick, isn't it?'

'It's about everybody's dick.'

'Guido, not everybody has a dick. Half the world doesn't have a dick.'

'I know that. The novel is told from the point of view of someone who hasn't got a dick.'

'A eunuch?'

'No.'

'A gelding?'

'No.'

'What then?'

'A woman.'

She clasped her breasts and feigned a heart attack brought on by hysterical mirth.

'A woman! Guido, what do you know about women? You have less knowledge of women than you have of zoos.'

I was tempted to tell her about Mishnah Grunewald, and all the other Mishnahs who gave the lie to our demi-Eden. What did I know about women? What *didn't* I know about women? But this was a moment to stay calm. 'I have listened to women, Vee. I have observed women. I have read about women. If Flaubert could write from the point of view of a woman, if James Joyce could write from the point of view of a woman, if Tolstoy —'

'Yes, yes. I've got the drift. And what is she like, this woman you know nothing about?'

I shrugged. 'Volatile, compassionate, beautiful, lovable.'

'And she's the zookeeper, I take it, this beautiful, volatile, lovable woman?'

'Yes, as it happens she is.'

I'd like to have added 'And she masturbates wild animals'.

'And there's a male character in this novel who loves her?'

'Yes.'

'And he's you.'

'It's a novel, Vanessa, not a fucking autobiography.'

'OK – so there *is* a male character in this novel who loves her. And it *is* you. Does he get her?'

'*Get her?*'

'Oh, for God's sake, you know what "get" means.'

'What he gets is his comeuppance.'

'Ah, so this is a story with a moral.'

'No, it's a story without anything. I'm a nihilist, I thought you knew that.'

'You're also a husband. You have a wife.'

'I know that, Vee.'

'Whom you wooed and won. And promised to be faithful to.'

Whom! Is it any surprise I loved her?

'Yes, I did. But the men in my novel are not me. They are not winners. They are losers.'

'And does the main one, the one who loves the lovable zookeeper, lose her along with everything else?'

I thought about it. 'It's ambiguous.'

She roared her laugh again. 'There you are then,' she said, slapping the palms of her hands like Archimedes proving a theorem, 'it's about me on every line.'

Quod erat demonstrandum.

I'd never seen her more volatile, compassionate, beautiful, or lovable.

The goddess Maieusis.

* * *

'Change the names, Vanessa,' I told her when she first showed me the opening page – which just happened to be the only page – of the novel she was writing.

Since I wouldn't call my novel *Vanessa*, that was the title she gave hers. The heroine was called Vanessa. The villain was called Guy. They met in a shop called Wilhelmina's. Vanessa had a mother called Poppy. That Guy was not feeling up Poppy was an accident only of timing and ignorance. I wasn't at the time doing it, and Vanessa – the real Vanessa – was ignorant of the fact that I wanted to. Which at that stage, beyond occasional drunken fancy, or as a consequence of an angry impulse to hurt Vanessa, so was I.

'If you think your changing the names fools anyone, you're a fool yourself,' was her answer.

But she misunderstood an essential fact about writing fiction. No matter how much you write about yourself, the minute you change your name you change you. And from that tiny germ of difference – as I never stopped telling Vanessa – a superior truth ensues.

'Bullshit!' was her considered response to that. 'What's a superior truth?'

'A truer truth.'

She'd pay me back with that eventually, when I caught her in a lying lie.

Change the names, anyway, is the novelist's credo. Change the names and you change what happened, and it's only by changing what appeared to happen that you discover what did.

So here, with the names changed, is the invitation to the big event – two years very nearly to the day after mother and daughter stepped up into Wilhelmina's which, for the sake of the truer truth, had now (if Gid was to be a goer) to be rechristened Marguerite's.

The Author and Pauline Girodias
Invite the Reader
To the Wedding of Valerie and Gideon

Why Marguerite? Why Valerie and Pauline? Because to my ear they have the ring of characters from superior French porn.

Now, as I write, I recall the only two women who ever roused me — Valerie and Pauline. After Pauline had laid out the outfit it had been decided Valerie would wear for her wedding night, the black silk stockings, the black gloves, the spiked-heel black suede shoes, she undressed slowly before the mirror, perfumed herself and began to rouge her own breasts . . . That sort of thing.

As for Girodias, Maurice Girodias was of course the founder of Olympia Press, which published my favourite otherwise unpublishable erotic fiction. (A prim tautology: shouldn't all fiction be erotic?) Not that Girodias was his real name either. He was in fact born Maurice Kahane. Girodias was his mother's maiden name, a *nom de non juif* chosen by his far-sighted, Nazi-sniffing father Jack in Paris in the 1930s. Maurice wrote warmly about his French mother, describing her as bubbly, charming and piquant, which is how I suppose I could have described my mother had I liked her more, or been possessed of a more charming personality myself.

The father, Kahane senior — born, I'm proud to say, just up the A34 from me in Manchester — was also a publisher of books of the spiked-heel, rouged-breast sort, as well as Henry Miller who was at that time banned in America. Heady days, these, for fiction, with novelists offending all and sundry, words having to be hidden from the authorities, and no one quite the person he said he was. Who was Francis Lengel, author of *White Thighs*? Alexander Trocchi, who else? Who was the innocuous-sounding Henry Jones, author of *The Enormous Bed* ('Our mouths met, but, at the same time, her hand shot as if uncontrollably down to my trousers and discovered my freshly proved manhood again')? The innocuous-sounding John Coleman, who other? What a thrill it must have been, how important a writer must have felt – and never mind the obscurity and the poverty – to know that governments trembled every time a woman's hand shot down as if uncontrollably to a writer's trousers. My tangling with the names of these pseudonymous heroes is a way of muscling in on the deception. Call it nostalgia. Writing will never be so much fun again.

Call it solidarity, too, if you like. The solidarity Mishnah had tried so hard to get me to show. I can't say I was ready for it yet, but I banked a bit for that certain futurity when I would lie there whimpering like Mishnah's father wondering where God had got to. One last check with the doctors and at the first shake of their heads I'd jump: give it the full Ableman; call in the rabbi; ask for a Sefer Torah to kiss. Meanwhile I saw this as a sort of halfway house, entwining myself with Jews who loved their mothers and had a passion for impolite literature. The Kahane boys! Mavens of the filthy and the ferocious. Jack and Maurice – my blessings on your heads. *Tsu gezunt.*

The fictional marriage of Valerie and Gideon, like the real one of Vanessa and Guy, took place in a registry office in the town, the party repairing for celebrations afterwards to the Merlin on Alderley Edge.

As far as the real marriage was concerned there were no Ableman issues. We weren't concerned about my marrying out of the faith. We didn't, as I have said, do faith. And Vanessa, for her part, didn't care or notice.

Pauline had expressed disappointment that her daughter had decided against white, and Little Gidding's mother had expressed resentment that the bride hadn't bought her outfit at Marguerite's. Being the cause of so much disappointment and resentment – Little Gid had expressed both when his wife-to-be told him she would not be towering over him in spiked-heels, would not be showing cleavage, would not be agreeing to honour and obey him, and would not be having sex with him after the wedding – gave Valerie a frenetic glow which made Little Gid tremble to the points of his patent dancing shoes.

The sex part was not entirely a surprise. Vanessa, correction, Valerie, didn't do sex when she was anxious, overexcited, happy, sad, angry, full (she planned to eat well at her own wedding), drunk (ditto), so dressed up that getting undressed would exhaust her, undressed already (and therefore presumed to be available), or otherwise placed in a position where sex was expected of her. The night Little Gid returned her mother home safely to the Knutsford cottage – the time Pauline had called him a cheeky monkey – Valerie, with whom he hadn't up to that point exchanged an intelligible word, let alone a kiss, ran out into the street after him and gave him oral sex in the doorway of a hardware shop. And that remained the pattern of their relationship. She would not have sex of any sort with him in a bed, on a rug, in the back of a car, in a field, or in response to his asking her for sex. Whenever Little Gid was not wanting or anticipating sex, she gave it to him. 'But don't think all you have to do is not want it and you'll get it,' she cautioned him. 'I'm wise to that.'

'I both will and won't be wanting sex on our honeymoon night,' he told her, hoping that way to have covered all eventualities.

'Then you both will and won't be getting it,' she told him, which he didn't understand but took to be a refusal.

'Why are you marrying her?' his mother asked him when he told her the news. 'You've nothing in common.'

'She's beautiful.'

She pulled a face, meaning she'd seen more beautiful. 'Not as beautiful as her mother,' she said.

'Maybe not. But I can't marry her mother.'

She pulled a face, meaning she didn't see why not. He liked that about his mother. She was unconventional when it came to the rights of older women. But she pushed on with her interrogation. 'And why do you think she's marrying you?'

He shrugged. Why was she marrying him? 'Stability?'

'Do you think you're stable?'

'That's not the point. She does.'

His mother wondered whether he ought to be marrying a woman who was such a bad judge of character that she thought him stable. But she kept the wondering to herself. In the end she welcomed a wedding. It meant dressing the guests, even if not, in this instance, the bride, and more importantly than that it meant dressing herself.

'There's still time, you know,' she told him on the morning of the wedding. She was already made up and half put-together, in a short slip and a beret with its steel antenna twitching. She had bought a new ivory cigarette holder for her electronic cigarette which was already switched on.

His father was walking behind her, the rest of her clothes folded over his arm.

'Time for what, Ma?'

'To bail out if you don't think you'll be happy.'

And here's where I needed Little Gid to be a writer, so he could say, as I had said to my mother in near identical circumstances, 'Happy? Novelists don't do happy. I'm in this to see what happens. I'm in it to register and record. Happiness be blowed!'

Little Gid enjoyed the wedding, writer or not. Five minutes

before he was due to make his speech Valerie grabbed his hand, led him to the women's lavatory, and gave him sex. Not just with her mouth either. The works. The full corporal.

After the gratitude, the curiosity. Had she decided on this course of action ages before? Was that why she had decided against a white dress?

What manner of thing was she, this woman he had married?

And what manner of thing was the mother-in-law as well? She, too, kissed him when the party was over. A chaste peck on each cheek.

'So,' she said, smiling at him. She looked wonderful, like some great South American bird of prey, a feathery fascinator wound into her red hair.

'So,' he said in return.

'So, I haven't so much lost a daughter . . .'

He waited. *As gained a what?* Go on, say it, Pauline. *As gained a what?*

A lover? An erotic opportunity? An invitation to hell?

He was drunk, remember.

He opened his eyes as wide, after an evening of marital sex in the ladies' lavatory, as he could be expected to open them. Go on, Pauline, say what you've gained.

She pecked his feverish cheek again.

'Cheeky monkey,' she said.

17

Old Times

His feverish cheek!

Enough! Move over, Little Gidding. Go live your own life.

Hard to keep it in the fictionalised third person when remembering the actuality makes your own head spin. Hard to be that altruistic. A writer such as I am feels he's been away from the first person for too long if a third-person narrative goes on for more than two paragraphs never mind a chapter.

He, him, his . . . Why bother when such words as *I, me, mine* exist?

Vanessa, in that case, *my* Vanessa, liked, in the early days of our marriage, *our* marriage, to keep me guessing sexually. And Poppy, I felt, was in on it. The giving and the withholding, but especially, it seemed to me, the withholding.

It's possible that the pain Poppy conspired in inflicting on me was her revenge on the junior diplomat who'd thrown her out for playing Brahms with the fiddler who'd photographed her nude at her cello. And there may have been a bit of making it up to Vanessa in it, too, for having taken her to Washington in the first place, for having failed to find a reliable second father for her. So I was the never-to-be-forgiven male figure around whom they could unite. They would hit the town together, anyway, mother and daughter arm in arm, unloosed like a pair of cats on the tiles, swaying into each other, bumping hips and laughing, enjoying the wolf whistles, revelling in what the sight of them did to their husband and son-in-law.

Was Vanessa unfaithful to me? And if she was, did Poppy encourage her to be unfaithful to me, as a way of being unfaithful to me herself? Was I being made a fool of twice over?

Only a writer or a pervert would have tolerated this. Gid, the happy retailer and sometime comedian, would not have survived a double infidelity. Whereas I, I was gathering material.

Teachers of Unglush Lut – such as Philippa the word-slut – demean novelists in the act of sentimentalising them. Fifteen years or so into my marriage with Vanessa I discussed this very question with the same Philippa in the Barossa vineyard, after literary sex.

'You novelists tell the story of the human heart,' Philippa said. 'You see what no one else can see.'

She was still holding my pruck as she was saying this.

'That,' I said, 'is because we tell the story of *our* hearts.'

'But when you look into your hearts you see humanity.'

'We don't. We see ourselves. We model humanity in our image. Jane Eyre and Alexander Portnoy, Joseph K and Felix Krull, Sam Spade and Scarlett O'Hara – do you think they're *characters*? They're not. They're writers by another name, feeling life's stings and disappointments just as a writer feels them.'

'But that makes luhterature about uhtself.'

'You've got it,' I said. 'Henry Miller called the writer the "uncrowned puppet-ruler". That's why I revere him. He didn't lie. The barely fictionalised scurrilous young reprobate probing the vagina of every woman that came his way was him. Henry. The novelist. Even the vagina was him. That's what we do. I make no apologies for it.'

What happened next in the vineyard was strictly between me and Philippa – the novelist and his reader.

If the power exchange between Vanessa and me, and even I dare say between me and Poppy, was of another order, I was still only party to it because I was the writer – what Miller called the 'wounded angel', and, heaven be my witness, I went on consenting to a wounding on an eschatological scale.

Sometime into our marriage – who's counting – we went, the three of us, to a casino. We were in Manchester, staying at the Midland Hotel for the fun of it, to see a lawyer, not about divorce, about matters relating to the death of Poppy's second husband. More money coming her way, whatever the explanation. She was one of those women for whose sake men died and left her things. You wanted her to go on thinking about you after you'd gone.

We hung around in the city so the women could shop for what Wilmslow did not provide, ate a Chinese meal, during which they flirted with the Chinese waiters – a near impossible feat – then, at Poppy's suggestion, took a taxi to the casino.

Writers feel at home in casinos. Self-asphyxiation, sentence-making, gambling – gasp, gasp, gasp, rub, rub, rub – they address repetitively the same itch. Feel bad at night, and then begin the day gasping and rubbing where you left off. I wasn't interested in the medium – horse racing or cards. I wanted the betting pure and simple, without any mediating spectacle: the spin of the wheel, me against the numbers, pure chance except that I believed I could supersede chance, just as through words I could supersede death, by systematising the sequence in which the numbers appeared. I watched the wheel for half an hour and saw that every time the ball landed in 25, numbers 28 or 29 followed. Don't ask me why no one else had spotted this. A half an hour later I had won five hundred pounds. It was like beginning and finishing a chapter with the same expletive. Another victory over randomness.

My women, meantime, were otherwise engaged. At a roulette

table at the other end of the room they had found an Egyptian-looking croupier they liked the look of. 'Handsome devil, don't you think?' Poppy whispered to me. 'He's taken to our Vanessa.'

Vanessa, more like, had taken to him. He had eyes like a scarab's and a shiny bristling moustache. There was something about him I recognised, but I assumed it was his resemblance to Omar Sharif. He had so obviously modelled himself on Omar Sharif he was a joke.

I mentioned this to Poppy. 'There are worse people to model yourself on,' she said.

'*One*self, or *my*self?'

She didn't know what I was getting at.

'Are you saying,' I said, 'that I should model myself on Omar Sharif?'

She had been gazing idly round the room but now paused to take me in. I'd say to look me up and down, but as she was in her highest heels up was not an option for her. Let's say she looked me through and through, then laughed. They were laughing at everything tonight. Poppy especially. Free drinks, I remembered. 'There's nothing wrong with you as you are,' she said, squeezing my arm.

It took me a minute or two to realise that she was turning me round, getting me to look elsewhere than at her daughter and the handsome-devil croupier. Long enough for them to exchange phone numbers?

'So, did you get it all?' I thought I heard Poppy ask her daughter as we were leaving.

'Get what?' I wanted to know.

Was there hesitation?

'I said "bet" not "get",' Poppy said.

'You were watching,' I said. 'You'd know if she'd bet it all.'

'Who's this "she"?' Vanessa wanted to know.

By which time I could continue only at the risk of looking a fool.

But the question remained. Did she 'get' it all? His address, the measure of his interest in her, a quick feel of the great god Horus under the roulette table – everything that 'all' in this context denoted?

And was Poppy the Vicarious in on it?

All good questions – gasp gasp, rub rub, scribble scribble.

Out on the street, Poppy realised she had mislaid her pashmina – a beautiful white-and-gold concoction, light as air, spun from eyelash of Himalayan goat, which had been a present to her from me. Pashminas of this quality were a Wilhelmina speciality. Vanessa, too, had several. 'You probably left it at the roulette table, on the back of a chair,' she told her mother, with one eye on me, making it clear whose job it was to retrieve it.

Was it deliberate? Was I to slip back in so he could slip back out?

I didn't refuse, anyway. You have to go with the story. I knew I should consider myself lucky to be in the company of two such expert manipulators of plot.

In the event I found the pashmina just as Omar the croupier found me. 'Guy!' he said. 'It is Guy, isn't it?'

I stared into the scarab's eyes. He had beautiful eyelashes, long and fine. You could have spun a pashmina from them. So where had I seen him before since he was so certain that he had seen me? Not in Egypt; I had never been to Egypt.

'It is Guy, yes,' I answered tentatively. Had Vanessa put him up to this for some reason of her own? Get me to like him? Get me to invite him back? Get me to lend him my wife?

He put an arm round my shoulder. 'Boychick!' he said. 'Well, fook me,' his pronunciation distinctly now from round here.

He waited for me to recognise him. Or to say 'Well, fook me, boychick' in return.

'Well, fook me, boychick,' I said in return.

But he could tell I didn't know him.

'I'm Michael.'

I stared.

'Michael Ezra.'

'Michael Ezra! Fook me!'

I had palled out a bit with Michael Ezra at school. He had been part of the Jewish clique to which I hadn't quite belonged, one of those who gave me that *we are all in this shit together* look and could no more do metalwork than I could. He'd been good at maths, though, I remembered. And poker. The prerequisites of a good croupier.

'Long time,' he said.

'You can say that again,' I agreed. 'I would never have picked you for you. You look −'

'Egyptian, I know. Turns out I had an Alexandrian great-grand-father. My skin turned half black when I was twenty-one. My parents had been expecting it but it was a bit of a shock to me, as you can imagine. Mind you, the birds like it. Not that −'

'I bet they do,' I said. 'You look like −'

'Omar Sharif, I know. To be honest, the moustache is what does it. Anyone with a black moustache looks like Omar Sharif. You, though − you haven't changed. You still look like the Pope.'

'The Pope! Which Pope?'

'How many Popes are there? The one that's against contracep-tion.'

'That doesn't exactly narrow the field, Michael.'

'The Polish one, for fook's sake. Waclaw or Vojciech, I don't know. You look like him anyway. Younger of course.'

'It's the paleness. Anyone who's pale looks like a Polish Pope.'

'Yeah, well, you always did. But you're famous now. And that gets the birds, doesn't it? A famous writer – who doesn't want to fook a famous writer?'

'Almost nobody,' I lied. 'About the same number who don't want to fook the Pope.'

'I believe it. I clocked you with your beautiful wife. What a stunner.'

I inclined my head. What else did he expect? my gesture implied.

'And her daughter, too. Also a knockout.'

I couldn't decide whether that was an insult or a compliment to Poppy, an insult or a compliment to Vanessa, or an insult or a compliment to me. But the mix-up, following hard on the heels of the flattery – knew I'd written a novel! thought me famous! – aroused me in a way I suspected it shouldn't. Had this been Vanessa's plan – to embroil me in one of those erotic confusions she knew I would never be able to think my way cogently out of?

'So what time are you on until?' I asked, assuming 'on' was the right preposition for tending a roulette wheel.

He looked at his watch. 'Another hour.'

I looked at mine. 'Well, listen, why don't you come around to the Midland? We'll be in the bar. It would be great to catch up. I want to hear about your Alexandrian grandmother.'

'Grandfather.'

'Him too.'

Men look at you strangely when they think you might be pimping your women. Invariably, I find, they touch their wallets to be sure you haven't begun fleecing them already. But his eyes flashed black light. 'I'll see you there,' he said.

'What do you know – your croupier chum and I are old school friends,' I told them in the taxi back. 'Looks like an Arab warrior but comes from Wilmslow. I've invited him to the hotel for a nightcap.' I squeezed Poppy's hand. 'He thinks I'm married to you,' I said. Then I squeezed my wife's. 'And you, Vee, are the daughter. Let's go along with it.'

'Why?' Vanessa wanted to know.

I made an experimental shape with my hands. 'Oh, for the fun of it.'

Poppy looked at Vanessa, Vanessa looked at me. She didn't say 'On your own head be it', but I read the warning in her expression.

So what was I doing? Trying to pair Vanessa off with Michael Ezra so I could have time alone in the Midland with her mother? Or was I simply interposing myself in whatever had been going on in order to claim authorship and control of it? Guy Ableman, ring-master. Not nice, but it beat being Guy Ableman, the dancing bear.

It would be satisfying to report that the four of us repaired to the biggest bed the Midland had to offer. And that I saw and did things there that would have made Satan's devils howl with shame and envy. But the great Olympia Press debauch I had been waiting for from the minute the Eisenhower girls showed up in Wilhelmina's – the rouging of nipples, the anonymous removal of wisps of lace, no one knew whose or by whom – failed again to materialise. Poppy made her excuses and retired soon after Michael Ezra turned up. 'No, no, you stay down here and talk to your friend,' she insisted, smiling at me sweetly. 'I'll be asleep when you come up.' Vanessa, on the other hand, made free with the opportunity which not being thought of as the wife afforded her, throwing back her head, arching her throat, and on one occasion running her fingers along Ezra's Egyptian moustache to see if it was as diabolically silken as it appeared.

'Oh, it is!' she said, withdrawing her hand and shuddering. It was as though she had put her fingers to a place the like of which they had never been before.

Later that night, I knew, she would put them to my nose.

She said she needed air and would see the croupier into a taxi. 'Go to Mummy,' she ordered me.

Ah, if only.

Michael Ezra and I clasped hands. 'Fook me!' he said, shaking his head.

'Fook me!' I agreed, shaking mine.

Vanessa, standing watching us, shook hers.

She took his arm and they left the hotel together. If it truly was a taxi she was escorting him to, she for some reason ignored those waiting outside the hotel.

Was she unable to wait until they were out of sight before giving him one of her famous street blow jobs, or was she merely stooping to brush something off his trousers?

How men deal with such uncertainties when they are not poets or novelists I have no idea. Do they, without the redemption of art, go mad?

God knows what blind Homer supposed was going on in front of his nose, never mind behind his back, but we owe the *Iliad* to his ignorance and the *Odyssey* to his suspicions. What lesser writers who never made it beyond a couple of short stories would have given for a Vanessa and a Poppy to torment them into creativity! Never let it be said I am not grateful to them myself. Before they ruined me, they made me. And out of ruins, too, can come deliverance.

18

Going Cuckoo

There was not time, not by so much as a preliminary shiver of a tremble, to gauge Poppy's reaction to the hand I'd let descend on her tautened thigh like a falling star from the Monkey Mia night. I no sooner made contact than I was upstaged by a rival. Who, at such a hair-trigger moment in my relations with my mother-in-law, was not a rival? My other hand, had it stirred, would have been a rival. This intruder, though, was not fanciful. It was the powder-blue boatman from the parvenu yacht, the one who had a phone ringing in every pocket. He made a beeline for our table as though he had seen us while on deck and from that moment wanted nothing more from life than to be in our company.

He came very close to us and bowed low. The gold chain he was wearing round his neck clinked against our wine bottle. He had sunglasses hanging from him too, which dangled in my drink. Purposely, I suspected, so that I would go to the bar and get another glass, and when I returned all three of them would be gone.

Not fanciful?

Well, he is no fancy of mine. Whether his outlandishness came out of a tropical sailor catalogue or simply his own imagination I cannot say, but his gold chain, the sunglasses he gratuitously dangled in my drink, his grossly obvious intentions, were no more of my making than was the extravagance of the night.

To me he presented the closed face of an implacable rival. To Vanessa he was elaborately courtly. But to Poppy he was as a man who had taken leave of his senses. The impression he gave of having seen us, that's to say having seen *her*, and then formed a desperate resolution to be among us, that's to say among *her*, was precisely the impression he wanted to give. She was, however, even more lovely than he had been able to tell through his binoculars.

'You've been looking at me through binoculars?'

'All evening, madame. We both have.'

She seemed not to hear 'both'. 'I haven't been here all evening.'

'All day, then.'

'I haven't been here at all today either, I've been out tickling the stomachs of dolphins.'

'I know. We watched you. It can't be necessary for me to tell you how envious we were of those fortunate creatures.'

She inclined her head to him. A woman accustomed to receiving the most preposterous of compliments. But if she was deaf to the boatman's salacious pluralising, this late into drinkies time, Vanessa most definitely was not. She signalled to a couple of empty chairs. 'Won't you join us?'

He bowed again. 'I, alas,' he said, 'cannot. But there is someone else who would like nothing more.'

Vanessa touched her face as though she were carrying a fan. Intrigue bubbled up in her voice like some cheap sparkling wine. Lambrusco, was it? 'And who would this "someone else" be?' she asked.

'Oh, for God's sake, Vee,' I muttered, in operatic sotto voce. I, too, wanted them to know, could descend into melodrama.

He, however, did it better. He looked around to see if anyone was eavesdropping and dropped his voice. 'My employer.' It sounded sinister. Even sexual. Something made me think of those ambiguously homoerotic South China Sea desperadoes that crop up in Joseph Conrad's novels. 'The owner of . . .' And he gestured with his shoulder to the boat Conrad wouldn't have been seen dead in.

'Ah,' I said, with unaccountable satisfaction, 'so it isn't yours.'

'Only to play with.'

'And who, then, is your employer?' Vanessa wanted to know.

At which moment, as though he'd been hiding all the while behind a palm tree – I don't know why I say *as though*: he had indeed been hiding all the while behind a palm tree as his employee broke the ice – there appeared a spectral figure, uncannily elongated but with big hands like a goalkeeper's, dressed in a worn rugby shirt and long, discoloured baggy shorts through which it was impossible to mistake the bell-like sway of sexual organs even bigger than his hands. Had he been older I'd have said they had begun their geriatric descent; but as he was roughly my age, I took him to be preternaturally over-endowed, as was sometimes the case with emaciated men.

'Dirk,' he said, extending his hand to each of us, though he might as well have been extending us a choice of genitalia. 'Dirk de Wolff.'

Poppy threw her head back and laughed. 'What's your *actual* name?' she asked.

He allowed the parchment of his face to crease, though not quite into a smile. 'What would you like my *actual* name to be?'

Poppy looked to Vanessa for inspiration. I held my breath. They might say anything, these women.

'Wolf de Wolff,' Poppy suggested, uncrossing her thighs, but Vanessa spoke over her, answering de Wolff's challenge with a challenge of her own. 'So why do you need someone else to do your dirty work?'

'Was that what you were doing, Tim?' de Wolff enquired of his lackey who had been stealthily backing away from us, the chinking of his jewellery growing fainter. 'My dirty work?'

'I most decidedly was not.'

'There you are. He most decidedly was not.'

Sadist, I thought. Sadist and masochist. Though not easy to be sure which was which. Or why, if whatever it was they did they did to each other, Poppy was of such interest to them.

He turned out to be a film-maker, our Dirk de Wolff. Poppy wondered why he hadn't, in that case, brought along his camera. Film-maker, not cameraman, he explained with great courtesy. If it was in regard to Poppy that the lackey had taken leave of his senses, he had clearly taken leave of them on his boss's instructions. Poppy was the reason for all this, whatever all this was.

'So which of your films will I have seen?' she asked him.

'I always say,' he said with polite painstakingness, 'that the only person who asks that question is a person who hasn't seen any. But you aren't alone. Millions haven't.'

'So which *should* I see?'

He took her hand. 'There is no *should* about it. I am glad you have seen none and recommend you going on doing so. I am not a friendly director. These days I make films I don't care if anyone sees or understands. It's the privilege of early success.'

Fuck you, I thought.

We were sitting by this time, the four of us, Tim having ferried himself back to the boat. I would have liked it had de Wolff more decorously crossed his legs. But then he'd have liked it had I more decorously disappeared.

Vanessa looked accusingly at me. Why couldn't *I* be so

insouciant about my work? Why did I have to go on caring whether I was read or liked?

De Wolff picked up the looks we exchanged. 'You think it's wrong of me to have such an attitude?' he wondered.

Vanessa answered for me. 'My husband's a novelist. Novelists want to be loved and noticed.'

He let out a small eruption of dry mirth. 'Of course they do. That's because no one any longer reads them.'

He waited for me to tell him I was wrong. But no words came.

'Then I have to ask why you go on doing it,' he went on. 'The novel died a hundred years ago, didn't it? Or whenever it was that people were given the vote and permitted to feel their opinions were of value. It is getting to be the same with film, but at least with film there is still the mystique of production. Though once everybody has a degree in media studies, that will be film finished too.'

'I love films,' Poppy said.

'And you also love books,' her daughter reminded her. It was humour Poppy time. But it was also notice Vanessa time.

'Forgive me, but do you know what I think?' de Wolff cut in. 'I think that people who say they love film or books or art, in fact do not. I don't mean you two lovely ladies – I am speaking generally. If you truly love film, you probably won't go to any. Same with literature: if you care for it there is scarcely a book you can bear to read. The actuality of art always lets down the idea you have of it.' He looked to me. 'What is your opinion?'

I was surprised to hear myself appealed to. I had gone into self-hating reverie, angry to be envious of this big-balled Dutch nihilist with whom I somewhere in my soul agreed. What was I doing in a moribund profession? Why hadn't I gone into film? Why hadn't I read media studies at the University of the Fenlands instead of creative fucking writing? But Shark Bay with stars dropping from the sky and dolphins grinning in the Indian Ocean and Dirk de Wolff's yacht ablaze with noise and light was no place to discuss the rival advantages of Thetford.

'The novelist Robert Musil,' I said with some pomp, 'once confessed that the more he loved literature the less he loved the individual writer. I make the same point. Don't ask someone as serious about the novel as I am, I say, to name you a novel he likes.'

De Wolff made to high-five me. Before he stole my women he wanted me to see we were brothers under the skin. Unless he just wanted them to see how much longer his fingers were than mine.

'But if actual art is always a let-down compared to the ideal thing,' I said, showing him I was no pushover, 'that's no reason to despise the poor consumers of it.'

'I didn't say I despised them. I only said I don't care what they think. Maybe it's you who despises your readers.'

'I don't have readers. No one has readers.'

'Then you confirm my point.'

'He has thousands of readers,' Vanessa said.

'Tens of thousands,' Poppy hyperbolically chipped in.

'But they don't understand you,' de Wolff laughed. 'I know all about it –' he tapped his heart with his enormous hand, to suggest a commonality of suffering – 'they want something to happen, and you don't want to give it to them. I too. The more they want, the more I refuse. "You want something to happen," I say, "then *you* happen! You want someone to change? *You* change! I hold my camera still. *You* do the squirming about." You should make a film, my friend. You should make a film about these two beautiful women. Just point a camera at them. Allow the features of the one to fade into the features of the other. And let the audience do the rest.'

Vanessa, high on his compliments, wondered if his films were Warhol-like. More Antonioni, he told her with another of his explosive laughs. Antonioni, without quite so much concession to event.

I lapsed out of the conversation again. Was he right? Did I despise the readers I didn't have?

Of course he was right. He had a boat and big balls. Doesn't a boat make you right? Don't big balls?

It was his boat he wanted us to see. No doubt his balls, too, but he wasn't saying that. I told him we were tired, that we had been on the water for a large part of the day, that we were leaving early in the morning for Broome, that we were not sea-faring people.

'That's not true,' Vanessa said. 'Is it, Mother? That we aren't seafaring people.'

She looked hard at Poppy, to be certain she was sober enough to conduct a conversation.

'Lived half my life on boats,' Poppy said, steadying herself between each word.

'Come and have a dekko at mine then,' de Wolff persisted, a master of the vernacular, looking from Poppy to Vanessa and back. Having ousted me in the matter of film versus the novel, that's to say in the matter of realism versus sentimentality, that's to say in the matter of success versus failure, he was now about to oust me in the matter of my women.

'Shall I?' Poppy asked, looking first at Vanessa and then at me.

'We'll all come,' Vanessa said. 'Unless you don't want to, Guido.'

'Oh, don't make him,' de Wolff said. 'There's nothing worse than being shown around something you don't want to see. I'm the same with other men's work.'

'No, come,' Poppy murmured to me, as though it would be our secret if I did.

'Best you stay and keep our seats warm,' Vanessa said.

So I stayed. Why? Because I am a novelist and a novelist, now that the novel is no more, must experience every last ignominy. That could be the novelist's final justification – on behalf of everybody else he drinks humanity's humiliation to the dregs.

I waved them off. Poppy looked round and waved back. Even blew me a kiss. Unless she was just blowing for air, the way old ladies do when they are three sheets to the wind. But there was as much of the schoolgirl about her as the matron. She turned a second time, put her hand to her eyes in pretend shock, and mouthed something at me. I couldn't be sure but what she seemed to be saying was, 'I can see his knob.' Vanessa, I thought, was going to have her work cut out.

She, of course, did not look round. No doubt she was annoyed with me. It was always my fault when her mother drank too much. And she wouldn't have been impressed with my capitulation to de Wolff's lawless cynicism. I should have fought harder to stop them going. I should have defended more vigorously my manhood, my husbandhood, my son-in-lawhood, and my profession. She never liked it when I was aggressive – 'A mad bull,' she called me – but she liked it less when I played the submissive – 'Faggot!' she'd say. We shared that contradictory view of me.

Alone, I watched Dirk de Wolff in his indecent floaty ball-bag shorts position himself between my women, one on either arm, and then lead them from the centre down a wooden ramp, their cork heels clopping on the boards, their hips swaying, to where a small boat was waiting to transport them to the big boat which seemed to burst into even more magnificent light the minute they set off.

Mad bull or faggot? Faggot.

*　　*　　*

In accordance with Vanessa's instructions I had not brought my notebook out with me. My pen I always carried, just in case. Even Vanessa couldn't prise me from my pen. I called the waiter – an overtanned boy-man (orange, his skin was) in calf-length pants that seemed to be made out of straw. I asked him to bring me something to write on. He looked puzzled. 'Like a drink mat?' 'No,' I said, 'like a piece of paper.' When he brought me what I'd asked for I sat in front of it, not writing a word. Was I going mad, I wondered. It was no longer existentially fashionable for a writer to be going mad, especially in Australia. But the last few weeks suddenly seemed chaotic and crazy. What was I doing here? What had I been doing in Adelaide reading my most obscene and antic passages to middle-class Australians who lapped up every word? You couldn't upset Australians once they'd found literature. They listened obediently to you whatever you read them, or even if you read them nothing, if you sat there with your stomach hanging between your legs, saying not a word, they brought down the roof of Adelaide Town Hall with their applause. Australia was reputed to have more readers per head of population than anywhere but Finland. How was one to process that information? Philippa had put New Zealand up there as well. And what had I been doing with her? In accordance with my usual post-coital moodiness I had hated her in retrospect for a week, and had then, retrospecting on the retrospect, begun to fall in love with her. Vanessa had got wind of her, though I denied everything, and was now paying me back with Dirk de Wolff and maybe Tim too. Giving herself to either or to both of them, or giving her mother? Vanessa was a connoisseur of pain. She would have worked out to a nicety how to hurt me. But for her to have worked out how to do that she would have needed to know how I felt about her mother. So did she? And would she sacrifice her mother's modesty – presum-ably even a woman in her sixties still has her modesty – just to hurt me? Was she laying her out on Dirk's bunk like a sacrificial virgin, bedecking her with lilies, as he turned his camera on them both, watching the one metamorphose into the other, even as I sat there, mouth-writing?

My pen hovered over the paper. Write the book. Write the book of me. *Mad in Monkey Mia*. No story, fuck the story, fuck anything happening – de Wolff was right: if readers wanted something to happen, let *them* happen – no event, no action, no furthering or unravelling of plot, just the brain (which should be plot enough for anyone) rolling around in pain like one of the dolphins beneath our rowing boat. 'One should go cuckoo!' Henry Miller had written. 'People have had enough of plot and character. Plot and character don't make life.'

But what if people had had enough of life?

I made life, anyway, whether they wanted it or not, I made life, going crazy over my mother-in-law whose knee I'd finally touched after nearly twenty years of thinking about it and who was now allowing a lascivious film-maker's quasi-sodomitic lickspittle in powder-blue pyjamas to pull at the lips of her vagina while the stars fell out of the heavens in amazement, or shame, or rapture.

Henry Miller, the devil he was, once transcribed the sound the petal lips of a vagina made when you opened them. *Squish-squish.* 'A sticky little sound,' he called it, 'almost inaudible.'

Squish-squish.

Jesus Christ.

Try getting away with that today. Try getting the sacred music of the labia past Flora McBeth.

And try getting a moment's peace, once you have heard it, yourself.

Squish-squish . . .

The things one suffers when one is serious about one's art.

19

The Baton of Literature

The first time I used the word 'cunt' in a book I lay awake imagining I would be struck dead. Not by Vanessa, by God.

In the morning I crossed it out.

The next day I put it in again.

In the morning I crossed it out.

It was my second book. I could never have used it in my first, whatever Archie Clayburgh's teaching and J. P. Donleavy's example. You need to grow into cunt.

In the end I asked Vanessa what she thought.

'Is it used in a swearing context or a sexual context?'

'Sexual.'

'Is it used with love or used with hate?'

'Well, certainly not hate. With desire.'

'Then be bold,' she said.

In the morning I put it back.

That night Vanessa asked to hear the passage with cunt in it. I read it aloud to her. 'Take it out,' she said.

I asked why.

'Because you're embarrassed. It doesn't come naturally to you. But if you want to leave it with me I'll fix it.'

The next day she handed me her amendment. Where I'd made

my way gingerly to the word, as though entering some holy of holies before which I started in mortal terror, Vanessa had peppered the page with cunt. He asked to see her cunt, she showed him her cunt, he said he'd never seen a cunt as beautiful before, she asked how many cunts he had seen in that case, he said he'd seen cunts enough, she asked how many cunts were cunts enough, he said he wasn't prepared to enumerate in the matter of cunts, she told him he was a cunt and he could fuck off.

'I think you'll find the scene works better now,' she said.

Without her knowledge I amended her amendment. Not entirely. I left in more than my original one. And felt all right about it too. But I hoped that when Vanessa came to read the book in manuscript she wouldn't notice my failure of nerve.

If she did she didn't say anything. But the reviewer in the *Financial Times* offered it as his view that 'Guy Ableman appears to have written this novel for the sole purpose of saying cunt'.

I was, needless to say, deeply hurt by this.

Vanessa wasn't sympathetic. 'You can't say I didn't warn you,' she said. 'The cunt.'

There are writers who start feuds with reviewers. They send furious letters accusing them of damaging a profession already beyond repair, they pick fights with them at parties, or they go out of their way to review with redoubled savagery any book the reviewer goes on to write. For over a year I kept an eye out in book catalogues for anything by the *Financial Times* reviewer. 'This book is written with the sole purpose of showing that its author is a cunt,' I planned to write, though I accepted I might encounter resistance from whatever literary editor I wrote it for. But in the end I forgot about it, and when he did at last publish a book it was a children's story about a cat that fought cancer, and I could see no way of harnessing a cunt to that.

The best way of handling a cruel review, a distinguished elderly novelist I had shared a platform with at a literary festival told me, was to write to the reviewer thanking him for his insightfulness, and further, if he did happen to be a writer himself, to review him, when one's chance came, with a magnanimity that would put him out of countenance for the rest of his working life. 'There's no shame harder to bear,' he told me, 'than that of being reviewed with enthusiasm by someone you've given a real drubbing to. Particularly if you never know for sure that the person you drubbed, and who has been so kind to you, is aware you drubbed him.'

'Is that a shame you've experienced yourself?' I asked him.

He nodded. 'In 1958,' he said, 'and I have lived in a torment of guilt and uncertainty ever since.'

We were sitting in the sun outside the writers' tent. Our event was just over. Neither of us had signed any books though there'd been four hundred people in our tent, each of whom had clapped enthusiastically at the end. Too old to afford a book, I presumed. Probably too infirm to carry one. You only have to do the mental arithmetic. Four hundred multiplied by the average age of the audience which was sixty-five. That's 26,000. Between them our audience had been alive longer than *Homo sapiens*. I don't say that's taxonomically accurate, but you get the picture. And it could only get worse. Eventually the average age of the audience would be a hundred, and there'd be more of them. Literary festivals filled a gap in the calendar of the retired. It was one stage before chair-dancing. Soon there'd be funeral parlours on site. You wandered into a tent, you clapped a writer you'd never heard of, you didn't buy his stroke her book, and you rolled over. Writers the same. The elderly writer I'd shared the platform with a case in point. Would he make it out of here alive? Would I, come to that?

A photographer, no doubt thinking along those lines himself, took our picture. Neither of us expected him to have anywhere to sell it, but it was nice to be noticed. Children sat on the grass colouring in books. I had friends who were writing colouring books as a last resort. 'You have to go where the readers are,' one of them told me. 'But colouring-in isn't reading,' I protested. 'It's all about the way you look at reading,' he said. Every day I combed the obituary pages of the newspapers, expecting to read he'd swallowed a mouthful of crayons.

'Ah, sun,' the old writer said.

I agreed with him. 'Ah, sun,' I said.

'Burning out, you know.'

'I know,' I said.

'Fortunately, I should just beat it.'

'Lucky you,' I said.

We must have both drifted off because suddenly there was a helicopter on the lawn. A famous television newsreader got out, pushing her hair back from her face. She had just published a novel about a poor girl who made a lot of money by becoming a television newsreader.

'Who's she?' the old writer asked me.

I told him what I knew.

'Live and let live,' he said.

This was not a sentiment I agreed with but he was too old to contradict, enjoying the last rays of a sun that was too old itself.

Before we parted he took my hand. The top of his middle finger, I noticed, was almost worn to the bone. I had read that he still wrote all his books with a pencil, and I wondered if the ruined finger was a consequence of this. 'In a manner of speaking,' he told me. 'This is the finger I erase with.'

'You never thought of using a rubber?'

He shook his head vehemently. A rubber was too technological for him. 'I have to touch the words,' he said, 'even those I reject.'

I nodded as though I were just the same, not wanting him to know the amount of electronic gadgetry I relied on to get a single sentence into the world. Shame on me. We were all busy wondering where readers had gone – there was even going to be a panel discussion of that very subject at the festival that evening; it was sold out – but what if the readers had simply followed the writers out of the room? You don't write as you should, they were saying – you don't touch words as the writers you admire once did, your keyboards take the living stuff out of language, your sentences no longer bear the warm impress of *you* – so why should we stick around to be short-changed?

'I have a confession to make,' the old author told me.

I waited. Was he going to say he'd been writing on a computer for years and that the eraser groove in his finger was a fraud?

He sat up in his chair and blew his nose. 'I once gave you a real drubbing.'

He made it sound as though we'd boxed each other as boys and he had won. An outcome I didn't for a moment doubt, had the fight itself only been chronologically possible.

He saw my confusion. 'In a review. I wrote some cruel things.'

I waved away his concern. 'Water under the bridge,' I said.

'Not to me,' he said. 'I fear I was ungenerous. Smutty, I called you.'

'Ah, yes.'

'You remember?'

'I remember somebody calling me smutty. I recall they said the same about Lawrence and Joyce.'

'Lawrence, yes,' he said, 'the one not of Arabia, I presume you mean.' He seemed uninclined to turn this into a conversation about the place of smut in literature. 'There was too much sex for me, you see, in yours,' he went on, 'but, well, that was a relative complaint. How much sex is too much sex?'

'However much you don't want to read about,' I said.

'But I don't want to read about any.'

We laughed at that together. I tried to remember the review, but couldn't. Unusual, to forget a bad review. Was he lying? Did he simply want to give me a bad review now?

He asked what I was working on at the moment. I told him it was a novel about my mother-in-law. 'There'll be no sex in that one, then,' he said.

I smiled and got up to go. He hoped I'd understand if he stayed where he was. Old joints. I nodded. His legs, crossed at the ankles in a little bow, were stretched out in front of him disconnectedly, as though they belonged to someone else. He wore white summer flannels which would not have been long enough on a man six inches shorter than he was. Above his schoolboy's black socks – black socks under white flannels! – his flesh looked sad and vulnerable. 'No man should ever expose that part of himself,' my mother had always said. In pursuance of which philosophy she forbade my father from ever crossing his legs. I was an avid pupil of her teaching myself. We die from the feet up. No matter how distinguished we are in mind, down there we are the ignoble, dying animal.

He apologised again for his damning notice and presented me with a proof copy of his new novel. One a year he wrote. One a year since 1958. All in pencil and all set in the same council offices in Chesterfield. Readers had loved him once, now he struggled to sell a hundred books. Word was that this would be the last he'd be able to find anyone to publish. The municipal novel, too, it seemed was over.

I got him to sign it for me. 'I'll treasure this,' I lied. What was one more lie?

He gave me the longest, sweetest smile. As though he were passing on the baton of literature.

Only afterwards did I seriously wonder if he could be trusted. Had he truly given a book of mine a drubbing? Or had he made all that up so I would take his advice and by way of revenge shame him with a good review?

But why go to such lengths of subterfuge? Did getting a good review still matter when you were eighty-five, when you had written more than thirty novels, and when there was no one out there to read the review *or* the novel, no one to give a monkey's either way?

Sick, the lot of us. Still sick, no matter how old and reverend, with the sickness that had made us novelists in the first place.

20

Big in Canada

I never discovered whether Vanessa actually slept with Michael Ezra. She had plenty of opportunities. Once that second novel of mine was published and I was able to hand Wilhelmina's over to Jeffrey Gorgeous, I moved my little family down to London, not immediately to Notting Hill, but to rural Barnes where I rented a cottage so that they shouldn't miss Knutsford too much, and there in a back room overlooking a garden, I wrote the next. Since I wasn't available for conversation, Vanessa planted sweet peas, explored the towpaths of the Thames with her mother, and when they got bored with that caught the train back to Macclesfield to visit friends in Knutsford or, while they were up there, to shop in Manchester. Why they needed to shop in Manchester when they had London I didn't understand. But Vanessa told me they had a routine worked out in Manchester, and I didn't question her. It was always possible that the routine included Omar Ezra, croupier.

When the writing was going well I didn't much care what her routine included. I was glad to have the cottage to myself. The women were a distraction when they were home, the sound of them talking as agitating as mice scratching about in the thatch, not making it absolutely impossible for me to work but always keeping me sensuously receptive to them. When they played the cello together they closed the door of what they jokingly called the music room – it was in fact Poppy's boudoir – but again I strained to hear them. And of course I imagined them playing naked. They played more plangently, I thought, when naked, more Dvořákianly, though this was baseless fantasy, sometimes good for me to indulge, sometimes not, depending on what I was writing. Once in a while they would burst into my study uninvited, like a delegation from the World of Fun, and bend invitingly over me, their hair aflame on my neck. Hadn't I done enough for the day? Didn't I want a short break? Didn't I want to join them for tea, biscuits, a game of Scrabble, a movie on the television?

Three in a bed?

My rancid mind. Scrabble was as far as it got. Though even there I once managed to find a spare 't' to which to add my seven-letter 'roilism', thereby earning 50 points for using all my tiles and beating down a wasted challenge from Poppy.

Disingenuous, was she? Playing me on a long lead? Or quite simply innocent?

It goes without saying that two women are more disruptive of a man's peace of mind than one. But Vanessa and Poppy were more than the sum of their parts. Each trebled the other's eruptive force. I've described the minor and even sweet disturbances to my work they caused, but some days, especially when they were not getting on, it was like living with a hundred women. They would fight over what to cook, what to plant in the garden, what day of the month it was, whether it was hot or cold, and which double cello piece they should practise. Poppy always wanted Vivaldi, Vanessa Brahms. Unless Poppy wanted Brahms, in which case Vanessa wanted Vivaldi. They would shout 'Hush!' to each other in their loudest voices so as not to disturb me – the 'literary fucking genius is trying to work' – but the literary fucking genius could go fuck

164

himself if Vanessa had a complaint about her mother's unreasonable behaviour to voice. Then, she would barge into my room with a list of grievances going back to before she was born, not scrupling to ask if I were free to discuss this or any other matter; whereupon, hearing herself traduced, Poppy would barge in behind her to appeal to my impartiality, her hair a storm of electric activity, as though Vanessa, among her other sins, had been wiring her up to the mains. It wasn't, of course, my impartiality she was appealing to; it was my partisanship on her behalf, a thing I was wise enough to conceal when I could, though on some occasions, as when Vanessa berated her for dressing like a slut, with her skirts 'pulled up to her arse and her tits half out', I couldn't help but take her side. Poppy argued that cleavage had always been a problem for her because her breasts started higher up than most women's, and I agreed.

I don't doubt that had I listened harder I'd have realised they were fighting over specific men, with whom, in Vanessa's view, Poppy had exceeded the propriety expected of the mother of a woman who was acting the slut herself.

Or maybe I listened just hard enough, knew exactly what was going on and liked it, because the wild-cat atmosphere made me feel bohemian, a writer of the pulsating night-time city living in a whorehouse at last. Even if we were only in Barnes.

To this degree, at least, their interruptions, though unlooked-for, were inspirational. I lost an hour to their technicolour commotions but wrote a week at full pelt on the strength of them.

If Vanessa were sleeping with the croupier, or indeed anybody else, her mother's always travelling up to Manchester with her had to be explained. Vanessa didn't need a chaperone, and I very much doubted they were enjoying him in tandem or by turn. For all their apparent freedom from convention, they were not liberated enough for that. So did Poppy just hang around in the foyers of hotels? And if that were all, why didn't she stay behind some days and share the solitude of the house with me?

How she managed to make me feel we were on the brink of having an affair all those years before we got to Monkey Mia without ever saying or doing anything that couldn't have been reported to Vanessa or the local vicar, I am unable to explain. Either she had a genius for innuendo in which nothing was really innuendoed, or drinkies got her into trouble which she was only by the skin of her teeth, or by the strength of her innate sexual refinement, able to get out of. To the third option, which was that I imagined the whole thing, I give a degree of credence – a feverish imagination being necessary to the business I am in – but only a degree. I didn't imagine the countless occasions on which she brushed against me when we passed drunkenly on the stairs or in the hall and she would pretend that the static we gave off kept us in the same magnetic field a fraction of a second longer than in truth it did; or the pressure on my shoulder of her breasts (which started so much higher up her chest than other women's) which was like being poked by a pillow; or the looks of fearful knowingness we exchanged some nights as though we stood on the rim of an active volcano; or the degree of domestic undress she permitted to become habitual between us, until Vanessa put a stop to it; or the unsubtlety of her flirting with my fellow writers when we threw a publication party, which I was able to explain to myself only as a plain manifestation of how badly she needed to flirt with me.

In this latter, she was no different from her daughter who found all social get-togethers of more than a dozen people of mixed gender sexually deranging, but a party thrown to celebrate the publication of a work of mine a provocation to vengeful licentiousness that threatened our marriage. She would rub herself up

166

against the most junior editors; she would whisper hotly in the ear of journalists who were there only to interview me; on one occasion she even sat on poor Merton's knee, causing him to turn the colour of the hair she had given him to nibble. But it was when I caught her in a huddle in the garden with a bald writer of novels about the joys and sorrows of single fatherhood that I read her the riot act.

'Not Andy Weedon,' I said. 'I draw the line at Andy Weedon.'

'Because he's big in Canada.'

Andy Weedon's *Can I Have the Bottle, Daddy?* had just won the Prix Pierre Trudeau.

'That's below the belt, Vanessa.'

But she had a point.

It was one of my beefs with my agent that I wasn't big in Canada, where a number of writers I affected to admire had been born and where I thought they ought in consequence to affect to admire me. I understood that novels about single fatherhood did well in Canada because Canadian women were so bored with their husbands that the majority of them ran off sooner or later with an American or an Inuit. But that didn't make me feel any better.

'Come clean,' Vanessa said. 'Canada is a bleeding sore with you.'

'I am not so petty, Vee.'

'You? Not petty? Next you'll tell me you don't admire the feeling way he writes about children.'

'I admire his way with children as much as you do, Vee,' I said. I didn't add, 'You unnatural bitch!'

There was something else I didn't add. I didn't add, though it was the truth, that I couldn't bear her kissing him because he wore inanition white T-shirts, like the one made famous in the film *Trainspotting*, and hugged himself in the way Ewan McGregor had, as though whatever he was on had made him shiver. 'If you're so cold, wear something more substantial than that fucking T-shirt,' I wanted to tell him. 'And when you're at a party of mine, show some respect and wear a jacket. You're not in fucking Leith.'

A further and, if anything, still stronger reason I couldn't bear to see her kissing him was that he was bald with the baldness of a man who had gone bald before he was twenty. You can always tell. Something indurated about the scalp. Like ground that has long gone unwatered. This wasn't a prejudice against baldness, or even premature baldness, in itself. It was a prejudice against men who had no natural vitality kissing my wife.

Later on at the same party I saw him doing it with Poppy. Not kissing exactly – to my knowledge, Poppy had never quite kissed anybody between Washington and Monkey Mia – but engaging her in a prematurely bald man's idea of intimate relations, holding her in heartfelt conversation about how hard it is for a single father to keep abreast of what's new in vinyl records, absorbing her attention, in short, bleeding her vitality in order to keep himself alive.

Ought I to have given him his marching orders? Beat it, baldy! Go suck the life out of some other writer's women.

It was my launch party, after all.

The trouble was, I wanted him to stay. Though in his fiction his broken reeds of men were invariably widowed or otherwise wifeless, in actuality he had a perfectly good wife of his own – Lucia, a Spanish or South American woman, as succulent as a wine gum. And while Andy was sucking the life out of mine, I was sucking – or at least trying to suck – the wine out of his.

Nothing serious – I didn't want to lure her away, which I suspect I could have done easily enough by presenting her with a locket containing a single one of my hairs. I simply enjoyed making small Judaeo-Protestant Wilmslow inroads into her Catholicism.

'This party,' she said, looking around her, perhaps catching sight of Vanessa sitting on Merton's knee, 'reminds me of a scene in one of your novels.'

'I have never put you into one of my novels,' I said.

'Thank God for that,' she laughed.

'You would illuminate any such scene,' I said.

She flushed. Close up I could see she had a darkly downy upper lip – a feature of Spanish women which I happened to love. So in what other regard, or in what other place, I secretly wondered, did she exhibit more of the signs of robust life than her husband?

'And here was me thinking you made it up,' she said.

'Oh, come on, this is hardly the *Satyricon*.'

It must have been at this point that she noticed Andy breathing up Poppy's nostrils. 'Well, that depends what you're used to,' she said.

'You will have to come to our parties more often,' I said, tossing first one sumptuous lock of hair, and then a second, out of my eyes. And left it at that.

It's a rule of the profession that novelists do not sleep with one another's wives or husbands. The reason being that you don't give a rival novelist the material for a book.

If they want to write about sexual jealousy it isn't going to be thanks to anything you've done.

And what about a fellow novelist who is not a rival?

The question is too simplistic to deserve an answer. There is no such thing as a fellow novelist who is not a rival.

There is a small-pond theory of why writers are an envious breed. So many fishermen, so few fish. But I doubt writers would be any different were the pond the size of Lake Superior. They simply obey the inverse human-kindness law that governs the practice of high-mindedness: the more apparently disinterested, exalted and 'creative' the profession, the less human kindness its members show to one another.

I first set my foot on this extending ladder of illiberality when I left Wilmslow for the University of the Fenlands School of Literature and Creative Writing, Thetford Campus, swapping the small provincial world of ladies' fashion for the open expanses of the mind they called humanities. Without doubt, people in Wilmslow, and further afield even than that, had been jealous of Wilhelmina's success. Owners of boutiques nothing like as well regarded as ours would spread unpleasant rumours about us, steal our ideas or try to block our supply chain, one of them, as I recall, going so far as to attempt to bribe Dolce and Gabbana not to let us stock their garments, and when that didn't work actually resorting to arson. It was to my mother's credit that when she opened up in the morning and found thirty spent matches on the carpet she didn't call the police. Anyone who thought to put her out of business with a box of Swan Vestas, she stood on the step of the shop and declaimed, presented no serious danger to her, to her family, or to the success of Wilhelmina's. But despite such sporadic outbreaks of warfare, a spirit of communal interest and mirth bound the shopkeepers of Wilmslow. We would meet at the bar of the Swan to share the day's travails; we'd swap notes on well-known local nuisances and time-wasters, or exchange stories about new arrivals in the area – Vanessa and Poppy, for example, aroused intense curiosity – and when a coachload of French schoolboys turned up in Wilmslow for no other reason than to strip our shelves, we were on the phone to one another issuing detailed descriptions of the *petits salauds* before they'd got away with more than a bar of chocolate and copy of the *Wilmslow Recorder*, which was free anyway. Then I went to East Anglia and encountered the savage mutual mistrust of scholars. And a few years after that I entered the begrudging, disconfederate world of writing, where every sentence I wrote was as a blade to the heart of every other writer, and where – just to be clear about this – every sentence they wrote was as a blade to the heart of me.

It was Vanessa, to her credit, who first dotted the i's and crossed the t's in the matter of novelists not sleeping with one another's spouses for fear of giving them material for a book.

It was after our disagreement about Andy Weedon. 'Christ, I've just worked it out,' she said. 'You couldn't care less about me giving Andy Weedon a fuck qua fuck, what you don't want is him putting me in one of his novels.'

'He wouldn't know what to do with you in one of his novels. He doesn't do living women.'

'And you don't want him to start doing them now?'

'If he wants to do one let him do his own.'

'That Spanish piece?'

'She isn't a *piece*.'

'Oh Christ, don't try that on me.'

'I happen to like her, that's all. She's got a moustache.'

'Oh yes, the moustache. The Jewess look. I always forget you have a weakness for that.'

I bridled at Jewess. I'm not sure why.

'I don't have a weakness, Vee,' I said. 'I just happen to like her.'

'I noticed.'

'There is nothing wrong in liking someone.'

'No, there isn't. Unless it's me liking Andy Weedon. So I can assume, can I, that she'll be turning up in your next book?'

'Why would you assume that?'

'From the intensity of your research into her personality and opinions.'

'I was being hostly.'

'I'd say you were being competitive.'

'With Andy Weedon? Don't make me laugh. If I wanted to be competitive with Andy Weedon I'd show him my eyelash.'

'Competitive with *me*.'

'You're different.'

'How am I different?'

I wanted to say *You're not a rival novelist*, but I knew where that would lead. So instead I just declared my innocence of any predatory intention towards Lucia Weedon. 'You don't sleep with a fellow novelist's wife,' I said.

'In case your own wife sleeps with the fellow novelist?'

'That's not the motive, but you're right, that's not done either.'

'Such sexual high-mindedness all of the sudden. What's the real reason, Guido?'

'Let's just say it's not my job to research his novels for him.'

Vanessa stared at me. 'What are you saying?'

'He doesn't light my fires, I don't light his.'

Vanessa stared at me some more. 'Are you telling me,' she said, 'that you'd rather miss out on a fuck with a woman with a moustache than give her husband something to write about?'

'Something like that. Though now you lay out so clearly what I'm sacrificing –'

'That's sick, Guido. That's the sickest thing I've heard. You're a fucking weirdo.'

'How can my being virtuous make me a weirdo?'

'When it's envy that makes you virtuous, Guido, you aren't being virtuous.'

'Envy makes it sound a mite mean-spirited, Vee.'

She laughed so loud at that her mother came downstairs to see what the matter was.

21

My Hero

I was asleep in the van when the women returned from the yacht. Vanessa clattered about. She was not considerate around another person's sleep.

'What time is it?' I asked.

'Two, three.'

'Had a good time?'

'What do you think?'

'Your mother?'

'What do you think?'

'Silly?' Silly was Vanessa's word for her mother when she'd had a drink.

'Very silly.'

Too silly to leave Dirk, I wondered. Too silly to keep him at arm's length? But I put the question slightly differently. 'She still on the boat?'

'Of course she isn't still on the boat. Had I left her on the boat she'd be halfway to India by now.'

'You didn't drag her away, I hope.' Liar.

'When don't I have to drag her away?'

There was a sudden hammering on the van. Desperate, as though a person was being attacked by wild animals – dolphins, pelicans, monkeys.

Dirk, I thought. Or Tim, doing Dirk's dirty business again, come to steal my women back.

Vanessa opened a window. 'Christ, Mother!' she shouted. 'What now?'

'Come quickly,' Poppy said. 'There's something in my room.'

Dirk, I thought.

'What do you mean, something?'

'Do I have to stand out here describing it? A beetle or a spider, I don't know . . . a giant cockroach.'

'Tread on it.'

'It's too big to tread on.'

'Then tell them at the hotel.'

'I can't find anyone. You've got to come, I can't sleep in there.'

'Just a minute.'

Vanessa shut the window and pulled the duvet off me. 'You'll have to help her,' she said.

'If it's too big for *her* to tread on it's too big for *me* to tread on.'

'I can't leave her out there.'

'Let her come back in here.'

'So she can snore, or sit up all night telling us what a good time she's had? Go and help her. You're the man.'

I thought of saying, 'Call Dirk, he's the man.' But what would that have achieved?

I threw on a pair of shorts, and remembered to put my feet in flip-flops. The ground writhed with venomous ants and ticks and millipedes out there. Snakes, too, for all I knew. I hoped Poppy in her panic hadn't mistaken a snake for a beetle.

She was still vibrating from the good time she'd been having. Her hair trembled like a halo of fire. Her dress steamed. There was so much alcoholic vapour coming off her she'd have gone up in flames had I lit a match a hundred yards away. And yet she appeared to be steadier, in mind at least. I wondered if she'd seen more of de Wolff's knob and whether that had sobered her up.

She took my arm and led me out of the campsite to her room, trying her key in a couple of wrong doors before she found the right.

'Silly me,' she said, echoing Vanessa's verdict, holding onto me in the dark.

'Easy,' I said, being the man.

She turned the light on and stood swaying in front of me. 'Prepare yourself for this,' she said.

I was hoping that whatever it was that had frightened her would be gone by now, scuttled out under the door or down the drain in the shower. But it had gone nowhere, whatever it was. It reclined on Poppy's snow-white pillow, its buggy eyes wide open, its shoulders hunched, its feelers twitching, a disgusting parcel of envenomed black fur like something a gorilla had coughed up.

'Christ!' I said. 'It could be a tarantula.'

'Don't kill it,' she cried.

'Don't kill it? It's him or me, Poppy.'

'Well, don't kill it on my pillow, I've got to sleep on that.'

I had no idea how I was going to kill it on her pillow or off it. 'I don't suppose you've anything like a tennis racket or a fishing net?' I enquired.

She took a moment to think about it. I could tell she wished her head were clearer. *Tennis racket, tennis racket . . . where did I put that thing?* In the end, placing a hand on my shoulder, she balanced on one foot and took her shoe off. It wasn't the first time she'd leaned on me to take a shoe off, but it was the first time she'd leaned on me to take her shoe off so I could kill with it.

The inside of the shoe was moist from Poppy's foot. At any other time I'd have put it to my face. It had a platform heel made of coiled rope, like a quoit. I took my cue from that and made a practice throw as though aiming at a spike. A lot hung on this throw. Since Poppy didn't want the blood and guts on her pillow I had to throw so as to give the spider a glancing rather than a decisive blow, but not so glancing as to let it escape or turn it angry, a blow sufficient to knock it off the bed stunned, ideally unconscious or having lost its memory.

'Don't hurt it,' Poppy said, as I was taking aim.

I imagined hearing her offering her mouth to me and saying, 'Be gentle. Be gentle with me.'

She was lopsided, one foot in a shoe, one not, like a heron standing on one leg. What is it about a woman standing on one leg that is so beguiling to a man? Even a woman Poppy's age. No, *especially* a woman Poppy's age.

'Give me your other shoe,' I said, 'just in case.'

She leaned on me again. Twice in one night, a woman I desired, and had no right to desire, standing on one foot. If only she'd had as many feet as the tarantula.

Shoeless, she was now lowered almost to my height, our eyes level, our mouths on the same plane. We could feel each other's blood pump.

I threw. Whether I hit I couldn't tell, but the shoe bounced off the bed and there was nothing on Poppy's pillow.

There were four, five seconds of silence.

'Now what?' Poppy said.

Now we make love on the floor and wait for it to die, I thought. Sex is never better than when something is expiring nearby, and I don't just mean a marriage. *Lust und Tod*, the Germans call it, and they should know. No doubt the Dutch called it something similar. Odds on, Dirk had made a film of that name. But in truth I'd have been too afraid of the spider coming to and biting us to have risked our rolling on the floor and taking bites out of each other ourselves.

Before I could say anything, Poppy screamed. The spider was up and running, still a bit shaken, but heading for the wardrobe on the other side of the bed.

'Kill it for Christ's sake!' Poppy cried. 'Kill it before it gets into my clothes. Quick.'

It's not possible to do quick in flip-flops. But I managed to get round to the other side of the bed before the spider disappeared – where I would have liked to disappear – into the silken, aromatic pleats of Poppy's dresses. There was a moment in which we eyed each other as rivals, then I stamped on it. I could feel its bulk, broken, sodden, but still resistant, beneath my foot. Killing an insect – no, an arachnid – is harder than it's cracked up to be. Or it is if you're squeamish and unarmed. I couldn't bear to press down harder or to release the pressure; I couldn't bear to look or not look. I thought I might have to stand there for ever.

'My hero,' Poppy said.

'Not exactly St George and the Dragon.'

'I wouldn't have been so afraid of a dragon.'

Nor, I thought, would a dragon have squelched so disgustingly beneath my flip-flop.

'I'm not sure where we go from here,' I said, still not wanting to move in case the thing remained horribly alive.

'I am,' Poppy said, pouring us both a brandy.

'I'm shaking,' I said.

'So am I,' she said.

I held out a hand. She took it. We both laughed.

Was I taking advantage of her drunkenness?

Yes. But she was of an age, wasn't she, to make it clear what she did or didn't want.

I pulled her to me and kissed her on the mouth. 'Good brandy,' I said. I laid my free hand on her hip, fingers pointing downwards, extending my palm to feel as much of her as I could.

She pushed me away, laughing more nervously this time. 'Go,' she ordered.

'I can't,' I reminded her, 'I'm standing on your spider.'

'You can't stand there all night.'

'Can't I?'

There are moments of trembling collusion in the lives of men and women, when the sacred rules governing decent society reassert themselves only to be broken. Right shows its face for the final time, in order that we can relish wrong.

Zoo time.

'Do it,' Poppy's expression dared me. 'Do it if you're man enough.' So I did it.

TWO

The Mother-in-Law Joke

22

Blocked

Not long after Merton's suicide, I discovered in the pages of the *Scrivener* – the house journal of the Scrivener's Society, one of the many authors' societies to which I subscribed – a yellow circular, a) remembering Merton and lamenting publishing's great loss, and b) setting out a plan of action for dealing with writers' constipation. The two were not seen to be connected, though in a profession as susceptible to suggestion as ours, one calamity easily triggered another.

Costiveness had long been known to afflict writers of every sort – though fiction writers in particular as they had the least reason to leave their desks and the most reason to be stressed – but of late it had reached near epidemic proportions. It goes without saying that we weren't rushing to make it public. On top of all the other stupid questions we were asked whenever we gave an interview – such as what time we started work, where we got our ideas from, could we name a book by any living writer we admired – we didn't now want to be asked to list our favourite laxatives.

But it was precisely that reticence, according to Thor Enquist, the General Secretary of the Scrivener's Society, that was the problem. The more reluctant to discuss constipation we were, the more constipated we became. We had, he said, to let go. A cliché which had on me, at least, the very opposite effect to the one intended.

Barely had that letter arrived than *Errata*, the journal of the Jotter's Club, devoted half an issue to writers' physical well-being, the greatest modern threat to which, in the age of the computer, was – and it behoved us as writers to call a spade a spade – confinement of the bowels. If members signalled it was their wish, they would convene a conference on the subject in Conway Hall in Holborn.

There followed a list of doctors who, as fellow writers and sufferers, were offering their services to members at a knockdown price. In the meantime, we could all do worse than pay close attention to the enclosed diet and fitness charts. And not to forget walking. The greatest threat to the modern writer was that we had forgotten how to walk.

I hadn't. Not that it was doing any good. But I liked, after a morning's work, to mouth-write my way along the Thames at Barnes, and then later, when we moved to Notting Hill, up and down Ladbroke Grove, avoiding any bookshop. I'd do the same around Fitzrovia and Soho after I'd called in on Merton or Francis, or Marylebone after I'd been to see my ophthalmologist. Other than the tramp who looked like Ernest Hemingway, I did more walking around London than any writer I knew. I was a feature of the city. Travel guides pointed me out to tourists. People smiled at me; sometimes they were ex-readers, most of the time they were not – mainly they just wanted to remark on the fact that they'd seen me on Jermyn Street a week ago, and on Wigmore Street yesterday, and now here I was on Savile Row. How amazing was that?

More amazing to me was that wherever I went I saw Ernest Hemingway, either sitting down outside a pub or café, or walking in the middle of the busiest main roads, oblivious to the abuse, writing, writing, writing. His shoes were down to nothing – mere cardboard pulp – and his buttocks were completely out of his trousers. How long before I looked the same? But I excited no companionable curiosity in him. Not once did he notice me. His eyes never left his reporter's pad and his hand was never still.

What was he writing? A journal of the city? The story of the circumstances that had brought him to this? Behind the beard was a strong face, inside the filthy clothes was a powerful frame; he could have been anybody – an actor fallen from favour, a dramatist who wrote plays too searching for these cardboard-pulpy times, a novelist who used words of too many syllables for his readers. Or maybe he was just one of us, no more tragic or unsuccessful, simply constipated and needing to walk his constipation off.

Though, in that case, why was he so often to be seen sitting down?

Because he was a writer, that was why. He'd begin his day, hoping a long walk would loosen his bowels, but then a sentence would occur to him, and that sentence would beget another, and soon he'd forgotten everything but the words.

He wrote and wrote, furiously at times, his fingers gripping his pen like a dagger, flipping the pages of his pad over as though even they were an unbearable impediment to the flow of his thought. Had Vanessa been with me she'd have urged me to get closer to read what he was writing, and then give him all my loose change, but on my own I lacked the courage for either of those acts of impertinence.

The surprising thing about the Scrivener's Society and the Jotter's Club was not the interest they had suddenly started to take in their members' bowels, but that they existed at all. Authors' clubs, whether mere bureaux offering services related to the business side of our profession or more elaborate watering holes for writers needing to get out, had mushroomed in the years I'd been writing. Some writers belonged to more of them than I did and yet my wallet could no longer hold the memberships cards I possessed, each offering me advantages I didn't want, such as help with my finances from a London firm of stockbrokers, the opportunity to buy books I would never read at a 15 per cent discount, or advice on self-publishing – the last refuge of those who dreamed of showing the world it had been wrong to reject them, though the world seldom was. Viewed from one perspective there was no explaining this steep and sudden rise in the membership of authors' societies. The logical consequence of there being fewer and fewer readers for any but a handful of books of the sort Merton had shot himself rather than publish was surely a reduction in the number of writers. Only the fittest survive and we weren't the fittest. But neither evolutionary nor market forces worked in literature as they did elsewhere. For every reader that went missing a hundred new writers appeared to take his stroke her place. Soon there would only *be* writers. Was one explanation, therefore, that authors' societies provided a sort of refuge for a profession for which there was now neither justification nor employment, a shelter for the otiose on the banks of the Styx where they could gather and console one another before the ferryman finally came for them?

We will all go together when we go – was that our motto?

Was it any wonder we were constipated.

Though constipation was incident to anyone who spent too much time sitting in one place, I didn't for a moment doubt that the severity of it I experienced was writing-related, the direct consequence of trying to make an art of language in an age of mechanical communication. When my words flowed and were allowed to flow, so did I. When they didn't, I didn't. A blockage is a blockage. I'm not talking writer's block, in which, as someone who was married to one, I happened not to believe. I'm talking the refusal of reciprocity. The warm reception of a book, first by Francis, then by poor Merton, then by Josephine Public, had always facilitated an easy bowel movement, whereas the hint of a demur from my publisher or my agent or a series of bad reviews made me feel niggardly of myself, resentful of all I had given, and determined to keep myself to myself from that time on. An American novelist friend, living in London, reported a direct correlation between the number of weeks his novels were on the *New York Times* best-seller list and the frequency of his visits to the lavatory. Too many weeks at the top and he would end up with acute diarrhoea and have to suck on an Imodium every hour, too few and his wife who happened to be a doctor put him on a diet of Miralax, Lactulose, malt soup extract and hot curries.

My experience was less extreme in its variability. For all the walking I was doing I was constipated full stop. And all the Lactulose in Christendom wasn't going to help me. So while I was secretly grateful for the lavishly illustrated stool charts which both the Scrivener's Society and the Jotter's Club had sent, I didn't hold out much hope of them doing the trick.

And then, to make things worse, Vanessa found them.

'What the fuck are these? Recipes for bread rolls?'

I told her she was disgusting.

'If you're frightened you've got bowel cancer go and have a colonoscopy.'

Vanessa had as many as she could fit in. Her mother the same. They were colonoscophiles.

In this they were not exceptional. Everyone we knew had had, or was having, a colonoscopy. It was like eating in expensive restaurants – it was all there was left to do. Soon they would be performed on the same premises, simultaneously. But until then I couldn't face the procedure.

'I'm not frightened I've got anything,' I said.

This wasn't true, but I was frightened I had so many things — being found dead and purple-faced on the lavatory after a heart attack, for example — that colon cancer was the least of my worries.

'Try walking more,' was Vanessa's advice. 'Try leaving the house. Try giving me my turn.'

I was constipated, by her reasoning, because she wasn't writing her novel.

So why wasn't *she* constipated because she wasn't writing her novel?

It was a mistake to have asked her that.

'Don't make unwarranted assumptions,' she said. 'Just because I don't kick up the fuss you do doesn't mean I'm idle.'

She put her index finger up to her temple and made a whirring motion with it, denoting a novel at work on itself even as we bickered.

I wished I could have said the same about my bowels.

Writing and marriage to me apart, Vanessa was a lucky woman. Constipation was not in her nature. Why, then, the colonoscopies? It's a good question. I could only assume that they were social events for her. That she liked watching the video of the camera travelling deep inside her colon. Or that she was having an affair with her colonoscopist. She was, anyway, someone who moved her bowels with consummate ease. Poppy the same. They were out of the WC before anyone knew they'd been in it. They were like wild animals. Had we lived on a savannah I didn't doubt they'd have nipped out the back door and used that. As indeed they did on the road from Perth to Broome via Monkey Mia.

Which had to mean, since neither of them was writing, that they weren't cut out to be writers. Just as my constipation proved that I was.

The Mother-in-Law Joke wasn't going well. I didn't like my hero, Little Gid. It was precisely my constipation that told me this. I'd rise early, full of writer's juice, take a pot of tea up to my desk, glance at what I'd written the day before, visit the lavatory not expecting complications, and feel my bowels seize. Little Gid's fault.

So what was wrong with him?

Not enough was wrong with him, that was what was wrong with him. He was too unremarkable. Inadequately, insufficiently feral.

You can feel like this about your own characters. Once they assert their independence from you – and if they don't do that you should try another job – you are free to dislike or even despise them. It can work the other way, too. You start off hating their guts and halfway through the book you can't imagine ever enjoying life again outside their company. This was something Vanessa never quite understood about novels. From the first page of the few chapters she'd written it was clear whom she intended to murder and obvious on every line thereafter that she would sooner take her own life than spare his. His stroke hers? No – just his.

'Novels aren't acts of violence on their characters, Vee,' I told her once. 'Flaubert didn't write "Emma Bovary was a fuckwit and deserved everything she got".'

'That's because Emma Bovary wasn't a fuckwit who deserved everything she got.'

'I'm so glad you see that.'

'*Charles* Bovary was a fuckwit who deserved everything he got.'

I rolled my eyes.

'You write yours,' she said. 'I'll write mine.'

In fact my novels started out as acts of violence too, but it was an article of artistic faith with me that I should relent. Or go in the other direction and fall out of love with those of my creations I'd originally been enamoured of.

But Little Gid bored me from the start and went on boring me. By putting too big a distance between us, by not making him a full-time writer or comedian, or at least some version of myself unchained – a chancer, a trickster, a word-risker – I ended up resenting him for getting what I'd laboured hard for without putting in the work himself. You could say I was jealous of him. Little Gid and Pauline/Poppy – never! I couldn't see what she would see in him. More than that, I couldn't see what *I'd* seen in him. Things were bad out there. There were a hundred writers for every reader, publishers were shooting their faces off, agents were going into hiding, some lunatic was depressing my sales on Amazon by overpraising my work, Primark would soon be selling books for the price of a bag of crisps, a national newspaper was rumoured to be employing reviewers who were still at school, awaiting their GCSE results, and my answer to this was Little Gid! What antidote to the great depression of our time did Little Gid provide? What walls would tumble when Gideon puffed out his cheeks?

What was it my old teacher Archie Clayburgh used to say? *Read viscerally, with your bowels, boys.* No wonder my bowels were failing. There was nothing visceral about Little Gid. The guy had no balls. He lacked rudery. He wasn't the cause of my constipation, he *was* my constipation. A hero I had to squeeze out of me but who remained resolutely locked inside.

What did that say about me? Was I locked inside myself?

Something made me decide to go to Wilmslow to visit Jeffrey Dearheart.

23

Less is Less

The day I'd earmarked for the visit north – I wasn't able just to catch a train to Wilmslow, I had to fill my diary with red exclamation marks, as though readying myself mentally as for a trek into the Interior – I received a phone call from Margaret Travers, Merton's secretary. Merton's replacement had finally been appointed and wanted to meet me. Could I make lunch the following Wednesday at 1 p.m.?

You must never sound too eager. 'I'll just check my diary,' I said, rustling paper. 'Yes, if I move a couple of things, yes, I can make Wednesday at 1 p.m. Just. Who is it?'

'It's Margaret.'

'No, who's the replacement?'

'There can be no replacement for Merton.'

I heard tears in her voice. Apparently she had wept every day since Merton did what Merton did. Had they been lovers? The word was not. Though she wore belted raincoats in the style of vamps from black-and-white films of the 1950s, and though her voice was suggestively husky, and though she had always pronounced the name Merton as if it were molten, Margaret Travers was a secretary of the old style, simultaneously faithful to her husband and her boss. When she said there could be no replacement for

Merton she meant in her heart, innocently, as well as in publishing.

'I know that. I meant who's his –' I couldn't find the word, if the word wasn't 'replacement' – 'who will I be having lunch with?'

She lowered her voice, as though not to upset Merton. 'Sandy Ferber.'

I knew a Sandy Ferber. He'd owned a highly successful minimalist gallery in Hoxton, providing one Turner Prize-winner after another, from which he went on to run a small but influential art press – Less is More – specialising in elegantly produced artists' monographs in octodecimo, after which, quite out of character, he popped up as the fiction supremo at a bookshop chain that soon afterwards went into receivership. In the short time he was there he'd rationalised fiction so that there wasn't any, boasting that he read at least one sentence of every novel published, deciding on its viability-or-not by opening it at page 100 and if there was too much happening in the way of words he wouldn't buy. I had celebrated his fall from eminence with an article in the *Bookseller*, offering it as my view that he chose page 100 to sample because any novel that had a hundred pages in it was already too long for his exquisite concentration. The closure of the chain that had appointed him was, in my view, the logical extension of his credo. As was the disappearance of the book, and, not a moment too soon, the disappearance of him.

But that had to be a different Sandy Ferber. Under Merton, Scylla and Charybdis Press had specialised in novels that ran to six or seven hundred pages, each densely printed and packed with verbal incident. The one time Merton quarrelled with my work it was because the amount of dialogue in it made for too many white spaces on the page. Sandy Ferber, a great champion of white in art, was not the man for such a list.

I postponed Wilmslow. Vanessa was disappointed. She was hoping to have the house to herself not to write her novel in.

And to my surprise, Jeffrey was disappointed too. It was too long since I'd been home, he told me on the phone. A man should see his family. I didn't agree with him but apologised for how long it had been. I'd reorganise, I told him. 'Good,' he said.

In the meantime I googled Sandy Ferbers but failed to find one with a publishing history that made him a suitable successor to Merton or indeed a suitable publisher for me. I decided I'd misheard Margaret. She must have said Sandor Ferber, or even Salman Ferber, a favourite of the parent company in Sweden drafted in from somewhere else, Hungary or the Indian subcontinent, it didn't matter where since books were in a healthier state everywhere else than they were here. Whoever he was and wherever he came from I looked forward to a new relationship.

Although Margaret had specified the boardroom, which could seat thirty at a pinch, I assumed lunch was going to be just him and me. What he would have wanted to meet *me* for, in such a hurry, I hadn't bothered to enquire. These days a new publisher could be in place for years before a writer met him, if he ever met him at all; but I was not without my significance on the Scylla and Charybdis list; I gave it a measure of muscularity which it would otherwise have lacked. Perhaps he wanted to male-bond with me, Hungarianly, over that. *We few, we happy few, we band of brothers* . . .

I turned up ten minutes early, anyway, in *à deux* spirits, having mugged up on the Hungarian novel and, to be on the safe side, Indian prose literature in general, and was at once surrounded by drinks waiters. A half an hour later thirty of us were taking our seats. All Scylla and Charybdis authors. Sandy Ferber was at the head of the table. Not Sandor or Salman – Sandy. *The* Sandy. He said hello to each of us by name without consulting a crib sheet.

'Hello, Sandy,' I said back, the words freezing in my throat before I could quite form them.

He had that effect. He chilled the room. It wasn't the cold wind of puritanism that blew off him, it was more an icy voluptuousness, as though he had just come from sleeping with the undead. He was that rare thing in publishing, a male anorexic. Relying on all my old skills learned at Wilhelmina's I measured him. A thirty-two-inch chest, I calculated. A twenty-six-inch waist. A twelve-inch neck. And there was still room inside what he was wearing for another man the same size.

Allowing for that, he was elegant. In a black suit, of course, and a priestly white shirt buttoned at the neck but worn without a tie.

His face moved independently of the words he spoke. Welcoming us all as the gods of articulation past and reminding us of the successes we had enjoyed over the years at Scylla and Charybdis, his eyes drooped with sorrow while his mouth fell away in what looked like uncontrollable fury. He would have smiled, I thought, but his face wouldn't let him.

'What a strange man this is,' I whispered to BoBo De Souza, the current holder of the Romantic Novelists' Association Pure Passion Award, who was sitting next to me. 'Here he is in charge of the meeting and yet everything he says comes out as though he has been passed over.'

'He has no lips,' she said. 'That's why. His face is capable only of opening or closing.'

I looked at him again. She was right. His mouth had not been finished. It was as though unsealed. I congratulated her on her observancy.

'Well, I've had the opportunity to study him at close quarters,' she whispered. 'I wrote a monograph for him once, in the days before Romance claimed me.'

'Is that a euphemism?'

'For fucking him, you mean? No. Though as it happens I have fucked him as well.'

'Sandy Ferber fucks?'

'Non-stop.'

'I'm not sure I need to know that.'

'I don't mean with me. I mean he goes from woman to woman. That kind of non-stop.'

'Why?'

'Ask him.'

'No, why do women let him near? Aren't they afraid they'll freeze in his arms? Does he have arms?'

'He's a challenge, Guy. You want to see if you can be the one to thaw him out.'

'And did you?'

'Ask him. But I found him exciting, in a cadaverous, lipless sort of way.'

'I have to say you haven't made it sound exciting,' I said.

'That's because you're a man. You don't know what an aphrodisiac power is to a woman.'

'You aren't telling me you find Sandy Ferber powerful?'

'It's nothing to do with what I find him. He just is.'

'Powerful? Sandy Ferber?'

'Immensely. He ran the art world for a decade. Now he's ready for literature.'

'He's just closed a bookshop.'

'Precisely.'

The reason Ferber had brought us together was to talk about exciting new developments in digital technology. When he said 'exciting new developments' I thought he was going to howl. When he said 'digital technology' he looked at everybody in turn as though he knew which one of us had raped his sister. He wanted us to think about the challenges that lay before us. The future of fiction was not in the traditional form; other platforms – that was the very word he used: '*platforms*' – were waiting to be exploited. To name but one – the story app. Reading no longer meant going to bed with a book you were ashamed to admit you couldn't finish. Reading was now as little or as much, as frequent or as rare, wherever you did or didn't want it, at the desk or on the move. We had a historic opportunity to rescue reading from the word. In a year he wanted to have a thousand story apps ready to go for the mobile-phone market. Bus-stop reading, he called it. Unbooks that could be started and finished while phone users were waiting for someone to call them back, or for the traffic lights to change, or for the waiter to arrive with the bill. In short, to plug those small social hiatuses of life on the run.

What was said next I have no idea. I fell into a black hole. How long I was down there I don't know. It was BoBo De Souza who returned me to the land of the living dead by asking what I was doing to myself.

'How do you mean?'

She pointed to the empty less-is-less notepad in front of me. It was covered in moustache hairs.

'Oh, I'm so sorry,' I said, touching what was left of my moustache with my fingers.

'Don't be sorry for me,' she said. 'Be sorry for you.'

'I'm sorry for all of us,' I told her.

'Oh, I'm OK,' she said. 'Or I will be if you let me borrow your moustache.'

'Help yourself,' I said, pushing the notepad full of hairs in her direction. 'In fact, you can keep it.'

'I don't mean the actual moustache. I mean the idea of pulling it out. It's a habit I'd like to give to one of my characters. It beats twirling.'

'Does that mean he's a bounder?'

'No. A sad sack.'

She pinched my arm.

Which I took to mean that she liked me but didn't find me aphrodisiacal.

Sandy Ferber was still alluding to the small social hiatuses of life on the run.

'I think he means you,' I whispered.

At that moment he looked directly at me. 'And I want you, my friends and colleagues,' he concluded to applause, 'to be the ones to plug them.'

He essayed a smile, but given the collapse of his mouth, he could have been addressing his executioners.

24

The Bosom of the Family

The next day I caught the tilting, sick-making Pendolino and journeyed to the Heart of Darkness that was Wilmslow.

Sun shining. Streams purling. Cattle dozing under trees. No
talent for natural description! Me?

I'm not sure why I made such a meal of it, given how little time
it took to get there. Vanessa and her mother still went up regularly,
sometimes on the merest whim, though to do what precisely I still
hadn't found out. But for me it was a jouney back to more than a
previous place, it was a journey back to a previous person. I felt
reclaimed, as though Wilmslow knew my secrets and had the power
to keep me or to let me go. It was that shop. Had I been my truer
self pinning up dresses at Wilhelmina's? Did my soul belong to the
cashpoint, as Jeffrey Gorgeous had taken to calling the till, rather
than the page? Shopkeepers never quite live down their lineage.
Mrs Thatcher was always a grocer's daughter. Was I, in the eyes of
other writers, always the boy from the boutique?

And then there was family which Jeffrey said I was neglecting.
Not like him to say a thing like that. Not like him to say anything.
'Gorgeous, darling, suck my dick, vroom, vroom,' was Jeffrey's idea
of conversation.

Suck my dick, I always thought, was for my benefit. I was no more homophobic than arachnophobic, which doesn't mean I wanted to tread on a homosexual, but I didn't get the same-sex thing, the proof of which is my supposing that suck my dick is something you say only to a woman. The truth is I didn't know what Jeffrey got up to, only that he got up to a lot of it.

I'd never much cared for him. It would be too easy to say that that was because my mother had, but my mother had. She was always picking him up when he fell, which meant he fell a lot. Once he fell down in a dead swoon after I'd rabbit-chopped him for tearing a page out of one of my school books. For a good ten minutes I thought he was dead. 'You could have killed him,' my mother said.

Could have, but didn't.

That night she took him into her bed.

He fell into dead swoons as a matter of course after that, and it was always assumed that I was the cause. Sometimes he would open one eye as he lay there, and wink at me. How a person faking his own death managed to turn so white I never found out. But he did it so well that even as he lay winking at me I feared I had killed him, no matter that I hadn't raised a hand to him. I was a threat to him, he succeeded in getting me to believe, simply by virtue of existing. He succeeded in getting my mother to believe the same. 'Get out of my sight,' she'd say, kneeling by his bloodless corpse.

God said something similar to Cain.

Whether my father liked him any more than he liked me I couldn't have said. In the end he was too transfixed by my mother to notice either of us.

My parents were still, in a manner of speaking, alive, both advancing into mutual dementia, sharing a small suite of airy rooms with yellow walls and orange carpets in expensively attended accommodation just a stone's throw from Wilhelmina's, which was thriving under Jeffrey Honeybunch's control. He had camped the shop up in line with the northern half of the country's current cultural love affair with homosexuals. The footballers' wives adored him, but then they were a species of honorary homosexuals themselves. In spirit he was doing no more than taking the shop back to its heyday when my mother had been the pantomime dame of Wilmslow. Its strictly masculinist period under me was now nothing but a forgotten interregnum – a passage between queens.

Was that why my mother had loved Jeffrey more? Because he was like a daughter to her?

A catty observation, I accept, but that was my problem with Jeffrey: he rubbed off on me.

I called on the Dementievas, as Jeffrey and I called them, before visiting him in the shop. He had suggested this when I told him I was coming up, presumably to wrong-foot me. I had always intended to visit them but now it looked as though I was only calling on them on his say-so. The bad son getting a lesson in filiality from the good. Although calling them the Dementievas had been his faggoty idea.

I found them doing a jigsaw of Chester Castle. The last time I'd visited them they were doing a jigsaw of Chester Castle. The likely explanation was that they no sooner finished it and called for a new one than they were given the old one back and either didn't notice or didn't mind. It wasn't so preposterous: half the readers in the country no sooner finished one book than they started another identical in all but the tiniest and most irrelevant details, and they didn't have senility as an excuse. Would the day come when one book would last a person a lifetime? Get to the end and then, as the Americans say, start over. Over and over and over.

My mother recognised me, my father didn't. Last time it had

been the other way round, so not everything had solidified into madness.

She was still glamorous, give or take a few dozen stains, in a mauve Chanel suit, the skirt a little woven tube that showed her tiny legs like those of the lucky tarantula on Poppy's warm Monkey Mia pillow. She wore her matching beret too, at its old rakish slant, though its antenna was bent and looked, frankly, no longer capable of receiving signals.

'What brings you?' she asked, looking over my shoulder.

'*You* do,' I said, trying to find her lips to kiss.

Where had they gone, her lips? The very question BoBo De Souza must have asked whenever it was that she and Sandy had made the frozen beast.

But my mother had an excuse Ferber didn't. A few years earlier she'd had an operation to make her look like an Italian porn star but had so hated the flytrap mouth the surgeons gave her she'd had the operation reversed. Now she had no mouth.

'Hey,' my father said, 'who do you think you're kissing, Mr Wise Guy?'

My mother shrugged. 'He's turned possessive,' she said. She put a finger up to her temple and made a whirring motion, just as Vanessa had when informing me that she didn't have to write to write.

'I'm just admiring your wife,' I told my father.

'Wife! Who told you she's my wife?'

It was a fair question. 'It's just something I know,' I said.

'Well, you know wrong. I had a wife. This isn't her.'

It was like talking to Othello.

'He thinks I'm his mistress,' my mother whispered. 'He thinks he's left me for me.'

'Well, I'm just admiring her whoever she is,' I told him.

It didn't upset me that he was demented. Here was the advantage of never having liked your parents, or never having known them entirely sane.

'Look at those legs,' he said. I could hear the saliva sluicing through his teeth.

'They're good,' I said.

'Good? They're magnificent. My ex-wife had legs like those, but not quite so magnificent. Hers banged together in the middle. These are the bee's knees.'

'Do you take this as an insult to you?' I asked my mother. 'Or a compliment?'

'Neither. I just take it that he's cuckoo.'

'You really don't mind?'

'He's company. He's actually better company cuckoo than he was –' She couldn't find the word for what he was.

'What are you two whispering about?' he asked.

'He was agreeing with you,' my mother said.

'About what?'

'About me.'

He pushed his face in my direction, trying to focus on me. An idea seemed to dawn on him. 'Do you want her?'

'Of course not.'

'Why, what's wrong with her?'

'Nothing's wrong with her. She's fantastic. I just feel I should leave her to you.'

'We could have her together,' he said. 'She wouldn't mind that.'

He winked a half-blind bloodshot eye at my mother and then turned again to me. 'Do you know what a spit-roast is?'

'All right, Gordon,' my mother said. 'That's enough.'

Through the dementia clouds my mother's words had their old effect. At once the life went out of him. 'Go back to your jigsaw,' she ordered him. 'You're doing the moat, remember. Just the straight pieces to start with.'

He did as he was told. It was the first time in my life I had ever felt sorry for him. Maybe I was feeling sorry for me at the same time, not because I'd missed out on spit-roasting my mother, but on account of the defeated wickedness we shared. It was so hard to be a black-hearted libidinous old devil any more. So hard to be scurrilous with grace. So hard to be a man, full stop.

Dementia was the only opportunity left, and even this they took away from us.

Now that poor constipated Little Gidding was a goner, I wondered about replacing him with my father. A new sort of hero for our clapped-out times – an old, mad, male fool, more Othello than Lear, who no longer knew who his wife was and so had taken her as his mistress, happy to share either with his son, except he was too crazed to know who his son was. How's that for visceral, Mr Clayburgh? That's if my father had any viscera left.

That's if any of us did.

He was back at his jigsaw, sorting out the straight pieces with bits of moat on them. (Me in forty years? Me in twenty?) My mother was watching over him, to be sure he was doing it right, but also because she was wanting me to go now so she could get back to it herself.

'But you're all right?' I asked her.

She gave me one of her big, expressive Wilmslow shrugs. I remembered her saying, the last time I visited her, that she wished she were Jewish like everybody else in the business. 'But, Ma, you *are* Jewish,' I'd told her. 'Am I?' 'Yes, we all are.' She'd thought about it. 'Well, that's all right then,' she'd said.

But something had changed. 'What did you just ask me?' she said.

'I asked if you were all right.'

'All right! What's to be all right about?'

I couldn't think of anything to suggest.

So what *was* Jeffrey? Was he gay or was he just playing at it? North of Nantwich, these days, there was no knowing who was or wasn't gay. Maybe it had always been like that and I had been too busy doing the other thing to notice. Perhaps that was why Quinton O'Malley had pressed me with such urgency to stay up north, in the hope I'd discover what was really going on and spill the beans.

Thinking about it now, I remember how my mother used to take Jeffrey and me to Manchester on the train to buy bits and pieces for the boutique – the plunder lines, she called them – non-designer scarves and stockings, sunglasses, impulse-purchase jewellery (not too expensive) for a single revolving stand that stood by the wooden till, now an electronic cash and PIN point. She always used the same porter when we returned to Piccadilly Station with boxes to take back on the train, a great burly bear of a man with round arms and red cheeks who never failed to give us sweets or comment favourably on what my mother was wearing. One evening when we'd stayed late in Manchester for a Chinese meal I saw him at a nearby table wearing lipstick and a wig. The other men he was with – railway porters or drivers, I decided, on account of their all-round muscularity and oiliness – were dressed as women too. He waved. He was wearing gloves such as you see in faded photographs of waitresses serving tea in Harrogate in the 1920s, fingerless and with lace around the wrists. The men at his table laughed as he made dainty movements with his fat porter's fingers. I wasn't sure whether to wave back. I wasn't sure I got the joke. When I looked a second time I realised he was dressed pretty much like my mother, particularly in the matter of the shortness of the skirt. Seeing my confusion, she explained that Derek – I hadn't realised she was on first-name terms with him – was experimenting with his identity. 'Are they all experimenting with their identity?' I asked. My mother said of course not, the others were just friends helping Derek through a crisis, but even at the time I suspected she was wrong – half the working-class men in Manchester were experimenting with their identity, and using wigs and lipstick in their hypotheses.

I wasn't tempted myself but Jeffrey Cuddly Wuddly, as he was then, might have been. It's possible he didn't in fact sit forward at the table and look intently into space when my mother used the word 'identity', but then again it's possible he did. You know quite early on, I suspect, whether any of this is going to appeal. Jeffrey saw something of himself in a railway man in a short skirt; where I, even before I knew what any of them were, caught my reflection only in scoundrels, perjurers, lechers and novelists.

It was late afternoon when I got to the shop. Jeffrey was in earnest conversation with a woman I thought I recognised from the newspapers. A bit still in the face for a footballer's wife, unless she'd come straight from Botox. And too old when I looked a second time. I guessed she was nearer Poppy's age than Vanessa's, but with that air of not knowing what you're for any more that you see on models no longer young but which I'd never seen on Poppy. Poppy knew what she was for. Inflaming me.

Jeffrey signalled to me to entertain myself for a few minutes. There were places in the world where a man who ran a provincial boutique would have been proud to introduce an important customer to his distinguished writer brother, but Wilmslow wasn't one of them. What I was hoping was that she'd recognise me and abash Jeffrey by saying she'd read everything I'd written, loved every word, and demand he introduce us. A hope that only goes to show there's a shlock novelist in all of us.

'Sorry about that,' he said, kissing me, after she'd left. He kissed me strangely, dodging my face as though frightened to get too close, unless he was frightened that I'd be frightened. He told me about the woman he'd been talking to. I was right. A model past her best. 'Beautiful still,' Jeffrey went on, 'though she's had a bit of work done.'

'*Bit of work?* Jeffrey, she looks as though she's been in taxidermy for the last decade. Can she smile?'

'Nothing to smile about,' he said. 'Her husband's just walked out on her.'

'It happens,' I said.

'Not when you've got a brain tumour.'

There was a slim chance Jeffrey had made that up to discountenance me — it was the sort of thing he did — but he looked furious with me for my unthinking flippancy and I couldn't risk challenging him.

I blew out my cheeks. 'Sheesh,' I said. 'Sorry.'

'Yes, sheesh,' he repeated.

'Well, you're looking well, anyway,' I said, after a decent interval. Though that too appeared to anger him.

He was taller and slimmer than me, a drainpipe man ambiguously foppish in an Alexander McQueen jacket with metallic lapels worn over a striped T-shirt and ripped jeans. Was he dressed up or dressed down? The secret to his style was that one never knew. He wore the lightest of mascara, so light I might have imagined it. His hair flopped about even more than mine did. At the moment of his kissing me he had flicked it out of his eyes so that it caressed my cheek like a whip made of feathers. The flick had petulance in it. Could be difficult if crossed, the gesture said. Then the kiss of the feathery whip.

Did he kiss-flick his women like that? Did he kiss-flick his men?

He always told me about his women, describing them in embarrassing detail, enumerating the things they did to him – it was always what *they* did to *him* – but I wondered whether he made them up, not to disguise his true interests but to help me see there were alternatives to Vanessa. It was an unspoken family fiction that I regretted my marriage to Vanessa and would escape her if I could. Though our father was a hobbled dormouse – or at least had been until dementia freed him into intermittent licentiousness – we entertained the fancy (by 'we' I mean my mother, Jeffrey and me) that Ablemen men were macho bastards who took no shit from anyone, least of all a woman. That I took shit from Vanessa needed some explaining and I wasn't going to explain it with reference to the feelings I had for Poppy. Not in Wilmslow. So I let them think I was simultaneously afraid of Vee and deeply sorry for her for being married to me. Which left them to suppose I could be won away eventually by stories of women no less beautiful than her, no less statuesque than her, but a hell of a lot more accommodating.

As though such a combination of virtues could anywhere have existed . . .

Jeffrey had found a new pub he liked on Alderley Edge, though what he really liked was powering down the lanes of Cheshire in a car that was built to rip up a racetrack with me next to him evincing terror.

'Problems with your exhaust?' I wondered.

'It's meant to sound like that.'

'Why?'

'Ha, ha!' he said. It wasn't laughter. He actually said the words. Separately. A 'Ha' followed by a 'ha!'

'Is that an answer?'

'Was yours a question?'

He was unable to believe I didn't covet his car.

He told me how quickly he could get from zero miles an hour to a hundred and fifty.

'Don't give a shit, Jeffrey,' I said.

He told me something about the steering.

'Give even less of a shit, Jeffrey.'

He shook his head and said 'Ha, ha!' again.

'Next you'll be telling me you don't know what we're in,' he said.

'Let me tell you something, Jeffrey – I don't know what we're in.'

'Is this a writer's thing?'

'What we're in? Well, no writer I know has anything like this.'

'No, is pretending not to care about cars something writers do?'

'I do care about cars. I care they don't crash when I'm in them.'

He lowered the roof with a button and hit the accelerator. The wind blew wonderfully through his hair, mine remained plastered down by fear.

'Ah,' he said, tapping me on the thigh, 'isn't this wonderful? Admit it, it's fucking lovely.'

Even when Jeffrey didn't say 'admit it', the command was implicit in all our conversations. In Jeffrey's view I was in denial. Denial about my marriage to Vanessa, women, cars, the success Jeffrey had made of the business, fashion, Wilmslow, money – in short everything I had and wished I didn't, and everything that Jeffrey had that I wished I did. 'Admit it' meant admit you want to be me. That I was the person I wanted to be, doing the thing I wanted to be doing, was not something my brother could conceive.

As it happened, though no thanks to his intelligence, his scepticism was well founded. I might not have wanted to be Jeffrey but

I hadn't particularly relished being me for the last four or five years. This was not my era. The times were out of joint etc. I was permanently constipated. I had a criminal record with Oxfam. They were giving me too many stars on Amazon – no one wanted to read someone as good as that. Even Poppy – who I definitely did want – would have been an easier proposition had I been someone else. Not her daughter's husband, say. Though you have to ask how much, in that case, I would have wanted her.

None of which, of course, was I willing to admit to Jeffrey Cutie Pie.

A funny thing about this getting me to 'admit it'. Jeffrey wasn't the only one. Vanessa's working assumption was that I lied about everything and would never be well – free of constipation, free of solipsism, free of self – until I came completely clean. Bruce Elseley was trying to get me to admit I was plagiarising him. My agent wanted me to admit I was secretly a thriller writer. Sandy Ferber wanted me to admit I couldn't wait to be the god of the thirty-second app. Mishnah Grunewald had wanted me to admit I was in denial about being Jewish. And there was someone else – the royal novelist and biographer Lisa Godalming who wanted me to admit I was a closet reader of the soap histories of Tudor monarchs she pounded out for Radio 4 listeners and only *pretended* not to give a monkey's whether Richard the Twenty-Seventh could or could not sire an heir while reforming Parliament and remaining a Catholic.

'Admit it,' she said when we last met at a party, 'underneath those sheets you're beavering away.'

'Yes, but not at your prose, Lisa.'

That wasn't gratuitousness. We'd been lovers briefly and so could be rude to each other with affection. And besides, she didn't believe me.

She blew me kisses when she left the party and promised to send me her latest.

It arrived early the next morning by courier. It was inscribed

For
My dear Guy,
Enjoy –
Your secret's safe with me

Not something you want your wife to find. But that wasn't the only reason I put it through the shredder. I didn't want posterity to come upon such a book on my shelves and take its author's assumption as a fact. No, I was not in denial. No, I was not beavering away at Lisa Godalming under my sheets. No, I did not have a secret hankering to read shit.

25

Terminus

'Admit it —' Jeffrey said, as we pulled into the pub forecourt in time to see the sun go down.

I stopped him there. 'Fuck off, Jeffrey,' I said.

He wouldn't let me buy the drinks. They had interesting vodkas here and I didn't know my way around them. Something else I was bound to be in denial about: how little, compared to my brother, I knew about drink. We'd had this out. 'I'm a wine man,' I'd told him. 'If you want to test your wits with me when it comes to wine —'

'Wits! You see? That's you all over. I'm having a drink, you're taking an intelligence test. And by the way, by drink we mean vodka up here. Wine's so out. Such a depressant — ugh.'

'I've read about the vodka rage,' I said. 'I've read you drink it through your eyes. That sounds more of a depressant than red wine to me. Doesn't it depress your sight?'

'You talking about eyeballing? Yeah. But that's students.'

'Not you?'

'Are you asking me if I've eyeballed? Of course, once or twice. Haven't you?'

'Why would I?'

'You're a writer? Aren't you supposed to experience stuff?'

'Not that kind of stuff. Jesus, Jeffrey, through your *eyes*? You're a human being. Aren't you supposed to treat yourself like one?'

'I don't do it any more. Not much. Not all the time. Just occasionally. These things come and go quickly up here.'

'So does your eyesight. But what's this crap about *up here*? We're in Alderley Edge not Cutting Edge, Jeffrey. Up here is the end of the fucking world.'

'Just because you've left?'

'No – I left *because* it's the end of the fucking world.'

'If you knew who lived here you wouldn't say that.'

'Who lives here?'

He reeled off names, ersatz, quasi Latin American names of the Ryanair jet set, the people who emailed you offers of Viagra and penis extensions—Felisha, Tamela, Shemika, Alysha, Shera, Teisha, Shakira . . .

'Are these Spanish waitresses?'

'Ha, ha! Don't pretend you don't know.'

'I honestly have never heard of them.'

'Shows how out of touch you are. Do you know how many top photographers and interior designers live in Cheshire?'

'Tell me.'

He made his hands flap like butterflies. 'You're in Happeningsville,' he said. And as though to prove it he rose from the table, went over to the bar, and returned with a plate of cold meze for each of us. Meze! Now call Cheshire the end of the fucking world!

'So who's fucking you right now, Jeffrey?' I asked him when he handed me my plate. 'Someone from Wilmslow? Someone I know? Someone whose mother I know?'

'Ha, ha!' he said. Ha. Ha!

'Is she a joke?'

'You wouldn't say she was a joke if you saw her.'

'What are her distinguishing characteristics?'

Before he could tell me, an Asian boy with a temple dancer's body and hair as floppy as Jeffrey's came over from the bar and kissed him on the mouth. He was wearing a Savile Row striped suit with a public-school scarf thrown around his throat. Something made me think of Billy Bunter's chum, Hurree Jamset Ram Singh, the Nabob of Bhanipur. Once again Jeffrey did not introduce us. We nodded to each other awkwardly.

'The confusedness is terrific,' I said to Jeffrey after the Nabob had left us.

Jeffrey did not pick up the allusion. He was not a reader. Maybe drinking vodka through your eyes was another explanation of why no one read any more: you opened a book and you saw not words but vodka.

'I couldn't remember his name, that's why I didn't –' he explained.

'Shakira? Tamisho?'

'He cuts my hair.'

'Jeffrey,' I said. 'Tell me something . . .'

He knew what I was going to ask him.

'Do I go both ways? Yes.'

'I wasn't going to ask you that.'

'What were you going to ask me?'

'How much it costs to get a good haircut these days.'

I expected him to say 'Ha, ha!' but it appeared he had stopped finding me amusing.

'It's just that Vanessa does mine,' I said, 'and I think it's time I put myself in the hands of a professional.'

'I agree with you,' he said, looking at my hair. 'I always wanted to ask you if Vanessa cut it.'

'You can tell it's not professional?'

'You can tell it's been cut by someone who doesn't like you.'

'You can tell that from a cut?'

'I can tell it from your unhappiness, Guy.'

'Ha, ha!' I said. 'Who's unhappy?'

Denial again.

'Suit yourself,' he said.

I leaned forward and held him by his wrist. It was slender and hairless. Did he shave his wrists? I wondered. Was the hair on his head the only hair on his body? Men were shaving their chests and their backs, their legs, their balls, their anuses. In Happeningsville Wilmslow, God knows where else. Did Shakira run his razor along Jeffrey's perineum?

'If you're sorry you told me you go both ways,' I said, 'don't be. I am not in the least judgemental. If anything I'm fascinated. I can't imagine it.'

'What is it you can't imagine?'

Shakira running his razor along your perineum, was one answer. Putting your dick inside a man was, frankly, another. But I didn't see that we could go that far back into Jeffrey's psychology, or indeed into mine. And I accept that whatever it is you can't imagine is a mark against you, not for.

'This bi business,' I said. 'This wanting both. Isn't a sexual choice by its nature an act of separation – this not that, her not her, and even more, though by the same logic, her not him?'

'But who's asking you to make a sexual choice?'

'Isn't that just what we do when we pick a mate – we reject the others? Isn't it discrimination that gives desire its savour?'

'Christ! Is that from one of your books?'

Have I said that I'm a mind-reader? I could read Jeffrey's mind, anyway. 'Then no wonder they don't sell,' he was thinking.

'All right,' I said, 'I'll put it bluntly. When I fuck a woman I am, among other things, very definitely and deliberately not fucking a man.'

'What about another woman?'

I took too long to answer. Behind Vanessa, sitting astride me and calling me Guido, loomed the shadow of her mother standing like a heron on one leg.

'There you are,' Jeffrey went on.

'There I am what?'

'There you are silently admitting to yourself that sex is not exclusive. If I'm sucking off a man while a woman's sucking off me, who gets precedence? Which is me doing to the one what I am very definitely and deliberately not doing to the other?'

I had no answer to this, in so far as I understood it, that wasn't prissy. What about love? I wanted to say. What about decency and self-respect, for fuck's sake? Deep down in the sewerage of my morality I even heard the Bible rumbling about 'abomination'.

Visceral, I told myself, think *viscerally*.

'So do you have no preference at all?' I asked.

'When it comes to?'

'Oh – oh – I don't know – oh – say blow jobs.'

I expected him to say, 'It's so over, up here, so yesterday, the blow job.'

But he answered me with candid directness. 'I prefer getting them.'

'No, I mean preference as to who you get them from.'

'Man or woman?'

'Man or woman.'

'Depends on the man or woman, Guy. These things don't divide on gender lines.'

The right-on prick! How had he done it? How – with his dick in one person's mouth and his own lips around someone else's – had he seized the moral high ground?

I changed the subject. Asked him whether his television series was still on track. He looked uninterested. They were talking, he told me. Asked him about the shop. Phenomenal. He looked melancholy about it.

In return he asked me about my writing, but didn't listen to my answers. He gave the air of not wanting to humiliate me.

And then, without any warning, he began to cry.

'Jeffrey,' I said, offering to put a brotherly arm around him. 'Jeffrey, what's the matter?'

He ran the sleeve of his lovely jacket across his nose. 'I lied to you earlier,' he said.

'That's OK.'

'Don't say that's OK. You don't know what I lied to you about. It's not OK. You remember the woman I was talking to in the shop when you arrived? Pamala Vickery? I told you her husband had walked out on her and she'd been diagnosed with a brain tumour.'

Ha, ha, so I was right. 'Yes, I did wonder,' I said.

'Oh, you *did wonder*, did you?'

'Jeffrey, it's OK. Truly.'

'*Truly?*'

'Truly.'

He wiped his nose again and then made a fist of the hand he'd wiped it with. I leaned back, fearing he was going to hit me.

He didn't. But what he said was worse than any blow. 'Fuck you, Guy,' he all but spat at me. 'Fuck you!'

I put my hand in front of my face.

He pulled it away. 'Let me tell you something *truly*,' he went on, 'you know-all cunt. There are things you don't know. And there are things that you can't tell me are OK.'

'OK,' I said.

'It isn't. Nothing's OK. Get that into your head – nothing is OK.'

I grew anxious. The last person who had said that nothing was OK was Merton.

'If that's how it looks to you, Jeffrey –'

'*Looks to me!* Christ, Guy, I might as well be talking to Dad. It's not Pamala that's got a brain tumour, right?'

I waited, not wanting to know what I knew was coming. 'Oh, Jeffrey,' I said.

'Don't "Oh, Jeffrey" me. I haven't finished. I'm the reason Pamala's husband has walked out on her.'

'So she can look after you?'

'So she can live with me – what's left of me.'

'Are you playing at this?'

'Why would I play?'

'Oh, Jeffrey,' I said again.

'You don't have to be sorry for me. I've had fun.'

'I know you have.'

'You know nothing. I've had fun with everybody.'

He looked at me with a curious insistence. 'Everybody,' he repeated.

'You've told me – men and women. What you do is your business. But, honestly, how bad is it?'

'You've not understood. By everybody I mean *everybody*.'

And then I did understand. I read it through the vapours of vodka swirling about his eyeballs. By everybody he meant Vanessa.

So that was what she did in Wilmslow. My brother.

'Are you telling me you've been sleeping with Vanessa?'

'I've always liked Vanessa.'

'That's not an answer to my question.'

'I read an interview you gave to the *Wilmslow Reporter* once –'

'You wouldn't have been able to understand it. You don't read.'

'I read this. You said you liked writing about wild guys. Well, you're no wild guy. The wild guy in your marriage is Vanessa.'

'Which justifies you sleeping with her.'

'I'm winding you up.'

'Why?'

'Because you're a sanctimonious prick.'

'And I haven't got a brain tumour?'

'That too. And because you've never listened to a word I say. You aren't listening now. I said everybody. Not just Vanessa. Fucking everybody.'

His look was so wild I wondered if he'd been having an affair with Wilhelmina Dementieva. But no, no, not even Jeffrey Sweetheart fucked his mother.

But that thought triggered another. Not his mother, Vanessa's mother.

Goats and monkeys!

'Poppy!' I had tried to make it a question but it came out an expostulation.

He smirked at me. 'Unless I'm winding you up again.'

So was that smirk an acknowledgement that he knew his fucking Poppy would be even more painful to me than his fucking Vanessa?

I couldn't allow him to think he had my number there. I rose from the table and went to the bar. Not to pour alcohol into each eyeball or smoke a cigarette through my ear, but to attempt some deep breathing and ring for a taxi.

One came in ten minutes. On the way out I put a chilled hand on Jeffrey's shoulder. He didn't move. 'I'm sorry about your tumour,' I said. 'I'd be even sorrier if you'd allow me to be. But you will let me know if there is anything I can do for you.'

In the taxi to the railway station it occurred to me he might have been lying about the tumour, that this was just another of those dead faints he used to fall into to get me banished and himself carried into our mother's bed. I had no idea why. He had her to himself now. And I was already banished. To sugar the pill of his confession, maybe, assuming a confession was what it was. To explain his behaviour. It wasn't him that had been sleeping with my wife or mother-in-law, it was the lump in his brain. But then if he didn't have a lump in his brain, why had he bothered to confess?

It was only as I was getting out of the taxi that I took the full impact of what had happened that day. I'd had another of those encounters with my brother in which it was impossible to disentangle truth from fiction, or sanity from madness. My father had asked me if I fancied joining him in a spit roast of my mother. My mother had understood what he meant – which alarmed me – and was only fractionally annoyed. Had they done this in the past? On the *QE2*? All right, he was senile. But we go senile in a way that reflects our natures. I'd always wondered who my father was. Now I knew. He was a sleazebag. Perhaps with a lump in his brain himself. We were the sons of a whoremonger, Jeffrey Tumour and I. And maybe of a whore as well. We were the children of the damned.

Jeffrey wanted me to know he'd been sleeping with either Vanessa or Poppy, but what if he wanted me to know more than that? What if he'd been sleeping with them both?

I wouldn't write the books I write if I didn't have a tireless imagination. I get quicker than most men from a whisper to a kiss, from a kiss to an affair, and from an affair to a sexual barbecue.

One at a time was bad enough, but what if – between them – my wife and her mother had been spit-roasting Jeffrey?

Not easy, but I put nothing past them.

But spit-roasted or not, my brother was dying. And if he was lying? To lie about that was a sort of dying in itself.

An involuntary cry escaped me as I was paying the fare, a sudden stab in a place I couldn't locate, as though it was the memory of pain.

'You all right?' the driver asked me.

'Me? All things considered,' I replied, 'I'm fine.'

I had to run to catch my train.

26

Fat Checker

The journey from Monkey Mia to Broome passed off without incident. Poppy slept in the back of the van. Vanessa concentrated on the driving. We couldn't do it in one day, though Vanessa did suggest she and I take turns to drive through the night.

'I'm too tired,' I told her.

'Why, what have you been doing to be tired?' she asked.

I could have said, 'I've been killing spiders,' but I didn't. 'I've been thinking,' I said instead, rubbing at my eyes to suggest the labour that was thought.

Saying I'd been thinking was always a good way of shutting down conversation with Vanessa. She was frightened I'd bore her by telling her *what* I'd been thinking.

We arrived in Broome late the following evening and checked straight into a hotel with a view of the mangrove swamps. I spent an hour sorting out the Wi-Fi connections for my laptop and getting my messages.

'Can't you wait?' Vanessa said.

'For what?'

'For one more night without your career taking over our lives again.'

'What career?'

'That's exactly what I mean.'

But I heard the bad news humming in the machine and couldn't wait to retrieve it. Once upon a time it was the Oracle. Now it was the Apple. But disaster is still disaster, no matter who's foretelling it.

Among the Viagra and erection dross, I found an email from Bruce Elseley, who shouldn't have had my email address, threatening legal action and wondering if I wanted to come and hear him read in a bookshop in Kentish Town; another from Merton, at that time still alive, attaching a belated review of my last novel but two – the best review he had ever seen, in his opinion, a review of breathtaking insight, only a pity it appeared four years after publication and in a journal no one read; and *American Traveler* were querying a few points in an article I'd done for them about the Barossa Valley. The one thing all writers dread, no matter where they are, is any communication, short of 'can't find fault with a single word', from an American fact checker; but in a hotel in Broome at the end of a long and emotionally exhausting trip, an American fact checker with 'a couple of queries' is the least welcome person on the planet.

Hearing Vanessa and me discussing the fact checker the following morning over breakfast, Poppy thought we said fat checker.

'How do you know she's fat?' she asked.

'I don't,' I said. 'She might be fat for all I know. But the word is fact not fat. She checks facts.'

'Which is strange,' Vanessa said, 'given that you wouldn't know a fact if it fell on you.'

'Exactly,' I said.

'So what's she checking?' Poppy asked.

'It's a misnomer,' I said. 'What she actually is, is style police.'

'She's a fat-style policeman,' Vanessa said, pleased with herself, as though she'd made a joke.

Poppy thought about it. 'Then maybe what she checks *is* fat, after all,' she said. 'Like a butcher.'

'Are you saying I have a fat style, Poppy?'

We exchanged shy glances, like schoolchildren who'd been behind the bike shed all lunchtime.

I was secretly impressed with her. It took more critical sophistication than I thought she possessed to think of writing as akin to meat, capable of being too greasy, needing to be made more lean. Had she changed in the time I held her in my arms, with one leg on the tarantula? Had my kisses turned her into a literary critic?

In her honour, anyway, that was what I decided to call the woman from *American Traveler* from now on – the fat checker.

The consequence of my hearing from the fat checker, who was also worrying we were running late with copy, was that I had to stay in and work on my article while Vanessa and her mother began their exploration of Broome. There were three main areas of concern about what I'd written. 1) The fat checker didn't understand it. 2) The fat checker didn't like it. 3) The fat checker didn't think any of it was true.

These three were not unrelated. 'Hyperbole,' I wrote back to her. 'You are not to take what I wrote literally.'

'How then am I to take it?' she emailed back.

'As a grand gesture to an essential truth, without my stooping to the banalities of factuality.'

'So when you say,' she said, on the phone from New York this time – it must have been the dead of night or the dead of morning, that's how dedicated to checking fat she was – 'that the waitress at the Mount Pleasant Winery Barbecue and Bistro was a mermaid who had just stepped out of a barrel of Shiraz, her long flowing hair wet and purple with the grape, you mean she *looked like* a mermaid?'

'Yes,' I said. 'No. That makes it sound like a flight of fancy on my part, whereas the waitress saw herself as mermaid.'

'Can you substantiate that?'

'No, not really. It was my impression. It was the way she held herself.'

'So it *is* a flight of fancy?'

'Well, it's part fancy, part intuition. But I still wouldn't want to say she *looked like* a mermaid. The simile diminishes her, diminishes me, and diminishes the reader. She *was* a mermaid.'

'But she hadn't actually stepped out of a barrel of Shiraz?'

'Of course not. But she could have. And in the end, who's to say she hadn't? Are you worried that someone might try it in their own home?'

'Don't you think that patrons of the Mount Pleasant Winery would be put off their wine if they thought a mermaid had been swimming in it?'

'Well, I wouldn't. But I doubt she had actually been swimming in it.'

'Then why does she have wine in her hair? How did it get there?'

It's a law of writing for an American magazine that the fat checker always wins. 'I'll rewrite it,' I said.

'Moving on,' she said. 'When you describe the glasses of wine at the Henschke Winery as bouncing light like the window of a Bond Street jeweller's, do you mean like the window or the jewellery in it?'

I thought about it. 'I think I meant that the wine dancing in the glass reminded me of jewels bouncing light in the windows of, say, Tiffany's.'

'In Bond Street? Isn't Tiffany's in *Old* Bond Street?'

'Well, we call it all Bond Street, Old and New. But yes, *Old* Bond Street, if that would help your readers to locate it.'

'And *bouncing*?'

'Yes, bouncing light.'

Now it was her turn to pause. I wondered if she was talking to the subeditor who was talking to the commissioning editor who was talking to the publisher who was talking to the owner of the magazine. She, too, I could hear, was wondering. In fact, it sounded as though they all were. 'We are wondering,' she said at last, 'if we could find another way of putting that for our readers?'

'*That* being "bouncing"?'

'Yes, and "dancing" and "mermaid" and "barrel" –'

'And "Shiraz"?' I added, moving on.

'Yes, and that.'

I thanked her, rang off, and stepped out onto the balcony of the hotel. Had it not looked so poisonous out there, had the jellyfish not been waiting to put an end to the few cardiorespiratory functions the fat checker had left me with, I might have jumped.

Why was I in Broome? Why was I anywhere?

It can help to think about home when the nausea of travel strikes, but home was Elseley hanging from a hotel door in women's stockings with an orange in his mouth, home was Flora McBeth systematically removing from the shelves of the country's bookshops all books ever written by a man, home was . . . Where was home?

And this Broome the two witches had brought me to – what sort of hell from hell was this? I stepped back from the balcony in revulsion. Disgusting, the heat, the crawling mangrove ('Is it the mangrove that's crawling or are there crawling things in it?'), the slow undulations of Roebuck Bay whose waters moved like soup ('mushroom? tomato? jellyfish?'), the osprey gliding in their infinite patience, imperturbable in their conviction that life was food and food was life and that is all ye know on earth and all ye need to know . . .

Food and desire . . .

Where were they now, the witchy women of my life? 'And where, where, where is my Gypsy wife tonight?' – Leonard Cohen, last of the old school of daredevil masochists.

So where, where, where *were* my Gypsy wives? Pearl diving? On Cable Beach, showing off their figures to the musclemen? Riding a camel, one either side of his hump, Poppy's fingers clasped like a child's around her daughter's middle?

Out of the heat of my disgusting desire they rose from the Roebuck Bay mangroves, two mermaids shaking droplets of Shiraz from their empurpled toxic hair.

Something I haven't mentioned.

On the night I killed the spider, the night all moral time stopped still, I returned at last to the camper van and found Vanessa gone. On my pillow, as though in mocking replica of what had been on Poppy's, a note.

'Just taking the air, the night too beautiful to miss. Don't wait up for me. Kisses. V.'

27

Wildebeest

We stayed a fortnight in Broome. Vanessa wanted to stay for ever.

'This is the frontier life I've always longed for,' she said.

She'd never mentioned the frontier life when we'd lived thatched-roofed in Barnes or when we moved into the three-storey house in Notting Hill Gate. (At this stage Poppy was still living with us. She decamped to Oxfordshire only after we got back from Australia, for reasons of what I suppose you'd have to call decency.)

I registered surprise that the frontier life was what she'd always longed for, but Vanessa was proof against my ironies. 'I never used the word to you,' she said, 'because I knew you wouldn't know what it meant. You're such a townie.'

A townie, me? I reminded her I came from Wilmslow. 'From the window of my bedroom, Vee, I grew up seeing cows.'

'Describe a cow.'

'Sheep, then.'

But since she was so enamoured of it, I left Broome to her. She returned the van and hired the most machismo jeep she could find. She loved the architecture and engineering of outback vehicles, the bull bars and the big tyres, the cans strapped to the roof, the noise the doors made when you flung them closed, the red dust on everything. For the two weeks we were there she became a well-known personality, driving at speed through the town, honking her horn and waving at the friends she'd made. She bought a new wardrobe of khaki shorts and ankle boots. She spoke in Aussie slang. At night she went out and drank with the Aborigines, the sound of whose laughter and brawling could be heard a hundred miles away.

'This land is their land,' she said.

'*Land?* That's not one of your words.'

'It is now. They've taught me. It's in their blood.'

'Vee, what's in their blood is alcohol.'

'And whose fault's that?'

I knew the answer. The white man's. Vanessa wanted to stay and make things right for the black man.

'Let's not go back,' she said to me one night. She'd been out drinking and doing God knows what else and was coiled around me like a snake around a wildebeest. 'Let's never go home. We can have a life here. Don't you feel the wildness of it? How can we go back to west London after this? Smell the night.'

I smelt it.

The warm smell of camel hide or even elephant, blood, lizard, eucalypt, jacaranda – the sultry smell of pain and everything you applied to pain to soothe it, including after-sun lotion. But then the smell of more pain still.

'Listen to it.'

I listened. Though the sea was not moving you could hear it. The sound of muffled silence, a roar as from another planet. And the sounds of creatures killing or being killed. And the Aborigines screeching their terrible disinherited laughter. And Vanessa whispering in my ear.

She was right. How could we go back?

'What about your mother?' I asked.

'Up to her. She can stay with us or she can go home on her own. She's perfectly capable. Just you and me. What do you say?'

For a moment I thought she was going to shoot her hand uncontrollably in the direction of my freshly proved manhood.

I lay quiet, listening to Vanessa's excitement.

'Well?' she said. 'What's to lose? You can write anywhere and this would give you a subject that's not yourself at last. And me too. I could finish my book here. This is what it was always about anyway. I understand that now.'

'Your book was always about *Broome*?'

She bit my ear. 'Don't be a smart-arse, Guido. Not here. This is our chance to put all that smartness behind us. Start again. What do you say? Start again where life is real. No more book launches. No more publishers' parties. No more running out to get the papers to see the reviews and then going ballistic.'

'I'll think about it,' I said, remembering ballistic.

'Don't think, just do it.'

She was right. I hailed her courage. She was right for me as well as her. The great louche and ribald writers I admired would all have leapt at a life here, however brief. Gone mad in the heat, roared drunken through the streets, shot goannas in their gardens, and written scorching books about the experience. Maybe she would stay. Maybe she *should* stay. But not me. I lacked the courage. Unruliness was my goal, but unruliness in Wilmslow, not the far north of Western Australia where there were still creeks from which no white man had ever drunk. Did I say Vanessa lay coiled about me like a snake around a wildebeest? Some wildebeest!

I still shook with the transgression of the week before, or however long it was, when I'd put my hands on Vanessa's mother

226

and kissed her till my tongue ached. How much wilder did a man have to be?

And we weren't done with each other yet.

Done? We hadn't started on each other yet.

I'd blown my chance the night of the tarantula. Blame words. Words had always got me into trouble. Breaking for breath, and with my arms still encircling her, I'd said – cute bastard that I was – 'So there are monkeys in Monkey Mia after all.'

Spell broken. Poppy, I should have known, was of that generation of women who let themselves go only on the understanding that it is not alluded to while it is happening. They let their hair down somnambulistically, so that in the morning they won't remember. Only draw attention – 'This good for you?' or 'I'd rather fuck you than your daughter' – and the trance is shattered. That's how fine the veil is that covers their modesty.

And I had ripped it.

'Go!' she said, and that time she did not relent.

So I went back to the van and found the note from Vanessa on my pillow.

Had the tarantula been a ruse? A rubber spider to get me out of the way so that Vanessa could slip away to the boat and its seedy crew a second time, the night being too beautiful to miss, blah blah . . ?

Did she regret she'd allowed things to progress that far?

Poppy, I mean. Vanessa was on the back burner of my jealousy. I'd deal with what I felt about her later. One pang at a time. And anyway, what Vee had done, she'd done. She was a great masticator, when it came to herself, of anterior ethics. Anything she had done in the past

– even yesterday – she chewed up and spat out. Christ, Guido, that was *then*. Get over it. But with Poppy the question still had future in it. What did she think? What would she go on thinking?

I studied her expression when she didn't know I was watching her. If her conscience was troubling her, she didn't give any sign of it. She still slipped her hand into her daughter's arm when they were out and about; they still strode together side by side, elevated on their cork heels, their heads turning in unison whenever someone unexpected passed them, though little was more unexpected on the streets of Broome than they were.

Had she mislaid what had happened? Had it vanished in alcohol, like so much else, like the spider on her pillow, like the monkeys she had hoped to find at Monkey Mia but had forgotten all about until I'd unwisely reminded her, like Vanessa into the night?

There were things I needed to know. Such as how a mother felt about borrowing her daughter's husband? How treacherous it was from the mother's point of view? Essentially, I meant. Never mind what a timorous society whose rules were made by women's reading groups in Chipping Norton thought, how great a crime was sleeping with your daughter's husband in the moral scheme of things? Did matrons discuss it laughingly with one another at the counter of the nail-care salon?

'*You had your son-in-law yet?*'

'*Yes, you?*'

'*Thinking of it. Any good, was he?*'

'*So-so.*'

Or did they tear their hair and await with trembling the vengeance of the gods?

Questions, questions. But from Poppy not a suggestion that she'd asked herself any of them. Did that make her a villainess of amorality, or a heroine? Did it make her anything at all?

While they turned heads on Cable Beach, flirting with muscle-men or riding camels into the sunset – a camel each, Vanessa and Poppy, a hump apiece, think of that – I stayed indoors and googled Sophocles and Aeschylus. They were the boys with the answers. A man and his mother-in-law – how seriously did the gods view our transgression?

Nothing. No mention. Even Phèdre did no more than fall for her husband's son from another marriage – and that didn't come close.

Only the Roman dramatist Terence bore fruit – *Hecrya: The Mother-in-Law*. But that was a comedy, indeed something of a farce when it was first produced, losing its audience to a bunch of rope dancers performing on another stage. And I wasn't looking for laughs.

We stood next to each other, Poppy and I, in the garden of the Mangrove Hotel one night, watching the Staircase to the Moon, a low-tide spectacle in which the moon seems to climb into the sky up the ladder of its own reflection from the mudflats of Roebuck Bay. People come from all over Australia, driving thousands of miles, just to see this. But I could barely look. Was I the stuff of tragedy or the stuff of farce? Was Poppy still in or was she out?

Had the Staircase to the Moon shed light on questions such as these I might have given time to observing it. Vanessa was talking to a gang of heavy-drinking men; dressed as she was, in her territory shorts and boots, and in wild spirits, her abandonment to heat and company was a spectacle in itself. I pressed my hand to Poppy's thigh, fingers down and spread wide as though measuring a horse, exactly as she had finally allowed me to do the night of the tarantula. But she moved swiftly away from me. No plea to leave her alone. No reprimand. Just a step, as though to give a stranger space.

The matter was not raised the whole time we were in Broome.

I didn't press myself upon her. This might have been because I was sorry suddenly for Vanessa. She was not going to get her wish. For all her boldness, she wouldn't stay without me. I couldn't explain that. Perhaps her courage needed the complement of my fear. Perhaps she had hoped for Dirk to show up in his boat and he had forgotten her. He wasn't exactly the sort of man who kept his word, assuming there'd been a word. Perhaps the frontier excitement had begun to wear thin. She stopped laughing and drinking with the Aborigines on the street. A wild man in a leather Stetson rammed the back of her jeep for the fun of it, yelled something about her tits, and then drove off. She overdid the sunshine. Things were biting her. As the days went by she was spending more time in the chemist's than on the beach.

And I saw no sign that she was writing.

Only on the final night did she admit she was relieved to be leaving, though she made it sound like a capitulation to me.

'You win,' she said.

We were standing drinking and smoking on the balcony, looking out to the poisonous sea. Poppy stood beside her. Something in her expression seemed to echo that sentiment. *You win*.

Meaning what? That she could hold out against her hellish desire for me no longer? Or was she just pissed again?

28

How Much Did Your Last Book Make?

On the train back from Wilmslow I ran into Garth Rhodes-Rhind, the urban fantasist I'd befriended when he was down on his luck, not knowing where the next penny was coming from, or the next wife, come to that, the previous one having left him for a sixth-form prefect Garth had taught while working as a supply teacher at a comprehensive in Tower Hamlets. It was Garth Rhodes-Rhind who, later in his career and conjugal history, had thrown the 'Launch on a Launch' party on a yacht named *Lulu*.

At the time I met him he was a jobbing thriller writer who couldn't give a book away. We met in the café at the British Library. He introduced himself and told me he was a fan. I didn't believe him. Genuine fans never say 'I'm a fan'. They name your books and tell you why they like them. 'I'm a fan' means I'm a star fucker, means I know your face but don't ask me to know the title of anything you've written. 'So which of my books is it you like?' I asked him.

I didn't actually, but I should have. The trouble is, even when you know what they mean when they say 'I'm a fan', you still like to hear them say it, so seductive is it to be recognised.

He was dark and brooding, overweight and unshaved. Unbathed, too, I thought. Unless it was simply unhappiness I smelt. And of course envy, but then all writers smell of envy.

He wasted no time in getting to the nub of his interest in me. He wanted to know if I was rich.

If I *were* rich.

My mouth fell open. 'Rich? You mean rich already? Born rich? Rich before I lifted a pen?' As though anyone any longer lifted a pen.

No, that wasn't what he meant. He leaned forward and touched the lapel of my jacket. For a moment I thought he intended to feel it. But the gesture was placatory. 'I don't intend any offence by this,' he said.

'Offence?'

For an unembarrassable man, he looked oddly embarrassed all of the sudden. 'I mean I don't wish to stereotype.'

I bridled at stereotype. I'm not sure why.

'Let me rephrase the question,' he said quickly. I expected him to ask me if I were rich in learning or in love. Rich in spirit, rich in the things that mattered. I was wrong. 'How much do you earn per book?' he asked.

My mouth fell open even wider. Wide enough, I thought inconsequentially, to fit a two-bore rifle.

'We'll discuss this when we know each other better,' I said, unable to imagine a time when I would want to know him better than I already did.

But he caught me a few days later. 'Now we're friends,' he said, 'I want to ask you something.'

'Not how much I earn?'

'Bear with me,' he said.

'No,' I said.

The following week he bought me a coffee and a cinnamon pastry without my even asking for it. 'I know this isn't something even good friends are meant to talk about,' he said, 'but writing's a business like anything else, isn't it? I want to know what I'm making these sacrifices for. I'm earning nothing. I'd do better stacking shelves at Waterstones. But will it improve? What can a novelist expect to earn?'

I looked at the cinnamon pastry and sighed. 'Depends on the novelist.'

'I know that, but give me a ballpark figure. How much did your last book make?'

'I don't write thrillers, Garth.'

'Tell me. I'll make the adjustment.'

'How much did yours?'

'Two thousand two hundred and sixteen pounds. There you are, I'm not ashamed to tell you.'

I smiled a wan smile at him. 'That's not a lot,' I agreed.

'And you?'

The truth of it was, I couldn't tell him. The etiquette of discussing royalties with another writer apart, I couldn't upset him. I wasn't exactly coining it in, but I'd have had to be in a bad way not to be doing better than Garth. It would have been heartless to rub his nose in just how much better.

So I lied. 'A bit more than that,' I said.

'How much more? Five thousand?'

I tried to calculate what he could bear to hear. 'A bit more than that.'

'Fifty thousand?'

Where was he on the scale of endurance?

'Not so much.'

We settled in the end on a figure closer to the lower of the figures we'd been discussing. I plucked it from the air. Twenty. Let's say twenty.

Now that we'd got there he looked faintly contemptuous.

233

Twenty thousand pounds! Was that all a book of mine pulled in? I could see he regretted saying he was fan of such a nobody. For a moment I thought he was going to take back what was left of the cinnamon pastry.

It occurred to me to hit the insolent little bastard with the truth and watch his knees buckle, but my humanity prevailed. Three years later I read that he'd changed genres and sold the rights in his new novel to Disney for a million pounds. And that before it was even published. I kept away from the British Library just in case he had bought it, but he got his hands on my telephone number.

'Guy,' he said, 'it's Garth, I guess by now you've heard?'

I wasn't sure how best to play it. Say yes and give him the satisfaction of knowing that I'd been living with the knowledge, or say no and have him tell me.

'I'm busy this minute,' I began.

He didn't hear me. 'A fucking million pounds, and that's before we talk book royalties.'

'I'm pleased for you, Garth,' I said.

'Meet me for lunch,' he said.

'No,' I said.

He did this once a week for three months. 'Meet for lunch,' he'd order.

'No,' I'd say.

Now here we were on a tilting Pendolino together. He'd been in Manchester giving a reading at the university. 'I won't normally talk for under a thousand,' he told me, 'but I make an exception for students.'

I pulled a deprecatory face.

'You think I shouldn't have?'

'No, no. I think you're right to.'

'But?'

'There is no but.'

'I hear a but coming.'

'No, yes, well, I'm surprised you'll take a thousand.'

'Why, how much do you get paid?'

'I'd rather not say,' I said.

'Come on. Fifteen hundred? Two?'

'Five,' I said.

'Five thousand a talk? Christ.'

'Sometimes seven and a half.'

'Jesus.'

'I know,' I said. 'Highway bloody robbery, isn't it?'

He fell silent after that. He pulled a hardback novel out of his briefcase and began self-consciously underlining passages. It was one of his own.

'Good?' I asked him.

'It's my first. No one took any notice then, now it's a bit of a cash cow, to be honest, what with film rights . . .'

I reached over to see the title. *Death of a Dead Man*. 'Haven't read this one,' I said, my voice empty of curiosity.

'I'm surprised,' he said, 'to hear you've read any.'

I smiled at him. 'I haven't,' I said.

Before he could get back to underlining his own prose I asked after Lulu.

'Leaking.'

'I didn't mean the boat, I meant the woman.'

'Also leaking. Leaking my money.'

'Expensive things.'

'Girlfriends?'

'Boats.'

'Amen to that. How's your . . . ?'

He couldn't of course remember her name.

'I don't have a boat. Oh, you mean Vanessa. Blooming. Just finished a novel. Spielberg wants it.'

Before he could ask a question I leaned across and laid a finger on his lips. 'Can't say,' I said.

It was such a good journey back from Wilmslow I briefly forgot all the terrible things Jeffrey had told me.

29

Dying from the Brain Out

I decided to break the news gently to Vanessa.

'My cunt of a brother's got a brain tumour,' I told her.

'Jeffrey?'

'What other cunt of a brother do I have? Jeffrey. Yes. You remember him?' I made a fist and put it to my temples, to suggest a grenade about to go off and blow Jeffrey's brains out.

'Jeffrey! My God!' She opened her eyes wide, did a dramatic actress stagger, collapsed into an armchair and wailed.

I'd read about people wailing but I'd never with my own ears heard a wail. It was the tragic equivalent to Jeffrey's comic 'Ha, ha!'

'Oh, oh!' she said.

It seemed to me I had to pace my responses. And not to offer it as my opinion that the whole thing was just Jeffrey playing dead again to get me into trouble. 'I didn't think you liked Jeffrey,' I said, after a while.

'He was the one who never liked me. But that's not the point. No one in your family did, and I don't wish the poor boy ill.'

Poor boy!

Was that why? Was there someone else's bed he hoped to be carried into, white as his own ghost and winking all the while at me?

And if he was a poor *boy* to Vanessa, what was he to Poppy?

'Is that true that he never liked you? I thought he liked you a lot.'

She didn't rise to that. Gave not a sign.

She wanted to know whether it was malignant. I hadn't asked. I assumed anything that grew in your brain was malignant. Wasn't the brain itself a malignant organ? Wasn't Jeffrey's, at any rate?

'Call him,' I said. 'I'll give you his number.'

She didn't rise to that either.

The news had a profound effect on her. She sat around for days, looking into space, sometimes shaking her head as though in an argument with an unseen foe. She didn't eat. If I wasn't mistaken she even did some writing.

'You'd better get yourself checked over,' she told me.

'Do tumours run in families?'

'Don't ask me. Just do it.'

'I've already got a colonoscopy booked.'

'They won't find a brain tumour looking there.'

'That's what I'm hoping.'

Instead of turning on the radio or putting on headphones or in some other way blocking out the sound of me when she went to bed, she sat up and initiated a conversation. I couldn't remember how long it had been since we'd talked in bed. Talked, not brawled.

'Everybody's dying,' she said.

She sounded so fatalistic I wondered how her mother was. 'Oh, she's fine. She'll go on for ever. She's probably the only one of us that will.'

A thought occurred to me. 'You?'

She dodged the question. I didn't read anything into that. She'd always wanted me to think she wasn't long among the living. And she was a highly suggestible woman. A brain tumour was now just a matter of time.

'What's it for, Guido?' she asked.

'Oh –' I was about to tell her but she interrupted me.

'Apart from the books and the fame, what's it about?'

'Nothing,' I said. 'That's why you have to have the books and the fame.'

She gave me a long, penetrating look. 'Lucky you, then,' she said, 'for having both.'

'And for having you,' I said.

'Oh, me.' She flicked her fingers, as though that was all it would take for her to be gone. Already the tumour had started.

It suited her to be talking about death. Her tears apart, I'd never seen her so blooming. But I decided against rolling on top of her.

The next day – as though in fulfilment of the lie I'd told Garth Rhodes-Rhind – she took up her novel again.

I did the same. But without my alter ego, Little Gidding. Gid the gadfly was, to employ Jeffrey-speak, so over. Jeffrey too, but in another sense entirely. And I could give Jeffrey immortality of sorts, no matter that it wasn't the sort he prized.

He was the way forward for me, anyway. A hero for our times. He went both ways where Little Gid went only one. Jeffrey was dying from the brain out, Little Gid was merely stillborn. And Jeffrey had outraged decency, betraying his brother, perhaps betraying his brother twice over, and in combinations even my imagination had to race to keep up with. Poor Little Gidding, like me, hadn't got beyond popping his tongue down his wife's mother's throat.

Should it all turn out to be the lie I had now convinced myself it was – well, that was even better. Heroes are meant to be liars nowadays. Lying's the great cliché of the novel. Like *story*. Have your hero start his *story* – the false prick – with the promise that everything he tells you is a pack of lies and you'll cream off however many readers are left out there.

The literary lie is what you're reduced to telling when invention is no longer prized, when fact is thought better of than fiction and publishers print the words 'Based on a true story' on the jacket of a popular novel. The literary liar is art's last desperate cry for attention.

Did I really want to go in the direction of the unreliable narrator, when there'd never in the history of literature been a good narration that *was* reliable?

I didn't know what I wanted. I was aflame with possibilities. And I was jealous of Jeffrey, whatever he was up to. Jealous of him for dying. Jealous of him for lying. Jealous of him for not lying. And jealous of him for lying with my wife stroke mother-in-law.

Good. Jealousy works for some men. Especially if they're writers.

My jealousy was inseparable from my renewed creative excitement. I had only to picture Jeffrey with either of the women I loved and before I knew it I had written a chapter. What would happen when I got around seriously to picturing him with both of them God alone knew.

In my dying world, Jeffrey was tomorrow. I had it in my power to write the seamiest novel of an admittedly exceedingly tame century.

I no sooner saw him as my hero than my constipation eased.

30

Murdering Time

A month or so later –

'So that didn't last long,' Francis said.

'It wasn't a good enough idea.'

'Not the idea. Your ma-in-law.'

'Oh, that's still a goer.'

'Pity, I was hoping –'

'Hoping what, Francis?'

But he couldn't even be bothered to frame a lewd suggestion. We were clapped out.

He looked at his watch.

He used to look at his watch every thirty minutes. Now it was every five.

We were lunching in a new club in Soho. Clubs were like authors' magazines – the worse things got, the more of them appeared.

After he'd checked his watch, he checked the room. We were all doing this, looking to see who else was there. Though there was no one whose company we sought, anyone had to be better than the person we were with. We were murdering time. Now was no good. What happened next had to be better. And we'd think the same about whatever happened next, whether or not anything did. Life was some place, some time, some person, else.

And if it still wasn't to be found, it was probably on your mobile phone.

The food the same. Wherever we ate, we discussed the menu of somewhere else. No one on the planet was where he wanted to be, discussing what he wanted to discuss, eating what he wanted to eat. We'd all slipped a cog.

'Do you have another appointment, Francis?' I asked.

'Sorry, sorry, God no. I'm just on edge.'

'Me too.'

This time we both looked around the room. Everyone was on edge. People whom their dining companions didn't want to be with were the object of greedy curiosity, even desire, on the part of people who didn't want to be with whom they were with. We could have played musical chairs. When the music stops you change your life. It didn't matter if you got it wrong. It would turn out shit whoever you chose.

'You know what, Francis?' I said. 'I think we're being prepared for the end of the world. We're being broken gently into hating our lives so that we won't feel too bad about losing them.'

'I don't hate my life.'

I shrugged. I wasn't going to tell him he was in denial.

We sat silently, chewing children's food. Mince and mash. Soon it would be mashed peach and rhubarb.

'So,' Francis said at last. 'You've met Ferber.'

'If you can call it meeting.'

'He's the future, Guy.'

'There is no future.'

'Maybe you're right. But he's the future that isn't.'

'I've just been up to see my brother. He's the future that isn't.'

'I didn't know you had a brother.'

'Jeffrey. He runs the family business.'

'What's the family business?'

'Christ, Francis, I've written about it often enough. Fashion. We have a boutique in Wilmslow.'

'I thought that was fiction.'

'It was fiction, told through the false prism of truth.'

'Then you must be ashamed of it. Why has it only ever popped up incidentally? Why haven't you written the great boutique novel?'

'Good question. I'm writing it now. From my brother's point of view.'

'What's wrong with your own?'

See! Any minute Francis would be asking me to turn it into a memoir. 'Based on a true story.'

'I don't interest myself any more. My brother does.'

'How is he that different from you?'

'Well, for starters, he's gay.'

'Who isn't?'

'Well, *he* isn't. He's both. Plus he's dying. Unless he's not.'

Francis looked around the room. 'I'm sorry,' he said, eyeing off a raddled woman with a deep ravined, wrinkled décolletage. 'Is that what Poppy Eisenhower looks like?' he asked.

'It certainly is not.'

A pale perplexed waitress, from some country even further gone into hating itself than ours, wondered if we'd like to order a dessert. Jelly? Rice pudding? It was a pointless enquiry. We wouldn't like what came. We'd be better ordering something else and not liking that.

Francis, notwithstanding, asked for Bakewell tart with ice cream, custard and double cream. He was very particular about it, as though the order mattered.

The waitress returned to tell him Bakewell tart already came with double cream, so did that mean he wanted double, double cream?

'Yes,' I said for him.

'And two spoons,' Francis added.

'That's not two *more* spoons,' I helped out. 'Just the one that it comes with and then an extra one.'

The waitress nodded and turned on her heel, understanding only that she didn't understand.

'I think I want to write about a degenerate,' I said.

'You *were* writing about a degenerate,' Francis said. 'You're *always* writing about a degenerate.'

'No, I mean the real thing. An actual degenerating person. Someone who fucks men and women, at the same time. Someone who drinks vodka through his eyes. Someone who lies about having a fucking brain tumour. Unless he's telling the truth. In which case he's an even more degenerating person.'

'Is that all?'

'What else is there, Francis?'

'Abuse. Drug-running. Wife-beating. Pimping. Murder. Child rape. Sex tourism.'

'He probably does all that too.'

'In Wilmslow?'

'Why not? The place is full of footballers.'

'Excellent. Make him a footballer.'

'A footballer! Francis, it's all I can do not to make him a French philosopher. I don't think you've grasped what I've been saying. This is going to be a pornographic critique of the pornography of our time, which isn't pornography. The pornography of our time is our failure to admit the pornographic.'

He stared at me and put his fingers together. 'OK,' he said, or rather, 'OKaaay.'

'What do you mean *OKaaay*?'

'I mean good, sounds really interesting, but don't write it just yet.'

'I'm writing it already.'

'OKaaay, but don't finish it just yet.'

'Why shouldn't I finish it just yet?'

'Because I can't sell it just yet.'

'Because?'

'Because the pornography of our time is our failure to admit the pornographic.'

'I just said that.'

'Which goes to show I listen.'

'And when do you think that's going to change?'

'When do you think I'm going to stop listening?'

'No, Francis – when do you think we will once again be able to admit the pornographic?'

He shrugged.

'So what am I supposed to do in the meantime?'

'Fuck your mother-in-law, you lucky so-and-so.'

'For a *living*, Francis.'

He consulted his watch and then looked around the room.

At that moment Vanessa appeared, with Poppy on her arm.

Followed by the waitress with an apple-and-rhubarb crumble, and no cream.

31

Every Living Writer is Shit

Poppy hadn't stayed with us long after our return from Australia.

'I feel like a change,' she'd announced on the third or fourth morning back.

I sneaked a look at her but she didn't sneak one at me.

Vanessa was distraught. 'Ma, you've just *had* a change. You haven't even unpacked your suitcases.'

'Well, that's exactly what I'm thinking. While I'm packed I might as well do it.'

'Do what? You can't just head out into the street. Where are you going to go?'

'I thought the Cotswolds. Stay in a little hotel and see if I can find a cottage somewhere hyphenated to rent for the summer. Do a bit of gardening. It's not for ever.'

('It's just until your overheated husband cools down,' was the sentence I heard next, though she didn't speak it.)

I offered to help her find a hotel but my offer was declined. They would do it together. Without me.

It was like being left by two women simultaneously. 'I'll be back when I'm back,' Vanessa said. 'I'd appreciate it if you didn't turn the house into a brothel while I'm away.'

For the record, I had no history of turning this or any other house I'd lived in with Vanessa into a brothel. I didn't even have a record of bringing women back for tea. If solitude grew too unbearable after a couple of days I would go out, and what I did out was no business of anyone else. I was a writer. I needed to get out sometimes. And I needed to do things that were the business of no one else.

So scrupulous was I in the matter of keeping the outside separate from the inside that I put a distance of a mile between myself and home before ringing Philippa on my mobile. We hadn't spoken since Adelaide, not least as I had other things on my mind, but she had emailed me a couple of times in the immediate aftermath of whatever you call what we had done, and while I hadn't expected to contact her again, the sudden emptiness of my life made speaking to her a matter of necessity. I even wondered, not for the first time, if I'd been in love with her and hadn't known it.

'I find myself on my own,' I said. 'I don't suppose there's any chance of your flying out?'

'I'm in Auckland.'

'I know. Lovely name, Auckland. Come on. Jump on a plane.'

'I don't see it, Guy. How long have you been on your own for?'

I tried to remember. 'Three, four hours.' It had actually been two, three hours, but Philippa wasn't my wife: I didn't owe her the truth.

'And how long are you going to be on your own for?'

Again I thought it was enough to be approximate. 'Three, four days. Could be more.'

'And you want me to fly out to keep you company for that?'

'Well, we had only one night in Adelaide.'

'Yes, but we were both on the spot. Lusten, I don't think I'm up for thuhs.'

'*Thuhs?*'

247

'Helping you through your boredom.'

'You didn't mind in Adelaide.'

'I hadn't realised it was boredom. I thought we were talking luhterature.'

'We could do more of that.'

She fell silent. Then she said, 'Thuhs must be costing you a fortune.'

I knew a brush-off when I heard one. Suddenly I realised I *had* been in love with her. 'I could come to you,' I said.

There was another long pause. Then, 'I don't thuhnk that would be a good idea,' she said.

'Why not? Is there someone else?'

'I have a partner, you know that.'

'And I have a wife. I meant someone else on top of someone else.'

'Suhnce you ask – yes.'

'Another writer?'

It was a silly question. Of course another writer. Like many women who haunted the festival circuit with bags of books over their shoulders, she only did writers.

She remained silent.

'I take that to be a yes,' I said.

'Yes.'

'Anyone I know?'

'You don't *know* him.'

I heard a distinction being made. 'Know *of*, then?'

'It's Maarten.'

'Maarten Noort?'

Maarten Noort was the silent Nobel Prize-winning Dutchman with the pendulous belly.

'Yes, that Maarten.'

'Christ, Philippa! He's twice your age and size.'

'So?'

'He writes novels that are over by the second page.'

'You don't measure language in feet and inches, Guy.'

'He doesn't talk either.'

'He does to me.'

'He's better by phone, you're telling me?'

'We don't talk by phone . . .'

Ah! Now it was my turn to be silent. Ah!

So he was there, perhaps unbuttoning her as we spoke. I listened hard, imagining I could hear the heavy Netherlandish breathing that had transfixed the literati of Adelaide for an hour.

It was a well-beaten path for internationally renowned novelists: Adelaide, Melbourne, Sydney, Auckland, Philippa's bed – Philippa understood metaphorically. Adelaide, Auckland, prose junkie.

I accepted I couldn't have it both ways. I couldn't lament the death of reading and then criticise those who read. At least prose junkies were hooked on prose. But accepting I couldn't have it both ways didn't stop me wanting it both ways.

'He never made it back to his motherland then?'

'I don't know whuht thuht's supposed to mean. He's an international novelist. He travels the world. But yes, he's here wuhth me, if thuht's whuht you're asking.'

Wuhth her. Christ! Considering how recently she'd been *wuhth* me, I felt that we were conjoined in her, Maarten and I.

'So where's your partner while Maarten's *with* you?'

'He's here. He's a great admirer of Maarten's work. I told you we had an open relationshup.'

I wanted to ask about Mrs Noort and how open about her relationship she was, but all things considered I didn't feel I was in a strong position to take the side of wives.

'Well, I hope you'll all be very happy, Philippa,' I said.

'You too, Guy,' she said.

It was the most final goodbye I'd ever been on the receiving end of.

So that was three women who'd left me in the space of three hours.

I can't go more than a day without a woman's company. I'd have rung Mishnah Grunewald had I not heard that she had left the zoo, married a rabbi, and gone off with him to help officiate at a new synagogue in Cracow where Jewish life was said slowly to be returning.

Everyone was having a better time than I was.

Poppy and Vanessa found a nice hotel in Moreton-in-Marsh where they stayed for a week before Poppy moved into a red-tiled cottage with the little garden she was after in Shipton-under-Wychwood.

'She got her hyphens, then,' I said to Vanessa on her return.

'Leave her alone,' Vanessa said. 'If you'd been nicer to her she might not have gone.'

'Did she say that?'

'No, I deduced it.'

'How have I not been nice to her?'

'The way you're not nice to everybody.'

'How's that?'

'By being uncivil. By ignoring people. By being locked away inside your head.'

'That's called writing, Vee.'

'No it's not. It's called being self-fucking-engrossed.'

Since Broome, we hadn't exactly not been getting on, more getting on as we had always got on, only more so.

Now she was back, she blamed me for not allowing her to stay.

'*Allowing!*'

'Encouraging. Facilitating. Don't play word games with me, Guido.'

And now that she was back from the Cotswolds she was charging me with forcing her mother to leave us and go and live in Wychwood-Over-Wherever-It-Was.

I shouldn't pretend to be ignorant of the location. Two weeks after Poppy moved in I was at a symposium in Oxford and halfway through it I lashed out on a taxi to take me to her cottage, the address of which I'd never been given but had found among Vanessa's papers. The village looked as it sounded. Nice. Village green, village church, village pub, village idiots. I could imagine Poppy being very happy there.

With me.

She was in the front garden when I turned up, sitting on a wooden bench, reading shit under a large sun hat with flowers in it. She was wearing silky knee-length batik shorts, which both as a fashionista and a man I considered a mistake, but then I hadn't called to say I was coming. She narrowed her eyes when she saw me but didn't close her book. I decided not to let the taxi go quite yet.

'Just passing,' I said.

'That's a coincidence. Did you just happen to recognise me from the taxi?'

'Something like that.'

'Where are you passing from?'

'Oxford.'

'Where are you going to?'

'Notting Hill Gate.'

'This isn't the way.'

'I know. You couldn't give the driver directions, could you?'

'Tell him to go back to Oxford and start again.'

'A glass of wine before I leave?'

'No.'

'Tea?'

'No.'

'And you don't need me to kill any spiders for you? I would imagine the country is full of them.'

'Definitely not that. I'd rather have them living in my clothes.'

'I'll be going then.'

'Please.'

I tried to sneak a look at what she was reading. Writers do this. They are book-transfixed. They can't see a person reading a book without wondering what it is.

'What are you looking at?'

'Just wanted to see what shit you're reading.'

'Why?'

'Just curious.'

'No you're not. If you were curious you wouldn't call it shit.'

'I'm curious which shit.'

'Well, you'll have to stay curious.' She clasped the book to her bosom like a baby. *My baby, my baby – they want to take my baby!*

'Couldn't I just stay, full stop?'

'No. You can't even just stay, comma.'

'I could be your page turner.'

'I don't need a page turner. This book's so interesting the pages turn themselves.'

'Who's it by?'

'Just someone you think is shit. Vanessa tells me you think every writer is shit.'

'That's not true. Only the live ones.'

'You're a live one.'

'Not for long.'

'Well, this one is a live one and he isn't shit.'

'*He!* You're just trying to hurt me.'

'That's right. Now go.'

'If that's what you really, really want.'

'Please.'

'Really, really, really . . .'

'I beg you.'

She was firm about it, but I chose to look on the bright side. She hadn't told me never to return.

In some part of myself – no, in some parts of myself – I was relieved. The novelist in me needed this to go on indefinitely. An easy conquest was against the interests of a good story. I wasn't mad about plot, but I knew the value of suspense. The moralist in me, in so far as there was one, needed it to go on indefinitely too. Broome was one thing: Broome was off the moral map. But for Poppy to have invited me in and removed her silly shorts in Shipton-under-Wychwood would have thrown me into crisis. Could she really do this to her own daughter? Here in the very heart of England? Did she not know the difference between right and wrong?

Why she hadn't already told Vanessa that her husband was a wretch was a worry to me. Didn't a mother owe that, at least, to her own flesh and blood? Get rid of him, Vanessa, he's rotten to the core, always has been, always will be, just don't ask me how I know.

But the son-in-law in me, the lover and the child in time, ached for consummation. Broome might have been off the moral map but I still longed to be standing on the spider again with Poppy in my arms. And if she had said nothing to Vanessa didn't that mean that she longed to be back there again among the monkeys too?

32

Fetch, Fetch

The subject of the Oxford symposium I'd bolted from was the role of children's literature.

In what?

The education of children?

There *was* no education of children. If there was education of children – if there *were* education of children – there'd be proof of it in educated adults.

But then what did I know? I'd been invited only to be publicly humiliated – an adult sacrifice on the altar of the adolescent paragraph. The *short*, adolescent paragraph.

I'd agreed to participate – half expecting what was going to happen – only in order to have an excuse to check how my mother-in-law was settling in around the corner. Oxfordshire had suddenly become exciting to me.

For their part, the organisers wanted to make a spectacle of me because I'd said something on one of those desperate late-night Radio 3 arts programmes you know nobody is listening to, because you wouldn't be listening to it yourself if you weren't on it, along the lines of my *you'd expect educated children to turn into educated adults, and since there aren't any, there aren't any* point. Where are they now, I'd asked, those avidly literary toddlers who had queued through the night to get their hands on the boy magician? Either still reading about the boy magician or reading nothing.

It demeaned our children, I argued – daring anyone to challenge me on the sanctimony of 'our' on the lips of a person who was, in all but deed, a child murderer – to suppose they needed children's books in order to progress to adult books. What they needed was grown-up literature from the off, with a few concessions made to the areas in which they weren't yet grown. Thus you didn't give them *Tropic of Cancer*. But you did let them know that *Tropic of Cancer* was waiting for them as soon as they'd finished *Wuthering Fucking Heights*.

I couldn't pretend to know what I was talking about. I had no children of my own and didn't mix with people who did. We lived in a child-blind world, Vee and I, and supposed children to be, in the abstract, like us only smaller and messier. 'Not *that* much smaller,' I hear Vee saying, looking me up and down.

But why did I need to know what I was talking about? There was universal agreement that children's writing had never been stronger, and there was universal agreement that anyone under forty was struggling to read anything more demanding than a Tweet. Ergo . . .

I'd also said, in an interview discussing my own early reading – a subject about which I'd been lying for years, pretending I'd read Henry James and Henry Miller at kindergarten – 'Junk anything that addresses the child qua child.'

One of my stroke our favourite words. Not child, qua.

The idea of junking anything that addressed the child qua child had struck the organisers as a usefully fiery starting point for discussion. Hence my invitation.

'How do you propose to do that?' the chairman of the morning session asked me, rubbing his hands. 'Ban them? Burn them?'

'Burn the children?'

'We were wondering if you'd go that far.'

('Why do you detest children, Mr Ableman?')

He was the owner of the children's bookshop in which we were gathered. We were crammed into a stockroom, forty or fifty grown-up children's readers on foldaway metal chairs – I was surprised they weren't high chairs – and the three panel members, of which I was one, arranged around a small card table. On the walls were blown-up photographs of famous children's writers of the past, together with reproductions of the jacket of the chairman's own latest contribution to the genre, a picture book about a dog called Fetch. *Fetch, Fetch*, it was called.

I answered these offensive opening questions, calmly I thought, making the usual writerly noises about being against banning or burning anything – I even invoked the Nazis – though in my heart there was much I'd happily have seen banned or burned, including, as the day wore on, this shop, this event, and everyone attending it.

'Allow me a little rhetorical flourish,' I said, enunciating my words clearly in case the proponents of children's writing were unable to grasp what I, as a writer for adults, meant. 'I am, of course, against censorship of any kind. But we can lead our children into books without condescending to them. John Stuart Mill was reading classical authors in the original Greek and Latin when he was three. I venture to assert that this would not have happened had his father given him, at an early age, *Hairy Hettie and the Bullshit Factory*, or whatever else it is they're reading now.'

I can't say that I was making a good job of getting them to love me. Even Fetch, looking endearingly at his master from every wall – waiting for the call, 'Fetch, Fetch' – now seemed to bare his teeth at me.

One member of the panel made as though to leave, gathering up his rucksack from the floor between his legs – a small urban cyclist's rucksack with Paddington Bear key rings hanging off it – but it turned out he was only searching for a handkerchief.

'If that's an example of your sense of humour I'm not surprised you aren't read by children,' he said, blowing his nose.

I couldn't tell if he was going to lean across and punch me or burst out crying. Tears, I thought, were favourite. Everyone cried now. The world was awash with tears, the literary wasteland more watered with them than any other.

No wonder nothing was growing.

In the end he just blew into his handkerchief a couple more times. Heston, he was called. Heston Duffy.

'How do you know I'm not read by children?' I asked. I had never wanted to be read by children, but suddenly the thought that I wasn't upset me terribly.

'Well, you're not read by mine.'

'Nor mine!' someone in the audience shouted.

Heston Duffy proposed a quick straw poll. Hands up, how many people's children had read anything by Guy Ableman? No hand went up. Then he had a better idea. How many people had themselves read anything by Guy Ableman? Again not a hand went up. He sat back in his chair – an inappropriately grand man for a children's writer, I thought: more like a country solicitor or an auctioneer – and smirked. The smirk did not become him. His face was already too fleshly – not a face I'd have wanted close to a child of mine, had there been a child of mine – and the smirk only added to his unsavoury handsomeness. He wore a crumpled black T-shirt, slightly spotted with water-paint or Play-Doh. His petulant expression reminded me of Victor Mature's in the role of Samson, though I was the one trying to bury the Philistines in the ruin of the Temple.

'What you read or don't read is your lookout,' I said, addressing the audience directly, 'but I am amused by the idea that you think you know what your children read. Do you check under their

257

covers each night? I kept what I read – *Ulysses*, *The One Hundred and Twenty Days of Sodom*, Coleridge's *Table Talk* – secret from my parents. That was the fun of it. Or has the fun gone out of reading now, along with everything else?'

I glowered. They glowered back. Fun? They'd show me fun!

The other panellist was a woman with grey hair tied in a pigtail like a very ancient little girl. She had three silver rings in each nostril and two more in each ear. Her voice was high and fluting, as though not her own. Had a child possessed her? I wondered. She put up a placatory hand as if to calm a mob. I don't know why I say 'as if'. They *were* a mob and she *was* attempting to placate them. 'I'm Sally Comfort,' she said, though she'd already been introduced.

Everybody applauded her for the second time. I clapped for a second time too. So this was Sally Comfort! Another response was available to me: so who the fuck is Sally Comfort?

But that she was a god among the mortals of children's literature there was no mistaking.

'I think I understand what Mr Ableman's getting at,' she went on, smiling at me in a way that would have made me run for the safety of my mummy's skirts had I been a child (and had my mummy not been a whore who wore no skirts). 'I think he's trying to tell us – and I for one don't mind listening, for I am a great admirer of his work, yes, I am – that children must not be written down to. I'm sure I don't need to remind him that John Stuart Mill suffered a nervous breakdown as a young man, which perhaps should make us think again about the style of education he received, but that doesn't detract from the essential point I think Mr Ableman is making, which is that we sometimes ask too little of our children's intelligences and imaginations.'

'Hear hear!' I said, pleased with myself for not rising to the nervous-breakdown bait and saying 'For all you know, half your children will be gibbering wrecks at the same age. And they won't have the advantage of a decent education and an acquaintance with the poetry of Wordsworth to help them out of it.' Instead I applauded Sally Comfort with my fingertips, like a pantomime Chinaman shooing away a mouse.

I imagined blowing in her ear and thanking her for being nice to me.

'Well, certainly no one,' chimed in the chairman, a cheerful drunken-looking man with capacious eye pouches, 'would accuse either of our guest speakers today of asking too little of our children's intelligences or imaginations.'

More applause. Though not, this time, from me.

'Fetch, Fetch,' I thought.

Heston inclined his heavy, handsome head. Sally smiled and rearranged the rings in her nostrils.

I imagined blowing up her nose.

There was then a moment of silence in which it became clear that I was expected to pick up Sally Comfort's thread and run somewhere with it. Wychwood-Over-Shipton, I was thinking, sneaking a look at my watch.

It would have helped had I known anything about the books Heston Duffy and Sally Comfort had written, but once you've decided there is a virtue in arguing out of ignorance you have to stick with it.

'I guess the question has to be asked,' I began, digging deep into the manual of writerly bluff, 'whether quite so many wizards, daemons and other mythical creatures with pseudo-Icelandic names are necessary to stimulate the imaginations of the young. Are we not, when it comes to children –' though how the fuck I knew, would have been a fair response – 'too quick to assume that imagination equals fantasy, that –'

259

'Not in my case,' Heston interrupted. 'My hero Jacko is no wizard. He is an ordinary boy born in Sussex who becomes a soldier of fortune fighting in many of the world's most terrible war zones. There is nothing fantastical –'

'Hang on,' I said. 'You say he is a *boy* soldier of fortune. How old is he exactly?'

'Well, he ages from book to book. But he is nine when he first bears arms.'

'Nine? Doesn't that make him a fantasy figure?'

Heston looked as though he couldn't decide between flattening me and weeping again. 'There are parts of the world where children even younger than that are conscripted.'

'Yes, I know that. But Jacko is a soldier of fortune born in Sussex, you say, where as far as I know they don't have conscription. If this isn't fantasy, it is surely the wildest fancy.'

'Not a word anyone would use of your novels, Sally,' the drunken-faced chairman said.

'No, indeed. The book I am working on now, for example, is the last in what I call my Chlamydia Series –' she laughed – 'in which teenage girls are taught the dangers of casual sex. It's a matter of great concern to me that so many girls think sex is safe so long as they don't go the whole way, if they stop at oral sex, for example.'

She nodded her head as she spoke, as though in complete, if surprised, agreement with herself.

'That sounds more like a medical treatise than a novel,' I said.

She laughed again, this time at a higher register than I'd suspected the human voice capable of reaching. 'The last thing I aim to be is didactic,' she fluted. 'Ask the children who devour my books.'

I wanted to ask whether devouring her books might not carry as many dangers for a young girl as devouring semen, but decided against.

'The important thing,' Heston said, returning to himself, 'is not where your story is set. It doesn't matter in the slightest whether it's in a mixed comprehensive in Banbury or on a battlefield in Bosnia. What matters is that children are able to recognise themselves.'

'*Identify*, you mean,' I put in.

You don't bring irony – even steamroller irony – to a symposium on the role of children's literature. You bring innocence or you're a dead man.

'Yes,' Heston agreed. 'Learn to see themselves in foreign situations.'

'Or to see themselves differently in only too familiar ones,' Sally added.

'But isn't the whole point of reading,' I asked, 'to take you far away from what you know about yourself already, to send the mind out on a wonderful journey of discovery? Shouldn't a child's imagination be fed by all that's alien to it?'

(Maternal spit-roasting in Wilmslow, for instance.)

'Fantasy, you mean,' Heston said, laughing horribly. 'The very quality you decry.'

'I think he has you there,' the author of *Fetch, Fetch* said.

And that's when you know you definitely are a dead man – when someone says 'he has you there', no matter that the little bastard doesn't have you here, there or anywhere else.

The audience applauded his knockout blow and threw their heads back with spiteful laughter, showing me their scarlet throats. Another enemy of the child sent packing with a bloody nose. Had I rolled off the platform they'd have gathered round and kicked my brains out.

And left them for Fetch to fetch.

33

Read Me, Read Me, Fuck Me, Fuck Me

'So *you're* Poppy Eisenhower,' Francis said, taking her hand.

'What's with the *so*?' Vanessa asked.

What's with the *you're*? I wondered.

They kissed. Francis and Vanessa, I mean. They had always got along well. For Francis, Vanessa was a means of relating to me without the strain of having to relate to me, and for Vanessa, Francis was the opportunity to do something similar. They gave each other a holiday from the person without whom they would not have known, or had any need to know, each other. They flirted, is another way of describing the manner in which they got along. So Vanessa could, without intending much by it, charge Francis with taking too great an interest in her mother. But I was still alarmed. I didn't want Francis, in his excitement, to show how much he knew.

'*So* as in *so* why haven't I met her before,' Francis said.

'Because I want to keep you to myself,' Vanessa said.

The women joined us at our table.

'I promise you I had no idea you were going to be here,' Vanessa hissed at me. She felt that finding me here put her in the wrong, and so blamed me for it.

I told her it was all right. We had finished talking business. And it was nice to see her out with her mother for the first time in many months. Indeed, nice to see her mother after such a long sequestration in the country.

Poppy greeted me with just sufficient affability not to arouse suspicion. Francis's company appeared to intoxicate her, which reminded Vanessa, lowering her voice – 'No, *Maman*, you promised, remember. Not at lunchtime.'

'Oh!' Poppy waved her daughter's fussiness away and accepted Francis's suggestion of a mojito.

They'd been out shopping at Abercrombie & Fitch together.

'Buying T-shirts or ogling young men with bare chests?' I asked.

Francis didn't pick up the allusion. 'It's a shop at the Royal Academy end of Savile Row,' I informed him, pointing to the soft-porn carrier bags the women had pushed under the table. 'It's for tourists, the gullible, and women of a certain age willing to queue for hours to get a look at pretty boys with their tops off.'

Jeffrey, I was thinking.

'Sounds good to me,' Francis laughed.

'What's this "women of a certain age"?' Poppy wanted to know.

'Don't rise to him, *Maman*,' Vanessa said. 'He's just jealous.'

'Of pretty boys with hairless chests?'

Jeffrey.

'Of the business they do. There were no queues outside Wilhelmina's that I remember.'

I saw a queue. Where? In my mind's eye, Horatio. In my mind's eye I saw my wife and her mother queuing to be let into Jeffrey's attentions.

Francis wanted to see what they'd bought. There followed some horseplay with leggings and skimpy knit tanks and camis, Francis saying, now to my wife, now to her mother, that he wouldn't mind seeing her in *that*.

'Hold that one up to yourself. God, yes, I can see why you bought it. Now you, Poppy.'

I eyed the three of them narrowly. Francis beside himself. Vanessa holding up a striped Henley top to go with a little floral skirt. Poppy a rose-covered sundress with cross-back straps, dancing her shoulders behind it like a girl.

Were the two women capable of wooing a man so to speak in tandem? Were they able to flirt as a team? Foolish question. Capability didn't enter into it. Flirting as a team was what they did. It was their thing. It was, now I came to think of it, what they'd done in the course of wooing me.

A dreadful thought descended on me: what if I was the only man out there who *hadn't* enjoyed them in concert?

'So how do you spend your days?' Francis asked, looking Poppy in the eye.

I was interested to hear the answer. My mother-in-law had not returned to the bosom of her loving family as she'd originally promised she would. She had stayed in Shipton-under-Wychwood. She came up to see Vanessa frequently, so that they could go shopping or to a concert on each other's arm, and Vanessa regularly visited her, or *said* she visited her, but our hot little unspoken pact of togetherness was broken. I saw her rarely, and on my own had seen her only on two further occasions after the day of the murderous symposium on children's literature – one comment-worthy, one not.

How did she spend her days? 'Oh, doing this and that,' she answered, already halfway to being drunk.

'*This* being?'

'Gardening.'

'And *that* being?'

'More gardening.'

'No cello?'

I glared at Francis.

Poppy glared at me.

Vanessa glared at Poppy.

Francis smiled at us all.

'Music's fucked,' I said.

'How do you reckon that is?' Francis wanted to know.

'He thinks everything's fucked,' Vanessa said.

I mouthed the words 'You included and I know by whom' at her.

I saw Poppy trying to lip-read. 'And you,' I'd have added had I dared.

'He thinks everything's fucked,' Vanessa went on, 'because the world suits him that way. A fucked world explains Guido to Guido.'

'Who's Guido?' Francis asked.

'It's my wife's pet name for me,' I told him.

'That's nice. Do you have a pet name for her?'

'Two-timing bitch of a whore,' I said. But the words came out as 'Vee'.

'And you?' he asked, turning to Poppy.

'Do I have a pet name for my son-in-law?'

'No, do they have a pet name for you?'

'Popsicle.'

Vanessa and I had never been more together. 'We do *not* call you that.'

'My second husband called me Popsicle.'

'Mr Eisenhower?'

'Yes. And I called him Toblerone.'

'Because?'

'Because his family was Swiss.'

I saw Francis shaping up to do something with the idea of not minding her taking a bite out of his bar.

'No, Francis,' I said.

265

'No what?'

'You know what.'

'I was just going to ask your lovely mother-in-law whether she'd object to my calling her Popsicle.'

Poppy fanned her face with her hands as though all this gallantry had made her hot. 'If you like,' she said.

I examined Vanessa's expression to see if she was/were jealous. A mother is meant to give way and leave the field clear for her daughter. But Poppy was still on active service. Was that bound to be the way of it now that women had discovered how not to age: were mothers and their daughters doomed to slug it out until one of them was finally pitched, made-up and manicured, into the unresponsive earth?

And did this explain why Poppy hadn't blown the whistle on me? Because all was fair now between the generations?

Vanessa was aware of my scrutiny. 'I hope you don't think,' she said in a quiet voice, though with Francis and Poppy hugger-mugger there was no need of one, 'that I came here deliberately to sabotage your lunch.'

'Why would I think that?'

'Because you usually think ill of me.'

I felt sorry for her suddenly, mistrusted by me, eclipsed by her mother. 'I don't usually think ill of you at all,' I said, patting her hand. 'I think well of you.'

She opened her palm so that I could slip mine into it.

'I do, however, think ill of my brother,' I said.

She didn't move a muscle. 'You shouldn't,' she said. 'He's ill enough already.'

'Will my thinking make him worse?'

'You know my theory of illness.'

I did. Vanessa's theory of illness was that illness was all in the head – in your own head or in the heads of others. You made yourself ill if you wanted to be ill and other people made you ill if they wanted you to be ill, and your being ill explained everything you did. In this way we were all entirely innocent of our actions while being entirely to blame for them.

'And you?' I asked.

'Me what?'

I turned my face into a blazing interrogation mark. 'How are you?'

'In relation to what?'

'In relation to everything. In relation to me, in relation to Jeffrey, in relation to life.'

'How do you think I am? Ill.'

'Your illness being specifically what?'

She didn't hesitate. 'Erotomania.'

I looked around the room and made a sign suggesting she keep her voice down. Not that anyone was listening, least of all Francis and Poppy who were trapped like baby rabbits in the headlights of their tipsy fascination.

'I hadn't realised it had gone that far,' I said.

'You hadn't realised what had gone that far?'

'You. I hadn't realised *you* had gone that far. You and –'

'I'm not talking about me. You're the erotomaniac.'

'Me? An erotomaniac? I barely have a sex drive when I'm writing, as you know.'

'I know the theory, Guido. Words drive out longing. But they don't in your case. In your case words *are* longing. They sit up and beg for it. Read me, read me, fuck me, fuck me.'

I slapped my forehead in exasperation. 'How has this got back to me? I thought we were discussing your illness.'

'You *are* my illness.'

'*I'm* your illness? Well, that's convenient for you, Vee. Convenient for Jeffrey, too. So does it follow that you're *my* illness?'

'How can my illness not be your illness if it was your illness to begin with?'

Was it because I'd slapped my forehead that my brain suddenly felt very tired? But I tried to stay on track. 'So it was my illness that made you sleep with Jeffrey?'

'Who said I slept with Jeffrey?'

'All right, I get it. You gave him one of your famous spur-of-the-moment blow jobs.'

'Did he say that?'

'No.'

'What did he say?'

'He didn't. He just stared in a particular way.'

'A way that made you think I blew him? What did he do – puff out his cheeks?'

'The details aren't important, Vee.'

'Then why are we having this conversation?'

'Christ – Jeffrey's my brother.'

'Ah, family now! Since when did you care about things like that? You're unconventional, remember. You're a novelist, a free spirit. The Wilmslow Debauchee.'

'It's not a matter of what I care about. Didn't *you* care about *things like that*?'

'Me? I'm third in this pecking order. There's you, and you don't care. There's Jeffrey, and he has certainly never cared. That's the blood is thicker than water part of it dispensed with, and then there's me – no blood relation to either of you.'

'Wife, Vee? Wife!'

'Oh – *wife*! What about husband, Guido, *husband*?'

'Meaning?'

We had been holding hands throughout this. Only now did she release mine. 'Meaning, Guido, whatever you want it to mean.'

An indirect answer to what had been, no matter how colourful my language, essentially indirect questions. I'd charged her with sleeping with Jeffrey but then again I hadn't. You have to be blunt when it comes to getting to the truth of a suspected infidelity. Do you or didn't you? When did you? Where did you? How often did you? How much did you enjoy it? When are you planning to do it next? Anything less and you let the person you believe to have betrayed you off the hook. You talk dirty but you don't get the answers you are looking for, assuming answers are in fact what you are looking for.

You expect the accused to prevaricate, but why would the accuser do the prevaricating for her? Because directness was not in my nature or my profession. Actually to ask my wife when and where and how often would have been too crude. To intimate suspicion was one thing, to demand an explanation another. I was a novelist: I didn't want an explanation, I wanted a spiralling narrative of uncertainty, nothing ever known for sure, the story going on for ever. It's why I don't read whodunnits. I take no satisfaction in knowing who dun it. A mystery capable of being solved isn't what I call a mystery.

Whereas Jeffrey and Vanessa, Jeffrey and Poppy, Jeffrey and Poppy *and* Vanessa . . .

Ah! Or rather, Ah?

The interrogative mark beating the exclamatory any time.

Was Vanessa's saying I could take her to mean whatever I wanted her to mean her way of showing that she knew about me and Poppy? Had Jeffrey been her quid pro quo?

But if it was a quid pro quo that barely seemed to matter to her, did Poppy and I not matter to her either?

Or was the whole performance simply to put me off the scent of the real crime, which was Jeffrey and Poppy? And if so, why? Who or what was she protecting? Her mother's reputation? My feelings?

A crazed thought sought brief shelter in my disordered mind. Vee loved me, Vee knew about me and Poppy, Vee understood – I was a writer: Vee got that – but I was also a man, and Vee didn't want to see that man hurt.

See the advantage of having nothing ever spelt out clearly? See what vast territories of outrageous speculation it leaves you free to roam?

I must have been mouth-writing again because Vanessa said, 'Planning a book about it, are we?'

'No,' I lied. 'Why don't you write it, since you know so many more of the details?'

'Who's to say I'm not?'

I stared at her. She threw her head back, showing me her throat, laughing like a temple prostitute. It worked with me every time. Had she done that more often I might have thought about her mother less.

'What do you mean *who's to say I'm not*?'

'You ask why don't I write about it, I reply who's to say I'm not writing about it – whatever the "it" is.'

'Well, you should know what the "it" is if you're writing about it?'

'One thing's for certain, Guido – my "it" won't be your "it" .'

We'd been here a thousand times. I'm writing, I'm not writing. I've started, I've not started. I'm writing about this, I'm writing about that, mind your own fucking business what I'm writing about. So what made it different now? I couldn't have said. It just felt different. I'd been asked once why I didn't write crime, since crime writing was where it was at. Because, I'd answered, I wasn't interested in crime, I was interested in punishment. So was this the punishment I'd been expecting, the punishment it could be said I deserved – Vanessa finally with the wind in her sails, Vanessa victrix?

'Been keeping a little diary?' I asked. Insulting of me. But bravado was at work. The bravado of a drowning man, waiting for his punishment. Some might say inviting his punishment, for every truly moral man is a masochist.

'Think that if you like.'

It worried me that she hadn't called me a patronising prick. It worried me how sweet-tempered she was being.

'So come on – writer to writer – what have you been writing?'

She looked me directly in the eyes, hers as wild as the stars that fell from the skies over Monkey Mia. 'What's sauce for the goose, Guido.'

That meant only one thing in our house.

'A novel? Don't tell me you're writing an unchaste novel about my family?'

'Why would it be unchaste?'

'Just a feeling I have.'

'And why shouldn't it be unchaste anyway? You're always writing unchastely about mine.'

'That's not true. I have never written about your family unchastely or otherwise. Anyway, you don't have a family, apart from Poppy.'

'It's true if one knows how to read you, and I know how to read you.'

I didn't rise to that. If she thought what I'd written so far was improper, she should get inside my head. Or was that her point: that she *was* inside my head? Unless she'd stolen a look at what was on my computer. But in that event she wouldn't be here, toying with me now.

'Never mind mine,' I said, moving quickly on. 'Where are you with yours? You'd written one line when we last discussed it. "Gentle reader, get fucked!" I recall asking you to reconsider that as an opening.'

I wasn't exaggerating. *Vanessa*, the novel was called. *Vanessa* by Vanessa. And so did it begin. 'Gentle reader, get fucked!' If that's how she began, I could see why she had so much trouble finishing.

'Not so,' she said. 'It was "Gentle reader, up yours." Subtly different, I think. It's you that's been fucking off readers for years.'

'Vee, there are no readers.'

'That's because you've fucked them off.'

'So how have you begun this time?'

'Ah!' she said, pursing her lips. It was as though I'd asked the temple prostitute to quote for the cost of an hour naked in her company. 'You'll know soon enough.'

She wanted me to be frightened, and I was.

'How far have you got?'

Nothing. Just the inscrutable sacred harlot smile.

'Shown any of it to anyone?'

Still nothing. I couldn't afford her, that was what her look meant. Her services were too high class for the likes of me.

I waved a dismissive hand at her. 'I'll believe it when I see it, Vee.' But then remembered that I loved her. 'I want to believe it.'

She was still laughing. Both of them were still laughing – Poppy at Francis's jokes, Vee at me. 'Then prepare to be pleased for me,' she said. 'I even have a title.'

My turn to say 'Ah!' I knew Vanessa's titles. 'Don't tell me,' I said, '*Why My Husband Guy Ableman is an Opinionated Prick.*'

She shook her hair as though loosening the snakes entwined and knotted in it.

'You, you, you. There are some things, Guido, that have nothing to do with you.'

I didn't believe that either.

34

Life's a Beach

A week later she asked me to leave the house. Not for ever. And not the whole time. Just during daylight hours.

We'd been through this before. 'I can't hear myself think with you banging at those keys,' was her usual complaint. Normally I closed my door and took no notice. We lived in a three-storey house with an attic and a basement after all. And I was in the basement. But this time she had stormed into my room with her eyes wild and her fingers extended like an animal's claws. It wasn't for myself I feared, but for her. 'I'm begging you,' she had cried. I thought she would hurl herself at my feet. 'Give me my turn.'

I offered to soundproof my room, to pack the door with bedding, to suffocate my keyboard with the softest swansdown pillow I could find. 'I'll type through the feathers,' I promised.

But that wasn't enough.

'I need you out of the house from eight to eight,' she said. 'It's not just the noise of your fucking computer, it's the sight of you mouth-writing in the kitchen, it's the atmosphere of you all around me, it's the *idea* of your presence. If you're in the house I can't function. You take up all the creative space, you clog the magnetic field, you gluttonise the airwaves, Guido.'

I had no answer to that.

If Vanessa wanted me out that badly, I owed it to her to go. It wasn't going to be for long. I knew Vanessa. The moment she got the silence she craved she'd write a sentence – 'Gentle reader, sit on this!' or something similar – and then start polishing the silver or self-harming. I estimated that after two paragraphs she'd be finding ways of letting me know it was all right for me to return. Not in so many words, of course – Vanessa didn't do retractions. But she'd text me, wondering if I could order her an ambulance, or reminding me of a dinner party we were throwing (this would be the first I'd heard of it), to discuss the menu for which we needed to meet. And in bed at night she'd announce that writing was an overhyped activity, couldn't understand why I enjoyed it, and was thinking of taking up yoga or the tango.

Maybe even offer me a blow job if it would stop me writing.

But between the Vee-victrix tone of our conversation in Soho and the new Clytemnestra-like desperation with which she'd stormed my sanctuary, there was no room for any doubt. She was started and she intended to finish.

I thought about decamping to the London Library, before deciding that the bookish spell it invariably cast was inappropriate to the novel I was hatching. That consideration hid another: in the London Library you ran the risk of running into a writer – as like as not a writer of imaginative non-fiction – for whom things were going well. I had high hopes for my new novel, provisionally entitled *Terminus*, with *Trickster* as a fallback, the trickster in question being my brother Jeffrey, a sexually demented anti-hero with a timebomb in his head – his tumour the perfect metaphor for literature in our time: irresponsible, self-defeating, self-delusional, eating away at the brain of the culture. I'd found a phrase in Georges Bataille that suited my mood and explained to me what I was writing. 'Impious disturbance'. Jeffrey was that impious disturbance. He disturbed *me*, anyway. So I didn't want my confidence rocked by some unlucky encounter.

An alternative to the library was turning up at Poppy's cottage with my laptop under my arm, though I wasn't sure of the welcome I'd receive and, besides, Vanessa would probably view that as my still gobbling up her airwaves. Furthermore, I wasn't at all sure how things stood between us, not having seen or spoken to her for a while. The meeting in Soho hardly constituted seeing her or speaking to her. Poppy was a person you needed to see on her own to get the best of her.

So I took a room above a shop selling fifties kitsch on Pembridge Road, just a two-minute walk from home. I liked the feel of it – an old storeroom which I fitted out with a cheap desk and chair from a second-hand furniture emporium round the corner and an anglepoise reading lamp from the shop below. It suited the mood of the novel, or maybe it would be truer to say it suited how I felt about writing it – rough and ramshackle, on the edge, with nowhere else to go. This was it. The terminus.

Not impossibly, if Vanessa kept me away longer than I credited her with the patience for, I'd bring a woman back – not for sex, or at least not to satisfy any sexual cravings I had (I couldn't speak for the woman), but because bringing a woman back to a writer's room shorn of all but the most basic amenities would confer a degree of existential futility on my endeavour. Jeffrey was a colourful, impious fantastic who drove a car that was too fast for anywhere he was able to drive it and wore designer clothes so up to the minute that even I hadn't heard of the designer, but when I imagined him with Vanessa or Poppy in any combination I saw a room like this, desperate and secretive. Perhaps that was because I could only understand the women's motives for cohabiting with him as a sort of slumming. They had me for the high life. Through me they met twisted journalists, writers at the end of their tether, agents running rapidly to seed, suicidal publishers. I took them to literary festivals on yachts. I showed them the world. How else, but for me, would they have ever got to Monkey Mia?

Whereas Jeffrey Intracranial Neoplasm – what did he have to offer?

Nothing but the squalor of the provincial which no amount of fashionable bribery – I imagined him showering them with gifts of an intimate nature from Wilhelmina's, sliding his hands up the stockings he'd bought them – could alleviate.

So I wouldn't have been lying had I told Vanessa that things were proceeding very nicely on the writing front, thank you for asking, that my shabby room conduced to the very feelings I was seeking to inhabit. But I was happy to return if she was missing me. The only trouble was, she wasn't. Day followed day, week followed week, and still Vanessa didn't sue for my return, didn't text me to ring an ambulance, didn't once refer in bed at night to the tedium of writing, didn't bring up the tango. Nor did she proffer a diversionary blow job. I wasn't so wrapped up in my own work as not to notice that for the first time since we'd met she was wrapped up in hers. Sleeping soundly. Singing in the shower. And not blaming me for anything.

I wrote, she wrote. I had no idea how close to finishing she was. I wouldn't have put it past her to have finished long ago – 'Gentle reader, kiss my arse. *Finis*' – and not have told me. She would choose her moment. Keep me waiting and then let me have it full in the face. Perhaps at our favourite restaurant – though all restaurants were our favourite restaurants – over a bottle of Saint-Estèphe. Perhaps in bed. Perhaps at the very moment when our fractious individuality was dissolved and we became as one. Who could say – maybe we'd make a baby and name it after her novel. *Why My*

Husband is a Prick. Not much of a name for a baby but I could offer nothing better. *Terminus* – I didn't think so, as I'd heard people say on television.

I wrote, she wrote. It was becoming a test of nerve. Whose would be the first to snap?

Mine, of course. But it was not the doing of Vanessa.

'It's not exactly holiday reading, is it?'

The author of this impious disturbance was Flora McBeth. Sixth-sensed Flora knowing to a nicety the best time to strike. Just as my fluency was beginning to falter in the face of Vanessa's inscrutable confidence in her own – I'm not saying you can't have two productive writers in a relationship, only that it takes some getting used to; nor am I saying I begrudged Vanessa her productivity, only that it was beginning to unnerve me – Flora called me in to break the news that she was putting all my back list out of print.

I saw the irony of it at once. There wouldn't be two productive writers in our relationship. There would be just the one. And it wouldn't be me. In my mind's eye I made out the long line of readers queuing to get Vanessa's signature, a line that stretched out like Bunyan's pilgrims waiting to cross the River of Death into the Beautiful City.

And I? Well, I could always take tango lessons.

Though that wasn't how Flora sold it. By Flora's reasoning, being out of print was an advantage every author should welcome.

'How so, Flora?'

'Well, it's not like the old days,' she said, 'when no back list meant no you. Now we have print-on-demand.'

'And what's the advantage of that?'

'With print-on-demand, darling, anyone who wants one of your books can go on the Internet to get it run off and have it in their sticky little hand in a matter of days.'

'But anyone who wants one of my books now can go into a bookshop and have it in their sticky little hand there and then.'

'Not if you're out of print, darling.'

'Then keep me in print.'

If it sounded as though I was begging, that was because I was begging.

'But then we couldn't print you on demand.'

'But then I wouldn't need to be printed on demand.'

'Darling, there's no particular virtue in being in print. It just means being in the warehouse. It doesn't mean being *out* there. You say anyone who wants one of your titles can go into a bookshop and buy it, but when did you last see any of your titles *in* a bookshop?'

I racked my brains.

'Precisely,' Flora said. 'Whereas this way –'

'– no one will ever again go into a bookshop to look. At least when you're there someone might find you while they're looking for someone else.'

'But they can't find you if you're not there.'

She made it sound like my fault.

Before I could remind her it was hers, she said, 'Darling, I'm going to tell you what I tell all my non-celebrity authors – you have to stop thinking in terms of *in print*. *In print* is so yesterday.'

'What's so today?'

Her answer was in her look. 'Not you,' her face said.

She was wearing the clothes of someone half her age, and even on such a person they would have looked desperate: silky black leggings with a little floral skirt, boots and a sort of weightlifter's singlet. The strange thing was, the desperation made her desirable.

Would it have helped, I wondered, had we slept together? It crossed my mind to ask. 'Would it have helped, Flora, had we . . .'

I was sorry that we hadn't. Not just sorry professionally, but sorry personally. Though I didn't like her, and knew she didn't like me, I felt that I had missed out on a strange and rare experience. An act of cohabitation based entirely on loathing that would have tested my mettle as a man. Or as something other than a man. When I thought about it – and, gentle reader, I didn't think about it often – I saw myself taking her as an ape might, from behind, with my teeth in her neck and my claws in her belly. Quickly. Out of pure hate. In and then out and then in and then finish. And then looking round to see if anyone had tossed us in a banana.

Except that monkeys, Mishnah told me, don't fuck out of hate. Only *Homo sapiens* fucks out of hate. Only *Homo sapiens* has the developed consciousness that can make hate such a powerful aphrodisiac that there is no going back afterwards to love, sweetness, gentle caresses, cigarette smoke and soft music. So monkeys don't know what they're missing.

Did Flora, in her hyperconsciousness, feel the same? That hate would take us somewhere so overwhelming that it would finish us off for anything else?

It must have been imagining this that made me tell her, as a sort of post-coital gift, what I was working on. As a rule you don't talk about a novel until it's done. It brings bad luck. But sometimes, out of a superabundance of self-belief, or more usually a deficiency of it, you take the risk. Give it a little airing, see how it goes down, return to your desk heartened by the interest.

As far as publishing etiquette went – an oxymoron if ever there was one – Flora wasn't the first port of call. First you go – or rather your agent goes – to your hardback publisher, then he seeks what's laughably called 'paperback support' before he makes his offer.

'Offer' being another laughable expression. The book passes to Flora to be put out of print only after it has languished for a year as a hard-back, supposing anyone, that's to say Sandy Ferber, is prepared to 'offer' on it at all. These days none of us could be sure.

I suppose I must have thought that if I could enthuse her about Jeffrey and his metaphorical tumour, Jeffrey the lover of his broth-er's wife and mother-in-law, Jeffrey the son of a spit-roast mother, Jeffrey who drank vodka through his eyes, she would remember what I was good at – my famous louche-light touch, as they referred to it on Amazon – and keep all earlier examples of it in print, no matter that in print was passé.

'It's not exactly holiday reading, is it?' she said, interrupting what there was of plot.

'Not exactly what?'

'Beach reading – reading for the beach.'

'Should it be?'

'Well, that's the only place people read now.'

'I've never read a book on a beach in my life,' I said.

I found a scab behind my ear and began picking at it.

She looked me over. I was wearing a black suit. I always went to see my publishers in a black suit. As a mark of respect, I thought. It's always possible there was some unconscious funereal associa-tion too. But I wouldn't have let the black suit stop me taking her as a primate would. Zip down. In, out. Zip back up.

And the pair of us lost to any other sort of happiness for ever.

'Well, I can see that you aren't the beach type,' she said. 'Have you ever actually been on a beach?'

'To walk,' I said. 'And when I was little to collect seashells and make sandcastles. New Brighton. Blackpool. But I haven't as a grown man sat on a beach with a book.'

'Then you don't know what you're missing.'

Like the monkeys.

She stretched back in her chair, lithe and muscular, simultaneously old enough and young enough to be her own granddaughter, as though to show me what else I was missing. There were tussocks of black hair under her arms, like the growths you see in the ears and nostrils of elderly dark-skinned men who are too busy or serious to bother about removing them. But it wasn't seriousness Flora McBeth was showing me I was missing, it was the spirit of play.

I wondered what would happen if I dropped to my knees and nuzzled my face into these dark spaces beneath her arms. Would she keep me in print?

It was faint-heartedness that stopped me, not distaste. I would have liked to communicate that to her, tell her about Poppy, make it clear that I found older women far more attractive than younger ones, but affirmations of non-fastidiousness never come out right. 'An old body holds no terrors for me' would have been an honest account of my erotic principles, but I could hear it being taken in the wrong spirit.

'So what's the quality people look for in beach reading, Flora?' I asked instead. I had a feeling that I had torn the skin behind my ear and that it was bleeding.

'Readability, darling, what else?'

'And what is that exactly?'

'Readability?'

'Yes.'

She brought her arms down and laid her hands flat on the table. The tussocks of black hair were mine to admire no longer. I was undeserving.

'If you don't know what readability is, darling,' she said, as though this might be the last conversation we would ever have, 'you are beyond help.'

*   *   *

On the way out of her office I bumped into – actually banged against – Sandy Ferber, wearing the expression of a man whose entire family had just been wiped out in a tsunami. He chose not to recognise me. When I say 'chose' I mean more than made a quick, instinctive mental decision. I mean chose from his soul, chose as though his genes had been deciding to take no account of mine for however many millions of years they'd been gestating in the womb of humanity.

I didn't exist for him. Person to person, I could have dealt with that. I sometimes wondered whether I had ever existed for my mother. And Poppy was beginning to let me know that I didn't exist for her either. But writer to publisher, this was hard to swallow. Without being fancy about it, to publish is to bruit abroad, to proclaim publicly, to achieve notice for. Flora had made the word publish mean its very opposite. To be published by Flora was to be put out of circulation, made secret, obliterated. Flora's outstanding achievement was to win obscurity for her writers, many of whom had been celebrated before she got to work on them. But Sandy Ferber's ignoring of me went further: in Sandy's eyes I was not even there to be expunged. I was non-app man. The wordy past.

He too wore a black suit, but where mine was a mourner's, his was the deceased's. In reality this did not reflect our professional relationship: *he* had been hired to bury *me*. But his bones rattled when I banged against him, and I still had flesh on mine.

On the spot I decided to cast my vote for life. I would leave Scylla and Charybdis. Had I been bolder I'd have left the day Merton shot himself. You have to know when the writing's on the wall. I felt light-headed. New book, new publisher. The world lay all before me.

I called in to say goodbye to Margaret.

'I've had it, Margaret,' I said.

To my astonishment she knew exactly what I meant. Were all Merton's authors doing this? Was I the last?

She came from behind her desk and put her arms around me. Strange to say, I smelt Merton on her. I didn't doubt that they had done this countless times. 'I've had it, Margaret,' he would come in and say, and she would get up from behind her desk and put her arms around him.

So had they been lovers?

The question was irrelevant. I knew what she felt. She felt she had failed him. 'I've had it, Margaret,' he had said, and she had not taken the full measure of what it meant, not understood what desperation the man-haters and the word-haters drove him to. And so she was trying not to make the same mistake with me. 'I've had it, Margaret,' I said, and in silence she held on to me for dear life.

35

Too Late for the Apocalypse

New book, new publisher.

Light-headed, did I say I felt? Optimism doesn't last long in my business. New book, new publisher was all very well, but what if the book took longer to finish than I hoped; and what if, by the time I had finished, there were no publishers left to publish it?

Needing to see Francis urgently and the day being mild, I strode in the direction of his office, bought an unnecessarily complex cappuccino from a nearby Carluccio's, sat outside with it and, knowing that Francis didn't like anyone dropping in on him unexpectedly, rang his number. His line was permanently engaged. As like as not disconnected so that no one could get through to him. In my self-absorption I hadn't noticed that Ernest Hemingway was sitting two tables away from me, writing. One unwashed testicle was visible through his ripped trousers. It lay on his seat like an exotic fruit that had fallen off his plate.

Antonio Carluccio, the mushroom king, had long ago sold his chain of inexpensive Italian restaurants – how did I know that? because chefs and restaurateurs are the inverse of writers: people know about them and love them – but that still didn't make this branch a hang-out for dossers. The management would have been well within its rights to move him on. He wasn't eating or drinking anything. And his appearance might fairly have been considered detrimental to trade. I certainly would not have wanted to eat spaghetti and meatballs at an adjoining table. And yet there he sat, unmolested, an unfailing reproach to all novelists of faint-heart, flipping over the pages of his reporter's notepad as though he feared his time was running out.

Was he invisible, I wondered, to everybody but me? Was he the ghost of serious writing – all that now remained of us? Was he Ernest Hemingway himself, come back from the dead, to stir the conscience of a public that didn't even notice he was there?

I was too far away to see what he was writing. And I couldn't exactly ask. *How's the novel going? Have your sentences got any longer?*

I tried to catch his eye. 'I see you,' I wanted him to know. 'I applaud you.'

But he was beyond person-to-person contact. People didn't interest him. The world didn't interest him. He had stuff to write.

On and on, he went, writing at the speed of light and rolling his unwashed testicle around in his fingers as though it were a rosary.

I tried Francis again. This time I got his answer machine. 'Please pick up, Francis,' I said. 'I'm finally done with S&C. I need to talk to you now. I'm just across the road. If you look out of your window you will see me. Pick up or I'm coming over.'

You need a bit of luck if you're a writer in the age of the dying of the word. Mine came in the shape of Kate and Ken Querrey, the owners of Slumdog Press, a sensational new publishing house whose speciality was the debut novel. The Querreys had worked out that if you paid young unheard-of writers a small fortune for their first novel, that in itself was reason for readers, dreaming of writing their own debut novels, to buy the book. How and what the debutants

wrote was irrelevant; the being plucked from obscurity was all that
was needed by way of plot, the size of the advance all that was needed
by way of denouement. That the rise of the debut novel was the
cause of much bitterness to experienced writers whose debut novels
were behind them needs no explaining; but most of us took consolation in the necessary brevity of the debut novelist's éclat. They were
like the *Latrodectus mactans*, the male black widow spider of North
America – one fuck and they were dead.

I at least was still limping about, looking for another.

The Querreys, meanwhile, could practise fatalism and move on
to the next.

I knew them vaguely. I had been at university with Ken Querrey
who was said to be second in line to a baronetcy and I ran into him
and his wife occasionally at literary festivals. Kate Querrey had
even chaired an event of mine once, in the course of which she
said I was one of those writers who had the courage to learn as
they went along, which I took to mean I hadn't learned much yet.
But at least she acknowledged my existence. So when I saw them
leaving Francis's office, obviously on business – rather than having
to drag his bulk around to publishers when there were matters that
needed discussing face to face, Francis would entice them to his
rooms with lavish finger food and a selection of the best malt whis-
kies – I saw no reason not to wave and invite them to join me for
coffee. In all likelihood, they needed coffee.

We engaged in the usual literary small talk, who was hot, who
was not, which of Francis's authors they published (never heard of
them), how, speaking of writers one had never heard of, things
were going in the realm of the debut novel, and finally, how things
were going in the realm of me.

'You're S&C, aren't you?' Kate Querrey asked, pulling a strand
of hair out of her eye.

I say 'eye' intentionally. She had only the one. But she used it in a way that implied it did the work of three, darting it about to take in whoever else was sitting out at Carluccio's, looking at the person I presented myself as being, and looking deeper into the real me.

'Yes,' I said, 'for my sins.'

Ken Querrey took no time understanding me. 'Sandy Ferber?'

I nodded. The nod which said, *but not for much longer.*

Kate Querrey shuddered. Sandy Ferber – ugh!

In an ideal world the Querreys would now have leapt on me like out-of-print monkeys getting their revenge on Flora. Guy Ableman! What good fortune puts him in our way on the very day he decides to leave his old publisher? But if they were thinking anything along those lines, they kept the thought discreetly to themselves.

They'd been secondary-school teachers originally – or at least Kate Querrey had: no one was quite sure what her husband had been up to, only that he was second in line to a baronetcy – branching out into publishing on the back of an anthology of children's writing they'd privately printed. Not the *Fetch, Fetch* school of children's writing. The children whom the Querreys taught would never have seen a dog – except maybe in a stew. Addiction, abuse, gang bangs, consensual schoolyard rape – those were the lived experiences which the Querreys had encouraged their pupils to mine. Write about what you know, kids.

Ken Querrey wore a T-shirt with what looked like a rapper's face on it under a Ralph Lauren leather jacket. Kate Querrey, a woman who seemed always to be on the point of falling apart, was wrapped, as though to hold herself together, in several layers of brown cardigan. How she was able to be décolleté under so much knitwear, I couldn't work out, but no matter where I looked I couldn't avoid her long, ginger, milky breasts. I wondered how

Francis, a notorious breast man, had fared. Perhaps he'd kept his gaze fixed on her eye.

Since nothing was coming from them, I steered the conversation towards my new book. 'But your speciality is the debut novel,' I laughed, 'and I doubt I can pass what I'm writing off as that.'

They looked at each other quickly. 'Well,' Kate Querrey said – more out of pride than encouragement – 'we don't only do that. We're always on the lookout for breakthrough novels as well.'

Ken Querrey shaped his face into an interrogation mark? Had I broken through yet?

I threw them a who-am-I-to-say smile. The concept of the breakthrough novel troubled me even more than the concept of the debut novel, though they were, of course, in the nature of things incompatible. Breakthrough into what? Primark! Since I was stymied as to debut, I could see that breakthrough was my last chance. But it seemed to me I'd broken through sufficiently by becoming a writer in the first place. I was the son of fashion retailers. My mother took *Drapers* magazine and the *Sun*. My father had never knowingly opened a book. They had sent me to a nothing school (when they could have afforded to send me to a minor public one) in the hope that I would never knowingly open a book myself. I was a Jew – I know, I know, but I never said I was against using it when I needed it (call me a foul-weather Jew) – living in a Gentile country. How much more breaking-through was I obliged to do to stay in print? But I knew none of that was going to wash with a pair of ex-comprehensive-school teachers from Rochdale – the word was that Ken Querrey had taught there for a week – where breaking through in the sense I was using it meant licking cobblestones for a living when you were five years old, eating dog, sending your sister on the street to pay for your education and going up to Oxford with holes in your shoes.

'The last person to know the value of what he's writing is the writer,' I said, flushing a little to hammer home my modesty. 'But I do feel I'm going where I haven't been before. Greater sickness and deeper despair. It's about a man with a brain tumour –' I was about to add that the brain tumour came about as a consequence of his drinking vodka through his eye when I realised just in time that Kate Querrey might have lost her eye doing the same.

Were they listening? 'Fundamentally,' I said, 'he is a hero in the French mode –'

'Meaning he philosophises as he screws?'

'Exactly that. It has always seemed to me that the unexamined screw is not worth having. But also in the extent of his destructiveness. I see him, essentially, as an impious disturbance.'

I glanced to see if Ernest Hemingway had picked up the reference, but he had left the table and was wandering off, in defiance of horns and the shouts of hell-bent cyclists, in the middle of the road.

'What does he disturb?' Ken Querrey asked.

'The tramp?'

'Your hero.'

Kate Querrey wound herself tightly in her cardigans, in anticipation of my reply.

'The sexual decencies, for a start. Not only is he having an affair with his brother's wife, he is sleeping with her mother.'

It was shocking to me, but I could imagine that where the Querreys had been this was normative not to say exemplary behaviour.

'Didn't I once read a review of your work,' Kate Querrey asked, 'saying you couldn't decide whether you were Mrs Gaskell or Rabelais?'

Meaning she had decided for me. And it wasn't Rabelais.

'I think it was Charlotte Brontë or Apuleius,' I said. 'And I don't think it said I couldn't decide between the two, I think it said I was a happy synthesis. But this book is different. This time there's no happy anything. Everything gets blown sky-high.'

Everything? Well, I wasn't going to mention Wilmslow. Or explain that by sky-high I meant as far as Alderley Edge.

'It sounds,' Ken Querrey said, tapping his chin with his finger, 'as though what you're writing is a dystopian novel.'

'More apocalyptic,' I said.

'Ah.'

They fell silent again.

'Is apocalyptic a problem?'

'Only,' Kate Querrey answered for him, 'in that we have a number of those on our list already.'

'So I've missed the apocalypse,' I laughed.

It was evident that neither could understand why I had laughed.

'We aren't saying we definitely don't want to look at it,' Kate Querrey said. Down, down into the valley of her ginger breasts I peered. 'It might turn out that apocalyptic novels are all anyone is going to want to read over the next few years.'

'Assuming,' I unwisely added, 'that over the next few years there's going to be anyone here to read them.' I laughed again – 'Not that I'm trying to rush you.'

We let it go at that. I apologised for ambushing them. Especially on my agent's very doorstep. He wouldn't be very impressed, I laughed. How many times was that I'd laughed in the last ten minutes? They said they didn't feel at all ambushed. If anything they were flattered that a writer as successful as I was would even consider having them as his publishers one day. One day . . .

Indeed that was twice in a single afternoon they'd been flattered in this way by me. I wondered when the other time was. Well, when they said me they didn't mean me exactly. But Francis had told them, though it wasn't for public consumption – and I could count on their discretion – that Vanessa was my wife.

My ear, already hanging by a thread, so much skin had I pulled off it, throbbed and roared.

'Ah,' I said. 'You've been discussing Vanessa.'

Ken Querrey patted his briefcase. 'In here,' he said.

Vanessa victrix.

Kate Querrey's single eye ransacked my soul.

Twenty minutes and three strong black coffees later I was taking the lift to the seventh floor and pressing Francis's bell. It used to rouse me, doing this, wondering what new offers Francis had to excite me with this time, but those days were over. Now all I wondered was whether I'd get there early enough to find Francis still alive. If someone was going to kill him I wanted it to be me.

There was no response, which I took to be a sign of Francis's guilt. He was rearranging his features. Or rearranging my titles to prove I was still important to him. Ultimately a receptionist answered. A receptionist! How long was it since Francis had been able to afford a receptionist? I announced myself and waited. After a bout of unconvincing coughing – to give Francis more time to rearrange my titles? – she buzzed me in.

There, sitting behind the reception desk, wearing headphones and with her lipstick smudged (I could have imagined that), was Poppy Eisenhower, my mother-in-law.

THREE

Famous Last Words

36

A Fuckload of Good Luck

Some time later . . .

I don't think I need to be specific. Start counting years and all you are measuring is loss. Time passes – let's leave it at that. Mankind cannot bear too much specificity.

Some time, anyway, has gone by since I wrote those words – 'Poppy Eisenhower, my mother-in-law'.

I can no longer write them with equanimity. 'Vanessa Ableman, my wife', ditto.

These are the specificities of loss *I* cannot bear.

Otherwise not much has changed. Bookshops continue to go into liquidation, the word 'library' has passed out of common usage, immoderate opinion continues to pass itself off as art, chefs still take precedence over writers, less remains less. But I, amazingly – as long as I don't count the years – am in fine fettle. In my profession you need, as I have said, a degree of luck. And that's what came my way: a fuckload of good luck.

That's a phrase it's difficult for someone with my acute northern vowel dysfunctionality to say.

A focklord of god look? A fackloud of gerd luke? A ferklod of gud lock?

Which could be why I had to wait so long for it.

Mine now, however you account for it, it is. I am even endorsed by G. G. Freville, the son of E. E. who one day simply ran out of puff and retired. 'The rest is silence,' he is – I think apocryphally – reported to have said, knowing that no author would want those words on his book jacket.

But G. G. is proving to be, if you will forgive the pun, an able replacement. 'Guido Cretino,' he was kind enough to say for me recently, 'can make a stone weep.'

Yes, Guido Cretino. All above board. I am now *Guy Ableman writing as Guido Cretino*. It is not uncommon to do this when you want to show that you can drop a register but don't want all trace of your earlier, more highfalutin writing self to disappear altogether. Though, between ourselves, all trace of it has.

Whether I am indeed, as Guido Cretino, able to make a stone weep, isn't for me to say. But women do approach me after readings with their eyes rubbed raw. 'I feel you've penetrated my soul,' they say. 'I couldn't believe, as I was listening to you, that you were not a woman.'

I smile and bow my head and say that in another life – who knows? – maybe I was a woman. Sometimes I take their wrists, rather as a doctor might. The wrist is a safe place to touch a strange woman. Not that these women think of me as a stranger. My words leap all barriers between us. I know them better than their husbands know them, therefore, they reasonably assume, they know me better than my wife knows me.

Wife? What wife?

Nor is it only the women I reach. Men too – the very men who yesterday would not join me, satyr to satyr, in dancing with their goat feet the Antic Hay – today nod their heads and blink the moisture from their eyes. My mistake was to try calling up the monkey from their basement. Andy Weedon had it right: 'Dad' is the word that turns men on. Write 'paternity' and they get a hard-on. Write 'visiting rights' and they turn to jelly. Make 'em laugh, make 'em cry? Not any more. Make 'em cry, and then make 'em cry some more. Heartbreak, it would seem, crosses the gender divide. And, I suspect, the age divide as well. If I am not mistaken my audiences are getting younger. Soon I will be giving toddlers what they want. Even Sally Comfort writes to me, asking me to sign my latest for her nieces. So though I have still not yet blown into the silver portals of her ear or up her ring-guarded nostrils, it isn't out of the question that I will.

How I manage to connect so well with everybody I can't explain. But then I can't explain anything.

How it is, for example, that I have readers when there are no readers. That's what luck does: it calls black white, it makes a nonsense of the actual state of things, it excepts you from the general, and only what is general is true. So, although there is no reason for reading groups or Oxfam or the bookshops whose assistants were once unable to spell my name to love me – *me* – any more than they ever did, they do. Luck blinds, is all one can say.

I travel the world, anyway, saying what I always said, but now to crowded rooms and warm applause. I won't pretend I can have any woman I want – because the particular women I do want I most definitely cannot have, and the rest are usually in tears or blowing their noses when I meet them – but I do all right for a man not in the bloom of youth who used to walk the streets of London talking to himself and pulling his hair out. I am still envious of other writers' success, but this time the success I am most envious of is my own.

And I am not a little contemptuous of that success, no matter that it's mine. Where was it before? I ask. Where was it when I needed it far more, and deserved it no less? If you're a writer through and through you don't turn cheerful overnight just because the fates have finally decreed in your favour. Taste success when you have known failure and the memory of failure grows more bitter with every new laurel you win. Success is arbitrary and wayward; only failure is the real measure of things.

But I am not accused of ingratitude or acerbity. I smile and am smiled back at. I sign and sign. Suddenly, those are the two words they can't get enough of. *Guido Cretino*. I can do no wrong. When I expostulate the case against me and my shameful capitulation – though I abhor the expostulatory as much as I ever did – they applaud my words. And of course they don't believe it when I tweet against the crime novel, the detective novel, the crossover novel, the children's novel, the zombie novel, the graphic novel, the schmaltz novel, the debut novel (with one exception), iPads, Primark, Morrisons, Lidl (I purposely don't name the supermarkets which stock me: why rock the boat?), three-for-two, and Sandy Ferber's instant bus-queue fiction, now selling in its millions. Ladies and gentlemen, I say to them – ladies, gentlemen and children – you will clap me to an early grave.

They laugh at that, knowing that if mine were to be an early grave I'd have been in it long ago.

Like Poppy Eisenhower, my mother-in-law.

37

The Good Husband

I will not dwell on Vanessa's novel. Not because I begrudge her but because she would not allow that I could ever do it justice. And all considering, she is surely right.

'Just don't ever think of reviewing me,' she had said.

This, though, I can say: despite encouraging notices, it did not score any great success until it was made into a film. That the film was produced and directed by Dirk de Wolff will surprise no one who understands the way a good narrative works. Why would I have brought him onstage in Monkey Mia had I not had further use for him? There were many people Vanessa and I met in Australia about whom I have said nothing. I don't say I invented de Wolff, only that his turning up in Shark Bay lends his reappearance a premonitory inevitability. An astute reader – whether of books or life – must have known he was there only because he was coming back.

I recall with sad fondness, anyway – also of the premonitory sort – the exhilaration with which Vee and I read the billboards on the Underground:

ARE THERE MONKEYS IN MONKEY MIA?
DIRECTED BY
DIRK DE WOLFF

and in smaller letters, but still large enough to read:

BASED UPON THE NOVEL

BY

VANESSA EISENHOWER

'Darling, how wonderful,' I said, the first time we went down onto the platform at Ladbroke Grove Tube to stare at a poster.

She glimmered at me from on high and trembled like a galleon. 'Thank you,' she said.

I was being a fantastic husband. Had been from the moment I saw there was no point trying to be anything else. Once your wife's name is up in lights you might as well enjoy it.

We kissed passionately. We could have made a baby there and then. By preference a girl, so we could have called her Mia. Mia Ableman. The little monkey. Or maybe Mia Eisenhower, now that Eisenhower was the name to conjure with.

'You don't mind?' Vanessa, all sweetness, had asked me, once there was no longer any concealing that her book was finished, that an agent – my agent! – had read it, that it would soon be published, and that she was now Eisenhower, not Ableman.

'Of course not,' I had said. 'I think it's a smart move. Clinton or Obama would have been even better, but Eisenhower is good.'

In fact, I suspected that it was only when she decided to change her name that she'd been able to get cracking. It meant she had broken through the false allure of factuality which for so long had held her back. 'I only hope you've changed everybody else's names while you're at it,' I said. 'Including mine.'

'How many times have I told you you're not in it?' she said. 'I'm not writing about us.'

It was exactly what I'd always been telling her. A novel isn't the intimate diary of my life, Vee. It's not *us*. But in her case – not because I patronised her, or thought she lacked imagination, but because she had always argued so forcibly for writing things exactly as they were – I believed it was.

'Of course I'm not in it,' I said. 'So what have you called me – Guido Cretino?'

Monkey, as we referred to it – and no, the irony wasn't lost on either of us – became a film almost before it was forgotten as a novel. The only way of explaining the speed of it, in my view, was that Dirk de Wolff had put in an appearance earlier than Vanessa had let on to me, long before he'd 'stumbled' on the book, 'recalled' the author, and, as someone who knew the location well, believed himself to be the 'only man' to make the movie. My theory was that Vanessa had got me out of the house because de Wolff was in it, I don't say uprooting me as a husband, but certainly uprooting me as a literary mentor and influence. He had spurred her on to write the novel, was my guess – hence her uncharacteristic celerity – with a view from the very start of what he wanted from a screenplay. I presumed that on a prearranged signal – 'Come! The work is done and I am ready for you!' – he had followed her to England, as it was agreed he would during discussions of a creative nature on his vulgar boat in Monkey Mia, either on the first visit with her tipsy ma, or when she returned to it alone while I was standing on her maman's spider – that's if that indeed was what she'd done, though it was immaterial now.

I say I was a fantastic husband – supportive, selfless, unsuspicious and above all non-competitive – but there was a brief time, just after Poppy's defection and the first inkling I had been given by the Querreys of how Vanessa's life was about to change, when I faltered. The period preceding the publication of Vanessa's novel should have been one of high excitement, but I spent most of it in bed. The thing they don't tell you about nervous breakdowns is how calming they can be.

'That,' Vanessa said, 'is because you're not having a nervous breakdown. I've had a nervous breakdown and I can tell you it was nothing like what you're having. What you're having is a pet.'

'A *pet*? You call this a *pet*? Vee, at the corner of each eye I see parallel lines and flashing lights. My family is disintegrating. My publisher has died. I am in print only on demand. This is not a *pet*.'

And I hadn't even mentioned Poppy or my agent.

She didn't argue with me. Things were different now. She didn't argue with me because she didn't need to argue with me. Any argument of consequence she'd won.

'And by the way, when did *you* have a nervous breakdown?' I asked.

'From the day I married you until very recently.' Even that she made sound complimentary.

'I'm glad to hear you're all right now.'

'I would be if you'd get out of bed.'

She couldn't bear my lying there all day, licking my teeth, clawing at my fingernails, drinking Lucozade and listening to Radio 4, though there'd been a time when she'd have prayed for such an eventuality. Once, my lying in bed all day would have meant she could get on with her novel without the distracting sounds of me getting on with mine. But things were not what they had been. I was not writing and she had no need to. She had written. 'It's a wonderful feeling,' she said, 'having done it.'

'You've never "done" it, Vee. It's never over. You should be writing another one now. Just in case.'

That a screenplay was brewing, that by some means she was in contact with de Wolff, I had no idea.

'Just in case what?'

'Just in case – and I speak from experience and with love – just in case what you're hoping for doesn't materialise. Novel two is an insurance policy against the failure of novel one; novel three is an insurance policy –'

'I get the idea, Guido. But I don't want to be like you, never satisfied, always chasing your tail. I'll take my chance. Now get out of bed.'

There was a new purposiveness about her, as of a person who had completed a long and demanding enterprise – climbed a mountain, saved a country – and now wanted to live a little. In Vanessa's case, to live a lot. 'Let's go to the markets today,' she'd suddenly suggest. 'Let's buy a new carpet. Let's nip over to Rome.'

I pulled the duvet over my head. 'Too ill,' I said.

'Oh, for Christ's sake, Guido, get up.'

'Can't,' I said.

'I finish and you go to pieces. Now you know how it's been for me.'

'My going to pieces – and in fact I'm not going to pieces: if anything I am coming quietly back together – has nothing whatsoever to do with your finishing. Which is why I ask you, as your beloved husband, to start another. I'd be delighted to have you starting and finishing every day of my life. It means I can lie here and mend.'

'Mend from what? What broke you?'

I rolled my eyes. What hadn't broken me?

'Can't I just be ill?' I asked. 'Can't I just be *unwell*?'

'You're never just unwell. You're the healthiest person I've ever met – in body. It's your head that's sick.'

We both fell quiet, thinking of Jeffrey. Did brain tumours run in the family?

Vanessa read my mind. 'No,' she said, 'they don't.'

I asked for tea. She said she'd buy me tea out. Claridge's. I reminded her you needed to book Claridge's a year before you wanted tea. How people knew that far ahead when they'd feel like tea had always been a mystery to me. The Ritz the same. There were people in rural Hampshire making reservations for a birthday tea at the Ritz twenty years hence. It was like putting your son's name down for Eton before you'd met the woman who would conceive him. Vanessa, twice the wife she had ever been, listened to me list my objections. Paris, then. Madrid. Casablanca. Let's fly to Casablanca.

To her credit she never said, 'Then stay where you are while I go to Casablanca with Dirk.'

'This advance of yours must have been quite something,' I said, with a deliberate absence of pettishness. 'Someone clearly did a good deal for you. Francis, was it?'

For a million reasons, all of them sound, the details had not been discussed. Not the title, not the contents, not Slumdog, not the deal, not the part Francis had or hadn't played in it, and if not him, who? When a call came for her about the book she closed the door. Tactful of her. But the more pain I was spared, the more time I needed to spend in bed.

She ripped the duvet off me. Embarrassing. I had an erection. I always did get an erection when I was depressed. Flu and depression invariably engorged me.

'What's that?' she said.

'Evidence that I'm pleased for you.'

'What will it be like when I start bringing prizes home?'

'We can only guess, Vee.'

'Say you'll come to the market with me and I'll suck you off.'

'I'll come to the market with you.'

'You have to mean it.'

'I mean it.' And to prove it I opened my arms and sang 'I'm in the Mood for Love'.

Here was the measure of how things had changed: once upon a time she'd have said, 'No, you're not,' and walked out of the room; today she bent her head towards my feverish erection and joined in. We were both, though it hurts me to recall it now, in the mood for love.

By our standards, and allowing for my nervous breakdown, these were idyllic times. I had never seen Vanessa more happy or more beautiful. She whistled as she did housework. She cooked casseroles for me, sometimes one for lunch and another one for dinner. And what is more she served them wearing her highest heels and very nearly see-through blouses. She read me things that interested her from newspapers. She told me stories, jokes. The only thing she never talked about was the subject of her book. And this I took to be the proof that a nasty shock was waiting for me. But that didn't matter. I was shocked-out. Let her do her worst if it made her happy, and there was no mistaking that it made her happy.

Not impossibly, a contributory factor in my collapse was guilt: I had come to see how cruel I'd been to her throughout our marriage, what pleasure I'd been denying her by putting me first, by letting it be felt that I was the centre of all marital operations, that it was my career that counted, my flame the one that had to be fed and kept alight at all times. When you see a person you love happy for the first time, you must ask yourself what part you've played in all the misery that went before.

But I worried what would happen when this period of excited anticipation came to an end and she had to face the inevitable anticlimax: no readers, no sales, no book visible in a single bookshop, no Richard and Judy, fatuous reviews, no back list, no front list, the black hole . . . I tried to prepare her for it but on her

305

impossibly volatile nature no warning would stick. Tra-la-la, wasn't the writer's life grand! Partly, of course, she was showing me how to do it. *You and your endless complaining. You and your 'literature's finished'. Look how easy it can be. Look what a good time we could have been having – the pair of us. Instead of just you you you and your long face.* Forgetting that I too had been like this at the beginning, and that we had danced around the living room when I got my first royalty cheque, and then spent the lot on a holiday in Taormina, where we found plaques to D. H. Lawrence. 'One day it will be you, my darling,' she had said, and we had danced in Taormina too.

It would all come to no good, but for the time being, yes – and even though I was throwing a minor nervous breakdown – life was sweet. Anyone coming into the house would have smelt it immediately – the sticky aroma, like lilies just before the turn, of a man and his wife in love, the man, maybe, just a little bit more so.

As for Poppy, nothing was alluded to. They had fallen out, that was all I knew. And not – not ostensibly – over me. Had they fallen out over me I'd have known about it. I had to assume they had fallen out over Francis. That Vanessa, who could be prudish when it suited her to be, disapproved of whatever it was that was going on there. And what is more felt that Poppy's grabbing Francis for her purposes, just as she was grabbing him for her own, smacked a little too much of naked competition. No sooner did Vanessa have an agent than her mother had to have the same person for her . . . for her whatever she had picked him for. It was indecent. Vanessa didn't put it to me like that; indeed Vanessa didn't put it to me any way – but with my nose for indecency and how it was perceived by others, I just knew it.

What I didn't fully understand until I read Vanessa's novel was that the breach had already been made in her own mind. The book would finalise that breach, but was also the history of it. Mothers and daughters – a rivalry that exceeded even that of novelists and novelists.

38

Whore

With Poppy out on the night with Francis, bed was the safest place for me to be. Whether they were in any real sense *out on the night* or even just *out* – under what terms she had entered his employment and/or his affections – I had no idea, but the expression describes the coloration of my fears. I knew my jealous nature and knew that if I didn't disable myself I'd be hammering at Francis's office door demanding an explanation. Not least for taking on my wife as a client.

How could you do that to me, Francis? I'm your fucking client. I was your fucking friend!

He, of course, assuming I could get to him, would pretend not to know what I was talking about. There was no law that said an agent couldn't represent a husband and a wife. Yes, common decency opposed it – boundaries, Francis! – and at the very least you asked the existing client how he stroke she felt about your taking on the spouse; but I knew what Francis would say. *Hey, never for one minute did I think you would mind. People have family doctors and family lawyers – think of me as your family agent.*

As for why he didn't mention it – he was enjoined to secrecy. Vanessa wanted it to be a surprise.

Was it to surprise me, too, having been apprised of my desires, that you employed my mother-in-law – in whatever capacity? Never mind common decency, Francis, you must have known that the very heavens forbade that.

But that was just as much a question for Poppy.

How could you do that to me, Poppy? I'm your . . . I'm your . . . What was I? *I'm your fucking son-in-law.*

Would I call her a whore? Probably. I liked the word. I liked the sensation of saying it on my tongue, the vibrations on my papillae that emitting it occasioned. *Whore.* It's a word that heats the mouth up. But it had fallen out of fashion at about the same time as modesty. De Sade's sodomitic whores would simply pass today for girls out on a hen night. A man felt foolish now calling a woman a whore. The word had been reclaimed. There were places in the world where the most sedate matrons painted their faces, hitched their skirts and went on 'whore walks', though had one of them been asked to turn a trick for money she'd have gone back to being an easily affronted matron on the spot. Not to be entered into lightly, whorishness. Not for the faint-hearted, whatever their sexual politics. On balance I was prepared to risk it on Poppy, but what would I say when she asked me what was so whorish about working as a receptionist?

And was that all there was to it? I didn't think so. If Poppy was installed as Francis's full-time secretary, or full-time anything else, she couldn't still be living in Shipton-by-Wychwood. Too far to travel every day. So where was she living?

Vanessa would surely have known. But how was I going to broach the subject with her? *So where exactly is that whore your mother making the beast with Francis, Vee?*

For the reasons I have already given, such an interrogation was out of the question.

In the meantime I lay there with an erection half in Poppy's honour, half in her daughter's, and might have stayed that way for another year had I not received a call from Jeffrey.

'Dad,' was all he said.

'I'm not your dad.'

'Not you, him. You should be here.'

'Is he ill?'

'We're all ill.'

'How ill is he?'

'How ill does he have to be? He's your father.' With which he put the phone down.

An hour later he rang again to apologise for his abruptness. An apology was an extraordinary event in our family and itself told me that something serious was afoot. My mother once ran over a neighbour's cat, almost certainly deliberately, forwards and then backwards, then forwards again, and that was the only time I ever heard her or any one of us apologise. 'Oops, beg its pardon,' she said.

'I'm on my way,' I told Jeffrey. 'I'll be there in a few hours.'

But I was mystified by a couple of things I thought Jeffrey had said. 'Brothers are born for adversity' – could he really have spoken those words or did I dream them? And if I wasn't mistaken, he called me Gershom.

I took a taxi from the station and asked to be driven round the town a couple of times. Sometimes the place you grew up in can hold the answer to the question of why you have not made as much of yourself as you should. I got the driver to wheel by the school, and then the Scouts hall, and then the library where I always took out more books than I could read, kept them for months, and amassed enormous fines. We drove slowly past Wilhelmina's where the shutters were down. I loved and hated that boutique, and remembered I had first seen Vanessa and Poppy there. I had wanted out but it was upsetting to see it closed and, it seemed to me, uncared for.

The door to my parents' plush sanatorium of senility being unlocked – ah, the open-hearthed and open-hearted north! – I went straight into the bedroom where I expected to see my father laid out. He was sitting up in his bed, attached to a simple drip, with a rabbi in attendance. When he saw me he gave me a sardonic thumbs up – my father I'm talking about, not the rabbi. He had never made such a gesture to me before and I found it oddly affecting. Were we going to become chums at the last?

'Ah, so you're Gershom, the oldest,' the rabbi said, extending a hand.

'Old*er*,' I corrected him. 'There are just the two of us.' First things first. 'And my name's not Gershom.'

He shook my fingers. 'Well, I know you're not Yafet,' he said. 'Your brother Yafet I am acquainted with.'

'Yafet! I have a brother called Yafet?' It came out sounding wrong. I didn't know my own brother!

I thought I knew my brother well enough. He was a sexual pervert called Jeffrey with a dirty bomb in his brain. The dirty bomb *was* his brain. When it went off it would pollute half of Cheshire. Even Jeffrey was too good a name for my brother. And now Yafet? What was happening to me? Had my nervous breakdown lasted longer than I had known? I felt I'd gone to sleep waiting for Vanessa to do something about my erection and woken up two thousand years previously in the Holy Land.

The rabbi, a heavily bespectacled American about half my age and height, who could have done with pulling a few hairs out of his moustache and beard himself, appeared to grasp the reason for my confusion. 'Your parents have explained to me,' he said, 'that you've never set much store by faith – as a family.'

He touched the brim of his Homburg when he said 'faith'.

'Is my father having a deathbed conversion?' I asked, uncertain

310

whether I could ask the old man himself, uncertain whether he could hear or understand. He had never understood much.

'It's hardly a conversion,' the rabbi said from the side of his mouth. He had a wonderfully city-smart way of spitting out his words, more like a gangster than a rabbi, which was at odds with his dishevelment. To do justice to a voice like that he should have been wearing a striped suit by Brioni, with leather piping up the lapels, and two-tone alligator shoes.

'What is it, then?' I asked. 'Are the Lubavitchers holding him hostage?'

He seemed impressed that I knew him to be a Lubavitcher. In fact, I didn't. It was a guess. The Lubavitchers were the only Jews I'd heard of who dressed like this and who converted Jews to Judaism.

'The word for it is *bal-chuva*,' he told me, enunciating it with great care. Maybe he wanted me to repeat it after him. *Bal-chu-va*.

'And that means?'

'Returning to the way of righteousness.'

Leaving aside the sentiment, the last time I'd heard anyone roll words like that was in a 1930s movie about a Chicago hood. 'Happy boithday, Louis,' he had said, spraying sub-machine-gun bullets everywhere. Happy *bal-chuva*, Louis, you righteous bastard.

For a writer of impious disturbances I was and always had been unaccountably respectful, even obsequious, in the presence of men of God. In an odd way I felt we were in the same business: reverence and irreverence, the construction and destruction of icons – neither of us could function without the other. But I didn't appreciate a rabbi from the Bronx hovering, at this late hour, around the spirit of a man who could not conceivably be said to have returned to the way of righteousness, never having done a righteous deed or entertained a righteous thought in his entire life.

Worthless my father might have been, but it was his own worth-lessness. And now they were taking that last dignity away from him.

'What's happening, Dad?' I asked.

He gave me another mute thumbs up.

'He's resting,' the rabbi said, as though I needed to be told what my father had been doing as long as I had been alive.

I lacked the courage to ask the rabbi how he came to be here. To administer the last rites? Did we do last rites? Had the poor bastard called for a rabbi because he was afraid? Could he possibly have known there was such a thing as *bal-chuva* and that the time was now right for it?

I enquired after my mother. She was in the kitchen doing a jigsaw, the rabbi thought. Which I took to mean that my father's death was not imminent at least. But then again, a jigsaw was a jigsaw.

'Look, whose idea is this?' I finally found the bravery to say.

'*This?*'

'You.'

'Well, originally, my friend, the idea is the Almighty's, blessed be He. But I had a bit to do with it.'

You start a conversation with a rabbi of this sort at your peril. And I wasn't 'his friend'. But I gathered that he was new to the area and was stepping up the provision of pastoral care. Did I know the word *rachmamim*? No, I did not. First *bal-chuva*, now *rachmamim*. How long before I spoke fluent Hebrew? Well, *rachmamim* was something like compassion. And in the dutiful spirit of *rachmamim*, to which no Jew, never mind a rabbi, could be oblivious, he visited the Jewish sick and elderly. I wondered how he knew of our exist-ence as a Jewish family. We kept ourselves apart, subscribed to nothing, never went near a synagogue. We were on no lists, that I knew of. He threw me a God, blessed be He, works in mysterious ways shrug. Meaning, if there's a Jew in need out there, He will find him. Yes, well, I'd heard that one before. And how interested would the rabbi be in my father, how interested would God be, come to that, were he to recover his senses sufficiently to offer them a share in my mother?

'I might just go and find her,' I told the rabbi. 'My mother.'

He inclined his head. 'Go, my friend.'

She was indeed in the kitchen doing the Chester jigsaw, the surprising part being that she was doing it with Jeffrey. But there was something more surprising than that. My brother, last seen in an Alexander McQueen jacket with metallic lapels, had now grown a full beard, wore a black Homburg and had fringes hanging from his shirt. He rose to greet me. '*Tzohora'im tovim*,' he said, putting his arms around me and kissing me on the neck.

My mother, dressed as ever to receive signals from another world while flirting with the ship's captain, did not look up from her jigsaw. Imaginary ash hung perilously from the tip of her electronic cigarette.

'What the fuck, Jeffrey?' I said.

But I knew what the fuck. The family had finally lost its collective mind.

Though it wasn't a subject that interested her, Poppy alluded once to the Jew thing.

We were in the garden of her Oxfordshire cottage. My second and final visit. Nothing untoward. I had been invited to address an undergraduate society in Oxford and Vanessa had asked, since I would not be far away, if I'd drop a dress off at her mother's. Vanessa had bought it for herself but then decided it would look better on Poppy. I agreed. 'Try it on,' I said when I got there, 'I'll look away,' which I suppose was tentatively untoward, but she pretended not to hear.

'Be a darling and cut me some mint,' she said, handing me scissors. 'I'll make us tea.'

'Which is mint?' I asked.

'Ah, yes,' she said, 'I forgot – you're a Jew.'

'A Jew!'

'Am I mistaken?'

'No, just blunt. But what's being *a Jew* – if you have to put it like that – got to do with mint?'

'Absolutely nothing. That's my point.'

'I'm not aware,' I said, 'that Jews have a blind spot when it comes to herbs. We probably invented mint tea. *I* don't know what it looks like out of tea only because *I* grew up in the city and never had a garden.'

She laughed. 'Wilmslow is hardly the city, Guy.'

'It *was*, the way we inhabited it. When we weren't in the boutique we were away buying clothes for it in Milan and Paris. I'd been to a hundred fashion shows before I was twelve. Catwalks I knew – country lanes I didn't. As for mint – wasn't that the name of a model? Mint. I suspect I even dated her. She had green eyes and tasted –'

Poppy put up a hand. Some things, she mutely reminded me, were not to be discussed with your mother-in-law.

'Tell me,' she said, 'talking about the boutique – why have I lost contact with your mother?'

'You moved away.'

'Before that.'

'She went dotty.'

'It wasn't to do with you and Vanessa?'

'I don't think she liked Vanessa. But then I don't think she liked any of the women I brought home. Not because she didn't think any of them was good enough for me. It was more because she didn't like me.'

'Vanessa isn't easy to like,' she said, bypassing me.

'Poppy!' We were sitting in deckchairs. I almost fell out of mine.

'It's true,' she said.

'*I* like her,' I said.

'You love her. That's different.'

'And you're her mother – that's also different. A mother can't say she finds her own daughter unlikeable.'

'Why not?'

Why not. I leaned back and let the sun warm my face. 'Because of this,' I said, with my eyes closed, gesturing to her garden, the trees, the grass, the birds, the mint. My subject. 'Nature.'

'Oh, nature!' she said.

'It isn't even true,' I went on. 'I've seen you together. I've watched you make music together. You look like sisters.'

'And you think all sisters like each other?'

I didn't have a sister but I had Jeffrey. 'No,' I said.

'And at least if you're sisters people *expect* you to be rivals. When it's mother and daughter the mother is expected to move over.'

I shrugged. Seems fair to me, my shrug said. Though I could never have been accused of expecting Poppy to move over. Roll over, maybe. 'There's room for both of you,' I said.

She shook her head. 'Before you know it you have a beautiful daughter,' she said. 'You're still a girl yourself and suddenly you're a mother. I didn't do girl enough. I didn't do it well enough or long enough.'

'I seem to remember something about a naked photo shoot in Washington,' I said.

'Oh, that. Five minutes of my life, and then all hell to pay. Vanessa loses another father and I'm another ten years making it up to her. And even then I'm not sure I'm forgiven.'

I formulated a theory on the spot. You aren't meant to forgive

315

your parents. And they aren't meant to expect to be forgiven. You go on your way. Goodbye, Mother, goodbye, Father, thanks for nothing. Seventy years later you kiss and make up, but at least in the meantime you aren't a living torment to each other. Torment too strong a word? Reproach, then. Vee and Poppy had spent too much time together. That was the unnatural part. No wonder they couldn't quite like each other.

'I have not,' I said, 'heard Vanessa say she can't forgive you. For anything.'

Which was true. I had heard Vanessa call her a slut and a pisspot, but that was another matter.

Or was it? In so far as calling her mother a slut pointed to one of the ways her mother did not behave as a conventional mother should — that's to say to act her age and move over — well, I supposed there was reproach in that. Indeed, given the thoughts Poppy had inspired in me, to say nothing of Jeffrey Braindrain, well, Vanessa had a point.

So did they hate each other? Was that what that bouncing along arm in arm in identical cork sandals actually amounted to — hate?

And had I, in my own foolish way, been an instrument of that hate? A bit-part player in their psychodrama? A mere tool?

'Don't get me wrong,' Poppy continued. 'I think Vanessa's great. I think she's wonderful. I think she's wonderful for you. Born to be a writer's wife —'

'I wouldn't let her hear you say that. As she sees it I'm born to be a writer's husband.'

'Well, there you are, precisely. She isn't easy.'

'Must she be?'

'It would be nice if she had more patience. I don't feel I can count on her. If I had a Jewish daughter she would be more considerate.' She made it sound as though she'd chosen badly. If only she'd picked the Jewish daughter when she had the chance.

'She has sent you the dress I've just brought. Are you sure you don't want to try it on? I'll look away.'

Once a tool always a tool.

'Stop it,' she said. But then added, 'You see – you're considerate. I think that's because you're a Jew.'

A terrible thought struck me. Was that what Poppy had all along supposed I was being – considerate? Considerate the night shooting stars dropped into the Indian Ocean and I slipped my smoking fingers between her cellist's thighs? Considerate when I'd stood with my arms around her and my foot on the throat of the tarantula? Considerate as my eyes met hers in shocking knowledge on the uppermost rung of Broome's Staircase to the Moon? *Considerate!*

'I'm not considerate to *my* mother,' I said.

'You probably are,' she said dismissively, 'but even if you aren't you have a brother to share the responsibility.'

My brother Jeffrey. Had she thought he too was being considerate the night he kissed her, or whatever else he did, by way of solemnising my marriage to Vanessa?

'So is that the problem with Vanessa – that there's only her? That's a bit tough on her.'

'And a bit tough on me.'

'Tougher on her.'

'No, tougher on me.'

I wondered if we might make a game of it. Tougher on her, no tougher on me, no tougher on her, and end up falling in a heap together in the bed of mint, wherever the mint was.

But the conversation had not been heading in the direction of illicit sex. And to my dismay I realised it relieved me to think that. I don't say I didn't want her still, but she was not as irresistible as I remembered her. Could have been the clothes – jeans, flip-flops, sloppy sweater. I had always preferred her 'dolled up', to use a favourite expression of my mother's. Hoisted high and painted, the cleavage starting just below her chin. She looked a touch weary, too. A little flushed in the face and red around the neck. She pushed her face forward, I noticed, as though to assert mastery over her jaw. Her head seemed heavy for her. It looked like hard work keeping herself straight.

'I'm getting older,' she said, as though reading my mind.

'You don't look it.'

'I'm getting older.'

'And?'

'Vanessa doesn't have the patience. So who will look after me?'

'You need a nice Jewish boy to care for you, is that what you're saying?'

It was the first time I had ever used that expression. But she'd brought the subject up, and it seemed apposite.

Once upon a time she'd have patted my cheek and called me monkey. Today she just waved what I said away as though it were a summer fly. But I was just going through the motions anyway. I felt that my time had been and gone with her. And even that the time that had been was not the time I'd thought it was.

Had there been no transgression to speak of at all?

I almost felt inclined to shake her hand. No hard feelings, Poppy. That was a lot of fun we almost had.

For the second time that afternoon she read my mind. 'Well you *are* a nice Jewish boy,' she said, rising from her deckchair, 'whatever you say about yourself.'

And then she kissed me, full on the mouth.

39

Wild One

I had stayed the night in Wilmslow. Vee had texted at midnight to see how my first day out of bed had gone. Had I remembered how to walk. I texted back that I was fine but the family had converted. She texted me saying that if religion was the only way I could cope with her having written a novel, that was fine. Whatever worked. Though she was surprised that the whole family had needed to convert. PS – what to?

jews, I replied.

good, but weren't you always?

you knew?

you know i knew. your nose, remember

I went to sleep remembering. Hot nasal nights with my wife. That's what hotels are for. Remembering. Missing.

Vanessa was strange about religion. I picked her for a pagan when I first met her. She swore, she blasphemed, she gave blow jobs in back alleys. Anyone less godly it was hard to imagine; and yet she tolerated religious extremes in other people and at times went so far as to encourage them. I didn't know whether she'd been to see my brother after learning of his illness, and was unaware as yet that she'd nicked his tumour as a metaphor for her mother's state; but if she had nipped up to Wilmslow when I wasn't looking there was every chance she'd been as instrumental as the rabbi in turning Jeffrey into Yafet. I wouldn't even have put it past her to have suggested *bal-chuva*. It was the kind of thing she liked doing – showing that she knew what a person's true self was, and instructing him how to walk in the particular path of righteousness that was best suited to his needs. Other than ask me to give her orgasms with my nose she had rarely alluded to my being Jewish. God knows what she'd asked Jeffrey to do with his. But I could well imagine her getting him to turn to Yahweh as a means of dealing with his tumour.

I breakfasted at the hotel then took a taxi to the Dementievas where Jeffrey had agreed to meet me, though he didn't find that name funny any more. Funny about funny, how faith regained invariably has trouble with it. You find your old religion and lose your old sense of the ridiculous.

'I'd always known there was something there,' he told me. This morning he had shed his Homburg and was wearing a knitted skullcap.

'Something where, Yafet?' He wouldn't answer to Jeffrey. It was Yafet or it was nothing.

I wondered if he was going to touch his head and tell me that it hadn't been a tumour after all, just his unattended-to Jewishness trying to get out, swelling and knotting until he'd put on a skullcap and grown ringlets, and then the pain subsided. Maybe he was even going to prescribe being born again as a Jew as a cure for all cancers, not just cancer of the brain.

But by 'there' he meant his heart.

'You never felt it?' he asked, tapping away at his chest.

'Well, I've felt plenty of things in my heart. In fact, I think I'd say I've felt everything in my heart. But what you're describing, no. And don't tell me I've been in denial.'

'You haven't missed anything?'

'No, Yafet.'

'You haven't felt that there's always been some question waiting for an answer?'

'No, Yafet.'

Not true. There always had been some question waiting for an answer. But it wasn't my brand-new baby Jew-boy brother's idea of a question or an answer. The question was 'Where has the idea of the book as prestigious object, source of wisdom, and impious disturbance gone?' And the answer was on the five-for-four shelf at Primark.

He smiled at me. It was strange to see the difference a skullcap and beard made to his face. His eyes looked blacker and more brilliant, his mouth sloppier, his expression more spiritual. Even his fingers looked longer, like a healer's.

He had a pile of ornately bound books on the floor by his feet, the kitchen table being occupied by the jigsaw. From the other rooms came the sounds of the Dementievas? – or should it now have been the Dementiovskies – stirring in their sleep.

'We could study together,' he suggested.

'Why does the phrase "study together", Jeffrey,' I wanted to ask him, 'always suggest books you'd rather be eaten alive by rats than read?'

But that would have been more brutal than I believed I should be, though I believed I should be brutal. So I merely said, 'Only if we could study a subject of my choice after.'

'And what would that be?'

'The novels of Henry Miller.'

He closed his eyes, his lids heavier and darker, more Mediterranean, than I'd ever seen them. I wondered if he was using make-up.

'You ever read him?' I asked.

'No.'

'Then why the closed eyes?'

'I'm asking myself if his books are anything like yours . . .'

'I wish,' I said. 'But I don't know why you're asking yourself that. You haven't read mine either.'

'You know I've never been a reader.'

'I do know, which makes me wonder why you're reading what you're reading now.'

'Different.'

'You can say that again.'

I picked one up. Back-to-front writing, the script ancient, heavy and mournful, lacking the visible music of the vowel. Leopold Bloom's shocking, unforgivable, irrefragable words, re the Holy Land, hammered in my ears – *The grey sunken cunt of the world*. We were similar Jews, Bloom and I. Thin-skinned, on the qui vive for insult, double-edged – a *cunt*, after all, is no negligible thing, a cunt is where it all begins – but otherwise enough already.

Though apparently not.

'Did you ever write a book about us?' Yafet surprised me by asking.

'Us?'

In illustration of his meaning, he twirled a piece of hair which I suspected he was training to be a ringlet. Had I had ringlets, I thought, I'd never be able to keep my hands off them. Right now, for example, I'd be yanking them out, a hair at a time.

'There is no us, Jeffrey – Yafet. And no, I never did.'

'Why not? What's wrong with us?'

'I had no interest in the same way you had no interest. Just because you've undergone a whateveryoucallit, it doesn't follow that I must. You have a tumour. I don't. If this helps you, great. I'm pleased for you' – the number of people I was suddenly having to be pleased for! – 'but don't insult me with it.'

'You may have missed a trick.'

'*Might* have missed a trick. What kind of trick?'

'Rabbi Orlovsky told me all the best writers in America are Jewish. He said he's never heard of you. If you'd been writing about Jews he'd have heard of you.'

'That's in America.'

'He hasn't heard of you here either.'

'Kind of you to tell me that, Yafet.'

'I saw an interview you did once for the *Wilmslow Reporter*. You told them you liked writing about wild guys.'

'You've told me that. You told me that the time you told me you had a tumour.'

'Well, I'm telling you again. You like writing about wild guys? Well, who's wilder than a Jew?'

I gave him a long look. Not much wild about the baby ringlets and the fringes. Who's wilder than a Jew? Who *isn't* wilder than a Jew? But I could have been wrong. I'd been wrong about everything else. I'd assumed that Jeffrey had squeezed himself into Yafet in order to damp himself down, quieten the tumult in his head. But what if Jeffrey the impious disturbance was not only still in there but more impious than ever? Not a fraud or an impostor, I wouldn't have accused him of that, but still going both ways. The religious could do that: they could jeer at belief, rail at God Himself, from the very centre of their faith. In this, they were unlike your regular conscientious humanist, who was stuck with his one-track, literal-minded rationality. No, he said. And that was that. Jeffrey-Yafet, on the other hand, grinning with his wet red mouth, could just as easily have been mocking himself as mocking me. Belief contained its own parody; disbelief did not. As a matter of principle, disbelief closed down uncertainty and ambivalence. Whereas belief, particularly Jewish belief, from what I knew of it in the novels of the wild

American Jews I admired, played more games with itself than any other sort. Even the most solemn Jewish holy man was a trickster at heart.

I didn't know I thought any of this until I thought it then. So thank you, Yafet.

Did that then mean that he was right? That I'd missed a trick?

Well, I'd missed everything else.

'So how does your new belief system square with the wrongs you've done me?' I asked him.

'Not new. Recovered. Always in there, Gershom, always in there. In you, too.' He leaned across to touch my heart this time. But otherwise he pretended not to know what I was talking about. *Wrongs?* What wrongs?

'My wife? Her mother?'

'Oh, not that again. I've told you – I was winding you up.'

Did I imagine it, or was he beginning to turn a w into a v. *I vas vinding you up.*

'And how does *bull-chava –*'

'*Bal-chuva.*'

I couldn't be bothered. 'How does that square with winding me up – your own brother?'

'I was ill. And yes, all right, the night of your wedding with your mother-in-law. A little bit. A nibble. Love was in the air, Gershom.'

'You were the best man.'

'Best man, mother-in-law – it was a wedding.' (*A vedding.*)

'And what you said about Vanessa?'

'Well, the family has never liked Vanessa. But I do. I've never said a word against her.'

'But you have. You said a word against her to me.'

He straightened his skullcap. 'You told the *Wilmslow Reporter* you liked wild guys.'

'So I should like you?'

'No, you should like her. She's the real wild guy in the marriage.'

'You've told me that, too.'

'But you took no notice.'

'How do you know what I took?'

'I talk to Vanessa sometimes. She rings me. She rang me when she heard about my tumour.'

'And she told you I wasn't doing my best by her wild side? How do you treat a wild guy you're married to?'

'I don't know. I've never been married.'

'So what did she complain about?'

'She didn't complain. I could just hear it in her voice.'

'Hear what? Unexpressed wildness? Did she tell you I was stopping her from being Jewish?'

'You can tell when someone's not happy, Gershom.'

'Fuck off with the Gershom. And anyway – who's happy?'

Dumb question. 'I am,' he said, grinning at me with his wet mouth.

That was as far as we got. My mother called us from the bedroom. She embraced Yafet, straightening his skullcap and pinching his cheek. 'A good boy,' she said, looking at me but meaning him.

Me she shook hands with. The writer. The disappointment of the family.

My father was sitting up in bed without his tubes, scraping out a grapefruit. He didn't know who anybody was but appeared cheerful enough. I thought I saw him eyeing off my mother's sparrow legs.

'Look at him,' my mother said, with a hitherto concealed tenderness, pushing what was left of his hair back from his vacant face. '*Kayn ahora.*'

40

Whoremaster

So had I missed a trick?

Would I have done better as Gershom? *The Anne Frank I Never Knew* by Gershom Ablestein. *Mishnah Grunewald's Choice* by Gershom Ablewurt. *The Boy in the Striped Dolce and Gabbana Pyjamas* by Gershom Ablekunst?

Had I missed out on my wildness by missing out on being Jewish?

Almost as soon as I got back to London Francis rang. Or rather Poppy rang. 'Is that Guy Ableman? I have Mr Fowles on the phone for you.'

'Come off it, Poppy,' I said.

But the next minute Francis was on the line.

'Dear boy! I hear you've been under the weather.'

'Under the cosh, Francis, not the weather.'

'Sorry to hear it. You all right now? Lunch? There's a new brasserie opened near me.'

'There's a new brasserie opened near everyone,' I said.

'So what do you fancy instead?'

I suggested the matchbox restaurant where I'd seen Merton for the last time.

'Oh God, Guy, you can't move there and it's full of publishers.'

'That's what I fancy,' I said.

I knew why. Only a month after Merton's suicide the buyer for books for thirteen- to fifteen-year-olds for one of the lesser-known supermarkets had keeled over here halfway through her dessert. There'd been a much publicised brawl in the toilets, too, between the husband of a foreign rights assistant and an Italian novelist widely supposed to be her lover. And a veteran book rep, describing what he'd seen to a table of colleagues, dislocated his shoulder imitating the husband throwing punches. The word was out in the trade that there was a curse on the place. Though all that did was increase the business. The appeal of it wasn't lost on me. We all wanted to see the industry implode before our eyes.

The other, if you like unconscious, reason I'd chosen to eat here was brought home to me when I saw Francis trying to squeeze his bulk between a table made from an old Singer sewing machine and a banquette fashioned from a pew riddled with woodworm. It pleased me no end to see him so uncomfortable.

'You look the way I feel,' I said, not waiting for the menus before starting in on him.

I noticed that he'd cleaned his appearance up considerably – no slim-fit striped shirt hanging out over his trousers. And a tie. The tie, particularly, pained me. It looked like a gift.

'Oh Lord,' he said, pretending to shield his face. 'We're not going to have a set-to as well, are we?'

'That's up to you,' I said.

'Well, first of all I never thought you'd mind.'

'I knew you were going to say that. Which offence are we discussing?'

'Are there two?'

'For all I know there might be more.'

'Vanessa begged me to read her novel. She said at your suggestion. I read it and I liked it.'

'Francis, there are people up and down the country waiting
years to get a verdict from you on their manuscripts. Many of them
will die before they hear from you. And many more will die when
they do. How come Vanessa was able to jump the queue?'

'She's your wife, Guy. I was doing you a favour. What would you
have said had I refused her?'

'Thank you.'

'You don't mean that.'

'No, I don't mean that.'

'It's a good novel.'

'I believe you.'

'You haven't read it?'

'No. Not allowed to until it's published. And Poppy?'

'Poppy is not allowed to either. Not ever.'

'That wasn't what I was asking, Francis. *And Poppy* meaning
what do you have to say about Poppy?'

'That I love her.'

'You love her! She's a woman of sixty-six. How old are you?
Fifty-two? Plus she's the mother of one of your clients and the
mother-in-law of another. Plus, *plus* I told you *I* loved her.'

'No, you didn't. You told me you wanted to get into her pants
and write a novel about it. I warned you strenuously against it.'

'You warned me strenuously against the novel. You encouraged
me strenuously to get into her pants.'

Our conversation, speaking of strenuous, was being followed
strenuously by the other diners. People urged me on silently when
I caught their eye. Hit him. Go on, knock him down the stairs. No
doubt they were urging on Francis likewise. They didn't care who
did what to whom. They just wanted to see blood spilt. Publisher

328

and author, foreign rights assistant's husband and lover, agent and client – it all gave spice to the dying days of a finished profession. I should have brought Vanessa here. Wife novelist versus husband novelist – that would have been a beauty.

'You misled me,' Francis said, our altercation having been interrupted by the arrival of charred octopus. I hated charred octopus but ordered it from every restaurant in London. It was like sea bream. Something just made one say the words – I took the compulsion to be general, given the amount of it I heard people ordering – when what I really wanted, what we all really wanted, was shank of something.

I was distracted. 'Say that again, Francis,' I said. 'Did I hear the words "misled you"?'

'Yes, that was exactly what you heard and exactly what you did. You misled me.'

'Into believing what?'

'Into believing you were having an affair. And you weren't. You never were.'

'Poppy denied me, did she? At the crowing of the cock, was it? Don't be so fucking melodramatic. I never claimed we were having an affair. I said I was thinking of it.'

He banged the table. 'But she wasn't, Guy. Get that into your head. She wasn't.'

Was this worth pursuing? What had happened was so old a story it embarrassed me to be a part of it. Francis throws himself at her – a man without a wife and only a handful of years, all right two handfuls of years, younger than her, a man with whom she could look forward to some future as she most certainly could not with me (in truth what could she look forward to with me, her daughter's husband, except the occasional company of someone who would kill spiders for her?) – whereupon, unable to believe her

329

good fortune, she cleans out all the cupboards of her past so as not to spoil his idealisation of her. *Guy! Did Guy say that, the cheeky monkey? Don't make me laugh.* And now I'm the bad one for speaking retrospectively ill of the woman he loves. *Get out of having thought about getting into her pants, Guy.* No matter that he had once egged me into them out of his own vicarious lubricity.

'OK,' I said, 'she wasn't. I hope you'll be very happy.'

'There's no need to be sarcastic.'

'I'm not. I think she'll make you an excellent receptionist. Unless she's progressed to reading manuscripts for you by now.'

'Well, that's something else I wanted to tell you.'

'You're handing me over to Poppy? Do you know her taste in literature?'

'No, I'm not handing you over to Poppy – though I don't doubt you'd like it if I did. Poppy will be leaving. As will I. I've had it. I'm getting too old for this. It's not what it was. The fun's gone. The soul's gone. The words have gone.'

'What about Billy Funhouser?'

'I'm Funhousered out, Guy.'

I didn't believe his motives. He was saying half this for me. But I didn't doubt his resolution. I saw what was waiting for him. Cutting mint for Poppy in Whichever-over-Shitheap for the rest of his days. Lucky devil.

'Love in a cottage, is it?' I enquired. I didn't say I knew the very cottage. I didn't say the last time I'd visited my mother-in-law there she'd kissed me full on the mouth. *Full on the mouth, Francis.*

Why spoil things for him, just because he'd spoiled things for me?

Besides, I had other things to worry about. I was agentless.

'You make it sound confined,' he said, 'but I'll count myself a king of infinite space there after bloody London.' He made as though to move his arms, to cut his octopus. Impossible. All he could do was flap his elbows.

'And me?'

'What about you?'

'What do I do?'

'Well, you don't come to the country with Poppy and me, if that's what you're asking. Though you're welcome, of course, to visit.'

Full on the mouth, Francis.

But I said, 'What do I do about an agent? What do I do with *Terminus?*'

He took a deep breath. 'Do you really want me to say?'

'No, but you'd better say it.'

'Tear it up.'

'Tear it up? There's nothing to tear.' That was a lie, but I had to protect myself in my own eyes against this proposed vandalism.

'Tear up the whole idea. Burn the notes. Destroy everything you've shown me.'

'I haven't shown you anything.'

'Don't make this difficult for me. I've heard you speak about it enough. An anathema hero with a fucking tumour, adventuring around women who are now adventurers of their own, terrorising nothing but your own head. Those kinds of books are over, Guy. If Henry Miller turned up in my office tomorrow I'd show him the door.'

'That's because you wouldn't want him to lay a finger on Poppy.' A last, desperate, libidinous nostalgia seized me. I closed my eyes, remembering my mouth on Poppy's.

And remembering what hadn't happened, and now never would. Not ever, ever . . .

Squish-squish.

When I reopened my eyes I found Francis toying with the idea of being furious. 'Leave Poppy out of it. This is about you. *Terminus!* Guy, it would be your terminus all right. No publisher would touch it. Who's it for? What's the market? I should have been sterner with you. I should have asked for two pages from you on who you think your readers are, how old, what sex, how many. That's what other agents would be demanding from you before they read a word.'

'I'm published, Francis, don't forget. Readers know what they're getting.'

'More's the pity.'

Before I could answer that he rose to go to the lavatory. It always amazed me that the place had one. He was away fifteen minutes. So had Poppy cured his constipation? Or made it worse?

'What did that mean?' I asked after he'd lowered himself back into his seat. '*More's the pity*. Explain that.'

'Guy, you've got to face up to what's changed. Things are different. Books don't send tremors any more. You're living in a world that's got beyond shock.'

'Got beyond words, you mean.'

'All right. That too.'

'So what's it *not* got beyond?'

'Ah, now you're asking. I don't know. That's why I'm quitting. If you stay with the company, maybe Heidi Corrigan will tell you.'

'Heidi Corrigan?'

Heidi Corrigan was the tot Flora had insultingly suggested I beg an endorsement from.

Francis looked ever so slightly sheepish. 'Shush!' he said, keeping his voice down. 'It's not a done deal yet. She's still thinking about it.'

'Thinking about what?'

'Taking over.'

'The world?'

'The agency.'

'To do what with? Turn it into a brasserie?'

'Running it, Guy.'

'*Running it!* Francis, she's ten.'

'She's twenty-four.'

'Twenty-four! As old as that. I'm surprised you haven't gone for someone younger.'

'She's very bright. She's the queen of YA.'

I turned my face into a question mark.

'Young Adult. It's big.'

'Queen in the sense that she writes it or finds it?'

'Both. More – writes it, finds it, places it.'

'And the advantage to me in this?'

'None. But you'd like her.'

'Francis, I know her. I used to sit her on my knee.'

'Well then – you could always try that again.'

'What I need is to sit on hers. I'm in trouble, Francis. I require guidance. You've just ripped up my novel.'

'You'll thank me for it one day.'

'Will I? We shall see. In the meantime I'm without an agent.'

'Maybe Heidi will keep you on.'

'*Maybe!*'

'She's hot, Guy.'

'And I'm cold?'

He stared out of the window and pretended to whistle. Right at that moment the author of *The Old Man and the Sea* shuffled past on one of his circuits of the city, oblivious to humanity, writing in his notepad, wandering off the pavement into the middle of the road, careless of all the honking and the shouting. Every other passer-by peered briefly into the restaurant, attracted by the noise, and perhaps by the smell, of literature in its death throes. Only Hemingway was beyond curiosity.

Francis looked knowingly at me.

'What does that expression mean?' I asked.

'What expression?'

'You know. *There but for the grace of God* – is that what you're suggesting?'

He tapped the table with his stubby fingers. His nails, I noticed, were manicured. No prizes for guessing who was responsible for that innovation.

'Accepting change is always the hardest part,' he said, reading my mind at least.

'Who are you referring to? Poppy? Vanessa? Heidi Corrigan?'

He didn't even pretend to hesitate. 'All three.'

'You're a bastard, Francis,' I told him.

And that, essentially, was that.

I went on seeing him. You can't just part from your agent. There were royalty issues – small royalty issues – to address. There was the matter of who was to take me over when Francis finally left – introductions to make, hands to shake, hellos and farewells. And because no one ever truly leaves the literary life unless he does what Merton did, there were bound to be encounters in muddy fields at literary festivals, prize-giving dinners, summer books parties, winter books parties, funerals.

One sunny afternoon I stumbled upon him on the lawn outside a tent in Witherenden Hill which, like every other small town and village in the country, now had its own literary festival. Poppy, wearing a long, book-reader's skirt, was beside him. They were reclining in deckchairs waiting to go into the village hall to hear three eminent atheists debate the non-existence of a God nobody believed in. They didn't notice me, though I got close enough to see they were reading from matching Kindles. I liked to think they were on identical pages of identical novels, but I couldn't be sure. I wasn't familiar enough with the technology to know whether they could talk to each other through their Kindles as they read, pointing out favourite passages, laughing or shedding tears together. But they seemed very close. That Poppy had, by the look of it, become a serious reader now, and a frequenter of festivals to boot, I found upsetting. Had she been waiting for me to spark her into intellectual life as Francis had? Could this have been us, lying Kindling together in the sunshine, had I gone about things differently? Had I not told her, for example, that every book by every living writer was shit?

I crept away without their spotting me, gave a talk, generously sponsored by the Witherenden Women's Institute, on the subject of Frank Harris and the Faux Confessional Male Novel, to a couple of retired schoolteachers and a librarian from Etchingham, and grabbed a lift back to London with the young woman who ran the online department at S&C who still owned my print-on-demand backlist. She insisted I join Facebook. 'I have the power to make you,' she said when I declined.

Once upon a time that might have been exciting.

I saw Poppy and Francis, together, once more. This was at the premiere of Vanessa's film. Slumdog had not thrown Vanessa a publication party for the novel – few publishers threw parties even for their most successful writers any more: they couldn't risk the ire of their less successful writers – and when I'd offered to organise something for her she'd declined on the grounds that she'd have to ask her mother and didn't want to. There were things in the book that would upset her mother – namely, all of it – and she thought a party would be tactless. Whether Poppy had read the book she didn't know. Her guess was not. Francis, of course, being an old-fashioned agent, had, but she believed he would find a way of dissuading Poppy from going near it.

That she would not be curious, that she would not have devoured every word of it at once, I found hard to believe, but when I said that to Vanessa she told me I was a cretin and understood fuck all – I'm quoting her – of the dynamics of a mother/daughter relationship. Or any family relationship, come to that. 'Who in your family has read a word you've written, Guido?' she asked me. And that was the end of the conversation.

Whatever the dynamics I knew nothing of, Poppy could not be kept away from the premiere of the film. Though it wasn't the full Leicester Square red-carpet treatment – it was only a modest-budget two-hander, after all, filmed almost as though it were a play, the camera allowing the beauty of each woman to metamorphose into the other – the press viewing was not without glamour for all that it was largely without press. Francis turned up in a tuxedo with Poppy in full regalia on his arm. Blissful, they both looked. Poppy proud of her daughter, Francis proud of Poppy. Poppy tried not to look at me. I tried not to look at her. But I saw enough to see she'd got her desirability back. A black suit with a fur collar, the fur falling into her vertiginous cleavage. Ankle boots, high but not too. Vermilion lips. Some confusion with the seats meant she had to brush past me. Her thighs played Brahms. The Double Cello Concerto. Mine Bach. Christ on the cross.

They didn't stay long. Ten minutes into the performance, Poppy, breathing hard, got up to leave. Her thighs once more brushed my knees. On this occasion she was the bow, I the strings. Haydn this time. *The Seven Last Words*. Francis, a man with no ear for music, shrugged and stretched his chin at me, and obediently followed.

I was glad that Vanessa had opted to sit with de Wolff in the back row, taking notes, though with what intention I had no idea. I didn't want her big night spoiled. But afterwards, as we took our places at a nearby fish restaurant – more octopus and sea bream – she looked around for her mother and I could see was alarmed not to find her. She asked me what I knew. I said I suspected Poppy had gone down with a migraine.

'My mother doesn't get migraines. Did she stay for the whole thing?'

'Not all of it.'

'How much of it?'

'Oh, an hour, half an hour.'

'Tell the truth.'

'Twenty minutes.'

'So she missed the scene on the yacht?'

'Not sure.'

'Weren't you following either?'

'I was following the film, Vee, every second of it. What I wasn't following was your mother.'

Liar.

We drank champagne. Dirk made a toast. 'To Vanessa!' We drank to that.

Vanessa proposed a toast to the two unknown English actresses. We drank to them. Not a patch, I thought, on the women they were playing, either as beauties or as performers, but then I was privy to what others weren't, I had been on the journey, no matter that I'd been written out of it. I might not have mentioned that. There were no men in the movie as there were no men in the novel. Not me, not Dirk, not Tim. Even the beach-guarding pelican was a she.

'Did you really think the screenplay was good?' Vanessa said, in a voice just for me.

'I thought wonderful.'

'Truly?'

'Truly truly.'

'Have I surprised you?'

A trick question. 'I always knew you'd be good once you got going, but never this good, no.'

'What did you like most?'

'The beauty.'

'Well, that's Dirk.'

'The concentration of the thing.'

'Also Dirk.'

'But the verve was you.'

'Yes it was. Thank you. And the feeling?'

'Yes, the feeling. I cried. The whole row cried.'

'And that bitch couldn't sit through more than five minutes.'

'Ten.'

'The bitch!'

'You don't know she didn't have a migraine. She might have cried herself into one.'

'She doesn't get migraines. She's always boasted that she's never even had a headache. That's why I thought it was safe to give her a brain tumour in the story. That way she wouldn't make the mistake of thinking I was writing about her.'

'She left before the brain tumour was revealed.'

'All the bitchier of her.'

'She left, Vee, when it became clear you'd given her dementia.'

'But she doesn't have dementia in real life. Well, not completely. Apart from the monkeys. Why would she have thought the woman with dementia was her?'

I wanted to say *for the same reason you thought every woman I wrote about was you.* But tonight was about her work not mine, no matter what the irony in her mother doing to her what she had always done to me. 'Us doesn't mean *us*,' I used to plead with her to understand. 'I doesn't mean *me*. You doesn't mean *you*. It's fiction, for Christ's fucking sake!'

'Even though *she* is saying word for word what *I* say?'

'Even then, Vee. Even then.'

Myself, I found the whole thing mightily affecting. Their falling out, but also the reason for it. The novel, the screenplay, the film, the work – call it what you will. The imagining . . .

Daughter and mad mother alone in the outback, hoping to see the monkeys at Monkey Mia. No Guido Cretino in sight. Just the two women, brawling and affectionate in a manless, monkeyless landscape. No mystery why the film was modestly successful with audiences of mothers and daughters. They saw their own psychology. And psychology is psychology, no matter whether you're sitting in a cinema in Notting Hill or the West End or, finally, in Western Australia where Vanessa later put in a surprise appearance at a film festival. A surprise to me, that is.

Vanessa's handling of the audience's slow realisation that the mother wasn't suffering from Alzheimer's but a brain tumour (for which my brother Jeffrey should surely have been given a credit) was exquisite. Little by little one realised that the attribution of dementia was a kindness dreamed up by the daughter. We'll pretend you're dotty, Ma, that way neither of us has to face up to the terrible fact of what's really going on inside your brain.

I say 'Vanessa's handling' because I felt I could detach her touch from de Wolff's. His hand was clumsier, more allusively filmic, as when the mother's failed hopes to see what was nowhere to be seen conjured up memories of Rizzo's thwarted longing to make it to Miami in John Schlesinger's *Midnight Cowboy*. Or when the

339

crazed refrain, 'Are there monkeys in Monkey Mia?' half echoed the simple-minded Lennie's unbearable 'Tell me about the rabbits, George' in Lewis Milestone's *Of Mice and Men*.

The film was drenched in sadness anyway, to whoever's talents one attributed it. But you can't please everyone, and *Are There Monkeys in Monkey Mia?* did not please Poppy.

41

Tell Me About It

I had my own uneasy moment. It came around about here in the script:

Exterior. Night.
A caravan park in Shark Bay.

DAUGHTER: *Maman,* look! Did you see that?
MOTHER: No, what are you showing me?
DAUGHTER: A falling star.
MOTHER: I missed it. Will there be another?
DAUGHTER: There might. It was beautiful. Strange to think it fell millions of years ago.
MOTHER: How do you know that?
DAUGHTER: It's just something one knows.
MOTHER: If it fell millions of years ago, how can it be falling now? A star can't fall more than once.
DAUGHTER: No, but what we're seeing isn't now, it's then.
MOTHER: What are you talking about? What's then?
DAUGHTER: We're watching what happened millions of years ago.
MOTHER: Is this the Big Bang theory?
DAUGHTER: No, I think that's something different. This is about the speed of light.

MOTHER: Will we see the monkeys tomorrow?

DAUGHTER: I'll ask. I'm not sure. But we can row with the dolphins.

MOTHER: I'll have another drink.

DAUGHTER: Do you need one? Do you *really* need one? Look how lovely the sky is. You can almost feel nobody but you has ever looked at this sky. Have you ever seen so many stars?

MOTHER: Yes – when I met your father on the Isle of Wight. When I was a girl. And there were more stars then.

DAUGHTER: There couldn't have been, *Maman*. Maybe the skies were clearer in those days.

MOTHER: What do you mean there couldn't have been? If stars keep falling out of the sky there must be fewer of them than there were. Why do you contradict me all the time?

DAUGHTER: Look! – there's another.

MOTHER: There you are – one less.

DAUGHTER: I think someone's waving to you.

MOTHER: Where? Is this another one of your falling stars?

DAUGHTER: There. From that boat. Look – he's waving his arms about.

MOTHER: I know what you're doing – you're trying to distract me. Let's have drinkies.

DAUGHTER: Wait a little longer. Wait till dinner.

MOTHER: He does seem to be waving at me. Lend me your lipstick.

DAUGHTER: Your lipstick's fine. You look beautiful. You look so beautiful he's fallen in love with you from all that way away.

MOTHER: How do we know it's happening now and not a hundred million light years before? Maybe he waved before the Ice Age.

DAUGHTER: Maybe he did. But he hasn't fallen into the sea. He's still waving.

MOTHER: How do you know he isn't waving at you?

DAUGHTER: I can tell. It's you he's smitten by. It's always you they're smitten by. Have you forgotten?

MOTHER: When was any man last smitten by me?

DAUGHTER: You *have* forgotten. Only last week, in Perth. A jeweller proposed to you.

MOTHER: You've made that up.

DAUGHTER: Why would I make it up?

MOTHER: To make me believe I'm losing my mind.

DAUGHTER: Why would I do that?

MOTHER: So that you can have me put away. Life would be better for you with me out of the way.

DAUGHTER: If I wanted you out of the way I could have fed you to the dolphins this morning.

MOTHER: You wouldn't have got away with that. You want them to declare me senile, so you can get that power of attorney you've been after for so long.

DAUGHTER: I only mentioned it last week.

MOTHER: It shocks me that you mentioned it at all.

DAUGHTER: Only for your sake. I want to be in a position to look after you.

MOTHER: I don't need looking after. Why do I need looking after?

DAUGHTER: Because you're forgetting things. You've forgotten the jeweller in Perth. You've forgotten there are no monkeys in Monkey Mia. One day you'll go out and forget your name.

MOTHER: You're worried I'll spend your inheritance.

DAUGHTER: There you are, that's something else you've forgotten – I don't have an inheritance.

MOTHER: Blame your father for that.

DAUGHTER: *Maman*, I blame no one. I am happy. I could not be more happy. Look at the night.

MOTHER: Darling, do you know there are times when I see so much of me in you I could cry? It's as though we are sisters.

DAUGHTER: There it is. There's what's wrong. We aren't sisters.

You're my mother.

MOTHER: So act like it, is that what you're saying? If you want me to act more like your mother, don't you think you should act more like my daughter and stop pimping for me?

DAUGHTER: Pimping! When have I ever had to pimp for you? You've pimped successfully for yourself as long as I've known you. There wasn't a man I brought home you didn't make a pass at . . .

There . . . right there.

Though I knew from the novel that I had nothing to fear, that I had no part to play in this, that the generalities of the terrible rivalry between mothers and daughters left me out and let me off – that where such mighty opposites were pitted against each other, my petty and unconsummated sinfulness did not merit so much as a walk-on role – I held my breath in the cinema fearing she might tell it differently this time and I would finally be exposed.

But she didn't and I wasn't.

So was Vanessa entirely unsuspicious of me? Did she not guess? Did she truly know nothing? Was she being, for her own reasons, discreet? Or didn't it, in the bigger scheme of things, matter a jot to her?

An alternative reading presented itself. There was nothing *to* know?

42

Luss

Three weeks after the premiere she left me. 'Make this easy for me, Guy,' she pleaded. 'Let me have my chance.'

What's making it easy? Making a fuss, to show you care, to show your heart is breaking, or making none?

I made none, unless you call a flurry of tears a fuss.

I think I wept as much over the nature of her appeal as I did over the fact of her going. No man likes to think he has stood in another person's way – any person's way – let alone the way of someone he loves.

'Take it,' I said. And then wept a little more over my own words. They had such a ring of stoicism about them.

I had one final request. Would she slip her feet into her highest shoes while I sat on the bed and watched? There is no more arousing sight than that of a woman with beautiful legs stooping slightly, stiffening her calf muscles, angling her toes towards her shoes, and then wiggling her feet into them. The height she then attains when she straightens up can be arousing too, but nothing beats the metatarsal tension in that split second before entry, especially if the shoe is just the slightest bit close-fitting.

She obliged. 'Just one more time,' I said. And she didn't begrudge me that either.

I didn't ask about de Wolff. I couldn't take him seriously as a threat, though undoubtedly he was one. Sexual competition more often than not assumes a melodramatic form; rakes, lechers, seducers, femmes fatales, belles dames sans merci – what are any of them but figures that stalk the stage of our own lurid terrors? Quite frankly I am ashamed to have introduced so obvious a character. But what to do? Life shames every writer and once you start leaving life out you get magic realism. If de Wolff hadn't existed I'd have had to invent him – and that's the truth of it. I like to think that somewhere out there I have similarly stalked the stage of other men's inadequacies. Brought other men out in cold sweats. Andy Weedon, maybe, without going so far as to give him an idea for a book. What goes around comes around. If Vanessa had chosen to throw in her lot with de Wolff for five minutes (I certainly wouldn't have given them any longer than that), it only proved that all human life was farcical. 'I can see his knob,' Poppy had mouthed to me giggling – not a word I care to use, but there was no other – as she was led off to his boat and the night stars fell from the skies. She knew how ridiculous it all was. So I wouldn't so far demean myself as to mention his name to Vee in the solemn hour of our parting. I bowed my head before the inevitable absurdity of things and offered to move out. Let de Wolff have my bed. He was a figment, knob or no knob. When I returned there would be no sign that he had ever lain between my sheets. Vanessa thanked me but said it would not be necessary. She would be the one to go.

That shocked me more than her initial announcement.

'I'm so lonely I could die,' I said, the day she left.

'No you won't,' she said, kissing me on the cheek.

I held on to her for ten full minutes.

A month later I received a brief email from her in Broome. She was writing another book with a view to turning it into another

346

film. About Aborigines. A subject, she reminded me, in which she had always taken an intense interest and would have pursued much sooner but for my obstructionism. She hoped I was busy and happy, writing about whatever I was writing about though she didn't for a moment doubt that it would be myself. She thanked me again for making it so easy. Life had closed over peacefully, she felt, and it was as though 'we' had never been. Did I, too, feel that, she wondered.

It was only then I realised it was all over between us.

So between whom and me wasn't it over?

It was one thing to have no wife and no wife's mother, but I had no publisher or agent, either. My earlier complaint – that I had no readers – shrank before these new privations. But then you can't complain about having no readers when you aren't writing anything for them to read.

As for the agent, Francis had introduced me to his replacement, who was not – that was something – Heidi Corrigan aged twelve, or Heidi anything else for that matter. Carter, he was called. Carter Strobe. A bulky, intense man who looked you deep in the eyes and ceremented himself in tight Ozwald Boateng suits with scarlet linings, buttoning every button, knotting his tie at his throat like a hangman's noose, as though to contain what would otherwise fly everywhere – not just flesh but enthusiasm, his love for writing and for writers so exceeding reasonable bounds that there was no knowing where it might end up once it was released. I should have been grateful to have him as an agent. I *was* grateful. All of us who had inherited him as an agent were grateful. But the inordinacy of his pride in having us as clients cancelled out any feeling of being special. If we were all that good, were any of us any good at all?

Because he kept a tight rein on language, too, he was hard to understand. The first time he introduced himself I took him to be saying 'The art of Rome was insightful', and wondered how to reply. 'Yes, the art of Rome was indeed unsurpassably insightful,' I tried, 'unless the art of Athens could be said to have surpassed it.'

He looked deeper still into my eyes, then laughed wildly. He introduced himself again, just in case there'd been some mistake – 'Carter Strobe, delighted' – but kept the laughter resounding in his chest to show that if I had been deliberately joking, he had got, and would go on getting until eternity, my joke.

He got me altogether, that was what he wanted me to know. He always had got me. He even reeled off a sentence from each of my first two novels.

'Those were your plays,' he said.

I stared at him. 'My plays? I've never written a play.'

He laughed again, a basso profundo laugh from far in and deep down. Clearly he found me a riot. '*Days*. Those were the days.'

I knew what was coming. Those were those days but these are these days. Things had changed and we too had to change to keep up with them. Quite how much information of a personal no less than a professional nature Francis had passed on to him I didn't know, but he was aware that *Terminus* had hit the buffers and that I had come to something of a halt.

We were in Francis's old office which Carter had not yet had time to refurbish, hence, I supposed, there being none of my books on show. 'It's never been my philosophy to tell a writer what he should write,' he said.

'No,' I agreed, hoping he hadn't said that it had never been his philosophy to bill writers who were white.

'But Francis said you were overhauling your oeuvre.'

Those words I didn't even try to comprehend. I smiled instead.

'So let me just mention what I think you could address better than any novelist I know . . .' Whereupon he leaned very close to me and, as though he supposed I heard through my eyes, boomed the word 'Less' into them.

'Less?'

'Luss.'

'Luss?'

'Loss. *Loss*.'

'Ah, loss.'

'You look downcast. I haven't offended you?'

'Offended me? No. It's just that loss is not my subject.'

'But it is. You write about it magnificently. It's only because you've done so much else that readers don't even know it's there.'

'Not just the readers,' I said. '*I* don't even know it's there.'

He roared with laughter again – I wasn't only lossier than I knew, I was funnier than I knew – then looked down in surprise at his suit, as though he had just found another button to fasten, and fastened it. 'Some writers just tear you apart,' he said. 'For me you're one of those writers.'

I thanked him. 'But luss is not me,' I said, hoping to make him laugh again.

He put his hand to his throat. It was, I decided, a physical metaphor for putting his hand to mine. 'But you do,' he said. 'That monkey. Beadle. Unbearable. I feel I know him. I feel he's me.'

'Beagle.'

'Beagle, yes. Heartbreaking.'

'What's heartbreaking about Beagle?'

'What isn't? When he beats his chest at the end and bellows, Christ . . .'

'But he's bellowing for more, not less.'

'Loss.'

'Loss, luss, less . . . It's not me. I do amplitude and accretion. I do

349

booty, lilacs out of the dead ground, the spoils of the sexual war. I do crudity, Carter. I wallow in filth. I do zoo.'

I could tell what he was thinking. I didn't look that amplitudinous right now, a man with no wife, no mother-in-law, no book, no publisher and no readers. Or that filthy. And anyway, filth was over.

But he rejected the idea that it had to be one thing or another. You could be greedy and heartbreaking. He offered to show me a novel that was both regretful and ample. He'd just sold it for an unspeakable sum of money. First-time novelist. Twelve hundred pages, a tearaway wild child of a novel, about the agonising demise of every member of a family going back five hundred years. Innovative, in the formal, print-job, typeface sense, a book that looked like no other book, with pages set out like gravestones, doctors' prognoses, real bloodstains, death certificates, line drawings of cemeteries and sepulchres, the endpapers impregnated with the smell of death, you name it, but the feeling in it, Guy, the sadness, the fucking heartbreak . . . he put his fists to his chest like Beagle and ground away at himself. When he took his fists away, I wondered, would there be two deep gouges in his jacket going all the way through to his breastbone?

'What's it called?' I asked, making a mental note never to read it.

'*The Big Boys Book of Loss*,' he said.

'Meaning it's a big book or it's a book for big boys?'

'Both, both!'

This was a first-time author who had thought of everything.

'Young readers are going to love it,' he told me.

'The young are into loss?'

'Big time. Loss, heartbreak – they can't get enough. But with a bit of formal innovation. They like a book to feel different in their hands.'

'And in their nostrils . . .'

'Exactly. Let me show you . . .'

I thanked him for the recommendation but refused a copy. 'It's too big for me to store and too heavy for me to carry,' I said.

He shrugged. I was the writer.

He kissed me when we parted, took me into his tight embrace and held me fast. Now I knew what it was like to be those things in him he didn't dare release, so many particles of appreciative matter with the potentiality for wholesale destruction.

But it was nice to be kissed by somebody.

I went home and thought about burning myself in my bed. Heartbreak! Loss! What would Archie Clayburgh have said? *Visceral, boy, think visceral.* Loss wasn't visceral.

And then, out of the blue, a distraught phone call from Francis. 'It's Poppy,' he said, his voice reverberating as though from the furthest corners of space.

I thought the receiver would melt in my hand. Please don't let it be a brain tumour, I prayed. Better a heart attack – sudden, quick, painless – while lying in the garden in the sun, with Francis by her side, reading her Kindle.

It was neither, more's the pity. The good news was that she was still alive. The bad news was that she was still alive.

In imagining the smaller irony of her succumbing to the brain tumour Vanessa had given her, I missed the greater irony of its being the dementia Vanessa had given her. A daughter's curse.

I thought it was unheard of for dementia to seize someone still in her sixties. It was commoner than I thought, Francis told me, especially among women. And anyway, Poppy was a little older than either of us had believed.

Really?

But it was too late now to castigate her for deceiving us.

He couldn't cope, that was why he'd called me. He couldn't cope with any of it, neither the sadness nor the practicalities. And he just needed to hear himself say it: I can't cope. After which, maybe he would be able to.

She'd been deteriorating for some time, but the illness had accelerated and she was beyond his care. For a terrible moment I wondered if he wanted me to take her. Irony was piled upon irony, so why not one more? But that wasn't what was on his mind. Vanessa neither, though it was surely Vanessa's duty. 'Have you called her?' I asked. As yet, he hadn't. Did he want me to? No, no, he didn't. Vanessa, he feared, would make things even worse. 'You know what they were like,' he said. 'They fought so savagely.'

'Did Poppy tell you that?'

'Yes.'

'Well, it isn't true. They didn't fight.'

'Well, Poppy thought they did.'

I wondered if that was part of the condition. Dementia made the worst of everything, didn't it? Dementia left out the nice parts.

We continued the conversation three days later at the Soho club where no one wanted to be but where he and Poppy had first met. His idea, not mine. He wanted to dare sentimentality to do its worst. Which was why, presumably, he began by attacking me. 'So what were these nice parts?' he wanted to know.

'Between Poppy and Vanessa? Where do I start? They were like sisters, Francis.'

'Have you forgotten Vanessa's book? Being like sisters was precisely what she said was wrong.'

'Sure, in the book.'

'In life, Guy.'

I swatted away the word. 'Life!'

'Well, life is where it hurts.'

'But it was only Vee's film that hurt Poppy. In "life", as you call it, they strutted their stuff together, they were forces, and you couldn't tell which of them energised the other.'

He suddenly turned angry with me. 'You were simply besotted with the idea of them both,' he said. 'You were so busy making fucking literature out of them you didn't see what was in front of your face. Let me tell you something about yourself, Guy – you fancy that you are hardbitten and cynical but in fact you're a baby. You idealised those women, you idealised them out of existence.'

What could I answer? That it was not my fault that Vanessa was squatting in the dirt with Aborigines and that Poppy had dementia?

I bowed my head. 'I'm sorry about her,' I said, not looking at him. 'I'm more than sorry, I'm broken-hearted. Shall I go and see her?'

I imagined sitting by her bed and stroking her hand. 'Of course there are monkeys,' I'd have told her. 'There are always monkeys if you know where to look.'

Francis was dismissive of my offer. 'You wouldn't be able to bear it. You're not man enough.'

I bowed my head still more. Maybe I should have dropped to my knees and bowed my head until it touched Francis's feet. I wasn't sure what I had done wrong, but sometimes you don't have to know.

After a long silence, Francis asked me how I was getting on with Carter Strobe but didn't listen to my answer. His eyes filled with tears. His couple of years with Poppy, he confided, had been the best of his life. The worst of mine, I confided in return. I meant coincidentally. Nothing, strictly, to do with him and Poppy. Not entirely true, but true enough.

He let me into a secret. Poppy had read everything I'd written.

'With your encouragement and instruction, I bet.'

'No. Before we'd even met. She read every word. Devoured you.'

I wiped a bead of perspiration from my forehead.

'And here's something else,' he said. 'She reviewed you on Amazon.'

'Poppy?'

'Poppy.'

'It was Poppy who compared me favourably to Apuleius?'

'I don't know about that. That one was probably Vanessa.'

'Vanessa did it too?'

'The pair of them. They sat and cooked the reviews up between them. They did it for years, apparently.'

My mouth must have fallen open. At least it should have fallen open, and stayed that way for all eternity. Vanessa and Poppy, their heads together, over me! And never breathing a word. Never looking for a thank you, and now never likely to get one.

So there you are, I wanted to say when I regained control of my face and could just about trust myself with words again, they *were* like sisters. But I could see that I would be no less than ever open to the charge of idealising them — idealising and sentimentalising them in the act of sentimentalising myself.

You never know what's going to finish you off. I had to leave the restaurant. Me, me, me? Yes, all right. But there was only me I had to feel with.

'So what will you do?' I asked before I left.

He shrugged. I'd never seen a man look more helpless.

'Whatever I do is probably immaterial. I don't think there's long . . .'

I wasn't made to hear sentences like that. Francis was right — I wasn't man enough.

I put a hand on his shoulder. 'If I can –'

'You can't,' he said, and looked away.

I knew what he was thinking. *You! Help! How? By writing one of your fucking books? Then go ahead and see what good that will do.*

If I hadn't thrown a little nervous breakdown a couple of years earlier I'd have thrown one that afternoon. Womanless, I did not know how to live. Once, one of them had not been enough. Even not knowing what I knew now, I'd needed the bounty of them both. Now – well, now was now.

And I had no book on the go, either, no sentences to lose myself in. Together, Vanessa and Poppy had got me started. In obeisance to the one or in opposition to the other, I had kept on writing. With neither to intrigue or woo or infuriate or simply do verbal battle with, I had no reason to write and nothing to write about.

I walked the streets, occasionally running into Ernest Hemingway who as ever took no notice of me. I might have felt that we were twinned in our endeavours, the last of a dying breed, but he acknowledged no similarity. Fair enough: he was writing, I wasn't.

How many notepads was he getting through a day? I couldn't imagine getting through another page.

Ditto finding another woman.

Ditto looking for somewhere else to live.

Ditto, once I gave up the streets for fear of being shamed by the tramp, getting out of bed.

Everything that promised a future, promised only to finish me. I couldn't see myself there. The future existed only as a promise of oblivion. I belonged to the past. I existed only in the past. I was walking through my life backwards. If I kept going I would eventually get to people reading my first novel, then to my writing it, then to Vanessa coming into the shop and asking – making a sort of pergola of her arms – if I'd seen her mother, a woman as vivacious as an apple orchard in a tornado. Vanessa herself the tornado. Two burning bushes . . .

You can lie on your bed a long time, remembering when you were happy. Eventually the bed itself becomes the site of happiness. It was on this bed that you were happy only yesterday, happily remembering the day before, when you had remembered the time you'd been happy . . .

So how long did I stay in my bed? I don't know. The more interesting question is how long *would* I have stayed in bed? Though again I don't know the answer to that. For ever? But as chance would have it, my family came to my aid. Isn't that what families are for? My father died.

All the black-hatted Hasidim in the country, and many more, I suspected, from elsewhere, attended the burial. How did they know to come? Some instinct for funereality, was it? Or just Jeffrey sending out the word?

They congregated in the cold marble cemetery, anyway, careening and lamenting, like a murmuring forest with a raven in every tree. But for the electronic cigarette on which she puffed and which, in the late-afternoon gloom, was the only point of light, it would have been hard to make out my mother. She was dressed as though for a date, and I don't mean with death. A single Hasidic fedora would have provided enough fabric to make the little black mourning suit she wore, and then some over for a pair of gloves.

We'd done whatever perfunctory kissing was considered necessary earlier in the afternoon, in sight of my father's ineloquent coffin. Mmm, mmm, at a sufficient distance from each other to ensure I wouldn't get entangled in her jet earrings.

'Now what?' she asked me once we'd buried him with all defer-
ence to the Jew he'd never known he'd been.

'Now what what?'

'Now what am I supposed to do with myself?'

Prepare to meet your maker, I wanted to say, though from a look
at the amount of leg she was showing, or at least the amount of
near-empty stocking that was on display, I doubted her maker
would have allowed her into His presence. Mysteriously, though
her cigarette wasn't real, she appeared to be exhaling smoke. Had
she begun to burn up from the inside? With impatience to get
started on the rest of her life?

A voice I didn't immediately recognise commiserated with me
from behind. 'I wish you long life, boychick,' it said.

I turned and saw someone I didn't know. He put his finger
where a moustache should have been. 'Ah,' I said. It was Michael
Ezra, Vanessa's croupier. Though without the moustache he looked
like no one in particular. Certainly no one dangerously attractive.
Shorn, his darkness merely made him appear poverty-stricken in
the Mediterranean mode – a Sicilian apple picker, a Libyan goat-
herd. Here, but for his respectful suit, he would have made, I
thought, a serviceable gravedigger.

After the amount of time I'd spent lying in bed, I probably
looked no better.

I didn't understand why he was here. He had not been a close
friend of the family. But it was a free-for-all kind of funeral – most
of Cheshire in attendance – remarkable for a man who had no
friends. I guessed Jeffrey was the reason: he called, and every
croupier in Manchester, plus every Hasid in Brooklyn, came in
answer to his pain.

'So what have you done to yourself?' I asked him.

'Cleaned up my image,' he laughed. 'Your brother's doing.'

'Jeffrey got you to shave off your moustache?'

'Yafet, yes. He's been trying to make a good Jew of me.'

'Oh God, not you too. What was wrong with the Jew you were? Anyway, I thought that being a good Jew according to Jeffrey meant growing more hair not losing what you've got.'

'Eventually. But it's different hair. First I had to stop looking like a croupier.'

'But you *are* a croupier.'

'Not any more.'

'So what are you doing now?'

'Looking around.' He made it sound sinisterly spiritual. Looking around for God. Waiting on the word of Yafet.

I shook my head. 'Jesus!' I said.

He lowered his eyes.

After a moment or two of awkward silence, he enquired after my wife and stepdaughter. I couldn't remember which I'd told him, or which he'd thought, was which.

'We are no longer together,' I said, to be on the safe side.

His eyes shone compassion on me. 'I'm sorry to hear that.'

I thanked him. 'So now it's in the past for all of us,' I was surprised to hear myself say, 'you can tell me.'

'Tell you what?'

'Whether you had, you know . . . Whether you went off with her that night?' Now I'd started it was hard to stop. 'Whether you went on seeing each other.'

'You're asking me if I had an affair with your wife?'

I had to think about it. I had no head for subterfuge. Which *was* my wife, again? 'No, her daughter. Vanessa.'

'Why do you think that?'

'She seemed to take a shine to you.'

He shook his head. 'You . . . writers,' he said, checking his language because of where we were. 'You think the worst of every-body. You think everything is underhand and unpleasant.'

'I'm not accusing you. I'm only wondering.'

'But why are you wondering? Why should I have had an affair with your daughter or your wife? I met them only once. And I happen to be married myself.'

I checked myself from looking at him enquiringly, man to man, as though to wonder when being married had ever made a difference to anything. It was not, I decided, a look that would go down well with him.

'It was you,' I reminded him instead, 'who said looking like Omar Sharif pulled in the birds.'

'That was a joke. Can't a person make a joke with you?'

Not when it comes to sex, I thought about saying, then changed it to 'Of course you can. Joking's what I do.'

'Do you? Well, I can tell you're not joking now.'

'It's my father's funeral,' I said.

'Then treat it with respect.'

'Touché, boychick,' I said.

But he hadn't quite finished with me. 'It's not all the way it is in your novels,' he said, lowering his voice because Jeffrey was heading our way, hairy and refulgent, holding a holy book. 'People rutting like monkeys, people pissing in one another's mouths . . . where do you get this stuff from? Your father has just been put in the ground. Isn't it time you got serious?'

'People pissing in one another's mouths is serious,' I said. 'You don't embark on such a thing lightly.'

'Sick!'

'Sick, sane, who's to say?'

'You think it's sane to ask me, here, on such a day, whether I've been having sex with members of your family? If that's what you choose to write about, that's your business, and if you can find people who want to read it, good luck to you, but believe me, it's fantasy. Not everyone is fucking their brains out.'

(*His* brains out.)

'So what are they doing, Michael?'

Unless he was Mordechai now.

He didn't so much as hesitate. But then he had been a croupier, accustomed, while the wheel spun, to sorting bets and settling arguments quickly. 'Good,' he said. 'They're doing good.'

I learned later that Michael Ezra practised what he preached. He did good. His oldest child was severely handicapped and in a home. Every day he travelled thirty miles there and thirty miles back to see him. That was why he had worked as a croupier – so he could have the daylight hours free to visit his sick child.

Frankly, I'd rather not have known this. Just as I would rather not have known that my father, returning rapidly to dust, had performed remarkable deeds of charity or endurance in his otherwise contemptible life. Not that he had. But *had* he, it would have disturbed the equilibrium of my view of him to have learned of them. You can know too much about people. Find out all there is to know about even the most dull or scoundrelly and you uncover a thousand reasons for respecting them. And then where are you? Suddenly the world becomes one vast melancholy sounding box, vibrating to the still sad monotonous music of humanity.

Whereupon words will no longer frolic lewdly before your eyes.

And the next thing you know you're writing social-worker novels.

43

Apeshit

Tedious to admit, but I believed what he had told me about my women. Vanessa had not been slipping away to Cheshire in order to finger his bristling moustache. Poppy neither. I believed my brother too. Vanessa had not fucked him into or even out of a brain tumour.

Whatever it was that drew her so frequently to the north, leaving me to my literary labours in the capital – it wasn't Ezra and it wasn't Yafet. That left a multitude of other readings, of course; those weren't the only temptations the north of England had to offer. But a novel suggestion presented itself: Vanessa had not been deceiving me. Not in the sexual intrigue sense anyway. Not everyone, as Ezra sweetly put it, was fucking their brains out. And you don't get a more novel suggestion than that.

So what *had* she been doing?

Good. I decided she'd been doing *good*.

Was it possible?

Could it be that Vanessa and her mother were good women? Composing rave reviews of my novels for Amazon, and telling me nothing about it, was the work of good, loyal, selfless women, was it not? They weren't to know those reviews would screw up my sales. When it comes to evaluating goodness you can only count intention. Vanessa was now working with Aborigines – that was the mark of a good woman. Poppy had resisted my attentions and given poor Francis the best two years of his life – that, too, was goodness in action, was it not? Making a moody man happy. (Or in my case making a happy man moody.)

But what if there was more?

As a novelist I'd never been much interested in secrets. Secrets were plot and only a moron could be interested in plot. As a reader, when I got to the spinning of a secret I closed the book. Who wanted to spend the next three days wondering what the secret was only to discover it hadn't been worth keeping in the first place? As a man I'd been different. As a man I saw a secret every time my wife, or indeed her mother, left the house. As a man I gorged on secrets. But they were always secrets of the same sort. Secrets of betrayal. A consciousness of betrayal kept the juices flowing. Life was dull until the imagination had some betrayal to chew on. That I might have sent my imagination out on other errands I was gradually coming to realise. Age, was it? Or did this just happen to a man who was living alone with no women coming and going and therefore no one to betray him? Sex feeds on sex. So the opposite must be true – the more nothing happens, the more nothing happens. People with clean minds are simply people who have never started on the ladder of lubricity. And I had been off the ladder long enough to be thinking spotless thoughts, in the pale, ghostly glow of which Vanessa and her mother began to appear as angels.

What if their goodness, I asked myself, now that one was dying and another was as far away as it was possible to go, extended way beyond their concern for me and Francis? What if, for example, they'd returned to Knutsford as often as they had, and without asking me along, because . . . well, because Poppy, like Michael Ezra, had a son, which is another way of saying that Vanessa had a brother, living in a home . . . well, for the mentally disabled? What if loving-kindness explained their absences (as it would explain their being in Cheshire in the first place), and a deep underlying sadness explained the fractiousness which had latterly marred their relations with each other, never mind with me? Did he lie there, year after year, with his tongue lolling out of his mouth, wondering where the monkeys were, in a terrible pre-enactment of his mother's dementia? Was that what Poppy was unable to forgive when she saw Vanessa's film? Not the charge that she had been a sexual competitor, not me, nothing to do with me at all? But the implicit blame?

Now I was on the what-if roundabout I couldn't, or didn't want to, get off. What if, after a long and harrowing illness, the son and brother had died, maybe in the arms of his mother or his sister, and the women had been left to mourn a life that had never adequately been lived, which somehow, with more love, they might have made a little better, a life, what is more, that called into question their own genetic soundness? Did Poppy castigate herself for Robert – let's call him Robert – did she wonder what unsoundness in her had misflowered into this ghastly family anomaly? Had Robert been the reason, in fact, and never mind her nude posing with a cello, for the break-up of her marriage to Mr Eisenhower? And what if Vanessa was unable to forgive herself the shame she felt at having an imperfect brother? They had never once mentioned Robert to me. Aha! That denoted shame, surely. And perhaps a fear that I would run a mile if I knew what tainted blood coursed through the veins of the women I adored. Was that why Vanessa let me get away with my courtship of her mother – assuming she ever knew a thing about it – because she couldn't begrudge her an attention which for a brief hour would allay the fears she had about herself? Was I – no better than a fattened black spider made comfortable in this intricate web of consideration; no better than Beagle sitting self-satisfied in his cage, allowing troops of girl gorillas to pick fleas from his fur while he stared in admiration at his own blazing erection – the only one in our little clan thinking of no one but himself?

And so I had my subject. *The good woman.*

In the good old days (to use good in an entirely different sense) when Francis and I used to go out drinking together, before the last few readers had dwindled into no readers, we would while away the hours thinking up titles of books that would be sure-fire best-sellers by virtue of a single word. 'Anything with the word wife or daughter in it,' Francis once suggested. We exhausted every possibility then changed the game to titles that would never sell even *with* the word wife or daughter in them. I won with *The Fudgepacker's Daughter.*

But I had done with pyrrhic victories. And when I called on Carter Strobe and offered him, as though it were a floral tribute to his agenting, the title *The Good Woman*, I knew from the way he enfolded me in his Ozwald Boateng suit that I was onto a winner.

I had alternatives in my back pocket, just in case, but he was so pleased with *The Good Woman* that – with some nostalgic regret, I have to say – I left *The Monkey and the Mother-in-Law* and *The Spider-Monkey's Wife* where they were. No more monkeying for me.

I thought Carter was going to rub noses with me when I followed the title up with a rough outline. Or at the very least tell me that he loved me. He held me by the ears. 'This is the one I've been waiting for,' he said, though I hadn't known he'd been waiting for anything. 'I'm weeping and I haven't even read it,' he said.

I told him I was weeping and I hadn't even written it.

But that was the easy part. You start at the beginning and you go on to the end. Previously I had done it the other way round, giving away what was going to happen at the outset so that readers shouldn't be distracted into suspense. Now you know where we're going to end up you can forget about it and concentrate on the sentences, was what, in effect, I was telling them. Roll me around your tongues. Savour me. Reading should be like sex. The end is written in the beginning, so just lie back and enjoy the journey. Who knows, maybe this was no better a strategy than Vanessa's 'Gentle reader, get fucked!' I was done with it, anyway. The past was the past. Alone, distressed and sentimental, I sold my soul to story.

I had to cheat a bit to get the Holocaust in, but a dream sequence will always make a chump of chronology. Otherwise it was Sierra Leone, the Balkans, Afghanistan, I'm uncertain myself where I sent them, the two women passing themselves off as sisters, fleeing from hellhole to hellhole on the back of a plot so flimsy – but then what plot isn't flimsy? – that I blushed as I constructed it. How they survived what they saw and what they were subjected to; how they made the selfless choices they did, each one sacrificing herself to ensure the safety of the other, as they journeyed from horror to horror in pursuit of the sweet but simple-minded boy (the illegiti-mate child of Pauline, passed off as hers by Valerie, after they had both been raped on the same day by the same Biafran soldier); how they watched in helpless horror as Somali pirates stole him from a pleasure cruiser anchored off Shark Bay, and there and then vowed that they would ransack the universe to find him, I can only ascribe to courage. Not theirs, mine. Because it takes tremendous courage – far more than is ever credited – to write what I was writing.

Goodness, of course, sustained them. The goodness of their

devotion to each other, the goodness of their love for the boy, and the goodness they brought to the troubled people they travelled among. That it wasn't always possible for the reader to know which woman was which – which the Good Woman of the title – I account a master stroke, though I got the idea originally from Dirk de Wolff who had merged them cinematically. Such goodness transcends individuality – that was my point. It doesn't pertain to a particular woman, young or old – it is the distinguishing feature of *woman*.

As it happens, I had always believed that, anyway. I simply hadn't thought it necessary to spell it out. Where I got such idealism from I can't be sure: it certainly didn't come to me in my own mother's milk. Perhaps I learned it from watching women shopping in the boutique, dressing and undressing, looking at themselves in mirrors, uncertain what suited them, troubled by their appearances, having to think twice about the expense. It made me sorry for them. Not easy being them, I thought. From which it followed that I saw their lives as one long trial, balancing beauty and elegance with all the other calls on their sense of duty. In even the most flibbertigibbety of customers I thought I could detect an underlying heroical sorrow, the struggle to remain a good wife when loucher longings beckoned, to make ends meet, to find time for the tedium of children or relatives long past any usefulness or sense.

No loucher longings this time. No sex, except by intimation – on pain of death no *squish-squish* – and no jokes. Writers of pornography obey a single golden rule when it comes to laughter: there is not to be any. A single laugh and the trance is broken. Well, *The Good Woman* was the pornography of the sentimental, and the same rule applied.

So no seriousness, either. The age of serious sex was over.

I say it took tremendous courage to write it, but that's an

exaggeration. In fact it took none. These were coward's words and I am ashamed to say they came easily to me. I turned on the tap of tears and tears flowed. Once you let idealisation out of the cage, there is no getting it back in again. There are some, of course, who find such idealisation, when it is unloosed indiscriminately on particular women, the deepest of all insults to woman in general – misogyny in its most underhand and deviously destructive form – but they were never going to be my readers. As for historical background it's a cinch. Skim a couple of books by academics no one's heard of and invent the rest. Topography the same. When you've described one arid mountain range you've described them all. Ditto desert. I had watched the desert bloom with wild flowers driving up to Broome with Poppy and Vanessa. And as they had marvelled, I marvelled. Occasionally, in defiance of their captors, one of them would dismount a camel or an elephant or a blood-bespattered jeep to pluck a desert pea (I would, of course, check the genus appropriate to the terrain) and croon. 'See how beautiful,' she would say to the Somali pirate who had been a fisherman before toxic waste was dumped in the waters that had been his livelihood, and she knew he saw. Beauty spoke in every language. She would lie with him before he finally released her to a warship belonging to the Indian navy.

International politics for the men, wonderment for the women.

As for the poor and downtrodden whose lives my two women touched as they travelled, they were the poor and downtrodden of Wilmslow and Ladbroke Grove without the iPads. There isn't anything, I found, that I didn't know already. The Afghan tribes-men looked like Michael Ezra before he'd shaved off his moustache, the well-meaning but ineffective consular Englishmen were Quinton and Francis, the idealists were Merton Flak, the Muslim fanatics were Jeffrey (where's the difference?), and the Somali pirate with a feel for beauty was me. This was all just watercolour background anyway. I reserved the richness of oils for little Robert, modelled on half the simpleton novelists I knew, but with particular reference to the lashless Andy Weedon, and of course for Valerie and Pauline, who were painted with a thick impasto of sympathy, an intense luminousness of admiration and devotion that no one but I possessed.

'How do you know us so well?' the Chipping Norton, Chipping Camden and Chipping Sodbury women's reading groups asked me. It struck them as uncanny that I could understand women as I did. By way of an answer I unmanned myself facially for them. I thought of Vanessa and her mother and my eyes watered. That was how I understood – by letting go of all that stood between me and woman, which wasn't, to be truthful, very much. Secretly, I marvelled that they should think we were so different. Was there really an entity called 'woman' to understand? Was she truly of a different species to man? Before Archie Clayburgh got to me, before I had progressed to the Olympia Press, I had loved reading about Jane Eyre and Little Dorrit and Maggie Tulliver. Girls, now I come to think of it, were all I read about. That they were girls and I was a boy never once occurred to me at the time, nor would it have mattered if it had. We were sensitives in the shit together, that was all. I turned the pages and immersed myself in slightly prettier versions of me. Not that much prettier either, in Jane Eyre's case. And certainly no more emotionally fraught. Novels told the story of our common pain, girls and boys, men and women. On the surface, de Sade's indefatigable embuggerers, like Henry Miller's down-and-out lickers and fuckers, might have seemed worlds away from the easily bruised charity girls at Lowood Institution where that bastard Mr Brocklehurst unfairly branded Jane a liar, but dig a little deeper and they weren't. One way or another they all found life hard-going. I wouldn't be surprised if the embuggerers found it even harder than the charity girls.

If women readers were unable or unwilling to enter the damaged souls of men as enthusiastically as I had entered the damaged souls of women, that was their affair, but they were imaginatively the poorer for it. As for the understanding they believed they found in me now I was Guido Cretino, it was no more than a deliberate toning down of the language of self in favour of a demonstrative lavishing of tenderness on others. I don't underestimate that quality. Tenderness is a fine thing. But it is not understanding – you can be tender and a fool, you can be tender and grasp nothing – though in the age of the dying of the word compassion will pass as understanding. More than that, it will be preferred to understanding which, as often as not, is too cruel for people to bear.

'Go, go,' said Eliot's bird, 'human kind cannot bear very much reality.' It didn't have to be a bird that said it. I'd have gone for something furrier. But all that mattered was that it was non-human. It takes another species to see us for what we are.

So was that all they had ever wanted, those who had once iden-tified only with my dead characters – a bit more rosy undiscerning goo-goo? Did they read in order to be spared from seeing what was true? Did they read to be lied to?

Everyman, I will go with thee and blind thine eyes.

What I was writing now a monkey with enough time on his hands could have written. I mean no disrespect to my new book-mad, serial readers. Without them there's no knowing what I would have done. They saved me from losses too keen to bear. They shored me up. It's possible they lied to me every bit as much as I lied to them. No matter. I kiss the feet of every one of them. But the truth is the truth: what I was writing now a monkey with *no* time on his hands could have written.

And do you know what I suspect? Buried deep inside those readers to whom I am eternally grateful, in a place too remote and inaccessible for their conscious minds to penetrate, was the half-belief that a monkey *had* written it. Or if not a half-belief, then a half-wish. A velleity on the side of apes. Not my kind of monkey-wish, not a longing for the serious and single-minded libidinousness with which Beagle surveyed his burning putz – though there was little in the way of burning putz envy left in me now – but a secret, unexcavated suspiciousness of the artist who knew what he was doing and dedicated his life to doing it, who was not a selector of random words which occasionally came together to make a terrible sense, who ran down language with a will and with a purpose and wouldn't let it go until it had yielded meaning – *his* meaning, *her* meaning.

Too much self-knowledge and intent spoiled it for those who made a hobby of being cultured, who trotted from Tate Modern to the National Theatre and then on to one of the three or four reading groups to which they belonged, and who in their hearts believed they too had a story to tell and would have told it if only they had had the time (which they might easily have had had they only stayed away from galleries and theatres more), if only they had not had families to bring up, if only things had worked out differently for them, if only they had had the advantages or the education, if only the monkey in them had struck the right keys and come up with the right letters.

I was under no more illusion about my esteemed readers' affection for me than I was about my affection for myself, and I didn't like myself at all. They read the pap I put out not because they loved me, but because they hated Proust at his most dilatory and

Henry James at his most sublimely impenetrable and Lawrence at his most finical-erotical-prophetical and Céline at his most odious. In my new incarnation as a writer of what was 'readable' I was the antidote to art.

Poppy died before *The Good Woman* was published. Francis had, in the end, cared for her and was now wasted himself. 'They should bury me with her,' he said. 'Or at least they should bury my heart.'

Other than 'Oh, Francis', I had no reply. In my own heart I thought it would be right if they buried his. I envied him. Not his few short years with Poppy but the inordinacy of his grief. It denoted a steadfastness I feared I didn't possess, and of course a goodness I knew I didn't.

Vanessa flew back for the funeral and shook like a leaf through every minute of it. She looked very fine, golden from the Western Australian sun, though less queenly than I remembered her at Merton's funeral. She had marks on her face I hadn't seen before, deeper, I thought, than could be explained by this new sorrow. It was as though writing had turned her serious, but in the process taken away her vivacity. Not writing had suited her. In her rage and frustration she had bloomed. In her not writing she had been a prodigy of non-fulfilment. Now she was just another practitioner. One of thousands, millions even. Hush, and you can hear them; listen, on a quiet night anywhere on the planet, and you can hear the scratch of their pens or the dead click of their keyboards, as innumerable as the sand which is by the seashore.

But I could not tell her that. Let her find out for herself.

We embraced, like old friends who had fallen out, without passion.

'Are you all right, essentially?' she asked me.

'I am,' I said. 'I can see that you are – essentially.'

She nodded. 'It's good to be busy.'

'Yes,' I said. I wanted to ask if she was enjoying the frontier life she had surprised me in Broome with the news that she had always craved. But she would think I was being ironic.

Similarly, I thought, she refrained from asking whether I was still writing about myself and wondering why no one read me. 'Working on something?' she asked instead.

'Yes. You?'

'Yes.'

There is nothing to say once you have decided to call an end; the argument has no spritz in it any longer. And you can't remember why it ever spat and fizzed the way it did.

I wished she would tell me to stop stealing her airwaves, to get the fuck out of the cemetery so that she could think her thoughts. It would have pleased me to see her vertiginous with frustration again. Not because I wanted to see her unhappy but because I wanted to see her grand.

We avoided all talk of Poppy until we were about to part.

'I know it must have been hard for you sometimes,' she said, 'having both of us to cart around. I want to thank you for doing it with such good grace.'

'It wasn't hard,' I said.

And then it was my turn to shake like a leaf.

44

Spelt From Sibyl's Leaves

My follow-up novel to *The Good Woman* was *The Good Daughter*.
There was no stopping me now. I had *The Good Mother* ready to go.
And even before I began on that I was mulling over *The Good
Son-in-Law*. Though how I was going to keep sex out of that one,
I didn't know.

It was as I walking home from the launch party for *The Good
Daughter* that I saw the tramp Vanessa had called Ernest Hemingway
keel over, like a shot bear, in the middle of the road. I couldn't tell
if he'd been hit by a vehicle or had just lost his footing. At this time
of the night in Soho there was no saying what had caused what.
Minicabs and limousines and rickshaws were double-parked,
picking up and spilling out. Hen nights, stag nights, monkey nights.
People lay in pools of their own vomit, waiting for the paramedics.
You couldn't tell, from looking at what anyone was wearing, what
the season was. In Soho it had become a perpetual late summer,
shirts open to the navel, legs bare to the femur, no matter what the
temperature. The restaurants were all full, booked out, though no
one was eating in the restaurant that they really wanted to eat in.

(That *he* really wanted to eat in? Forget it.)

Smokers lounged outside, laughing and coughing, inspecting
their mobile phones with that air of urgent wonder that would

have made a Martian suppose they had never seen such things until tonight. Everyone had a message waiting, and whoever didn't, sent himself one. In restaurant queues the latest of Sandy Ferber's two-minute Unbooks helped while away the waiting.

No one noticed anything any more, there were no witnesses to any crime, because people did not raise their faces from their screens. How they any longer fell in love was a mystery to me. Eyes used to have to meet in long lingering amazement. But who had time to raise their eyes or be amazed? Perhaps they fell in love, at a remove, through their electronic devices. IthinkIloveyou.com. I felt self-conscious carrying an actual book. It was a first edition of *The Good Daughter*, still hot from the printer's, signed by everyone at my publishers, even Flora, though I might not have mentioned that I never did leave S&C – couldn't do it, couldn't do it to the memory of Merton, couldn't do it to Margaret Travers, his no less faithful secretary, who I felt needed me to stay for continuity's sake, and into the dark interior of whose crackling unbelted raincoat I couldn't bear no longer to slip my arms, and anyway, with books as verdant and unapocalyptic as I was writing, there was nowhere else to go. Slumdog Press? I was too popular.

Verdant or otherwise, was I the only person in Soho, I wondered, carrying a book qua book? Ought I to have hidden it inside my jacket? I was the only person in Soho wearing a jacket, too. Or down my trousers?

It was as I was thinking about where or whether to conceal it that I saw Ernest Hemingway go over. It must have been a heavy fall, however it happened, because his notebook had come apart and leaves from it were being scattered by the careless feet of pedestrians. It was only paper. The streets of Soho were full of paper.

People are good, whether they are readers who respect the page or they are not. My new humanitarian philosophy: keep people away from art and judgement, where they are as lost souls, and they are, behaviourally speaking, wonderfully good. Was that another title for me? *People Are Good* – and no sooner did the tramp fall than passers-by rushed to see how he was and to assist him to his feet. 'I'm trained in first aid,' I heard one woman say, 'tell me where it hurts.' Shame she didn't ask me. But on Hemingway it was a wasted, thankless piece of kindness; he did not raise his sightless eyes to her or to anyone else, and would not, frankly, have been very pleasant to make physical contact with.

We are all good in our own way. Some looked after the man, I went after his papers. Assuming this was the same book he'd been working on since Vanessa and I first encountered him, and possibly for years before that, it was a magnum opus, the labour of many hundreds of weeks. In which case every page was precious. And who else but I gave a damn about them? I chased down as many as I could, standing on them before bending to pick them up, the way I imagined the acolytes of the Sibylline oracle would have run after the leaves of her prophecy when they blew from the mouth of her cave. The Cumaean Sibyl had 'sung the fates' on the leaves of oak trees and when they scattered they scattered. What she had prophesied was lost. What did she care?

Ernest Hemingway, too, seemed not to care. Let his leaves blow where they chose.

But *I* cared.

It was my intention to return the pages I had retrieved, whether he wanted them or not, but I was word-deranged – a man who could not walk by a discarded cigarette packet without pausing to read it – and I could not resist stealing a look at what he had been writing all these years. Not a vulgar, competitor's curiosity, I hope, not a thief's or a scoffer's, but the respectful wondering of a fellow worker with words. How good was he? What did he know that the

rest of us, who lived lives so much more compromised and comfortable, who preferred not to let our testicles hang out of the holes in
our trousers, who lacked his austere, friendless dedication – what
did he understand that we did not?

I quickly saw that for all their density not one of the scattered
leaves of his notebook was different from any other. What he had
to say, he went on saying, for page after page. And what he had to
say was forceful, incontestable, not to say beautiful, in its
clairvoyance:

O

OOOOO
OOOO
OOO
OO
O

O
OO
OOO
OOOO
OOOOO

O

A NOTE ON THE AUTHOR

An award-winning writer and broadcaster, Howard Jacobson was born in Manchester, brought up in Prestwich and educated at Stand Grammar School in Whitefield, and Downing College, Cambridge, where he studied under F. R. Leavis. He lectured for three years at the University of Sydney before returning to teach at Selwyn College, Cambridge. His novels include *The Mighty Walzer* (winner of the Bollinger Everyman Wodehouse Prize), *Kalooki Nights* (longlisted for the Man Booker Prize), the highly acclaimed *The Act of Love* and, most recently, the Man Booker Prize-winning *The Finkler Question*. Howard Jacobson lives in London.